ALL-OUT RAVES FOR THE BLOODHOUND FILES

"Snappy writing, a page-turning story, and fresh world-building make *Dying Bites* a satisfying meal of a book."
—Kelley Armstrong, *New York Times* bestselling author of *Men of the Otherworld* and *The Awakening*

"*Dying Bites* is wacky, unpredictable, fresh, and amazing. I would kill to write as well as DD Barant. Seriously."
—Nancy Holder, author of *Pretty Little Devils*

"This engrossing debut adds another captivating protagonist to the urban fantasy ranks...Barant's well-developed world offers intriguing enhancements to mythology and history. Jace is remarkable, strong-willed, and smart, and she sets an unstoppable pace. Look for the Bloodhound Files to go far."
—*Publishers Weekly* (starred review)

"A heroine with plenty of guts, moxie, and a sense of the absurd. [A] fresh and original take on urban fantasy...Huge kudos to Barant for spicing things up with a story that expertly integrates detective work, kick-butt action, and a wacky sense of humor. Make sure you get in early on the outstanding new Bloodhound Files series."—*Romantic Times*

"DD Barant builds a strong world and fills it with fascinating characters that will delight and entertain. *Dying Bites* is a well-written urban fantasy with a gripping plot and a heroine who is quite believable with her very human flaws. I'm looking forward to seeing more in this captivating world."
—*Darque Reviews* (starred read)

"Barant does an excellent job introducing a whole new world where vampires make up the majority of the population... quick and engrossing...a great new series."
—*Romance Reader*

St. Martin's Paperbacks Titles

by DD Barant

Dying Bites

Death Blows

Killing Rocks

BETTER OFF UNDEAD

BOOK FOUR OF
THE BLOODHOUND FILES

DD Barant

St. Martin's Paperbacks

This is a work of fiction. All of the characters, organizations, and events portrayed in this novel are either products of the author's imagination or are used fictitiously.

BETTER OFF UNDEAD

Copyright © 2011 by DD Barant.

For information address St. Martin's Press, 175 Fifth Avenue, New York, NY 10010.

ISBN: 978-0-312-54505-5

Printed in the United States of America

St. Martin's Paperbacks edition / October 2011

St. Martin's Paperbacks are published by St. Martin's Press, 175 Fifth Avenue, New York, NY 10010.

10 9 8 7 6 5 4 3 2 1

BETTER
OFF
UNDEAD

ONE

There's something about being driven to prison that makes you think about the past.

The bad parts, especially: lost loves, mistakes you made, chances you never took, choices you came down on the wrong side of. Me, I'm thinking about a werewolf physician named Dr. Pete who saved my life on two separate occasions and got himself killed on attempt number three.

Well, not so much killed as erased, replaced by an alternate version of himself—a version with a different history, a different past in which he'd made some bad decisions. Hard to believe that gentle, caring Dr. Pete could ever have been a member of a crime family, but we all have skeletons in our closets, don't we? If I hadn't gotten a degree in criminal psychology and joined the FBI as a profiler, my own violent youth could have progressed into me becoming the kind of person I now hunt.

Okay, maybe not the people I hunt now, more like the perps I used to catch in my native reality—the one with *M*A*S*H* reruns and butterscotch ripple ice cream and thrift-store silver jewelry. Here, nobody even knows what a gun is, silver is a controlled substance, and butter-scotch—for some bizarre reason—hasn't been invented. *Here* being a parallel world, an alternate version of planet Earth that exists in a dimension right next to the one I came from. I didn't travel here willingly, either; I was yanked out of my own apartment in a dreamlike stupor, with nothing more than my laptop, a large hand-gun, and a crate of ammunition for company. Seems the residents of this reality had a problem with a crazed human psycho killing them off, and they needed an expert to deal with it.

I call this world Thropirelem, because the word neatly encapsulates the three main types of citizens: werewolves (thropes), vampires (pires), and golems (lems). Human beings make up a meager 1 percent of the worldwide population, less than a million people, and I'm one of them.

So far.

I now work for the National Security Agency, based out of this world's Seattle, and I've largely adapted to my new existence. My current employers keep insisting they'll send me home one day, just as soon as I catch one Aristotle Stoker: descendant of the infamous Bram, leader of the Free Human Resistance, and prolific serial killer. Hasn't happened yet, though I've come close a few times.

In the meantime I'm being kept busy. The supernatural races are immune to most diseases including mental illness, which means they have very little experience with full-blown crazy. That is, they *had* little experience—until Stoker circulated a subliminal message buried in an Internet video, footage of an Elder God designed to make everyone who saw it into two things: (a) living mummies, trapped inside their own immobile bodies for all eternity; and (b) nuts.

With Dr. Pete's help I managed to reverse the first condition, but the second one has proven more pervasive. Since millions of thropes and pires worldwide saw the video—humans and lems couldn't perceive it—insanity has become a booming industry. Many, many fanged or furry lunatics, and just one person who understands how the homicidal ones think.

Me.

All of which is weighing pretty heavily on my mind as Stanhope Federal Penitentiary gets closer. I've accomplished some good since I got to this world, but I've screwed up plenty, too—and right now it feels like I'm heading straight for my biggest mistake of all.

"Nickel for your thoughts?" my partner says. That would be Charlie Aleph, a golem composed of three hundred pounds of black volcanic sand poured into a transparent plastic skin and wrapped in a seven-hundred-dollar double-breasted suit with matching fedora.

"Where I come from it's a penny."

"Same here. You just look like you might have more than one." He pauses. "Could be wrong, though."

Charlie owns the copyright to the word *deadpan,* and he's filed an application for *wiseass.* Think Humphrey Bogart by way of the Terminator and you'll have an idea of his style. But he dresses better than either of them.

He's the one driving me to Stanhope, where I have an appointment with a lycanthrope named Tair. That's what he calls himself these days—but when I knew him, his name was Adams. Dr. Peter Adams.

"Thinking about Dr. Pete," I say.

"He was good people."

"I know. My fault he isn't anymore."

"No, it's not. You didn't stab him with the Midnight Sword."

"He shouldn't have even been there."

"His choice. Gotta respect that."

"Me and respect aren't exactly best buds, Charlie."

He nods, one glossy black hand on the steering wheel. "You got me there."

"More like Facebook friends. You know, the kind that lurks in the background and never posts anything."

"Right."

"Then you unfriend them and they send you an angry three-page e-mail demanding to know why you think you're better than them and that they've never forgiven you for stealing their boyfriend in the fourth grade."

"Sure."

I sigh. "Tell me I'm doing the right thing, Charlie."

"Why? You suddenly gonna start listening to me?"

"No, but it's a good starting point for an argument."

"Like that's a requirement. Most people need a reason to argue—you just need a place."

"I do not."

"Yeah, you're right."

"You call this an argument?"

"If I do, will you disagree with me?"

"Probably."

He shrugs. "What the hell. You're doing the right thing, Jace."

"I sure hope so . . ."

The last time I was in Stanhope, I was almost bitten by a redheaded werebitch named Cali Edison. This time I intend to be a lot more careful.

The guy handling intakes is a stocky lem with the same high-gloss, transparent skin over black sand Charlie has, and the same slightly irritated, slightly bored demeanor I've seen in too many prison guards. He checks our credentials, makes us stand in a warded circle to tell him if we're carrying any mystic contraband, confiscates

Charlie's short sword and the two spring-loaded holsters filled with silver ball bearings he wears up either sleeve, and more or less ignores my gun. It's not that he's incompetent—it's that a global spell cast in the twelfth century has made the very concept of a firearm seem ridiculous here since then. Despite the fact that my Ruger Super Redhawk Alaskan has the power to put a basketball-size hole in his chest, the guard is incapable of viewing it as anything more than a toy.

"What is that thing, anyway?" he says, eyeing it in my holster. "Some kind of hair dryer?"

"Yeah. Does a real good job of blowing things away."

The guard shakes his blocky, hairless head. "Well, keep an eye on it. Lot of thropes in here are vain enough to want something like that. Probably try to steal it if you give 'em a chance."

"I'll keep that in mind."

Tair's already waiting in the interview room, sitting on a wooden chair and chained at the neck, wrists, and ankles to a steel post with just enough silver in it to make him *very* uncomfortable if he tries to change form. More precautions than they took with Cali, but Tair's already developed a rep as a dangerous customer in the short time he's been incarcerated here. Of course, a life sentence for treason will give you a pretty solid foundation to build on.

He smiles at me when Charlie and I walk in, the same open, slightly wry smile that Dr. Pete used to give me. I wonder if he's been practicing it—the way Tair leered at me every time we met was a lot less subtle. He's wearing an orange jumpsuit, he's still got the streak of gray dyed into his shaggy brown hair, and he still reminds me of a young Harrison Ford.

"Hey, Jace," he says affably. "Good to see you. You bring me a cell-warming present?"

There's a table in the middle of the room, with two chairs behind it. Charlie and I sit. "Maybe I have, Tair. Maybe I'm here to tell you that all your troubles are over, all is forgiven, and there's a big pile of cash just outside the wall that'll cushion your fall when you pole-vault over it to freedom."

His smile gets wider. "I missed you, too. You looking after her, Charlie?"

Charlie's stare is as flat as a snake on the interstate. "Always."

"Good. I know Special Agent Valchek has a tendency to get herself into situations she can't get herself out of."

"Unlike you," says Charlie.

"Ha!" Tair barks. "Well, you got me there, pal. Or should I say, you got me *here*."

"That could change," I say. I keep my voice as neutral as possible.

"Oh, I doubt that." Tair sounds more amused than fatalistic. "I'm not going to testify against my former employer, Jace."

"Even though he's dead?" Tair used to work for an international arms merchant named Silver Blue—until Charlie decapitated him.

"His organization is still up and running. In fact, they've already made at least two attempts on my life since I got here." If this bothers him at all, it doesn't show.

"I haven't heard anything about that."

He shrugs, the chains giving a metallic tinkle with the movement. "Took care of it myself. Didn't want you to worry."

Maybe it's the mood I'm in, maybe it's Tair playing me—but just for a second he sounds *exactly* like Dr. Pete. It's the kind of thing he'd say.

"I'm not here to get you to testify, Tair. I'm here with a different kind of offer."

The sly look this produces on his face is a lot more like the Tair I know. Dr. Pete and I went on exactly one date, and nothing much happened—but going out with Tair would have been very, very different. Not that I would have let him get far, but . . .

Damn it. Did I mention he looks like a young Harrison Ford?

"If you're thinking about conjugal visits, we'll have to get married first," he says. "If, that is, I say yes. I mean, this is awfully sudden—"

"How'd you like to have your sentence reduced?"

He pauses, studies me. Sees that I'm serious. "What did you have in mind?"

"Sorcery. There's a Shinto priest who says he can reverse what the Midnight Sword did to you. Return your original persona."

He looks at me blankly for a second, not giving anything away. "Bringing back your beloved Dr. Pete. And I would do this because?"

"It would greatly reduce your sentence. Enough that even early parole would be possible."

"Ah." He thinks about it for a second, staring at a space just above my head. "You can't do this unless I give you my permission, or we wouldn't be having this conversation."

"Yes," I admit.

"Uh-huh. So this isn't about what you can *get* from me—it's about what you're willing to *give* me."

Charlie stands up. "C'mon, Jace. Let's go. This mook doesn't know a good deal when he hears one."

"Tell your pet sandbag to sit," Tair says. "Let's discuss this."

I nod at Charlie, and he sits back down.

"You're asking me in essence to commit suicide. Why should I?"

"It's not suicide. You'll still be alive—you'll even retain some memories of your time as Tair. Mostly, that'll seem like a dream—but the priest assures me that at your core, you'll still be the same person. You'll have the same soul."

"Interesting metaphysical dilemma. A psychic lobotomy in return for a get-out-of-jail-free card."

"It's better than spending the rest of your existence in prison. What's a thrope life expectancy these days—three hundred years?"

"Depends on the bloodline. Plus your diet, getting regular exercise . . . oh, and not getting shanked for your pudding. But let's say I'm provisionally interested."

"The procedure would be performed at a Shinto shrine—"

"Hold on. You haven't heard my provisions yet."

I raise an eyebrow. "You think you're in a position to bargain? I'm giving you an opportunity here."

He shakes his head, still smiling. "No, you're not. You're giving *yourself* a chance to get a friend back—good old safe, boring Dr. Adams. I'm not getting a damn thing; he is."

"Then why ask for anything? You're not going to benefit anyway."

His smile fades. "Because there's more to me than just self-interest. The doc and I had the same parents, the same friends, the same childhood. Hell, I still have the same genes. You really think I'm not capable of caring about anybody but myself?"

That stops me. Tair may be arrogant, he may be ruthless, but everything he said is still true. He and Dr. Pete used to be the same person—it's the reason I cut Tair more slack than maybe I should.

"Before I tell you what I want," he says, "I need you to understand a few things. About me and my history."

"Which one?" Charlie growls.

"Let's start with what you recall about good ol' Dr. Pete. About what happened to him and how he became the person you know—sorry, knew—and loved."

I ignore the last two words of that statement—Tair is convinced Dr. Pete and I had a thing, mostly based on his own inflated ego. He's wrong. Mostly. "I know he was studying human medicine. He did some moonlighting as a biothaumaturge to help pay for his education—activating illegal golems for the Gray Market."

"Golems that were used, essentially, as disposable slaves." Tair glances at Charlie. "How's that sit with you, Charlie? Whipping up members of your race for a little hard labor, then turning them into cement mix when they're worn out?"

Charlie doesn't rise to the bait. He just stares back, unblinking, about as readable as a block of granite.

Tair shrugs. "Better than no life at all, I guess. If you can call what you do living—no sex, no food, no chemical recreation. Hey, I heard a great lem joke the other day—what do you call a golem with no eyes and no ears? A levee."

Charlie smiles. It's not a friendly gesture.

"Enough," I say. "I know Dr. Pete was approached by the Gray Wolves, this world's Mafia. They wanted him to work for them full-time. He turned them down—and they slaughtered his entire pack."

Tair says nothing for a long moment. His face is carefully, completely composed, and when he finally does respond, his tone is casual.

"Yeah. That's what happened, all right. And that's where the good doctor and I parted company."

The Dr. Pete I knew had gone to the authorities. They had introduced him to the Adams pack, a group composed of orphans and outcasts with no place else to go.

I'd met them—they were a large, boisterous clan, closely knit and fiercely loyal. They'd given Dr. Pete the strength to pull himself together, to keep going and become the healer he'd always wanted to be, while their affiliation with the NSA had protected him from reprisals.

But that was before an insane shaman had plunged a powerful artifact called the Midnight Sword into Dr. Pete's chest. The Sword had altered key points in Dr. Pete's personal history, changing good decisions in his past into bad ones and physically kicking him back a week or so in time. He'd woken up with a head full of memories that had never happened and a name he'd chosen for himself years ago: Tair.

He tries to keep his tone light, but I can hear the emotion he's trying to hide. "See, *I* didn't run to the cops. I just ran. The killers tried to make it look like a robbery gone wrong, but I wasn't fooled. Didn't add up, didn't make sense, not any of it, not at first. Know what my reaction was, when I finally got it? When I finally figured out that this was meant to *recruit* me? I was *insulted*."

I don't say a word. Neither does Charlie.

"I mean, they thought I was so *insecure,* so *gullible,* that I would just blindly accept the murder of my entire pack as some sort of horrible act of random violence. That I would *welcome* their invitation to join them without even *thinking* about it."

The stress in his voice is trying to break out, hitting certain words harder than others. He doesn't let it.

"When I realized I wasn't in any danger, I surfaced. Let them contact me. Let them . . . *comfort* me." He almost spits the two syllables out. "Got inside their defenses, got them to trust *me*. It was a game I played—how good could I become at fooling them? How far could I go to prove I was worth trusting?"

His gaze has lowered to the floor while he's been talking, but now he raises his eyes to meet mine. They're very, very cold. "Turns out I was willing to go pretty far. And when I was well and truly in their inner circle, I sold them out to a rival family. And helped kill every single one."

I study the challenge in his eyes. He's just admitted multiple murders to a federal agent, while in custody. No details, but enough to get him into several lifetimes' worth of trouble.

If any of it had actually occurred.

But, of course, it hadn't. His revenge was part of a past that didn't exist except in his mind. And he knew it.

"That ship has sailed," I say. "A long time ago. Dr. Pete dealt with it—the *right* way. An investigation was opened, arrests were made. The people responsible for your pack's murder have paid for their crimes."

"Oh, I know. Once I'd adjusted to my rebirth, I looked into it. I had two very powerful mystic items in my possession for a while, and then I went to work for an international arms dealer. Believe me, before Charlie here separated Silver Blue's head from his shoulders, the man had every criminal organization in the world on speed dial. Using his contacts to find out what the Carcione family was up to these days wasn't hard."

He stops and waits for me to process that.

I nod. "I'm guessing the Carcione family isn't around anymore."

"I wouldn't know. But I also wouldn't be surprised if some of them ran into a little bad luck." He pauses, then lets the steel show in his voice. "In fact, I'd guess that bad luck affected *every—single—one of them.*"

I frown. I thought he was building up to some kind of pitch for revenge—but it sounds like he's already taken care of that. "Tair, what do you *want*?"

"Back in the day—the nonexistent day, you understand—the Carciones' biggest rivals were the Falzo family. They were the ones I betrayed the Carciones to, the ones who wiped them out. I didn't do it on a whim; I was very, very careful. Revenge has to be meticulous to be successful—otherwise it'll blow up in your face. I did a lot of research on the Falzos, studied them, got to know who they were and what they were about. A good assassin has to know his weapon, and the Falzos were going to be mine. I did this at the same time I was trying to convince the Carciones that I was a loyal and faithful employee, turning out illegal lems in an underground factory. It wasn't enough to just be convincing—I had to be *perfect*. I immersed myself in their world, became what they wanted me to be. Holding just enough of myself back to remember why I was there in the first place."

He falls silent, gathering his thoughts. I have no idea where he's going with this.

"It changed me," he says at last. "Made me who I am today. But it wasn't all bad."

"Yeah," says Charlie. "Look where you are now."

Tair ignores him. "See, it's never as simple as who's good and who's not. People are complex. Some of the people in the Falzo family turned out to be honorable, if not law-abiding. I made more than just alliances, I made friends. After the Carciones were wiped out, the Falzos offered to take me in. I accepted."

"No, you didn't," I say. "None of that actually happened, remember?"

"As far as I'm concerned it did. I *know* them, even if they don't know me. Which is why I approached them after I'd dealt with my . . . unfinished business."

After you'd executed your pack's killers, you mean. "And they were receptive?"

"Considering recent events I'd had a hand in—events that proved quite favorable to them—yes. The Don, in particular, was intrigued to hear about my situation. He was skeptical at first, but I knew things he would only have revealed to a close friend. Examinations by his own shamans verified my condition."

"So you and Don Falzo rekindled a relationship he didn't know existed. So what?"

"So that's what I want in return for my cooperation. I want you to do a favor for Don Arturo Falzo."

TWO

I'm pretty quiet on the drive back to Seattle.

Charlie generally respects my silences, probably because he doesn't get too many of them—maybe *enjoys* is a better description than *respects*.

This time, though, he just can't keep quiet. About twenty minutes go by before he says, "Bad idea."

"I'm not so sure."

"You being sure has nothing to do with it. Bad idea."

"What could it hurt?"

"You're a federal agent. He's the head of one of the largest organized crime families in the state. Yeah, no way that could go wrong."

"It's not much of a favor."

"I'll bet the guy who got those theater tickets for John Wilkes Booth had the same thought."

"Booth assassinated Lincoln here, too? With what?"

"Wooden gavel with the handle sharpened to a point."

"Huh. Anyway, I still don't see the harm."

"Look harder."

I give him a glare instead. "I'm not big on helping

out *La Lupo Grigorio* either, okay? *But it could get Dr. Pete back.*"

"I doubt that."

"Why?" I demand. "I had Eisfanger check out the whole procedure. He says it could work."

"*If* Tair cooperates."

"He'll have to, or I won't give him what he wants."

"Sure. Let me ask you one question, okay?"

"Go ahead."

"What would you say is the single defining aspect of Tair's personality?"

A number of terms scroll through my brain: *Cocky. Ambitious. Obnoxious.* But there's only one that really applies to the whole package.

"Ego," I say.

"Yeah. You really think a guy like that would willingly give up his sense of self in order to help *anyone*?"

That, of course, is the question that's been bouncing off the inside of my skull for the last thirty miles; I've been trying to find a different answer than the one that keeps popping up.

"So he's playing us."

"Like a three-card monte dealer. What's to stop him from pretending the procedure took when it really didn't?"

"Eisfanger says there are tests, ways to confirm that."

"Tests can be beaten."

"So can know-it-all partners. Shut up and drive, okay?"

Which is exactly what he does. No matter what I may say to his face, as a partner Charlie really *can't* be beat.

It's the end of my working day, so Charlie drops me off at home. I live in an apartment building in an okay part of town—respectable, not too flashy, a little larger than

I could have afforded at my previous job as an FBI profiler. Of course, in a world largely populated by supernatural beings there's a lot more nocturnal activity, but
I've adjusted to that pretty well. I was always something
of a night owl, and my current work schedule has me
starting my shift around 7:00 PM and getting off at 4:00
in the morning. It's around four thirty when I open my
front door.

And encounter pandemonium.

A middle-aged, paunchy man with brown-and-white
hair, wearing nothing but baggy, bright pink sweatpants,
is charging around my living room on all fours. He's got
a toddler riding on his back, holding on to his ears with
both hands and screaming with glee, while a teenager
with a double row of razor blades embedded in her skull
is sitting at the dining room table, tapping away at a laptop with earphones on, managing to look bored and impatient at the same time.

"Um," I say. Nobody appears to notice me.

"*Um,*" I repeat, then, "HEY!"

The rodeo comes to a crashing halt against the dining room table. The toddler looks at me and giggles.
The teenager—Dr. Pete's niece, Xandra—looks annoyed
and tries to yank the headphones off, but the cord catches
on one of the razor blades, which severs it neatly.

"Jace!" the man says, radiating joy. His name is Galahad, and despite appearances he's actually a St. Bernard—
one with the lycanthropy gene in his DNA, probably
introduced when an ancestor survived a thrope bite. He's
a dog were, transforming into a mostly human being
every night when the sun sets. He's also boisterous, good-
natured, loyal, and can brew a pot of coffee on command.
What more could you ask for in a pet?

The toddler is my friend Gretchen's daughter, Anna.

Anna's barely a year old, but she's amazingly advanced; I guess vampire babies have certain natural advantages.

"Guh buh *bep*!" Anna blurts out from her perch on Galahad's back, and points at me imperiously. She's as dark as her mother is blond, with beautiful brown eyes, dusky skin, and coal-black hair. From her father's side of the family, I guess.

"You said it." Thank God the full vampire speed and strength don't kick in until they stop aging—regular babysitting duties are stressful enough without worrying about a toddler who's faster and stronger than you are. Not to mention more resilient—even at this age, Anna's more or less invulnerable to everything except sunlight, garlic, anything sharp made of wood or silver, and decapitation. She still cries when she bonks her head, though, and I don't think I'll ever get used to the bottles of pink milk.

"Hey, Jace," Xandra says. She looks a little like a tropical fish with two stainless-steel fins on her head. "How'd it go?"

"Complicated. Thanks for covering for me with Anna."

"No problem. Gally did most of the work, anyway. Anna thinks he's a horse."

"I can see that."

"Yeah, so, I'm gonna take off now." She gets to her feet, grabs a backpack from the table, and stuffs what's left of her headphones into it.

I head for the kitchen, Gally trotting along behind me on his knees. Anna squeals. "Really?" I say over my shoulder. "I was hoping we could hang out for a bit. You could fill me in on the new hairstyle."

"It's called blading," she says. "Implants, with a charm that lets the skin and muscle grow around it to keep it in place. Otherwise, it would just kind of get pushed out as it healed." And as a thrope, she doesn't have to worry about infection. What is it with teenagers and sticking things in their bodies that don't belong there?

My brain replays that last comment inside my head, and I'm really glad I didn't say it out loud. I mean, that's basically a teenager's job description, right?

"It looks very . . ."

"Don't say sharp."

"I was going to say dangerous."

"Yeah, isn't it great?"

I shake my head as I dig out the coffee and the grinder. "Yeah, absolutely. You're gonna spend a lot of money on headphone cords, though."

"S'okay. I was about to go wireless anyway." She slings the backpack over her shoulder. "Sorry I can't stick around, but I'd rather not be here when the Gretch arrives."

Gretchen and Xandra don't really see eye-to-eye. Well, Gretch is a 130-year-old vampire and intelligence analyst for the NSA, while Xandra is a teenage werewolf with authority issues. Go figure.

"Okay, but we're still on for the actionfest, right?"

"Hey, would I miss Charlie Chaplin and John Wayne kicking some serious ass?" On the surface, Thropirelem looks a lot like my world—but dig a little deeper and you uncover all sorts of weirdness. Hollywood plus vampires plus werewolves equals some truly bizarre productions. I have a particular fondness for the action-comedy buddy-cop genre—maybe because I live one every day—and you can't do better than Chaplin and the Duke.

"*The Little Trampire* and *True Grit Three*," I say. "It's the best one in the series."

"You won't say that when you see number five. *Truest Grit: Down and Gritty.*"

"We'll see."

"Later!"

The door bangs shut and then she's gone. Too bad—I really could have used someone to talk to about the situation, and I already have Charlie's point of view. Xandra would have taken the opposite stance, I'm sure— Dr. Pete was her favorite uncle, and she misses him terribly.

I take off my holster and gun, lock them away where neither Anna nor Galahad can get to them, then pour myself a cup of coffee and get some food ready for the baby and the dog. Anna gets a bottle of pink milk warmed to body temperature, and Galahad gets a plastic baggie filled with kibble, which he promptly sits on the couch to eat, like a kid with a bag of potato chips.

Anna's halfway through her bottle when there's a brisk knock at the door. Gretchen, no doubt. She's a little early, but that's hardly a surprise; Gretch's never late for anything, and when it comes to her child, I'm amazed she lets Anna out of her sight at all.

I get up, cradling Anna in one arm while she greedily slurps back her dinner, and open the door. "Hey there, Mother—"

Of the three guys standing in my hallway, none of them is Gretch.

"—sucker," I say.

All three are thropes, and two are in half-were form— hulking, muscular wolf-men with long muzzles full of razor-sharp teeth and hairy, clawed hands. They're wearing expensive, hand-tailored suits, a lot of gold jewelry, and some god-awful kind of cologne designed for thropes that smells like a wet dog who's been rolling in week-old liver.

The third guy stands between the two brutes. He's wearing much the same thing, but he's in human form so he's a lot smaller. His hair is black and oiled, he's got a greasy little mustache and sideburns, and in general reminds me more of a ferret than a wolf.

"Good evening," he says. "Jace, right? We'd like to offer you—"

"Not interested," I say, and slam the door in his face. Or I would have, except he puts out his hand and blocks it.

"—like I said, we'd like to offer you a ride to your meeting."

"What meeting?"

"Your meeting with Don Falzo."

"I don't have one." I'm painfully aware of the toddler I'm cradling in one arm.

"No? Your invitation musta got misplaced—I apologize for any inconvenience. Shall we go?"

"I'm sort of occupied. If you could just wait until her mother shows up—"

"I'm afraid time is kinda of the essence. The kid can come along, though—we love kids. Don't we, guys?"

The two well-dressed thugs growl in response. Right.

I weigh my options. No weapon, baby in the line of fire, three of them and one of me. Galahad would get his throat ripped out in a second. God*damn* it.

"Okay," I say. "But if she needs a diaper change, I'm gonna expect some help."

So they hustle me downstairs and into a waiting sedan, a long, black thing that looks like they stole it from a funeral home. The ferrety guy drives, while the two thugs keep me company in the backseat. Anna just keeps working on her bottle, more or less oblivious. A predawn light is creeping up the horizon, but it doesn't worry me too much; I grabbed a hooded blanket on my way out the door, big enough to protect her from the sun if we're out that late.

The car takes us from my modest neighborhood to a much more upscale one known as Queen Anne. Its houses—or should I say, estates—are perched on a hill, with the best views on the west side overlooking Puget Sound. The Falzo grounds are pretty close to the top, surrounded by high, red-brick walls topped with silvery razor wire and security cameras every twenty feet; I doubt if so much as a ninja mosquito could get in without setting off alarms. The Don's obviously paranoid about security, and probably has extremely good reasons for it.

There are more thugs at the gate, armed with crossbows, and I see at least another half a dozen once we're inside the grounds. The house is an appropriately monster-size fortress, more castle than mansion, with the odd turret sprouting here and there from the roof like granite mushrooms. All the windows seem to be barred, and behind its mahogany exterior I think the front door used to seal a bank vault.

None of this impresses Anna, or me. I've been around rich crooks before, and generally they use houses the way a middle-aged man uses a sports car: as compensation for insecurity. The more ostentatious the furnishings, the easier it is to spot the dirt-poor, two-bit criminal yelling at the world: I am *too* somebody! Yeah, somebody who doesn't understand he's living in a cliché. So I'm gonna skip the description of the rugs, paintings, marble statues, wood paneling, and all the other crapola that wise guys seem to think exude class, and just say it was a big house with a bunch of expensive junk in it being guarded by professional killers.

Plus a vampire baby and an extremely irritated NSA agent.

I don't take well to being kidnapped. I take having a child along as an implied hostage even less so, and having it done by guys who smell this bad is just about making my eyes cross.

They take me to a room. A home theater, it looks like, with five rows of comfy, plush seats, a screen that takes up one wall, and a quaint little popcorn machine on a cart. There's a single chair at the head of the room, in front of the screen and facing the rows of seats—maybe they expect me to do some stand-up. I can see the backs of three heads in the front row.

The goons stay at the door, as does Ferret-face. I walk in, hearing the door click closed behind me. Anna's fallen asleep in my arms—car rides seem to do that to her.

I walk to the front of the room, but don't take the chair. I study the three men in front of me, trying to get a feel for just what I've gotten myself into before I open my mouth and probably make things worse. Hey, knowing your weaknesses is a strength.

Don't see that many fat thropes, but I guess the guy on the end has been putting away the pasta as well as the veal. He spills out of his seat on either side, dressed in what seems to be a velvet tracksuit of deep purple, with matching leather loafers. He's got a jowly face, thick lips, and a shiny black pompadour in an oily, frozen tidal wave on top of his head. This is what Elvis would look like if he'd retired and gone into the fried chicken business.

The second guy is wearing a sharkskin suit in a dark gray, the body inside it lean and muscular. He's tall, pale as a hemovore, and has only the barest dark fuzz covering his bony scalp. He makes up for that with a pair of bushy black eyebrows, waxed into curving points like devil horns.

Number three looks like an aging football player—wide shoulders, gut starting to bulge, thick arms ending in big hands. He's got salt-and-pepper hair, neatly combed back. He's wearing a suit, a simple black number with a thin tie, like he's on his way to a funeral. Hope it isn't mine.

"Miss Valchek," number three says. Deep, rumbly voice. "Thank you for joining us on such short notice. My name is Dino. This is Louie"—he indicates Mr. Sharkskin—"and Atticus."

"Atticus?"

The fat guy shrugs. "*To Kill a Mockingbird* was my mom's favorite book. Whatta you gonna do?"

"Well, you know who I am," I say. "Why am I here?"

That's a question I already know the answer to, but I want to see what they tell me. Tair might not have given me the whole story.

"We need your expertise," Dino says. "In a very sensitive matter."

"Sensitive," Louie says, leaning forward with his forearms on his knees, "as in it doesn't leave this room."

"Hit me," I say. "Uh—I mean, tell me."

Louie raises one demonic eyebrow at me, which is a little like watching a caterpillar do a push-up. "It's about the Don," he says.

"Yeah," says Atticus. "We have what you might call a delicate situation."

"Sensitive *and* delicate," I say. "Does it involve lacy things, too? 'Cause you've got to hand-wash those."

"What do you know about *La Lupo Grigorio*?" Dino asks.

"Quite a bit. Seeing as how I work for the National Security Agency and all."

"You know how we decide leadership issues?"

"Sheep-eating contests?"

That at least gets a grin from Atticus, though Louie scowls. Dino seems to have decided that the best response is to ignore my attempts at wit, though he's going to regret that. It just makes me try harder.

"We do have contests, yes. Just like packs in the wild, we choose our leaders based on strength. Strength of mind, strength of will, strength of endurance. I can't give you any details, but believe me when I say that the only way you get to be head of a family in the Gray Wolves is to be the toughest, wiliest, meanest son-of-a-bitch within a thousand miles."

"Okay, let's agree that's exactly what Don Falzo is," I say. "Which means you three *aren't*. You're capos, right? Dino, I've got you pegged as consigliere. So let's skip the chase and cut to the kill—why are three of the Don's flunkies talking to me about their boss?"

"Because we think he might be getting goofy," Atticus says.

"Getting Goofy? He's put out a contract on a Disney character?"

Dino sighs. "At this point, I wouldn't put it past him. See, he's—he's acting unstable. Not himself."

"Mentally unwell," says Louie.

"Like I said," says Atticus. "Goofy."

They all sound a little hesitant, unsure of themselves. That's because the supernatural races, being mostly immune to disease, have little experience with either the fact or the terminology of the mentally ill. Little—but not none.

"What about Hades Rabies?" I ask.

"He's been tested," Dino says. "Negative. We think

he must have watched that video on the Internet. Won't tell us, one way or the other."

I nod. Hades Rabies is a cursed virus, one that infects thropes and makes them crazy. If that wasn't what was affecting the Don, odds were good he'd been exposed to the Ghatanothoa meme—but I needed more to go on.

"So what's he done?"

Dino glances at Louie. Louie glances at Dino. Atticus says, "He's been eatin' the furniture."

"Really?"

"Yeah. Chowed down on most of a couch the other day."

Now Dino and Louie are both looking at Atticus. They're not happy, but Atticus just looks back and shrugs again. "Hey, she wanted to know. What, I should tell her about the Jacuzzi?"

"What about the—"

"Never mind," Dino growls. "Look, all we want is for you to check him out, let us know if he's losing his mind or not. You can do that, right?"

"Maybe," I say. "Depends on whether or not he cooperates. And whether or not I do."

"All due respect, Miss Valchek," says Louie, "I'd advise you to help us out in this matter." He stares at me, unblinking, a predator with his prey cornered. I feel my own hackles rise in an automatic response—I don't do well with being bullied—but I bite back on my anger. The fact that I have a sleeping infant in my arms helps. "Besides," he continues, "I understand you have something to gain, too."

So he knows about Tair's offer. "Yeah? Can you guarantee Tair will follow through on his end?"

Dino smiles, a big, wolfy grin. "Oh, he'll follow through. Being in stir—and not too popular with certain other parties—he's pretty much committed to keeping us happy."

Well, that makes sense. Tair would double-cross me in a second, but he'll think twice about doing it to the Mob, especially in his circumstances.

"Let's say I do this. How would you want to—"

"Right away," Louie says. "He won't let a shaman near him, but he's agreed to talk to you. He could change his mind at any moment, though—you have to do it *now*."

Now I understand why I was yanked out of my apartment in the middle of the night: They're worried the Don will do something a lot worse than chewing on the upholstery and figure they better take a shot while they still have one.

"One question before I start. Which way are you hoping this will go?"

"It's not like that," Dino says flatly. "We gotta *know*, that's all. If he's losing it, he'll get replaced. But we have a code about things like this, on account of dealing with Hades Rabies. He's got to be examined by a professional, one everybody signs off on. Replacing the head of a family, that's not something that gets done lightly."

No, of course not. It occurs to me that I have an opportunity here to remove a major criminal figure from a position of power—but who's to say his replacement won't be worse? For that matter, how do I know I won't screw up some ongoing investigation by another agency?

I look down at Anna, trying to think.

"Don't worry about her," Atticus says. "We're family people, remember? She'll be just fine while you and the Don talk. Then we'll take both of you home." He gives me a jowly, Elvisoid smile.

"You better," I say. "Or I'll come back with a black

ops team and put a silver-tipped crossbow bolt into the left eye of everyone in this house." I give him a smile of my own, and it's not nearly as jolly. "Now let's get this over with."

THREE

The defining aspect of the Mafia, on my world and this one, is greed. Greed is at the root of all seven of the deadly sins: Lust is greed for more sex, anger is greed for violence, sloth is greed for more rest, envy is greed for something someone else has that you want. Pride is just greed congratulating itself on a job well done.

And then there's gluttony.

It may be a cliché that Italian mobsters are obsessed with cooking, but in my experience it holds true a lot of the time. Aside from the fact that Italian cuisine is obsession-worthy all on its own, gluttony is one of the seven deadly sins that they can indulge in without worrying about the law. Well, that and sloth, but in a world of carnivores that's more likely to be a main course than a hobby.

In fact, it may even be what the Don is cooking when I walk through the kitchen door. As a vegetarian I'm not that crazy about the smell of cooking meat, but whatever he has bubbling in that giant pot on the stove, it isn't something my nose can identify.

He's absorbed in his work, stirring the pot with a

wooden spoon and adding a handful of spices. Don Falzo is a robust, large-framed man, with a full head of iron-gray hair that looks more leonine than lupine. His features are strong, angular, and wrinkled, with a squared-off jaw and a Roman nose. Deep-set eyes beneath craggy eyebrows darker than his hair. He's wearing a plain blue chambray shirt, tan slacks, brown leather loafers, and an apron that proclaims MY MAMA LOVES TO COOK!

"Don Falzo?"

He doesn't look at me, just sticks his head over the pot, closes his eyes, and inhales through his nose. I guess whatever he's got simmering is doing well, because he smiles. He doesn't look crazy—he looks like somebody's grandfather puttering around in the kitchen.

Then he opens his eyes and turns to me. "Ah. You must be Jace. *Buongiorno.*"

"Hi. You know who I am?"

He turns back to the pot, stirring it slowly. "Yes, of course. You work for the NSA, no? You are the one they call the Bloodhound."

I shouldn't be surprised—wise guys often have as much information about us as we have about them. "That's right. But I'm not here as part of a criminal investigation. Your—associates wanted me to talk to you. If that's all right with you, Don?"

"Please, call me Arturo. Yes, I will speak with you. You do not mind if I continue while we talk? The dish needs tending."

"No, of course not."

When trying to determine someone's mental state during an interview, there are at least twenty different factors you have to consider, from psychomotor behavior to social functioning. You can learn a lot from simple observation—I can already see that his emotional affect is good, he's capable both physically and mentally of paying attention to involved tasks, his mood is open and friendly. His clothing is neat and appropriate, his grooming careful. To learn more, I have to get him to talk.

"I understand you've been a little unsettled lately."

He shrugs. "Perhaps. I am no longer a young man, and so my concerns are not those of youth—but there are always concerns, no? The older you become, the more heavily the world weighs upon you." He's not making eye contact, which could indicate hostility or nervousness—though his tone and attitude seem to contradict that.

"Concerns like losing your position as head of your family?"

He glances at me sharply. "That is not a problem. Every year I face a challenge to my leadership, and every year the challenge fails. My strength is not diminished."

From what I can see, that's true. He has the body language of someone years younger, with none of the stiffness or hesitancy you might expect to see in someone of his age—his apparent age. What his true age is, I have no idea; he could have been around when radio was the big idea. His posture is firm, proud, without any signs of agitation. So far, he seems pretty normal.

I decide to take a more direct approach. "I also hear you ate a couch."

He frowns. He turns back to the pot, lifts the spoon to his lips, and takes a taste. Goal-oriented behavior, good control. He nods, then holds the spoon out toward me. "Taste this."

"I'd rather not." The spoon holds a viscous brown liquid, steam rising off it. I still can't identify what it smells like—oregano, vanilla, and wet paper, maybe?

"Try it." It's not a question, and I can hear the trace of a snarl in his voice. Definite increase in hostility, with abrupt change of emotional affect; he seems more focused now, more suspicious. Before he wouldn't meet my eyes and now he's watching me like a hawk.

"Tell me about the couch, Arturo."

"It was not a couch. It was a demon. It was lurking in my house, waiting for me to sleep so it could slaughter me and take my place. I killed it and sucked the marrow from its bones." His voice is getting rougher, deeper, and his eyes are shifting from black to yellow. Coarse gray fur sprouts from his skin. Bones creak and joints pop as his skeleton grows and his mass increases.

I take a step backward. On the world of my birth, a statement like the one he just made would definitely be grounds for a psychiatric assessment—but here, he could actually be telling the truth.

The last word he growls before his mouth deforms too far for human speech is, *"Look!"* He sweeps one long, hairy arm at the pot on the stove, knocking it to the floor and splashing boiling-hot liquid all over the place. I scramble backward and only get a few drops on my legs, but they burn like hell. I can see what he's been cooking now, lying on the kitchen floor in a steaming brown puddle.

Shoes.

A loafer, a sneaker, a bedroom slipper, and a ladies' high-heeled pump. The Don has switched to sign language, which is what thropes use to communicate in were form. *You see? The cloven hooves of the damned!*

"Sure," I say carefully. "And you were cooking them because?"

I was boiling out the evil! He pauses, his long, clawed fingers stroking the air like he's playing an invisible harp. *Once you do that, you can make a really nice manicotti from them. I used the couch for bouillabaisse.*

So *that's* what happened with the Jacuzzi. Well, I know which way my diagnosis is leaning . . . and then he notices *my* shoes.

He points with one long, wicked claw, and growls. I'd really rather not part with them, but I'd like it even less if he decides to remove them himself. He might not take them off my feet first.

I kick both shoes off, using the opportunity to take another backward step toward the door of the kitchen. I'm really not sure if it would be better to run or yell for help—

And then he leaps.

For the shoes, luckily. While he's concentrating on demonic footwear, I bolt for the door.

The lean one, Louie, is just outside—listening in on the conversation, no doubt. He raises a curved eyebrow at me.

I try to bring my breathing under control. "In my considered professional opinion," I say, "he's in a state of nocturnal airborne rodent feces."

"Huh?"

"He's batshit. Crazy as a square cueball. Off-his-rocker-around-the-bend-out-of-his-mind. Your Don is riding the crazy train, *compadre,* and I think he's bought a first-class ticket."

"That's—"

I don't get to hear whatever Louie is about to say, because right then the Don bursts through the door, a seven-foot gray-furred werewolf in a frilly apron with one of my shoes hanging out of the side of his muzzle. It would be hilarious, if I weren't unarmed and facing down an insane lycanthropic mobster.

"Hey," says Louie. "Take it easy—"

With a single backhand swipe, the Don disembowels him.

I won't go into detail here, but it's about as messy and violent as it sounds; I can tell Louie's a man with backbone, because I can see it. He slumps against the wall with an expression on his face that's part shock, part disbelief, and mostly pain.

The Don throws back his head, letting the remains of my shoe drop from his mouth, and howls. "AAAOOOOOOOOWWWHHHH!"

This is it. I'm dead. If he'd do that to one of his own men, then obviously a purveyor of satanic pumps will be shown no mercy. I hope he at least makes it quick.

He glares at me for one long moment, his yellow eyes blazing with madness, and then he turns and bounds away down the hall and around the corner. A second later I hear the smash of a window breaking, and then a tortured screeching that has to be iron bars being ripped out of their frame.

Louie, on his knees on the floor and already trying to stuff various loopy bits back into his belly, stares at me. "Nuts, huh?" he says. "Y'think?"

Thropes are extremely resilient; if the weapon that delivered it isn't made out of silver, they can pretty much come back from almost any wound. Louie's not going to have much of an appetite for a while, but he'll pull through.

Don Arturo Falzo, however, is gone.

Not just gone in the sense of no one home upstairs—he isn't home at all. After leaping out a window, he ran down the hill and jumped in the ocean. His men tried to track him, but even a wolf can't track a swimming thrope. For all they know, he's decided to swim right back to Sicily, by way of the Panama Canal.

I know this because they won't let me or Anna go until they figure out if I had anything to do with him taking off. I know Louie would vouch for me, but he passed out from lack of blood shortly after he found his spleen. I don't think he put it back in the right place, anyway.

They've got Anna and me stuck in the home theater, I guess because they're paranoid about a federal agent seeing the rest of the house. Anna's woken up and she's not happy—I think she needs to feed, but I don't have anything with me and I'm not about to let her latch onto my jugular.

Dino comes in, closing the door behind him. "Sorry about this," he says. "But there's one more thing you got to do before you can leave."

"It better be fast," I say as Anna starts to wail.

"It'll only take a moment."

He motions for me to follow him. I do, carting an unhappy vampire baby under one arm and my remaining shoe in the other. Not the combination of barefoot, pregnant, and in the kitchen that my mother envisioned, I'm sure.

Dino leads me down the hall, to another room about the same size as the home theater. Just outside the door, Atticus is waiting; he takes Anna from me, and her wails get louder. The thick door closing behind me shuts them out completely.

This room is obviously for meetings: It has a long, black slab of a table, with twelve high-backed chairs around it. The walls are hung with portraits of thropes, most in half-were form and wearing some kind of formal outfit that dates them to previous centuries.

There are four flatscreen monitors in a row down the center of the table. Each of them holds the black silhouette of a man's head, features hidden in shadow.

"Honored Dons," Dino says. "This is Dr. Jace Valchek.

She's here to deliver her medical evaluation of Don Falzo."

"Proceed," one of the figures says, though I can't tell which.

"Uh, I didn't have time to do a thorough analysis," I say. "I only talked to him for a few minutes."

"Jace," Dino says. "Just tell them what you told us."

"As near as I can tell, he's mentally ill. Delusional, possibly even schizophrenic."

"Schizophrenic?" one of them demands. "What does that mean?"

"It means he's had a psychotic break. He can no longer tell the difference between what's real and what isn't."

"Demenziale," one of them mutters.

"Yeah. That's my considered opinion, anyway."

"Grazie," somebody says, and all four monitors turn off.

"Are we done now?" I ask. I've lost my shoes, I have a cranky infant in my care—one whose mother is going to show up at my door any minute now, and is entirely capable of mobilizing the Marine Corps to ensure the safety of her child—plus it's almost dawn. I'm starting to head toward cranky myself, and I generally don't have very far to travel at the best of times.

"Almost." Dino's voice is very flat, very cold, all the Mediterranean charm drained out of it. He got what he wanted, and he doesn't have to pretend to be polite anymore. "There's still the little matter of the Don."

"What? I did what you asked me—"

"No. You were supposed to have a little talk with him, feel him out. What you did was drive him over the edge."

"Hey, I am *not* responsible for your Dogfather flipping out—"

"You know who those four men were? The ones you just talked to?"

I know exactly who they must be, but I'm not in a cooperative mood. "A barbershop quartet that forgot to pay their light bill?"

"Those were four of the heads of the Five Families. Don Falzo being number five. And now he's out in the world, running around with a skull full of crazy, and I'm the one that's got to hold things together until we resolve this."

"Isn't that what we just did? Can't you remove him from power now?"

Dino scowls at me. "No. There are rules, a procedure that has to be followed. He's got to be brought back and put down—until then, nothing can be decided. And *you're* the one who's going to do it."

I stare at him in disbelief. "Looks like he's not the only one that's short a few aces in his deck. Why should I—"

"Because if you don't, we'll kill you." Dino meets my eyes calmly, not bothering to ramp up the scary. He doesn't have to. "And your friends. And your family. And your little dog, too."

FOUR

And then they take me and Anna home.

I've got a lot to think about on the drive back. A lot of it is pointless revenge fantasies about what I'd like to do to Dino with a silver meat cleaver, but I force myself to calm down and strategize.

It's obvious why they want me to catch the Don—I'm the one with loads of experience hunting homicidal lunatics. If I fail, Dino has a ready-made scapegoat to publicly slaughter, and if I succeed he can take all the credit. Basic office politics, applicable in the boardroom and the back room.

They drop me off in front of my building, and I get Anna inside and upstairs just before the first rays of dawn creep over the horizon. In typical toddler fashion, she's fallen asleep again. I put her down in the play yard set up in the living room and sink onto the couch.

Galahad pads out of the bedroom. With the sunrise he's become a big brown-and-white St. Bernard, no longer able to pee standing up but compensating for it by generating prodigious amounts of drool. Not really a fair trade, in my opinion.

He comes over, sniffs at the play yard, then puts his head on my lap and gazes at me soulfully. "Thanks, big guy," I say. "Frankly, I could use a little support. How are you at chasing down renegade Mafia Dons?"

He licks my hand, which I take to mean, *I have no idea what you're talking about but I love you.* It helps.

And now I have to figure out what to do.

The first and most attractive option is massive retaliation. Threaten an NSA agent and you're essentially threatening the intelligence agency charged with keeping the United States safe. One brief conversation with my boss and I can have that whole estate overrun with cold-eyed professional soldiers who make the Don's men seem like pimply-faced high school bullies. If I happen to mention that Anna was along for the ride, they might just burn the whole thing to the ground to make a point.

But that's not going to get Dr. Pete back.

I can't really let the NSA know what's happening until after Tair lives up to his end of the deal. Then I can call in reinforcements—but not before.

Looks like I'm going back to prison.

Gretchen shows up about fifteen minutes later. Gretchen is blond, British, and a pire. She's also an NSA intelligence analyst, one of the smartest people I've ever known, and a very good friend.

She's already shed her UV-resistant mask, goggles, and gloves by the time I answer the door. "Hello," she says. "How's the little nightcrawler?"

"Fast asleep. Went through three bottles and two naps."

She strides inside, leans over the edge of the play yard, and sighs. "Good God," she murmurs. "She's so perfect, isn't she?"

"Absolutely," I say. When it comes to her child, all the other things Gretch is fade away and she's just a mom. A mom who knows about fifteen different ways to kill you with her bare hands, but just as gooey-eyed and sentimental as every parent is when looking at the love of their life. Me, I have to make do with a dog.

She asks me the usual questions about feeding and diaper changes and so on, and I don't have to lie to her once. That's good, because Gretch is far, far too experienced at picking up on the slightest thread of falsehood.

"How did things go at Stanhope?" she asks.

I tell her. "So apparently the Don is loopy. I've agreed to do an evaluation for them later today—I can't really see any downside to it."

"Make sure you take appropriate precautions."

"Of course," I say. "Nothing to worry about."

Which is how, a little less than five hours later, I find myself in a room at the Tsubaki Grand Shrine School, observing a Shinto ritual being performed by a vampire on a werewolf.

Shinto is big on Thropirelem, though it's evolved into something considerably different from the Japanese religion I'm familiar with. Here it's a magic system, one based on an intricate bureaucracy of deities, spirits, and ancestors. It's animistic in nature, which means one of its central tenets is the belief that everything has a soul: people, animals, plants, weather, even rivers and mountains. The Shinto on my world relies on praying to these spirits and hoping they do you a favor; here it's less about sucking up and more about negotiation. A high-powered Shinto priest is essentially a wizard, with various forces of nature at his command.

The one in the center of the room is a man named Julian Wiebe, a pire with wispy blond hair wearing a loose white robe belted with a wide red sash. He's kneeling before a small stone shrine shaped like a miniature pagoda, while Tair—somewhat incongruous in his bright orange prison jumpsuit—kneels beside him. I'm standing just inside the door, observing.

Tair's not wearing manacles, which makes me nervous. Julian insisted they be removed because they'd interfere with the ritual, and I had no choice but to agree.

I know Julian Wiebe through his brother, Helmut, a bail jumper who once took me hostage for all of two minutes. After a bounty hunter named Silverado hauled Helmut's sorry, Cloven-dealing ass back to jail, I had Gretchen verify Julian's story that he'd been trying to get his brother back on the straight and narrow; when it proved to be true, I'd pulled a few strings and helped Helmut get a reduced sentence. Julian had been grateful—and gracious—enough to thank me by offering me the use of his dojo. The Tsubaki School is in Granite Falls, a little too far from Seattle to drive on a regular basis, but I had gone out once or twice; Julian's head of Aikido Studies there, and we'd even sparred a few times. He took it easy on me, for which *I* was grateful—a pire is hard to beat in a fight as it is, but fighting a pire with martial arts training is like trying to hit lightning with a Wiffle bat.

So why am I nervous? I've got armed guards outside the door. I've got a high-powered sorcerer and aikido master keeping a lid on things. My own .454-caliber insurance is slung in a holster under my arm. Everything's under control.

Uh-huh.

The air is heavy with the smell of burning incense. Julian is chanting in a regular, sonorous voice, an invocation for the Spirit of Beneficent Restructuring to intercede on our behalf. When I said the Shinto spirit-realm was a bureaucracy, I wasn't kidding; the whole thing is intricately layered in a hierarchy that covers everything from bacteria to the sun. The Spirit of Beneficent Restructuring is apparently a popular guy in corporate circles.

But what we want him to do here is restructure not only memory, but a little bit of time itself. To take Dr. Pete's memories from the last moment they actually existed, and bring them into the here and now. Normally the present is continually overwriting the past, but Julian is going to try to subvert that, getting the historical to impose itself on the current—bringing in a ghost to repossess the body it once inhabited.

Bringing back Dr. Pete, and killing Tair.

Okay, it's not really murder. Magic created Tair and magic will uncreate him, but it still feels like a cold-blooded execution to me. I'm trying to view it as a medical procedure, like removing a brain tumor that's changed someone's personality, but it's not working. Tumors don't generally make passes at you.

The chanting stops. I can feel something electric in the air, a building charge of mystic energy. Without a word, Tair and Julian pivot on their knees so they're facing each other. Julian places one hand against Tair's chest, palm flat and fingers spread, and the other on his forehead. A white light begins to emanate from where Julian's skin touches Tair's.

Time stops. I mean it literally freezes—all sound, all motion just ends, like somebody hit the PAUSE button on a really high-quality TV.

And then it starts going backward.

Julian warned me about this beforehand, but it's still kind of a shock. The weirdest part is how it feels; you might not think you'd notice the difference between the blood flowing in your veins one way and then flowing the other, but you do. I can hear Julian chanting in reverse, which will apparently stop once he gets to the beginning of the ceremony—

But he never reaches it.

The ritual trappings of magic are usually just methods of focusing the user's will, and past experience has shown me that Tair has plenty of that. Which is how he somehow manages to raise his hand, knocking Julian's away from his chest.

The effect is immediate and explosive. A flare bright enough to sear retinas bursts from the broken connection, the whole world going an agonizing white. Time remains suspended, and in the eternal instant that follows I realize that Tair's eyes were closed.

And then everything shudders forward again, like a train jerking a line of boxcars into motion. All I can see are dancing spots, but I go for my gun just the same.

It's not there anymore. Pires are fast, but thropes are no slowpokes, either.

The spell that makes it impossible to take firearms in this reality seriously affects Tair the same way it does everyone else—so he uses it to *club* Julian instead. It's not easy to coldcock a pire with something that isn't made of silver or wood, but the backlash from the interrupted spell has already knocked Julian for a loop; being smacked between the eyes by a desperate thrope wielding a few pounds of cold steel is enough to knock the priest out for the next hour.

I reconstructed all this later, of course. At the time, I was still trying to blink away the damn spots in front of my eyes and yelling my head off for the guards to get in there.

Stupid. That was exactly what he wanted.

My vision's still blurry, but I can see that Tair's shifted into half-were mode, a snarling, six-and-a-half-foot wolfman with claws as long as his fangs. He doesn't seem to have my gun anymore, but he's picked up the stone shrine itself and pitches it overhand at the guard charging through the doorway, smashing the lem out of the room and into the hall.

The other guard, a thrope, has his bow drawn and ready. He does his best to put a silver-tipped shaft into his target's heart, but Tair's already moved, putting me in between him and the guard. That's not going to work for long—

And then I feel something very, very sharp slice through the fabric of my pants, on the inside of my thigh.

I look down. There's a thin line of red getting thicker every second, blood welling up from the deep cut. Tair's just slashed open my femoral artery with his claw.

It's a fatal wound. Without medical assistance I'll bleed out in minutes. I look up at Tair in shock.

Save her or chase me, he signs to the guard. *Your choice.*

And then he bounds straight through one of the rice-paper walls.

Gone.

FIVE

Twelve hours later I'm standing in front of my boss, David Cassius, trying to explain myself. I'd really rather be sitting—my stitches hurt like hell—but some combination of guilt and stubborn pride won't let me.

Cassius stares at me with an unreadable expression on his face. He's a pire who's probably thousands of years old—nobody seems to know for sure—but he looks like a blond college-aged student who'd rather be at the beach. He wears an immaculately tailored dark blue suit and gray tie, and his blue eyes bore into mine as I give my report.

"After that," I say, "the guard stayed with me and called for medical attention. Tair ripped his way through several more walls and exited the facility on the south side, where it's heavily wooded. Trackers chased him to the banks of the Stillaguamish River, where they lost the trail."

"We'll find him."

"Yes, sir." I never call Cassius sir, but this is all my fault.

"How's the leg?"

"I'm still standing."

"You're lucky one of the pupils at the school was minoring in baseline human physiology. It's not exactly a robust science anymore."

He's right—the last time I tried to get some medical attention, they were ready to use leeches on me. But a faculty comprised of powerful shamans—plus one eager student with an esoteric interest in an endangered species—meant all I had to show for the encounter was another interesting scar to add to my collection. They even had my blood type in storage.

Except, of course, for one other, teeny-tiny detail. Nobody's said much to me about it, and I haven't had the nerve to ask. Right now it's the elephant in the room— the big, bad, hairy elephant.

I take a deep breath, and let it out slowly. "So."

Cassius doesn't rush me. He lets me get to it in my own time, which I appreciate.

"I guess *that time of the month* is about to take on a whole new meaning, huh?" I say.

He doesn't respond, just sits there and looks at me. Trying to figure out if I'm about to go batshit myself, I suppose. I'm really not sure, either.

"Well, it's an excuse to go shopping for a whole new wardrobe," I say. "Should I go stretchy or tearaway? And hey, I can finally celebrate Moondays with all the other whuh—*whuh*—"

And suddenly I can't breathe. Cassius is at my side so fast I swear he must have teleported, and then he's got his arms around me as I let go with what sounds a lot more like wailing than crying. I'm not much of a bawler, but when I do I can howl with the best of them . . .

And now, I guess I can do even better.

It goes on for a while, and he just holds me and lets it happen. It finishes as abruptly as it started—with me, that's usually the case—and he hands me a tissue when I finally pull away and step back. I hate him a little for that—he must have had it ready and waiting, because what the hell does a vampire need a Kleenex for?

"It's not as bad as you think," he starts, but I cut him off with an angry wave of my hand.

"No, it really is. I'm not *human* anymore, do you get that? I'm not *me*."

"Not true. You've been infected, but you haven't changed, not yet. You're still human—that wound, for instance, would have killed you."

I laugh, then blow my nose for added emphasis. "Thanks for putting things in perspective. I almost died, *and* I've been turned into a—" I still can't say it.

"Maybe not," Cassius says.

"What?"

"There may be other options."

"You mean like a cure?"

"Nothing as simple as that. But I don't want to get your hopes up—before I say anything else, I need to have you examined."

"I thought the shamans at Tsubaki did a pretty thorough job."

"I'm sure they did. But I want to have one of our own people do it, because there are very specific things I need them to check."

"Like what? What size collar I take? An allergy to flea powder?"

He shakes his head. "I've already briefed Eisfanger. Get over to his lab as soon as you can."

"Eisfanger?" That doesn't make any sense to me— Damon's a forensic shaman, one who specializes in evidence collection and analysis. "What's he going to do, take claw impressions? We know who did this, remember?"

"I'll tell you afterward, all right?" Now the worry is evident in his voice and face, which tells me just how serious this is. Cassius doesn't usually worry about anything less than the collapse of a country.

"Okay, okay. But before I go, there's something else you need to know."

With Tair on the loose, there's no reason to keep our deal a secret—in fact, right about now I need all the help I can get. Cassius listens without comment as I tell him about the favor Tair asked for, my abduction by the Gray Wolves, the Don's breakdown, and the subsequent threats.

"I wish you would have come to me with this earlier, but I understand why you didn't," he says when I'm finished. "We'll keep you safe, of course. I doubt they'd have actually gone through with any of their threats; *La Lupo Grigorio* are vicious, but they're not stupid. Probably thought they could simply intimidate you into doing what they wanted."

"About what I figured. After all, they're the big scary monsters and I'm just a puny little human, right?" I shake my head. "At least, I used to be."

"Go see Eisfanger," Cassius says. "Please."

Damon Eisfanger's lab is equal parts clean, modern research space and primitive anthropology museum. He has tribal masks in large, Plexiglas display cases, mummified snakes stored under bell jars, gleaming chrome autopsy tables adorned with feather-and-bone fetishes. I usually find it creepy yet entertaining, like a morgue built from parts of an old amusement park haunted house.

But not today. Today all that whimsy is stripped away, and I see everything for exactly what it is. Those shrunken heads aren't made of rubber, that ceremonial knife isn't a prop. I'm surrounded by the tools of an ancient, world-shaping technology that I don't understand, made to influence powers completely beyond my control. It's all very, very real.

And then Eisfanger comes in wearing mouse ears.

They're not really mouse ears. They're some kind of protective glasses with white plastic frames, the kind on hinges that flip up and out of your way. Except he's forgotten that and pushed them up on top of his head the way some people do, and with the lenses flipped they stand straight up like—well, like Mickey Mouse ears. Damon's a thrope who gets his build from his mother's side of the family and his coloring from his father's; the maternal side has pit-bull genes in the mix from an ancestor bitten by a thrope-infected dog, while the paternal half were arctic wolves. Damon's wide and stocky, with ice-blue eyes and short, bristly white hair on his head and above his eyes. That plus the white coat he's wearing make him look like the world's biggest lab rat.

"What?" he says.

"Never mind," I say, grinning. I suppress the urge to give him a hug—Damon's just geeky enough that the social incongruity might set him back years. "Just in a wacky mood. You get the word from upstairs?"

"Oh, uh, yeah. How are you—you know, holding up?"

He looks anxious, and I resist the urge to tease him. Inappropriate humor, while more or less my standard operating procedure, just seems like a little too much effort right now. "I'm doing okay, aside from the leg. Charlie, not so much."

My partner had been on the warpath ever since I told him about the Gray Wolves' visit; it took some serious arguing to persuade him that storming the mansion with a battalion of agents was not the best response. He muttered something about "sending a message of my own" before stalking off, and I suspect that more than a few of the local wise guys were going to be joining Louie in the scoop-your-own-innards-off-the-floor club.

"Has he heard?" Damon asks.

"Not yet. He's still out in the field, and telling him would be like pouring rocket fuel on a bonfire. I'm going to wait until he's cooled off a little."

Damon nods. "Yeah. Warn me first, okay? I think I'll want to be in a different city. Maybe a different state."

"He's not going to take it out on all thropes, Damon."

"Easy for you to say. You're not—" He stops dead. His pale skin flushes.

"Not yet. Which is why I'm here—Cassius wants you to examine me?"

"Yes. Take your jacket off, please, and have a seat." He points me at a chair sitting next to a stainless-steel table with a number of items on it, both familiar and esoteric: a stethoscope, a brightly painted rattle, a syringe, a bowl with some dried white berries, a number of things I can't identify. I slip out of my jacket, hang it over the back of the chair, and sit down. "Cassius wouldn't give me any details, other than hints about this helping with my . . . condition. What can *you* tell me?"

He starts by listening to my heart, then my lungs, then my stomach. "Not much, I'm afraid. I don't know what he's got in mind, just that he asked for a very specific set of data points." He scrawls some numbers down on a clipboard, then squeezes one of the berries between a thick finger and thumb and rubs the pulp into the hollow at the base of my throat.

Great. Once again, Cassius plays it so close to the vest that even his own people don't know what he's up to. I feel a surge of anger, but I know it's misplaced; you can't really blame the head of the NSA for keeping secrets.

I'm not really angry at him, I'm angry at myself. Strangely enough, I don't seem to be angry with Tair.

"Okay, then. What can you tell me about what's *going* to happen? To me?"

He shakes a rattle under my chin, then asks me to open my mouth and sniffs my breath before answering. "You mean the change."

"No, I mean the effects of eating a sauerkraut-and-mushroom pizza before going to bed. Yes, of course I mean the change."

He scribbles more notes, then picks up a tuning fork covered in embossed runes. "Well, it's a federal crime, for one thing. Tack another thirty years onto his sentence when he gets caught."

"That'll be a great comfort when I'm marking trees with my own urine. What about *me*?"

He raps the tuning fork against his palm, then holds it over my heart. "Your first lycanthropic transformation won't happen until the moon is full. But you'll experience other effects before then."

"Like what?"

He listens carefully to the tone of the tuning fork, then puts it down and jots another number. "Well, let's see. Sharpened senses, especially smell—that will come and go, increasing in intensity as the full moon gets closer. Changes in appetite, with an increased intake of protein. Insomnia, restlessness, irritability, heightened aggression, possibly an achiness in your joints or head, abnormal hair growth—though that's less of a factor in women—and feral urges."

"*Feral* urges? Do I even want to know?"

He shrugs and looks uncomfortable. "It's about what you'd expect. There aren't that many instances of intentional lycanthropic infection these days, but I've read a few case studies. *Disrobing in public* is a phrase that seemed to pop up a lot."

I groan and close my eyes. "I can't believe this. It's not enough that I'm being turned into an animal—no, it has to be *embarrassing, too.*"

Damon doesn't respond to that, and then I realize what it is that I've just said. "Not that there's anything wrong with being an animal—I mean you're *not* an animal, obviously, except in the sense that we're *all* animals—"

"It's okay, Jace." He gives me a look that's more sad than offended. "I'm sorry this happened to you. I can't imagine what you're going through right now, but it must be hard."

"Yeah. I know I don't always come across as the most lovable person around, Damon. Thanks for putting up with me."

"No problem. Uh—there's something else you should know about, too."

I roll my eyes. "Great. What now, am I going to have to get neutered or something?"

"It has to do with the thrope who passed along the lycanthropy. Until the first full moon, you and he will share a mystic bond. It's sort of like imprinting, except with a junior and senior thrope instead of a mother and offspring. The senior thrope is supposed to prepare you for your new life."

I stare at Eisfanger in disbelief. "You're kidding."

"No, no, it makes perfect sense from an evolutionary perspective. It ensures that important survival skills are passed on in the most effective—"

"You said *bond.* What kind of bond? How does it work?"

Eisfanger looks apologetic. "I, uh, don't know all the

particulars. It doesn't apply to somebody who's born a thrope, so I've never gone through it. In fact, it only pops up in certain bloodlines—but your attacker belongs to one of them."

"Great. I won the genetic lottery, too."

"I seem to recall that it allows the senior to share experiences with the junior, and to let the senior keep track of the junior's location."

"What about the other way around? Can I use it to locate *him*?"

"I'm not sure," he says hesitantly, "but I don't think so."

Which, again, makes sense from an evolutionary point of view: If the survivor of a werewolf bite can track the one who bit him, pretty soon you either have a bunch of dead werewolves or a bunch of werewolves who don't leave survivors. Either way, it slows population growth in the lupine sector.

I haven't even finished processing this latest bit of good news when I hear a voice that makes me swallow my gum. Okay, I'm not chewing gum, but if I were it would be either halfway down my digestive tract or in a flat midair trajectory after being spat out.

"Hello, Jace."

I swallow, and turn slowly in my chair. "Hi, Gretch. How are things?"

She's standing in the doorway, dressed in a tweed skirt and high-collared white shirt, her blond hair as usual pulled back in a bun. Her hands are behind her back. She smiles at me, gently. Gretch and I are good friends, I'm the godmother to her daughter, I would—and have—trusted her with my life. But she also scares the living crap out of me sometimes, and this is one of them.

"I guess you heard, huh?" I say, trying to convince a smile to show up on my face.

"Heard what, Jace?" Her voice is as soft and friendly as a teddy bear. I wonder how far I could get if I ran. Probably not very.

"That Sicilian werewolf gangsters kidnapped your baby while I was looking after her?" Sometimes honesty is the best policy. Besides, at this point I'm sure she has more information about what happened than I do.

"Oh, that. Not to worry—it all turned out fine, didn't it? I never doubted you for a moment."

Oh, damn. I am so far past hooped they'll be naming basketball courts after me. And she's not going to make it quick, either.

"Gretch, I can explain. They came right into my building, I didn't have my gun—"

"Mmm."

"Well, okay, the gun was there but it was out of reach and I was holding the baby—"

"Mm-hmm."

"Yeah, you're right, I could have just strolled over and picked it up, they wouldn't have taken it seriously, but it was also behind a locked door plus then I would have had to shoot all three of them—"

"Ah."

"Okay, okay, I *should* have shot all three of them, but—but—" I run down slowly. She looks at me and nods once. Gently.

"I'm glad you see where you went wrong. Now, let's concentrate on capturing Tair, shall we? I understand he managed to give you a bit of a scratch."

And with that, she turns and leaves.

"Brrr," says the descendant of arctic wolves.

I probably deserved that, but it stings all the same. Great. Charlie's hellbent on revenge, Cassius is keeping me in the dark about my own possible future as a lycanthrope, and Gretch is pissed at me. I decide to celebrate by visiting Dr. Pete's family and telling them I failed completely.

The Adams pack, despite the name, is not altogether ooky. In fact, they're a large, rambunctious group made of strays, orphans, and outcasts—or the descendants thereof—who have created something of their own. As usual, a bunch of them are spilling out of the house and onto the lawn as I pull up, squealing children being chased by growling wolves who are then chased in turn, old ladies in shawls knitting on the front porch under the moonlight, conversation and laughter rising and falling from the open windows.

I park on the street and get out of the car. Usually, my arrival means being surrounded and pestered by a horde of kids, some in were form, which is like being mugged by puppies. I see heads turned in my directions, I see ears go up and noses sniff—

And then, nothing.

The kids go back to playing. The adults are all looking at me—some just glance, some outright stare. Nobody seems angry or upset; a few appear confused, while the older ones are carefully neutral.

"Uh-oh," I say.

I make my way up the walk and toward the front door. People smile and wave at me, their discomfort disappearing behind a mask of politeness.

I smile and wave back.

None of the kids comes near me.

The house is big, a three-story sprawling rancher painted a bright green, with a pool in an immense yard. I find Leo out on the back deck, holding court with a group of young thropes, a mug of beer in one hand. Leo's the patriarch of the Adams clan, a large, burly guy with a hefty paunch and two wiry gray tufts of hair sticking up from his head like a lycanthropic Krusty the Clown. His grin is wide, his canines prominent and very sharp. He's wearing his usual outfit, a baggy pair of shorts covered in a tropical design and a loose-fitting silk shirt of pale yellow. He stops in mid-sentence when I walk in. All heads swivel around, all eyes focus on me.

The smile on Leo's face drains away. He looks very, very sad. "Oh, Jace," he says quietly. "You poor girl. I am so very, very sorry."

I don't know how to respond to that. I'm not the weepy type—my little meltdown in Cassius's office will do me for quite some time—so when Leo gets up, walks over, and enfolds me in a big, compassionate embrace I'm a little lost. Damn it, I didn't go to all the work of bottling up my terror, anger, and grief behind a solid wall of cynicism, sarcasm, and denial to have one hug tear it down.

"Thanks, Leo," I say into his shoulder. "Guess the wolf's out of the bag, huh?"

"I knew as soon as I smelled you. It is a scent I have not encountered in a long, long time—but one never forgets. How did it happen?"

I pull away and brace myself. "Tair. And it gets worse."

Leo frowns. "It didn't work?"

"If by work, you mean give Tair the opportunity to slice open an artery in my leg and escape while I was bleeding to death, then it worked like gangbusters. Otherwise, not so much."

Leo glances back at the group of thropes he's been talking to and says, "You must excuse us. Jace, please come with me."

He strides away, not back into the house but out into the yard. I follow him, wondering what's going on.

He leads me around the pool, past a cluster of patio furniture, and all the way to a stand of trees that borders the property. There are no lights, but I can see multiple trails leading through the undergrowth, no doubt worn by children tearing through their own private forest. Leo pauses at the edge of the trees, waiting for me.

"I thought it better if we talked alone," he says. "It sounds as if we have much to discuss."

"Yeah." I tell him the whole story—the Gray Wolves, the deal, the escape. He listens attentively, and doesn't speak until I'm done.

"Again, I am so sorry," he says. "This is all my fault."

"Leo, you know that isn't true—"

"No. It is. I was the one who told you about the procedure. It was a foolish risk, one I should not have asked you to take. At the very least, I should have been there as well."

"It wouldn't have helped. And security procedures wouldn't have allowed it, anyway."

He turns away from me, toward the dark, rustling shadows of the trees. "It was my own weakness that triggered this. I just—I miss him, Jace. He is like my own son. But now, you are the one who must pay the price."

"I miss him, too, Leo. But he's gone."

Leo nods, then turns back to me. His face is somber. "Yes. But you are not—you are here. And you must listen to me very carefully now, all right?"

Leo is the driving force behind the Adams clan, the one who took Dr. Pete in when his own family was slaughtered. He's done the same for countless others, binding them all together with the kind of love and loyalty they needed. I have a huge amount of respect for him. "Of course."

"What I am about to say to you, I do not say out of guilt. I do not say it out of duty, or even compassion. I say it because it is something I have thought long and hard on, and I know in my heart it is the right thing to do—right for you, right for us. I want you to join us, Jace. I want you to join our pack."

I try not to sigh. I knew this would happen—Leo's made it obvious that I have a place in the Adams pack anytime I want it, doing everything but offering to bite me himself. "I'm flattered, Leo. I really am. But things are moving kind of fast, and I'm not ready for that kind of commitment yet." I pause. Up until now Leo's affection has been sort of playful, but this is the equivalent of a wedding proposal. I hope I haven't hurt his feelings.

He chuckles. "I didn't expect you to say yes—not right away, in any case. I just wanted to make it plain that we're here for you, that there's no question of that at all. You aren't alone in this—not if you don't want to be."

"Thanks. But I'm not sure I even belong in a pack—even when I was working for the Bureau I was kind of a lone wolf."

"So were many of the Adams clan. You would find much in common with many of them, I think. They would respect your privacy, if that is what you desired."

He's offering me a chance to belong, to really fit in for probably the first time since I got to this world. It makes me feel a lot better and terrifies me at the same time. "I'm not saying no, Leo."

"That's good enough for me. Now let's go back inside—I promise you, no one will pry."

"Tell me *exactly* how it happened," Xandra says. "Every *detail*."

Leo's promise, it seems, doesn't extend to the curiosity of teenage girls. Teenage thrope girls full of hormones and angst, especially.

We're in her bedroom, where she's dragged me for a full interrogation. It's covered in posters for musical acts, all of which look genuinely frightening; the term *hair band* takes on a whole new meaning when you throw lycanthropy into the mix. The ones I find the most disturbing, though, are the equivalent of skinheads: a completely shaved, seven-foot-tall werewolf behind a drum kit is a sight you can't unsee.

I lean back against the wall and groan. We've both kicked off our shoes and are sitting on her bed. "There's not much to tell, Xandra. I didn't even see it happen— just felt something slice open my leg."

"Did he threaten you first? Was he all like, *Choose— join me or die?*"

"No. He was all like, *Let her bleed to death or try to catch me.* And he said it to the guard, not me."

She nods, somehow satisfied. "Yeah. Cool."

"What do you mean, cool? I could have died!"

"Nah. If he'd wanted to kill you, he would have. He took that shooty thing away and you couldn't even *see*, right? He *totally* could have killed you."

She's right. "I know. He played it smart, like Tair always does. He knew he could disable at least one guard and the priest, but he found a way to take me and the other guard out of the equation, too."

She rolls her eyes. "Nuh-*uh*. He did it because he's *afraid* of you."

"Excuse me?"

"That's why he didn't take you hostage *or* kill you. He's got feelings for you that he can't handle, so he hits you and runs away."

"Xandra, please—he's a hardened criminal, not a ten-year-old boy."

She gives me a pitying look. "They're *all* boys, Jace. Anyway, this just proves what I've been saying all along—Uncle Pete's still in there."

I study her for a second before answering. Dr. Pete was Xandra's favorite uncle—she used to volunteer at the anthrocanine shelter where he worked part-time. I know she misses him, even more than Leo or me, but I don't know if it's kinder to encourage her hopes or kill them.

I go with what I know. "Xandra, Dr. Pete's gone. The process didn't take. All that's left is Tair, and he's an escaped convict on the run. I don't think this is going to end well."

"No," she says, softly but firmly. "That's not true. He interrupted the spell halfway through, right? So it might have half worked."

I don't know enough about magic to argue. "Even if that's true, it doesn't change the facts."

"You'll see, Jace. I *know* it." She speaks with the unshakable conviction of the young, the confidence of a child combined with a teenager's assured immortality. Well, she may not live forever, but she's probably good for another three centuries, anyway. I hope she's right.

But I don't think she is.

I get a text from Cassius in my car, telling me to get back to the office ASAP. I wonder if Tair's been sighted, or maybe even captured, but I doubt it. He's too wily for that.

As I drive, I think about what Xandra told me. *He's got feelings for you.* Just the world seen through a teenager's romanticism? Women's intuition? Or had Dr. Pete said something to her? Maybe it was even a thrope thing, the way he smelled when I was around. Pheromones.

I wonder how *I* smelled when Dr. Pete was around.

It's the middle of the night when I pull into the underground parking for the NSA building and head upstairs. That means the middle of the working day here; there are agents everywhere, drinking hot cups of blood cut with cappuccino, rustling through paperwork, rushing from one office to another clutching files or evidence folders. I nod at people as I stride down the length of the office, and get nods in return. I don't have a lot of close friends here—Gretch, Eisfanger, and Cassius are about it—but I'm grudgingly accepted by most. I do my job and I do it well, which cuts you a lot of slack no matter what world you're on.

But they still snicker and call me the Bloodhound behind my back. Human hearing may not be as good as a pire's or a thrope's, but that doesn't mean we're oblivious. I wonder what they'll call me a month from now.

Maybe it won't change, I think as I knock on Cassius's door. *I'll still be a professional tracker. I'll still work for a pire with a history of dating humans. And I sure as hell won't be any less bitchy.*

Cassius tells me to come in, and I do. He's sitting at his desk, holding the notes I saw Damon scribbling earlier. There's a massive and ancient-looking leather-bound book in front of him, unopened.

I walk up to the desk but don't take a seat. "I see you've heard from Eisfanger. What's the verdict?"

He puts down the notes and leans back. "I have a proposition for you, concerning your condition. It's dangerous. It may not work, and the consequences of failure are unpredictable—but I felt I had to at least offer you the option."

"The option of what, exactly?"

He studies me carefully for a moment before answering.

"The option," he says, "of letting me drink your blood."

SIX

I stare at him. I blink. Nothing happens, so I try it a few more times.

"That," I finally say, "hadn't occurred to me."

"No, I didn't think that—"

"Wait, let me get this straight. And by that, I mean so totally and completely level you could build a skyscraper on it and balance an egg at the top. You're not talking about a quick aperitif, right? Not let's-just-decant-a-few-drops-into-a-thimble-and-see-what-she-tastes-like, right?"

"No, that's not what I—"

"Good, because—while I can understand your curiosity—a girl's really got to maintain a little mystery, and I think having my boss know the flavor of my hemoglobin is crossing the line."

"I wasn't suggesting any—"

"On the other end of the scale, I really, really, *really* hope you're not talking about turning me into a Big Gulp. Because I'm pretty sure I would taste like coffee and probably keep you from sleeping for a few years."

"Jace, will you *please*—"

"And bitter. Did I mention the bitter? Me getting bitten, you get the bitter. The biter gets the bitter."

I'm babbling. I'm babbling because I don't want to have this conversation and I'm pretty sure I know what's next and I don't want to hear it.

"Jace, hear me out."

"I—no, you—*you want to turn me into a vampire!*"

He raises an eyebrow. "*Want* to? God, no."

"Well, good, because—wait, what?"

"Have you around *forever*?" He shakes his head. "I've done some bad things, but even I don't deserve *that*."

Now I'm glaring. "Very funny."

"At least it got you to stop talking. Are you ready to listen, or do I have to wait through another ten minutes of stand-up?"

"All right, all right." I sink into a chair. "What's your proposal?"

"First of all, you know that there's no such thing as a pire thrope, don't you?"

I did—in fact, I'd had it graphically proven to me when Aristotle Stoker exposed a human captive to both thrope and pire blood at the same time. It would have killed him even if the rising sun and injection of colloidal silver hadn't. "I'd forgotten about that. So if you can't turn me into a pire, what are you suggesting?"

He leans back in his chair and opens the tome in front of him to a bookmarked page. "I'm suggesting we try anyway."

"I'm not following."

"Both lycanthropy and vampirism are transmitted through a sorcerous virus. Usually the thrope virus is passed on through a bite, but it also lives on the surface of their claws. The version that lives on claws, though, differs slightly from the one that lives on teeth."

For the first time, I see the barest glimmer of light at the end of the tunnel. "So it's not as virulent?"

"Actually, it's more virulent."

"Ah." That light isn't an approaching train, it's a low-flying 747.

"No, that's a good thing. Because the virus is hardier, it's harder to kill. Attack it on a biological level and it will fight back, possibly even survive."

I'm starting to see where this is going. "You want to declare war on it. And use little pire viruses as your soldiers."

"In essence. Normally, when two such viruses fight it out, the sorcerous aspect causes a kind of equilibrium that makes it impossible for either one to win. The body's resources are co-opted and consumed by both sides until the host is destroyed—a long and painful process."

"Yeah, this is sounding better and better all the time."

"But it's possible to change that equation. To bolster the body's immune system mystically, while blocking viral access to its resources. Letting the battlefield survive, while forcing the two armies to fight to the death."

I think about that for a moment. It makes sense, in a goofy, pseudo-biological way. "So it's a case of last virus standing. But either way, I still wind up undead or furry."

"Those are two possible outcomes, yes, but there are two more. If the two viruses battle each other to a standstill, your own mystically enforced immune system might be strong enough to eliminate both of them."

"Huh. The old let's-you-and-him-fight strategy. Let them kick the snot out of each other and then step in and nail them both."

"Exactly."

"What's the other?"

"You could die." He looks me in the eye as he says

this, not sugarcoating it or hesitating. I appreciate that a great deal—it shows me how much he respects me. "Your system might not be able to handle the mystic charge. It could burn your immune system out like an overloaded electrical circuit."

"Let's say I do this. How is it going to happen? Do I get an inoculation? Is a shot glass full of blood somewhere in the picture? Am I going to have to be strapped to a hospital bed for thirty-six hours while I hallucinate and talk to giant rabbits named Harvey?"

And now, strangely enough, he looks a little uncomfortable. "You won't have to drink anything, or be injected. But in order for this to work, you can't simply be exposed to the pire virus. It will have to be directed, guided, kept from rampaging freely throughout your body. To further the military analogy, there has to be a general in charge of the viral troops."

I frown. "I'm guessing that would require a shaman, right? A pire shaman."

"Yes. But as far as I know, this is an untried method; there are no shamans, pire or otherwise, experienced in what we're going to attempt. The best we can do is use a pire well versed in certain control techniques. One who knows how to maintain a mystic connection between himself and the person he's bitten, one who can suppress or enhance the progress of the virus as he chooses." He pauses. "There aren't many such pires in the world. The techniques I'm talking about take a long, long time to master." He's looked away while he was talking, but now his eyes search out mine again. There's a question in them he doesn't have to ask out loud.

"Uh-huh. The general being you, which is why you asked about drinking my blood. I'm guessing there's nobody else that can do this?"

He shakes his head slowly, never taking his eyes off mine. "Not that I trust. Not that you would, either."

"This . . . directing you'd have to do. How, exactly?"

"I would have to introduce the virus directly into your bloodstream."

"You'd have to *bite* me."

"Yes."

Well, the phrase has entered my mind more than once when dealing with Cassius, but I've never said it out loud. Something tells me it's an insult that never really caught on here. "And then there would be the drinking. How much?"

Now he looks even more uncomfortable. Who would have thought discussing bloodsucking with a centuries-old pire would be like talking about sex with a nun?

"Not very. The length of physical contact is more important to establish a proper connection—there would have to be several, ah, sessions. I would restrain myself from taking more than a few ounces each time, and each session would last several minutes."

There's something he's not telling me, I can see it in his eyes. "Okay. Where?"

And now he looks truly miserable. "The site of the original thrope wound would be best."

"Actually, I just meant where would this procedure take place. But now that you've brought it up . . ." I study him carefully. I really shouldn't be enjoying this, but you take life's little pleasures where you can. "So. The inside of my thigh?"

"Yes."

"More than once. For several minutes at a time."

"That's correct."

"Your lips pressed to my skin."

He doesn't say a thing. But he doesn't look away, either, and I realize that the conversation has slid away from me teasing him and into something else. Suddenly I'm the one who's uncomfortable.

"It would be dangerous," he says.

"It . . . sounds like it."

"I'd understand if you weren't willing to risk it."

"Come on. You *know* I have more guts than brains."

"I know no such thing. You have both, and plenty of them."

"Yeah, yeah . . ." I mutter.

How did he *do* that? A second ago I was tormenting him and now he's got me on the defensive, feebly warding off compliments like an awkward schoolgirl. Sometimes I forget just how old and good at manipulation he is. In fact, him spending a year or two maneuvering me into a position where I *ask* him to drink my blood isn't hard to believe at all—but not too far in that direction is also an alley with a big neon sign that reads PARANOIA LANE, and the entrance is a lot easier to find than the exit. Occupational hazard when you're a government spook, even worse on a world filled with the supernatural.

"I'm going to need some time to think about this."

"Of course. But don't wait too long; the closer the full moon gets, the more of a foothold the lycanthropic virus gains. You have four nights to decide."

"Great. So the longer I take, the worse my chances get. *That's* a terrific formula for good decision making."

"There's another possibility that may make it easier. Kill the thrope who infected you before your first transformation, and the virus will die, too."

He says it flatly, intending to shock me. It does.

"Kill Doc—kill Tair?"

"Yes. There's a temporary mystic link between certain breeds of thrope and someone they've bitten. Unfortunately, it's one-way—"

"I know, I know. Eisfanger filled me in."

"You can't use it directly to locate him, but we could set a trap."

"Why would he bother?"

"He's fascinated by you, Jace. Surely you've noticed."

I shake my head. "He's a horndog, that's all. I doubt he'd come within twenty miles of me now that he's on the run."

Cassius doesn't look convinced. "All the same, I want Charlie to stick close."

"He will, once he cools off."

Cassius picks up his phone. "He'll do it *now*."

Cassius doesn't want me to leave the NSA building until Charlie comes in. I can't stand the thought of waiting in Cassius's office—not with the offer he just made pulsing in my brain—so I go down to the staff cafeteria.

There's not a lot I can eat there—it's mainly meat, meat, and more meat, with an extensive blood bar—but I get some frozen yogurt and a cup of tea. I'm usually more of a coffee drinker, but I can be flexible.

Just *how* flexible is the question on the table.

I spot Gretch sitting at a table for two by herself, sipping her own cup of tea. I find myself really needing to talk, but a conversation with her right now could be like walking into a blizzard. One where all the snowflakes are made out of sharpened steel.

She sees me, though, and waves me over. I square my shoulders, both mentally and physically, and join her.

She looks me over coolly, then smiles. "How are you doing?"

"I'm . . . a little shaky," I admit.

"You must be." Now I can hear genuine concern in her voice. "I'm sorry, Jace, truly I am. I forget sometimes."

"Forget what?"

"That you're not invincible. None of us is, really, though we supernatural races have a distinct physical advantage. But *you*—you simply ignore that fact, most of the time. Except when someone else is at risk. Then you become much more cautious. Usually."

"I'm really, really sorry about Anna, Gretch."

She shakes her head gently. "No, I overreacted. You did exactly what was necessary in order to keep her safe, and I owe you an apology. Consider this it."

"So we're good?"

"I am. What about you?"

"Freaking the hell out, actually . . ." I tell her about Cassius's plan.

"Hmmm. Interesting." She stares into space, thinking.

"Is it doable?"

"Of course it's doable—Cassius wouldn't have suggested it otherwise. But the risks are considerable."

"Believe me, I'm considering. And you can help me—with some of it, anyway."

"What do you need?"

I hesitate, not really sure how to put it. "Well—what's it *like,* being a pire?"

A slight frown creases her face. I imagine that after over a hundred years of undead existence, it's a little like asking a fish what it's like being wet. "That's a very broad set of parameters, Jace. Can you narrow it down a little?"

"Okay, okay." I concentrate, feeling like a little kid asking a grown-up about the birds and bees; I have the absurd urge to say, *Mommy, where does hemoglobin come from?* "Temperature. I've noticed pires seem pretty well immune to the cold, and they definitely don't sweat. What's that like?"

"More or less exactly like you just described. I can

feel slightly cool, and I can feel slightly warm, but only when exposed to extremes. Most of the time, I don't notice the temperature at all."

Well, that was helpful. Not her fault, though. "How about your senses? They're sharper, right?"

"Than yours, certainly. To me, of course, they seem perfectly normal. I could get you some hard data on comparative acuity between hemovore and human sight and hearing, though the others are more difficult to quantify—"

"No, no, that's not really what I'm after." I think harder. "You weren't born a pire. What do you remember the most, when you changed?"

"When I died, you mean? Hmm. I haven't thought about that in decades . . . I believe it was the *lightness* of everything."

That wasn't what I expected. "What do you mean?"

"Pires are much stronger than human beings. When you first arise, it's as if the pull of gravity has become no more than a gentle tug. I found myself astonished that every step I took didn't catapult me into the air."

"What about—you know, switching over to a liquid diet?"

"Well, it wasn't an overwhelming desire, more like simply needing a drink. Any squeamishness I had vanished. I remember thinking how odd it was that something salty could also prove so satisfying at quenching my thirst."

"Did you *feel* any different? Were you still *you*?"

"Oh, certainly. Except for the occasional compulsion to bite the heads off kittens, I was entirely the same person."

I'm good at sarcasm, Charlie's mastered the deadpan delivery, but nobody combines the two quite like Gretch. "Right. Anything you miss? Other than being able to stroll past pet store windows with a clear conscience?"

"I used to quite like a dish my mother made, a soup with lots of garlic. The very thought turns my stomach now, so I can't say I miss the dish itself . . . but I miss the *idea* of it. I miss the enjoyment it used to give me, sitting in front of the fire on a snowy day in London."

Her face softens, and for just a second I see the young girl she used to be, living in the same city that Dickens did, maybe even walking down the same streets at the same time.

I hope it's okay to ask this. "How did it happen, Gretch? Was it . . . voluntary?"

"Hmm? Oh, yes, absolutely. I'd thought about the matter long and hard. I think, in fact, it was the winters that decided me—London was never terribly sunny in those days, and giving up a meager amount of sunshine in return for immortality, eternal youth, and a good wage seemed far more attractive than an existence plagued with disease, hunger, and uncertainty—"

"Wait. A good wage? You were *paid* to become a pire?"

"Oh, yes. London was full of recruiters, offering competitive terms. The Royal Blood Bank had just been established and the National Sustenance Act had passed Parliament the previous year; no pire needed worry about starving to death, and employment opportunities abounded. I wound up working for Scotland Yard, myself—but my history is a long and convoluted one, and I doubt its particulars are what you're after."

She pauses to take a sip of her tea. Like everything pires consume, it's either been magicked to let the caffeine affect her or been cut with blood. I try to picture myself waking up to a nice Colombian-dark-roast-and-O-negative blend in the morning, and can't quite do it.

So I consider the alternatives. Life, death, or thropehood. Life is good—or at least preferable—while death is something a cop lives with every day; it's always part of the equation, always lurking in the background. My attitude has always been that there's no use worrying about the inevitable, so I decide to stick with that.

Which leaves the furry option.

It's the one I hate the most. I shouldn't; thropes are a lot closer to baseline human than pires. I wouldn't have to give up garlic or sunlight, and I even have a pseudo-family willing to embrace me and help me through the rough bits. The worst part of the whole thing is the three nights of the full moon, when all thropes have to transform whether they want to or not, and even that comes with the compensation of the seventy-two-hour monthly party known as Moondays. Really, becoming a thrope should sound like a great deal.

But it doesn't. *Because it wasn't my choice.* It was something that was *done* to me against my will, a violation of who and what I am, and I just can't accept that.

I *won't*.

"Thanks, Gretch," I say. "I think I know what I have to do."

Three minutes later I'm back in Cassius's office. "I've made my decision," I say.

I hope it's the right one.

SEVEN

Which is right when Charlie barges in.

Charlie is a champion barger. If there happens to be something in his way while he's barging—like a door, a wall, or another person—that thing often ends up in less-than-pristine condition. Cassius's door was lucky, but then it's used to dealing with Charlie and may have had its pristineness fortified.

"I'm here," Charlie growls from the doorway. His usually immaculate suit—this one a soft dove gray with narrow lapels—is torn in several places. There are large stains here and there, of a decidedly red hue. And he's not wearing a hat, which in Charlie's universe is like walking down the street without any pants.

"Good," Cassius says. "As you can see, so is Jace. Stay by her side until further notice."

"Right," Charlie says. He stalks into the room, slamming the door behind him.

"Geez," I say. "Get into a tiff with your sewing circle?"

"There was a discussion with certain elements of the local community."

"I can see that. Looks like some pretty sharp verbs were thrown around."

"Nouns, too."

"Such as?"

"Table. Mailbox. Refrigerator."

"You threw a *fridge* at someone?"

"I didn't say that. There was throwing, yes, and a refrigerator may have been involved. Don't go jumping to conclusions."

"Sorry. Clearly, I was *way* out of line."

Cassius makes a sound halfway between an impatient sigh and an annoyed snort—a snigh, if you will. "Charlie, I'm afraid that *until further notice* will have to be amended to *immediately after Jace and I are finished*. Would you mind waiting outside?"

"Nah. I should really pay a quick visit to the repair department, though. Could use a few patches."

"Go ahead. I'll make sure she's still here when you get back."

Charlie nods, then stomps back out, this time slamming the door a fraction more gently. It's times like this that remind me that Charlie's driven by the spiritual essence of a long-dead *T. rex,* carefully distilled by government shamans from crude oil. Part sandbox, part *Jurassic Park*—that's my partner.

"You were saying?" Cassius says.

"Yeah. I guess I was." I feel a sudden wavering of my resolve, which is very out of character and usually pushes me to do something drastic in order to prove it. "I hate that I have to make this decision, but I'm glad that at least I get a choice. The smart thing, it seems to me, would be to hunt Tair down and kill him."

"You'd be all right with that?"

I shake my head. "No. It would make things easier, but I couldn't just execute him. Anyway, I said that was the smart thing to do, and since when is *that* my first choice?"

"Just catching him won't help your situation, Jace."

"I know that. But he wouldn't be on the loose if it weren't for me, so I have to try." I take a deep breath and let it out. "And whether we catch him or not, I'm not going to let what he did to me define me. Not without a fight."

"You're sure?"

"Hell, no. But I don't have *time* to be unsure, so let's get this party started. You good with that?"

He nods, slowly. "All right. But we need to bolster your immune system first. You'll need to undress."

Sure, nothing weird about getting naked in your boss's office. I take off my jacket, my socks and shoes, and then my pants, trying very hard to be brisk and professional. When I'm done, I stand there in only my silk top, arms crossed, not embarrassed or uncomfortable at all. I pretend I'm wearing a bikini under a T-shirt and I'm a lifeguard on duty at a beach. A *military* beach.

Cassius opens a drawer, pulls out a few things, and places them on top of the desk. A vial, a Japanese flute, a long strand of leather with tiny bones tied to it at regular intervals. The leather goes around my neck, while the vial contains something red and earthy smelling that gets daubed onto my forehead, my stomach, my throat. When that's done he positions himself a few inches away from each mark and plays a few odd, dissonant notes on the flute.

I guess that's it, because he straightens up, puts down the flute, and says, "I'm ready whenever you are."

There's a leather couch in one corner of Cassius's office; I remember sitting there, wearing nothing but a T-shirt with a panda on it, when I first got to Thropirelem.

It's where Cassius explained to me where I was and why I'd been brought here, and at the end of the explanation I'd thrown up and passed out. Not from the emotional impact of what I was going through, but the physical—being taken from one reality to another had given me a condition called RDT, Reality Dislocation Trauma. An herbal concoction called Urthbone had proven to be an effective treatment; maybe I'd get lucky again.

One major difference, though: Last time it had been Dr. Pete who'd cured me. This time, he's the cause.

I can hear Cassius telling the NSA switchboard operator to hold all his calls. I lie down on the couch, the leather smooth and cool against the bare skin of my legs. At least the stitches on my thigh have stopped itching. I peel off the white gauze taped over them and see that not only is the wound healed, but the stitches themselves are gone. I find them stuck to the underside of the bandage in a little zigzag pattern.

"Your body rejected the thread." Cassius walks over and drops to a squat beside me. "It's how thrope metabolism handles any foreign object not made of silver."

He reaches out with a forefinger. "May I?"

I nod. He touches the tip of his finger to one end of the pink line that runs down the inside of my thigh like the border of a stocking. "It's healed almost completely. By morning you won't even have a scar."

"Too bad. I was looking forward to adding it to my collection."

"Will you settle for a replacement?" He has the barest trace of a smile on his lips.

I swallow. "Guess I'll have to."

"I'll go slow. The initial incisions will sting, but the procedure itself will cause no pain."

Incisions. Procedure. He's trying to make it sound as

clinical as possible, but what's going to happen is he's going to bite me—with two very long, very sharp fangs—and then drink my blood. He's going to *feed* on me, while I lie here half dressed and try not to pass out.

"Just do it already," I whisper.

He takes his tie off first. Doesn't want to get stains on it, of course. The smart-ass gland in my brain notes this, comes up with at least three good cracks, and seizes up before any of them can reach my suddenly dry mouth.

His eyes flood with crimson. His incisors lengthen and sharpen. My pulse kicks up a notch, and my back-brain starts screaming about predators and survival and how running away would be a good thing. I ignore it.

He places one hand on my hipbone, over the hem of the silk blouse I'm wearing. The other goes just above my knee. His hands are as smooth and cool as the leather I'm lying on.

He leans over and puts his mouth to my skin. His lips are warmer than his hands. I feel two simultaneous sharp jabs, no worse than pricking myself on a rosebush. I gasp anyway.

A little circle of warmth grows around the bite. Blood, spreading out, stopped by the boundary of his lips. I realize I'm all tensed up, and make a conscious effort to relax. My hands won't stop trembling.

When he starts to drink, something happens.

The warmth pulses out in a ring, up my thigh and down my leg. I look down to make sure I'm not bleeding to death, but all I can see is the top of Cassius's blond head.

It's more than warmth now. There's a tingle that goes with it, a kind of almost-tickle that's maddening and pleasurable at the same time. I've started to breathe harder, even though I'm doing nothing at all.

I close my eyes.

The warmth is radiating through my whole body

now. *This is all wrong,* a voice in my head whispers. *Exsanguination is typically accompanied by a feeling of cold, not heat.* I tell it to shut up. What I'm feeling isn't medical, it's mystical; it's *him,* the supernatural equivalent of his DNA, flooding my body.

But it's not alone.

I didn't feel this way when Tair sliced me open, but the thrope virus is on a lunar cycle while the pire one is obviously more immediate. Now I have both of them in me, and neither one is happy.

I remember what happened to Roger, the man Stoker killed in front of me by exposing him to both pire and thrope blood and then adding sunlight and silver. Before the rays and the metal killed him, he'd gone into convulsions. One of his eyes had turned blood red, the other bright yellow.

That doesn't happen. I can feel the thrope virus waking up, biochemical alarms bellowing that an invasion is under way; a tremor goes through me from scalp to toes. I feel a weird spike of energy at the same time a kind of lethargy settles over me, like I'm about to run a marathon in my sleep. I can't move, even to open my eyes, though every muscle in my body is tensed for action.

My senses are going crazy. I can smell the starch in Cassius's shirt, the polish on his shoes, the ink in the pen in his pocket. The couch is an overpowering burst of tanned animal skin and chemical dye. My mouth is a crazy blend of toothpaste, coffee, and this morning's cinnamon bun.

Other senses seem to have shut off completely—crack teams of virus commandos must be blowing up bridges all over my central nervous system. My body is suddenly gone, leaving me floating in a weightless void; my hearing contracts down to the single, steady throb of my own heartbeat.

My eyes are still closed, but that doesn't mean I can't see. Vivid bursts of color pinwheel across my vision, brilliant reds and yellows like the color of Roger's eyes before he died. Some kind of symbolic representation of the battle going on, though it doesn't make any sense—no neat little lines of soldiers fighting each other for possession of a lung, a foot, an endocrine gland.

But when I focus on the red, I can feel Cassius.

Not his lips on my thigh; that's as far away as the rest of my body. No, I can feel *him,* his . . . I don't know, his consciousness, his essence.

His soul.

The more I focus on the red, the more the yellow fades into the background. The explosions of color get a little more solid, coalescing into multiple radiating networks of lines, like a thousand scarlet spiderwebs hanging in space, branching in every direction. The longer I look, the more intricate and detailed the connections become, until I finally recognize what I'm seeing: his mind. Millions and billions of interconnected neurons, the memories and thoughts and feelings of centuries of existence, spread out like a cosmic skein of life. I'm a bug that's blundered into the headquarters of the world's most overachieving arachnid.

But that's not how it *feels,* not at all. It feels *alive.*

It's his emotions that come through the strongest. They pulse through the network in waves, one after the other, each with its own flavor. The sharp, metallic taste of aggression; the cold electricity of logic. The mind-set of a commander, one who's devoting all his attention to a military campaign.

There are other feelings, too, buried deeper in the web but just as strong. Without knowing how I'm doing it, I reach out and touch them.

A surge of heat brings my body back into existence. I

can feel every inch of my skin and everything it's touching: the silkiness of my blouse, the grip of my underwear, the tension of the couch pushing back against my weight.

And Cassius's mouth on my thigh. I know the shape and texture of his lips as intimately as if they were crushed to my own. I feel the rhythmic pulse of his throat as he drinks. And I feel the growing insistence of his need.

When Dr. Pete treated my RDT, he warned me that there might be side effects—specifically, that the Urthbone I was taking might heighten my empathy. That turned out to be true, so much so that I stopped taking it; I just couldn't handle being constantly bombarded by other people's emotions. But before I quit, I did develop some skill in probing what other people felt—especially if they were trying to hide something.

Like Cassius is doing right now.

It's there, a few layers down, buried somewhere in the scarlet thicket of his mind. Maybe it's because I don't want to dwell on Cassius's bloodlust, maybe it's because I can't stop being a cop; whatever the reason, I just have to know what's in there. I reach out again—farther, deeper.

I don't get very far. He's had a long time to build his defenses, and I'm just an intruder outside the castle walls with a rickety ladder. But he's distracted and I'm better at this than he thinks, so I actually get the briefest glimpse of what's behind the curtain.

Pain. That's it, that's all I can tell. A fleeting sensation of something immense and suffering, like a giant squid washed up on the beach and dying by inches. Or maybe the kind of creature that would eat giant squids like calamari.

His response is immediate. Fury surges through the

network, overriding everything else—everything but the desire. That amps up as well, hunger and anger in a feedback loop of bloodlust.

My leg starts to feel cold.

I don't think he even realizes what he's doing. I can feel my life rushing out of my femoral artery and down his throat, and my head is spinning and I can't think straight. If he doesn't stop he's going to kill me.

No. No, he's not.

It's the thrope infection that saves me. It wants to survive as much as I do, and it's not going to let me just give up and get downed like a plasma shooter. I grab his blond, surfer-boy hairstyle in both hands and yank on his head as hard as I can, trying to break the seal and his concentration. It doesn't work; he's stuck on me like a leech.

So I throw my head back and howl.

That gets his attention. Probably the attention of everyone else in the office, too, but I've got other things to worry about than my reputation. He looks up, blood on his mouth, and *hisses* at me.

I growl back.

It's a surreal moment, but it doesn't last. He comes back to himself with a visible exertion of will, his fangs receding and his eyes returning to their normal deep blue. I stare at him, panting like we just went three rounds in the ring instead of three minutes on a couch. Or maybe it was thirty minutes—I'm a little hazy on that point.

"My . . . apologies," Cassius says. He gets to his feet in one swift, easy movement. "I didn't expect that."

I get my breathing under control. "That?" I manage. "*That?* Just what the hell *was* . . . that?" I sit up, hugging myself. Funny, I expected to feel cold, but instead I'm all sweaty.

"Your immune system—it's been altered by the Urthbone you used to treat your RDT. I had thought you were fully acclimated, but I didn't realize—" He breaks off and shakes his head. "I'm sorry. Battling your own defenses as well as the thrope virus was more difficult than I'd imagined. My instincts kicked in."

"So you went all *vacuum cleaner* on me? Jesus, Cassius, I *trusted* you!"

The look of shame on his face is real, and it reminds me of the buried emotion I'd encountered in his mind. But now doesn't seem like a good time to bring it up.

"Again, I'm sorry. But I'm afraid this changes things, Jace."

"You think? I'm not going to be able to look my boss in the eye again without wondering if he sees me or the blue-plate special!" I try to stand up, but I'm still a little dizzy; I sit back down again.

"It won't happen again."

"Damn straight it won't! The next time you're feeling peckish try takeout, 'cause the Jace buffet is *closed*."

"That's not going to work, either. I've infected you, but in a very careful and measured way. Should we let matters run their natural course, you will not survive."

I let the *careful and measured* remark go. "So we're locked in now? No turning back?"

"Yes. We must—*reconnect*—in order for me to influence the course of the infection. But even that may not be enough."

This just keeps on getting better and better. "So now I have to add being *sucked dry* to my list of options?"

"That's not going to happen," he says patiently. "But the situation has changed. I may need . . . additional resources." He sounds reluctant.

"Like what? A couple of really long straws?"

"Like Tair. Alive."

"What? I thought you said—"

"I know what I said. I was wrong. This is— Magic isn't science, Jace. It's inexact, it shifts and changes according to circumstance. I thought you knew that." Now he sounds mildly disapproving, like a teacher chiding a student who isn't living up to her potential.

"Okay, whatever. We need Tair, I'll find Tair. Just promise me this isn't going to result in me being the main course at an all-you-can-eat thrope and pire banquet, all right? Being the chew toy of one supernatural being is already too much."

"I promise you, that will not happen."

"It better not." I get to my feet again, slowly. Grab my clothes from the floor and get dressed, wipe the ritual marks off my skin. There are two tiny little slashes of dried blood on the inside of my leg, more like stripes than dots, a little *equals* sign.

Equal to what, though?

Charlie's waiting for me when I leave Cassius's office, perched on the edge of a desk and talking to a clerical lem named Seymour. They're using that deep, almost subsonic rumble that passes for a lem language, one I hardly ever hear in public. Seymour looks at me, curiosity in his eyes, as I walk up.

"Hey," Charlie says. He's wearing a different suit, a high-waisted zoot-style number with wide lapels in a houndstooth pattern, and a wide-brimmed Panama hat instead of a fedora. Anyone else would look like a pimp, but Charlie manages to give the ensemble a certain dignity.

"All patched up?" I ask. Seymour's still staring at me, so I add, "What?"

"He's just wondering something," Charlie says.

"Yeah? What's that?"

Seymour cocks his head to the side, studying me like an entomologist who's run across a rare bug. "How did you get bitten by a monkey in Seattle?"

"A what now?"

"A cursed howler monkey," Seymour clarifies. "You know, the one on the recording you played for Director Cassius."

"That wasn't—that was—" I stop and just glare at Charlie.

"Yeah, those howler monkey bites are nasty," Charlie says. "Pretty soon, she'll be making the same sounds. Swinging from the trees, too."

"My condolences," Seymour says.

"Thanks," I manage. "It's a real blow, what with the recent demise of my partner and all."

I stalk away from Seymour's confused look and toward the elevators. Charlie catches up with me there.

"Thanks for covering for me," I snarl.

"Hey, it's what I live for."

"Cursed howler monkey?"

"You know anything else that howls?"

I think about it. "Well, no."

"You're welcome. Hey, you want to swing by the cafeteria? I hear they have banana cream pie today."

"Thanks, but this primate thought she'd go talk to Gretch. We need to find Tair."

"I was working on that myself when I got called in."

The elevator shows up and we get on. "We have to take him alive, Charlie. Cassius is trying to put together a fix for my condition, and Tair's an essential part of it."

"Yeah? You sure?" He sounds disappointed.

"I'm sure." I pause. "Okay, he doesn't have to be in mint condition."

"That's good, because I wasn't planning anything spice-based."

We get off on Gretch's floor, the intel division. We find her in her office, a large, windowless space with several flatscreen monitors mounted on the walls. Her desk is large, square, and made of steel. Her door is open, and she looks up when we walk in.

"Hello," she says. "*Howler* monkeys?"

I just stare at her. Gretch doesn't really have the whole office bugged, nor is her hearing so sharp she can hear conversations through several concrete floors—but nobody keeps on top of the flow of information like she does.

"The length of an elevator ride," I finally say. "I think that's a new record, Gretch."

"Collecting information *is* my job, Jace. Just as it is to know what particular pieces of information in a vast sea of data will be of the most use at any given moment. I think, for instance, that you may find *this* especially valuable right now." She hands me a file folder.

I flip it open. It's a copy of a local FBI file on a night-club called the Mix and Match, including surveillance photos and the jackets of a number of known felons who frequent the place. A moment's reading tells me that the M&M is just a front for a bookie operation, one run by the Mob.

"Why am I looking at this?" I ask.

"Because we just received a report that Tair and Don Falzo were spotted there about an hour ago."

"Thanks!" I call over my shoulder. Charlie's already halfway to the elevator, fishing the car keys out of his pocket.

EIGHT

I read the file while Charlie drives. The Mix and Match isn't your ordinary sort of bar; it's a fetish club.

On the world of my birth, that would mean leather and rubber, whips and chains, masters and slaves. On Thropirelem, though, it's something very different. Whereas most thropes and pires seem attracted to only their own kind, there's apparently a subculture known as crosskink where the opposite is true. And it's not just about members of one supernatural race dating another—there's also an aspect of it devoted to pires posing as thropes and vice versa. Transexual Transylvania, indeed—though maybe *transpecies* is a better way to describe it.

I'm feeling a little transpecies myself. Everything seems unnaturally sharp and bright. I can smell the fast-food wrapper in the backseat, and the squeal the power steering makes every time we turn a corner is setting my teeth on edge. Speaking of my teeth, my gums are tender, and I can't stop running my tongue over my canines and incisors, trying to tell if they're any pointier.

I think I can taste the inside of my own mouth, which is about as weird as it sounds.

The bar is in Capitol Hill, an artsy and slightly seedy part of town, and by the time we get there I'm ready to jump out of my own skin. It's nearly 3:00 AM when we pull up across the street, and I can hear the music booming from the place even before I step out of the car. Lots of bass, distorted guitars, deep growling vocals. Angsty, no-one-understands-me-and-it-pisses-me-off rock, closer to the violent than the whiny part of the spectrum. I kind of like it.

"I'd advise earplugs," Charlie says.

"Don't have any handy," I say. "I'll survive. We'll use LSL when we get inside." LSL stands for "Lycanthrope Sign Language," which I've gotten pretty fluent in. Handy when you're interrogating a suspect who has a muzzle instead of a mouth.

We cross the street. There's a line to get in, the doorman one of the largest pires I've ever seen: a tall, bulky bald guy with a tattoo of a bat on his forehead like the world's biggest unibrow. I walk right up to him and realize his mouth is deformed, too, his jaw unnaturally long.

I pull out my badge. "NSA. We're going in to look around."

He doesn't say a word, just nods and motions for us to go in. Up close, I can see that he isn't a pire at all; those red eyes are contacts, and his mouth is the beginning of a wolf's snout. It takes a lot of willpower and effort to maintain a partial transformation like that—he must practice every day, and shave every few hours. It gives him the size and strength he needs to do his job, sure, but it would be a lot easier for him to just go half-were.

Yeah. And it would be a lot easier for men in drag to

not pluck their eyebrows or shave their legs or find high heels in a size 12. But they do.

Inside, the club is about as noisy, dark, and crowded as I'd expected. The music is recorded, not live. The dance floor is crowded with people, and at first it just looks like an assortment of pires and thropes; it's not until you peer a little closer that you notice the fake fur, the dental prosthetics, the artificial claws. It's the faux-thropes that stand out the most; mimicking a seven-foot werewolf is a lot harder to pull off than pale skin, an overbite, and red eyes.

We make our way over to the bar, where a slender woman who looks exactly like a pire but smells like a thrope is pouring shots of something crimson into plastic glasses shaped like test tubes. I order a glass of club soda—Charlie doesn't drink. Or eat, for that matter. I asked him once what lems ran on, and he just said, "Willpower." I didn't argue the point.

The file said the bookie business is run from the second floor. The only entrance is a stairwell behind a metal door, and that's in a room behind the bar. There are, of course, ways for the staff to alert the guys upstairs, as well as security cameras that mean they probably already know we're in here. Charlie isn't exactly unobtrusive.

That's fine. Subtlety, in my opinion, is highly overrated.

The DJ booth is on an elevated platform at the head of the room. I can see the DJ, a thrope or thrope wannabe with long, spiky fur and wearing a pair of shades and headphones, bopping along to his own groove.

I know the bartender is keeping an eye on us. When I wave her over, her casual saunter is entirely feigned. I show her my ID, and lean in close so she'll be able to hear me. "Get the DJ down here, now," I say pleasantly.

She cocks a dubious eyebrow. "Hey, I don't always

agree with his taste, either, but I wouldn't *arrest* him for it—"

"Yeah, you're hilarious. He's here in thirty seconds or you're out of a job tomorrow."

Funny how threatening someone's livelihood will often get results a lot faster than mentioning jail. She practically sprints over to the booth, has a short but intense exchange involving pointing, staring, and probably a lot of bad language. It produces the desired results, though: He pulls off the headphones, and he and the bartender leave the booth.

Charlie nudges me and signs, *What do you expect that to get you?*

A clear line of fire, I sign back, and draw my gun.

There's certain things I can get away with on Thropirelem that would land me in the unemployment office or prison on my own world. For instance, the fact that no one is even capable of taking my gun seriously means I can use it for the most frivolous purposes, with almost no legal consequences—like getting the attention of an entire club full of partying thropes and pires. The Ruger makes an impressive bang, but with the music this loud I know that's not going to be enough.

So I shoot the sound system.

The music comes to an abrupt stop. Everybody on the dance floor looks confused, then annoyed. I climb up on the bar and hold out my ID for everyone to see.

"This business is now closed, for reasons of national security! Please leave in an orderly fashion! Anyone still here in ten minutes will be going to jail!"

I repeat this a few times for the sake of those hard of hearing, slow on the uptake, or just drunk. Then I climb down from the bar and take a sip of my club soda.

"Nice," Charlie says. "You could have just asked him to turn it down."

"Not the message I wanted to send." Plus, sometimes I just really have to shoot something, and right now feels like three of those times.

The DJ, a short little pire wearing what I can only describe as a punk thrope toupee, charges up to us quivering with righteous indignation. "You can't do that! You can't just barge in here and wreck expensive equipment—"

"Charlie?"

Charlie leans in close to the pire. Lets him see what's in his eyes. "You pay for any of that equipment yourself?"

"Well, no—"

"Then shut the hell up, because the person who did is the one we want to talk to."

The DJ sees which way the wind is blowing, and decides to go with it. He stops long enough to grab a bag from his booth, and then he's gone.

The bartender's standing a few feet away, her arms crossed, studying us. No telling how old she actually is, but she's got the body of a twenty-year-old and is showing it off with tight-fitting jeans, a belly shirt, and no bra. Bigger tips that way, I'm sure.

"Don't you have someone to report to?" I ask her.

She shrugs. "Hey, they know what's going on."

I smile. "Then I guess we wait."

The crowd files out slowly. It takes closer to twenty minutes than ten, but time is cheap when you're immortal. Thropes only have around three hundred years, give or take a decade, but they don't seem to be moving any faster than the pires. Ah, the blissful ignorance of youth.

Finally, there's nobody left but us, the bartender, and the bouncer at the front. "Mind if we start cleaning up?" the bartender asks. "Since it looks like we're closed for the night."

"Go ahead," I say.

And then—finally—I hear the big metal door in the back *chunk* open. A moment later a guy walks out and stops behind the bar. He's a thrope, dressed in a pale blue linen shirt, hair black and shiny as an oil slick. Looks around thirty. He puts his hands on top of the bar, leaning forward in an open, relaxed sort of way. "I'm the proprietor," he says. "There a problem, Officer?"

"Not anymore," I say. "You've had more than enough time to clean house upstairs, so you don't have anything to worry about, do you?"

He shrugs. "We try to look our best for visitors."

"Inconvenient, though. Slows things down, cuts into the profit margin."

He sighs. "Cost of doing business. That why you're here? To talk to me about my profit margin, and how certain taxes are unavoidable?"

I shake my head. "You've got the wrong idea. We're after a little information, not a bribe. We don't get it, we'll have to do this again tomorrow night. And the night after that, and the night after that . . ."

"What do you want to know?"

"There was an escaped convict in here earlier tonight. He was in the company of a certain Sicilian gentleman. I'd really like to know where they went after they left."

He sighs, again. "Look, I'd like to help you out, I really would. But this is a busy place, dark, with a lot of people coming and going. People who might be attired in a way that would render them hard to recognize, if you get my drift. So even if these gentlemen were here—and I'm not saying they were—I wouldn't necessarily know about it."

"Sure. I can see that. But the thing is, the Sicilian gentleman in question? *Somebody* would have recognized him, no question at all. And that somebody would have gotten word to you, very quickly. Which means you—quite understandably—are lying to me."

"Hey, I wasn't even here until an hour ago. Maybe this gentlemen came in ealier."

I'm having a hard time concentrating. The loud music and crowded room was actually easier, because it was such a torrent I could just shut it all out. Now I keep getting hit with specific sounds, specific images. The glint of the overheads off this mook's oiled hair. That dripping tap under the bar. And the smells—good Lord, the smells. Spilled beer and vomit and wet fur and cigarette smoke and—

Hold on.

"Who are you, anyway?" I ask.

"Ignacio Prinzini. I manage the bar."

"Uh-huh." I lean in close, take a deep breath in through my nose. "That's not all you do, Iggy. You *reek* of something else—what is that, exactly?"

His easygoing grin gets a little wider. "Let's just say I have an appreciation of the feminine form in all its varieties. You got a sharp nose."

I pull back, suddenly a little repulsed. Okay, so what I'm smelling is thrope musk, obviously from more than one donor. And when I concentrate on it, it *is* obvious— the different smells separate themselves out in my head, like listening to a piece of music and focusing on a single instrument at a time.

But one of them doesn't fit. It's heavier, deeper, a bass drum booming over a string concerto. And it's *familiar*.

"Interesting," I say. "A club like this, I guess you get your fair share of females. I wouldn't have thought your tail wagged that particular way, but live and let live."

And now the grin is gone. "Hey, my bitches are *real* bitches, okay? Just because I sell them drinks doesn't mean I—"

"Oh, I know they're real, Iggy. I can *smell* that. Just like I can smell the hair remover and white makeup they use to give themselves that nice, pale, smooth skin." Every Mob guy I've ever met was a raging homophobe, so it's not surprising that a thrope version would be deeply offended at my insulting his red-blooded wolf-hood. Sometimes insulted is good; it can lead to a suspect saying things he shouldn't.

He glares at me. "I don't got a thing for shampires, awright? I like my babes furry, four-legged, and howling at the moon."

I believe him. But if that was true, why the hell was he running a transpecies club? I can't think of a single case of the Mob operating a gay bar, even as a front. Which means there has to be a really, really good reason for it—and when it comes to the Mob, that means really, really profitable.

And then, out of the blue, it hits me where I know that smell from.

"You know," I say, "I'm sorry I implied you were anything less than an alpha male. Matter of fact, you're such an irresistible hunk of man-wolf I think I just have to spend some quality time getting to know you. In a small, windowless room with a one-way mirror in it. Let's go."

"You're taking me in? What the hell for?"

"That intoxicating scent you're wearing. It's a mix of the industrial delousing agent they use down at Stanhope and boiled shoe leather. I don't know why I can't smell either of the guys we're hunting—maybe they're suppressing their natural odor with magic—but they were definitely here. That's enough to bring you in."

"That's bullshit," Iggy says. "I can't smell a damn thing, and neither will my lawyer."

"We'll see." Mystic forensics can do some amazing

things; as long as I'm not hallucinating, I'm sure both Tair and the Don were in close physical proximity to this guy. The whole turning-thrope thing is starting to look a lot more attractive. But why can I smell it and he can't?

"It's the link," Eisfanger says.

Ignacio's in an interview room, waiting for us to talk to him. Charlie and I are on the other side of the reinforced, one-way glass, and Damon's just arrived with the results of the tests he performed on our guest. Sure enough, he has traces of the delousing agent on him—but that's not enough to charge him with harboring a fugitive.

"You're probably right about Falzo and Tair using magic to hide their natural scent," Eisfanger says. "Those kinds of charms are highly specific, though, and won't usually affect secondary odors. Even so, the readings I got were very, very faint. You shouldn't have been able to detect the chemical at all."

"So this mystic bond Tair and I have is making me hypersensitive?"

"It's a fairly common side effect of prelycanthropy. It's not reliable, though—it'll come and go, and won't necessarily pick up what you want it to."

So much for having superpowers—dependable ones, anyway. "So we know that Tair and the Don were there. We know they talked to Iggy. But why? What kind of game is Tair playing?"

Charlie shifts in his chair. He's been studying Iggy on the other side of the glass silently ever since we put him in there; times like this, I can see the reptile in Charlie's soul. A cold-eyed, patient predator, just waiting for his prey to make a mistake. "He's a con man, and he's got the Godfather in his pocket. Who knows what Tair's convinced him of?"

"Maybe," I say. "Or maybe the Don's the one doing the convincing."

Damon frowns. "I thought you said he was irrational."

I shrug. "Craziness is like magic: its boundaries shift and blur. He seemed completely out of it when I talked to him—ripping the guts out of one of his own men pretty much persuaded me he wasn't faking—but he could still have lucid periods. If Tair owes the Don as much as he says he does, he might be willing to trust him to a certain point."

"Still doesn't answer the question of why they were there."

"I've been thinking about that. They're both on the run—how did they hook up? Was something prearranged, or did they have some kind of safe house they both bolted to? And why risk going out in public?"

"They needed something," Charlie says.

"Yeah. I ran Prinzini's file—he's got a lot of priors, but not for running a bookie operation."

"Let me guess. Fraud or forgery."

"They needed documents," Eisfanger says. "A new identity for both of them."

"That's what I figured," I say, "but I was wrong." I pick up the file I'd had Records drop off and hand it to Charlie.

He leafs through it, scanning the pages quickly. "Huh. How about that. Iggy was telling the truth—in a bottom-feeding kind of way."

"Not sure how it ties in to Tair and the Don, but I've got a few ideas."

"I've got one of my own," Charlie says. "Let's go ask him." He jerks a thumb at the one-way mirror.

Ignacio looks up when we enter the interview room, and smiles. "Hey, if it isn't my favorite cop. You figured out yet that you got nothing to hold me on?"

"I'm a little slow," I say, taking a seat on the other side of the table. Charlie stays on his feet, arms crossed. "Bear with me, okay?"

"I'll bear it if you will," he says. His eyes slide down to my chest and back up again. Guess that's what passes for flirting in the Mafioso set.

I flip open the file and pretend to study it. "How's the bookmaking business?"

"You'd have to ask someone who makes books, I guess. I wouldn't know."

"'Course not. That was your cousin Vincenzo, the one who's doing a few years in Stanhope. The Bureau figured you'd taken over, set up shop over the Mix and Match, but that's not really your style, is it? You don't have a head for figures."

"Oh, I've got a head, all right." His grin is gradually turning into a smirk. "And it's one that's interested in figures, too."

"Sure, just not the ones we thought. You're a pimp."

His eyes get a little wider, but that's the only reaction I get. "You know, Agent Valchek, I think I'm insulted. Just because I have a certain amount of success with the opposite sex is no reason to—"

"You're running hookers out of the club. I don't why you chose the M and M for a front, since you're clearly not interested in their regular clientele, but I know there's a reason. I'm going to find out what it is."

Now he looks a lot less cocky. "I don't know what you're talking about."

"Sure you do. And now you're getting nervous, because you went to the trouble of setting up a phony bookie joint as a decoy, with a kinky nightclub downstairs you normally wouldn't be caught undead in. You picked it for a reason and you wanted it to stay hidden. That's all over now."

He doesn't look like he's flirting with me anymore. He looks more like he'd really like to rip my throat out and is trying not to let it show.

"There's a reason they call me the Bloodhound. Once I get a scent, I follow it all the way to the end. And I've got yours."

I get to my feet. "You're free to go, Iggy. I'm already looking forward to our next little chat."

NINE

"Why would Tair and the Don go to a pimp?" I ask. Charlie and I are in an NSA car, Charlie behind the wheel while I eat. It's not easy getting a vegetarian burrito here, but I've found a place that will stick strictly to black beans, cheese, salsa, and some token strands of lettuce. We're parked, the windows rolled down, while I eat and talk with my mouth full.

"You're asking me? Golems don't do sex."

"Or food, or drink, or any of those other squishy biological things. I know. But two guys running from the cops *and* the Mafia are not going to be stopping for a little nookie."

Charlie's got a newspaper open on the steering wheel, reading while I chow down. "You sure? Seems to me like you non-mineral types will take your clothes off and jump in the sack first chance you get."

"Some of us, maybe. But I don't think Iggy's running a brothel—the place wasn't set up right for that. More likely an outcall service, where the girls are sent to hotels or private residences."

Charlie nods and turns a page. "You don't need a

bricks-and-mortar location for that. Cell phones and a Web site work just fine."

I chew, swallow, and ruminate. "Yeah. No need for an elaborate cover-up. So what's that leave us with?"

"Maybe the pimp angle is a dead end. Could be Tair was looking to get back into his old business."

"The Gray Market?" Tair used to work as a biothaumaturge, activating undeclared lems that were used as illegal—and disposable—slave labor.

"Can't run without money. Lem activators are always in high demand."

"Maybe—but there's no way the Mix and Match is a lem-production site, either; you'd need industrial facilities for that. You'd think the Don could at least point him at the right place."

Charlie shrugs. "Might be that's the answer. Tair says, *Hey, where's a good gravel pit where I can get some work?* Don says, *Follow me,* only his brains are scrambled and he takes his pal to a bookie joint instead."

"Not even a real bookie joint, a fake one. Maybe the Don knew that. Maybe he knew what the place really was, and why it was disguised."

"Which brings us back to where we started. Congratulations. We finished, or do you want to do a few more laps?"

I shake my head in disgust. "You're right. This is getting us nowhere, and this burrito is a lost cause." I stick it back in the paper bag I got it in, and toss it in the backseat to get rid of later.

"I thought you liked this place."

"I do. It just doesn't taste right today, that's all. And I'm still hungry."

"Great. Only thing I like better than spending my time watching you stuff organic products into a hole in your face is looking for a new location to stuff organic products into a hole in your face."

"Forget it, let's just go. I'll eat later."

"I'm sure you will. Where to?"

"You know where any of these local *gravel pits* are?"

"I know some guys we could ask."

"Then let's go ask."

We head to the waterfront. Not the touristy part with the boardwalk, but down by the working docks, where the cranes loom like the yellow steel skeletons of giant praying mantises. We park in a large, half-full lot beside a squat industrial-looking building with LOCAL 109 emblazoned over the large wooden double doors of the entrance. Longshoreman's union—or the Thropirelem equivalent, anyway.

I let Charlie lead the way. Inside, there's a long, wide room, lined with benches on either side and a double row back-to-back in the middle. It's a little after 5:00 AM. At this time of the morning I'd expect to see a mix of the supernatural races on those benches, maybe weighted a little lighter on the pire side; hemovores prefer to work inside, which means they gravitate toward white-collar jobs.

But there aren't any pires here at all. Or thropes, for that matter; the benches are occupied solely by golems, maybe fifty or sixty in total. Yellow in color, which is the default for their race. All of them wear heavy-duty work clothes, overalls or jeans and thick wool jackets, with steel-toed boots on their feet and hard hats on their laps. The overhead fluorescents gleam off their plastic skin where it isn't covered by denim or flannel.

There's a counter with a glassed-in booth on the far wall, a bored-looking lem behind it. He's the only one not dressed for industrial labor, in white short sleeves and a dull brown tie. Charlie strides right up to the window, me in tow.

"Morning," Charlie says. "Looking for Mason Zeta. He working today?"

"Lemme check." The clerk taps a few keys with thick, beach-colored fingers. "Yeah. Pier six, unloading a Danish ship. Been on since eleven."

"Okay, thanks."

Once we're back outside, I say, "That was easy. You didn't even have to flash your badge."

"It's called being civil. You should look into it."

"Nah. I like to stick with what I know."

We get back in the car. "Lot of lems in there," I say. "That a union thing?"

"More or less," Charlie says, starting the engine. "Lems didn't invent unions, but we know a good idea when we see one. Might be different pretty soon, though."

"How's that?"

"Nevada changed everything. For the first time, lems have a say in their own production. That's causing repercussions all over the world." The entire state of Nevada—thanks in part to me and Charlie—is now a separate golem nation; they even tried to headhunt Charlie into being their top cop. He turned them down, muttering something about a prior commitment to a lunatic with a gun. "Washington is trying to impose new regulations on the industry, and everyone's afraid that Nevada's either going to flood the market or freeze production and demand reforms. Congress is voting on a bill next week—supposed to make it harder for renegade operations to exist, though I can't see it. Just drive them deeper underground, probably. Typical Washington solution—more laws make us safer, right?"

"Yeah. Never mind that every substance or act we

make illegal generates more income for groups like the Gray Wolves."

Pier six is a short drive away. We park beside a heavy chain-link fence, on the other side of which is a mountain range of shipping containers. More like a block of tenements, actually—no hillside was ever that squared off.

We get out, find the gate. A thrope security guard lets us in once we show him our credentials. Charlie approaches the first worker we see—another lem—and asks him if Mason's around. He points and gives us directions.

Mason's up in the cab of one of the cranes, jockeying big metal boxes from the ship to the dockyard. Charlie flags down a lem in a bright orange vest carrying a walkie-talkie, and gets a message relayed. Then we head over to a utility trailer where the lems take their breaks and wait for him.

We have the trailer to ourselves. It has neither bathroom, coffee, nor vending machines, though it does have two couches, an ancient TV, and a stack of magazines. I leaf through an old issue of *Entertainment Weekly,* while Charlie channel-surfs through recycled sitcoms, talk shows, and infomercials. After ten minutes or so the door opens and a lem walks in.

Charlie gets to his feet and puts out his hand. "Mason. Good to see you."

Mason looks about the same as most lems I've met, and he's wearing a checked blue flannel shirt and jeans. I'm starting to understand why Charlie goes out of his way to have a flashy wardrobe.

"You, too," Mason says, shaking Charlie's hand. "What's up?"

"Need a little help," Charlie says. "Looking for a gravel pit."

Mason frowns. "Yeah? Why come to me?"

"You know why," Charlie says. His voice isn't as friendly anymore.

Mason stares at him for a long moment, then his eyes move to me. He gives me a hard, evaluating look, then says something to Charlie in Lem—a single, bass syllable that reminds me of dropping a brick into a barrel. Charlie's reply is a little longer, but still in Lem. They go back and forth like that a few times.

Only 7 percent of face-to-face human communication is relayed through words. Thirty-eight percent is intonation and inflection, while the other 55 is body language. Lems aren't human, but the overall principle still applies; I can pretty much follow the emotional flow of the conversation, even if I can't understand the specifics. It goes something like this:

MASON: Meatbag!

CHARLIE: She's my partner.

MASON: Meatbag *meatbag*!

CHARLIE: I trust her. And you owe me.

MASON: Bag. Of *meat*. Further racial slur. (pause) And anyway, whatever you're referencing, it was a long time ago.

CHARLIE: That thing I did for you. And then all that stuff happened. Don't you remember? Don't you love me anymore?

MASON: Oh, *that* thing. (long pause) Boy, that was really something, wasn't it? The Good Old Days, when thropes were thropes, pires were pires, and lems were tall, man-shaped piles of rock that everybody agreed were Really Cool. But now the world is worthless crap and there is nothing anyone can do, ever.

CHARLIE: There, there. I commiserate in a manly way. Now how about that thing I mentioned?

MASON: I am deeply gloomy, but you have reminded me of better times before all hope and joy were crushed from my spirit. (even longer pause, with searching looks) I will help you, but you must pretend to be grateful for my loyalty even though it's really because I'm scared gritless of you.

CHARLIE: I know.

And then Charlie turns to me and says, "Mason might have a lead for us."

"Huh," I say. "How about that."

Back in the car, with me driving. Charlie would happily drive all the time, but I hate being a passenger. Control issues, Charlie says. Which is a phrase he picked up from me, since psychoanalysis on Thropirelem is about as advanced as alchemy on mine.

We're on our way to the address Mason gave us. Now that we're alone again, I ask Charlie what the deal is between him and Mason.

"We were in the army together," he says. "Saw some stuff. Did some stuff. You know."

Since the closest I've ever been to the military is watching reruns of *Hogan's Heroes,* I say, "Not really. Care to elaborate?"

"No."

I don't ask him the obvious question, which is how a lem would know about an illegal lem-making operation. Same way a slave knows about the Underground Railroad, or an undocumented immigrant knows about border crossings.

We drive for a while in an uncomfortable silence. I'm really not sure how to approach the subject that has to be brought up, so I finally just haul it out into the light and let it flop around. "So. How do you want to do this?"

"You won't like it."

"Try me."

"Quietly."

"Why wouldn't I like that?"

"No need to raise your voice."

"I'm *not*—oh. Yeah, you're hilarious. Okay, I'll use my inside voice."

"And no gun."

"Fine. No gun."

He gives me a skeptical look. "Just like that. No argument?"

"I don't need the gun. I'm packing the scythes today. I've got you. That's plenty."

"I mean it. It stays in the car."

"Fine, it stays in the car."

Charlie's good at rolling with the punches, but when confronted with the yawning abyss of the unknown—me giving up without a fight—he's not sure how to respond. So he settles for trying to drill twin holes in the side of my head with his stare.

"I don't like putting civilians at risk," I finally say.

"There won't be any civilians there. Just a crooked biothaumaturge, some hired muscle, and a bunch of illegal lems."

"I don't consider the last group to be criminals."

"The US government disagrees."

"How about you? Do you disagree?"

He doesn't answer for a while. He turns his head, stares out the windshield at the road. "I do my job," he says at last.

"Yeah? And what happens to illegal lems when they're discovered?"

"They're confiscated. And destroyed." His voice is flat.

I shake my head. "And you're okay with that? Really?"

"Let it go, Jace."

"Jesus, Charlie—"

"Jace. *Please.*"

I've seen and done a lot of things since I came to Thropirelem, but the one thing I never thought I'd encounter would be a note of pleading in Charlie Aleph's voice. It shocks me into silence, and it takes me a full minute or so to answer.

"Okay," I say.

He doesn't reply. Just stares out the window at the road rolling past.

Charlie gives me directions to an industrial park. Upscale, busy, lots of different kinds of businesses: software, import–export, wholesalers. One of those areas with weird little cul-de-sacs and lots of one-story bland shoebox buildings jammed together in a continuous row, like council houses in England but lower and flatter. Everything lit by the harsh glow of sodium vapor streetlights, with a moon hanging in a predawn sky. A moon that's a little too close to full for me—and after it sets I only have three more moonrises to catch Tair before I leave my humanity behind forever. I park next to a chrome-and-glass sign with a list of six different companies on it.

"Which one—" I say, and then Charlie cuts me off.

"I want you to stay here," he says.

"What? Come on, I'm sorry if I stepped on your size thirteens—"

"It's not that. But some of these places—they react the same way a drug dealer does when you knock. Try to flush everything down the toilet before you kick the door in."

My reply is out of my mouth before I can stop it.

"So? Thought you didn't care about what these places produce."

He doesn't get upset, though. He just says, "If I go in first, I can play it soft. Convince them all we want to do is talk. Less threatening than both of us."

I never thought I'd see the day when Charlie would describe himself as "less threatening," but it seems today is full of surprises. "And if you get into trouble?"

"I'll have one hand on my phone, on speed dial. Your cell beeps, you charge in. You can even bring your gun."

I don't like the idea of sending my partner into an illegal operation on his own, but if anyone can take care of himself, it's Charlie. I give him a grudging nod. "I guess. But I'm setting a time limit—five minutes, no more. Then I'm coming in."

"Five minutes is fine." He starts to get out of the car.

"Hey, what's the name of this place?" I say.

He pauses, one leg already outside. "Karma Imports. Just like the sign says."

"All right. Be careful."

He gets out and shuts the door. Walks up to the glass door, pulls it open, and steps inside. The glass is tinted, so I can't see him after that.

And then I start to worry.

Five minutes is a long time. And if things go bad, they'll go bad with swords and crossbows and steel-cored ball bearings thrown just under the speed of sound. No gunfire to tip me off.

Tick, tick, tick.

It doesn't smell right. It doesn't *feel* right. I've always trusted my instincts, and right now they're screaming at me. Problem is, I don't know if it's the thrope virus ramping them up or something more genuine. Whatever the root cause, it keeps telling me something's *wrong*.

And four and a half minutes later, I realize what it is. *You can even bring your gun.*

At the beginning of the conversation he specifically asked me *not* to bring my gun. Not because it's dangerous—he doesn't think of it that way—but because it's *loud.*

Then he reverses himself completely a few minutes later. At first I thought it was because he doesn't take my gun seriously—he can't help it, nobody on this world does—but that's not it. His previous objection still stands. So why the abrupt change of heart?

Because it doesn't matter. I can bring any damn thing I want, no matter how noisy or ridiculous, because I'm not going to the same place he is.

I get out of the car, walk into the building. Karma Imports isn't hard to find; there's a central lobby with a hall going left and right, and signs telling you which way to go. A brown-skinned pire with a bindi on her forehead looks up when I walk into the Karma Imports office, and asks if she can help me. I ask if a lem in a panama hat has been by in the last few minutes, and she shakes her head. I show her my badge and ask if I can look around, and she looks mystified but gives her okay.

I don't find anything. Just an office, filled with cubicles and people working in them. No gravel pit, no lems, no Charlie. He probably left by a rear exit; he could be anywhere in this whole complex by now.

I try calling him. No answer, straight to voice mail: "This is Charlie. Thrill me."

Oh, I'll thrill him, all right.

I go back to the car and wait. I spend the first few minutes envisioning what I'm going to do to my conniving, devious partner when he returns . . . and then I cool off a little and start thinking about exactly *why* he did what he did.

He comes back about twenty minutes later. He gets in and closes the door, then looks at me expectantly. Waiting for the explosion.

"I *know* it's not because you don't trust me," I say. "But reassure me, all right? I deserve that much."

"I trust you with my life, Jace."

I nod. "Just checking. So let's play a what-if game. What if a federal agent were to stumble across an illegal lem-making operation? By law, she'd have to report it, right?"

"Absolutely."

"And if she didn't—and someone ever found that out—there would be some nasty repercussions."

"Almost certainly."

"She might even lose her job."

"Yeah. Which wouldn't be so bad. Unless, you know, she had some sort of contract to return her to her own world that would become null and void if she were fired."

"Right. And reporting this illegal operation would result in the destruction of all the lems—lems whose only crime was existing in the first place."

Charlie doesn't respond right away. When he does answer, his voice is soft. "Golems have to be careful. Deactivation for Gray Market lems is automatic—but so is *assisting* lems like that in any way. The big monster in the closet for thropes and pires is the idea of lems controlling their own production. Afraid we're going to start breeding like rabbits or something. They bring the hammer down hard on anything like that."

"So helping illegal lems is a death sentence for another lem?"

"Yes."

I pause for a moment to let that sink in. "It's a real shame," I say at last, "that the tip we got didn't pan out."

"Waste of a whole morning."

I shrug. "What can you do? That's life . . ."

Charlie doesn't smile often, and he doesn't smile big. But that little upturn of his lips is the best thing that's happened to me in a couple of days.

"Any brilliant and completely spontaneous ideas about where to go next?" I ask, starting the car.

"As a matter of fact, I have this sudden hunch."

"Is that what that is? I thought you just slept funny and something shifted."

"I think we're approaching this from the wrong angle."

"Angle? Most hunches are kind of round . . ."

"I don't think Tair is looking for work. I think he's looking for an exit, and he's planning on taking the Don with him."

"Exit? To where?"

"Out of the country. He was hooked up with an international arms dealer for a while—he'll have contacts overseas."

Makes sense. "So why were he and the Don talking to Ignacio?"

"Because Iggy's connected to a smuggling network, one that moves lems across borders."

"Ah. So we need to take a harder look at Iggy?"

"We need to take a harder look at the club."

By the time we get back to the Mix and Match the sun is coming up. I park a block away and Charlie and I strategize; this time, we're going to use a little more discretion. Okay, a lot more.

"Hey, I thought they closed the place for the night," I say.

"Looks like somebody forgot to tell her," Charlie says.

There's a woman standing in front of the club. Even from this distance, I can tell she's a Fake Furry; the shaggy boots and gloves are more like a fetish version of lycanthropy than any attempt to duplicate the real thing. She's wearing a little black dress, her legs long and pale and her cleavage pronounced. Three-inch heels, an over-size fur hat, and some kind of toothy necklace.

She raps on the door. A moment later it opens, and she steps in.

"Maybe she works there," Charlie says.

"Not in those heels. She's dressed more like a customer than an employee."

And then a long, black car pulls up in front of the club. No more than a minute later, the same woman steps out and gets in the car. Backseat.

"Uh-huh," I say. Things are starting to make sense. I start the car and pull out. "Charlie, get out the bubble, will you?"

He pulls the light out from its nook and puts it on the dash. "We doing a traffic stop?"

"Yeah. I have a reasonable suspicion that we're witnessing a violation of the law."

"Which one?"

"I'll decide later."

I get behind the car and hit the switch, flooding the street with blue and red light. The car pulls over to the curb. Charlie and I park behind them and get out.

The driver of the car is a thrope, a young, tough-looking guy in a flashy suit—from his appearance, he might even be related to Iggy. He stares at us with no expression at all on his face. "There a problem?"

"Yeah," I say. "But not with you. Can you exit the car, miss?"

The door opens slowly, and the woman gets out. Up close I can see how beautiful she is; one of those classic, high-cheekboned faces, full lips, large, expressive eyes. The fur accessories make her look more like some exotic Russian aristocrat than a thrope wannabe.

"Do you have any ID?" I ask.

"No," she says. "I left it at home."

"Funny thing to forget when you're out clubbing. Let's go have a little chat, okay?" I nod at Charlie, who's keeping a careful eye on the driver.

The woman looks . . . bewildered. A little afraid, a little confused. She glances in the driver's direction, but she can't make eye contact from where she's standing. She's on her own.

"Strictly routine," I say. "You're not in trouble. Just take a minute."

She nods hesitantly, then follows me over to my car. I open the rear door and motion for her to get in, then go around to the other side and do the same.

"What's your name?" I ask.

"Csilla. Csilla Janos."

Her accent is Hungarian, as is her name. "Csilla, I know what you've been doing. But that's not what I want to talk about."

"I've—I've done nothing wrong."

"I don't care about the prostitution, Csilla. But I need to know how you entered the country. I need to know where the lems are going out and the women are coming in. Tell me that, and I promise I'll protect you."

Now she looks miserable. "I can't tell you anything. They'll kill me."

"No, they won't. See, you're going to tell your boss this is a shakedown for money. They'll believe that. And all I want is an address—I'm not asking for names." I pause. "Look, I understand you're trapped. But don't you want to make a friend? A friend who can help you from the inside? I can be that friend, Csilla. You think I like seeing women treated the way you are?"

She gives me a troubled glance. I know what she's thinking. She's played this scenario out in her head before, maybe even fantasized about it, wondered what she will do if offered the chance.

A chance she decides to take.

"The place you are searching for," she says quietly, "is called the Black Port."

TEN

Iggy isn't just a nightclub owner, or a pimp, or a lem smuggler. He's a human trafficker—or in this case not-so-human.

I'm familiar with the practice from my own world. Desperate women from impoverished countries agree to exorbitant fees to be smuggled into the United States. They work off their debt through prostitution, which is bad enough, but the people they're in debt to are professional thugs like Iggy; thugs who make sure the debt is never quite paid off.

That's why the Mix and Match is the perfect front. Nobody notices if women come and go all night long, and the crosskink angle lets them disguise the women as something else. No hookers here, Officer; just freaky party-people playing dress-up.

It might seem a little elaborate for an escort service, but there's more than that going on here. This is slavery, plain and simple. Iggy's got a pipeline going, and in typical wise-guy fashion has decided to make it twice as profitable by having it operate both ways. Lems go out, women come in. He's not keeping them at the club, though—it's just an intermediary station, in case something goes wrong. The women and lems are kept somewhere else—probably two separate locations.

But that's not what I'm after. I want the Black Port.

As it turns out, Iggy's specialty is pires. The reason for it is simple, one a famous fictional vampire figured out over a century ago: If you're one of the living dead and you want to travel undetected from one country to another, the best way to go is as freight. A coffin in a ship's hold will work, but you have to ensure you can come and go during the trip; a sea voyage is relatively slow, so you'll need to duck out to snack on crew members now and then. Going by air is much quicker, but in a world full of pires you can't get away with something that obvious.

Iggy hit upon the same solution human smugglers did in my world: freight containers. Big metal boxes full of manufactured goods, which crisscross the globe in such large quantities that it's fairly easy to hide one in the middle of a bunch of others. Punch a few airholes in it, provide some basic amenities like a bucket and maybe some water—

But wait. Pires don't need air. Or water. Or a bucket, for that matter. They need blood, but that's about it. And they're really, really resilient.

So forget about all those amenities. Run a hose through a hole, one you can stick a funnel in. Bribe someone on the ship to pour some blood down it every now and then.

And then stack the pires like cordwood.

"It was horrible," Csilla whispers. She's not looking at me, having gone someplace inside her head. Not a good place. She stares out the car window, her voice low and strained. "The ones on the bottom rows had it the worst. The hose would not quite reach. We tried to cup some in our hands and pass it to them, but there was no room to move. And the blood ran out on the third day, anyway."

I can't imagine what it must have been like. Hundreds of pires, crammed together, filling the container to the top. Csilla was somewhere near the middle.

"A pire deprived of blood is a beast," she says. "The ones on the bottom, the hungriest ones—they lost the ability to reason. They began to scream. It went on for days . . . they tried to bite those nearest them. This is not possible, of course—pire teeth will not penetrate pire skin. But they tried. They searched us beforehand, to make sure we had no wood or silver. That was a good thing—if the ones on the bottom had possessed such items, they would have killed those around them in an attempt to feed."

There's more, much more, but I don't have time to hear it. The longer I listen, the more danger I put her in, so I gently interrupt her and ask her what I need to know. She tells me. I send her back to her driver, and hope I haven't just signed her death warrant.

And then Charlie and I go back to the office to get some warrants of our own.

Sometimes working for the NSA has its benefits.

For instance, you can whistle up a covert ops team with highly specialized skills and equipment on a moment's notice—as long as you can convince your boss you actually need them—and let them do the heavy lifting. Or in this case, the heavy swimming.

Almost twenty hours after my little chat with Csilla Janos, I'm sitting in an inflatable Zodiac boat out in the harbor. Seattle's lights twinkle at me, far enough away that the skyline is no more than a suggestion of blocky peaks and valleys. The moon looms overhead, an inescapable reminder that I'm down to two days of pre-wolfiness.

I've taken scuba training before, but I'm a little nervous; this equipment was designed for thropes, and thropes can't actually drown—though the agents who are ferrying me out here, Tony and Ben, have plenty of stories about thropes who tried.

"Hey, you remember that guy on the Hawaii dive?" Tony asks. He's a big guy with a black crew cut.

"The one who spaced out, got rapture of the deep?" Ben asks. He's Puerto Rican, small and wiry.

"Yeah. Drifted right down to the bottom, passed out. Took a long time to bring him up after we finally found him." You can't raise someone too fast when they've gone really deep; nitrogen bubbles will form in the bloodstream, causing intense pain.

"Except this guy, he got impatient," Ben tells me. "He's had his lungs full of water for hours, which is agonizing—you're basically drowning over and over again. So when he gets high enough to see sunlight, he loses it. Just starts swimming straight up, as fast as he can go."

I swallow. "What happened?"

"What do you think? He exploded," Tony says. "Well, more like ruptured, I guess. Different organs, arteries, all kinds of stuff. Real mess. Took him a couple weeks to heal."

"His skull even blew out," Ben says. "He was never the same after that."

"Thanks, guys. One of you want to make sure I've got everything hooked up right?"

Tony chuckles. "If you don't," he says, "you'll find out pretty fast."

Ah, cop humor, so dark it would give a black hole indigestion. Not that I'm any different—just a lot more fragile, rupture-wise. Or at least I used to be . . .

I slide into the cold, wet embrace of the water, on my back, the night sky above me going blurry and then fading away completely. I switch on my headlamp, orient myself, then check my wrist compass. I swim down and toward the south at a steep angle; what I'm looking for is right on the bottom.

My field of vision doesn't extend very far in this blackness, so it comes into sight abruptly. One second there's nothing but silt swirling in my light's beam; the next there's a wall in front of me. A white, curving wall, encrusted with barnacles.

The Black Port.

I don't see the entrance, so I swim to the right, running over the instructions I was given in my head. I can pick out details now, like the row of little square windows that line the wall.

And then I come to the wing.

It's got a semi-trailer fuel tanker resting on top of it upside down, a big chrome cylinder with its wheels pointing up like a stranded turtle's limbs. There's a patchwork of steel plating connecting it to the 747's fuselage at the base of the wing. That gives me a better idea of where I am; the entrance is on the other side.

I swim up and over, the lamp's beam sweeping along the structure. It's grotesque and beautiful, an immense crippled mechanical hybrid lurking on the bottom of the ocean. The other wing is completely gone, but the body of the plane butts directly against the wreck of a large freighter. Rusting steel pipes welded to the ship's hull extend from it like angular tentacles, ending in a variety of bulky shapes: shipping containers, smaller boats, even a few wheeled vehicles like panel trucks. I can't decide if it looks like a larger creature feeding off a bunch of smaller ones, or giving birth to them.

The hatch I'm looking for is inside the freighter itself. An agent is waiting for me, hovering in the inky water a few feet above the slope of the deck. This one's a pire, and doesn't need any breathing gear; in fact, all he's got on is a pair of black swimming trunks and fins, and some sort of headset. He's holding an agency-issued speargun in one hand and motions with the other one for me to follow him. He glides down and through a square black opening in the deck, not even bothering with a headlamp. I guess his night vision's a lot better than mine.

I'm not worried about running into resistance—like I said, the assault team did the heavy lifting before I got here. The Black Port is now in the hands of the NSA, and after we've learned all we can from it the whole facility will be destroyed.

We're in what must have been the hold. Curving walls, rusted iron strutwork. Seaweed sways gently, nudged by our passing. The agent leads me to a square steel box welded to one side of the hull, big enough to hold both of us, with a sealed oval hatch on one side. The agent grabs the spoked metal wheel in the center of the hatch and turns it. The hatch swings open, and the agent motions me inside. He doesn't follow.

Water conducts sounds quite well, and the noise the hatch makes as it shuts behind me reminds me of a safe door closing. The inside of the box is featureless except for a grille in the floor and a second hatch on the far side, this one with a small glass plate set into it.

I hear the rumble of a motor starting up, then a chugging. I'm pulled toward the bottom of the box as pumps suck water through the grille. A few minutes later the box is full of air and wet NSA agent as opposed to liquid.

A panel behind the glass plate slides aside, revealing it as a window. A familiar-looking pair of ice-blue eyes beneath snow-white eyebrows peer at me, and then the inner hatch opens.

"Jace," Damon Eisfanger says. He's wearing a black neoprene wet suit, his wide, pale feet bare. His squat, powerful body looks like it's about to bulge right through the fabric. "I haven't finished processing the scene yet—there's a *lot* to go through."

"As long as the site's secure," I say, unbuckling straps. I shuck off the diving rig, having already taken off the fins while I was waiting for the air lock to empty. "I didn't bring much with me."

"That's probably a good thing. Your weapon does have an unsettling tendency to make large holes in things, and down here that would be—bad."

Down here is the choke point for the trafficking trade in Seattle. It was run almost entirely by pires, who capitalized on the fact that they didn't need to breathe to build their own little underwater way station. Not that they did any of the physical work themselves; they used Gray Market lems for that, since lems don't breathe, either. The pires didn't show up until after the place was finished—and, of course, all the workers had been destroyed to keep the place a secret.

And then the merchandise had begun to move. Lems assembled in factories on land were marched across the seafloor to the Port, where they were transferred topside to ships bound for other countries. Those same ships would drop containers full of illegal immigrants into the water, and the process would happen all over again but going the other way. The containers themselves would become part of the Black Port, holding cells connected by pipeline tunnels where they could stick lems or illegals while waiting for a ship or a delivery run to the mainland.

I take a look around. The forensics team that got here first has set up electric lanterns for light since the Port's own power source was disrupted during the raid, and they throw harsh shadows onto the curving walls. I'm inside the fuselage of the 747, which has maybe a third of its seats remaining, all on one side of the plane; the doors to the overhead bins have been ripped out, and the windows covered with sheet metal. An inch or so of seawater sloshes underfoot, and the air reeks likes a New Jersey beach at low tide.

I walk over and take a look at the seats. They've all been modified, heavy chains replacing the seat belts, with manacles for wrists. Like some warped, modern-day version of a slave galley, without the oars.

"We think this is where they processed them," Eisfanger says. His voice doesn't echo at all, damped down by the wonders of twenty-first-century aviation acoustic design. "The fuel tanker is basically a larger version of the air lock you came through. They were herded in here from there, where they could be evaluated and assigned to wherever they were going."

I try to imagine it. Row after row of lems, sitting stoically, chained to their seats. Waiting to be shipped off to become slave labor or part of some Third World dictator's private army. Lems can be manufactured anywhere, but the United States has the highest proportion of skilled activators and lem-friendly minerals, mostly mined in Nevada. A brisk trade in illegal lem precursor soil has sprung up since the state declared itself a sovereign golem nation.

But that image, chilling as it is, isn't as bad as imagining row after row of pire women chained to these seats.

The lems wouldn't really understand what was happening to them; they'd only be days or even hours old. But the women . . . they'd be terrified. Starved for blood. Many of them wouldn't even speak English—but that didn't mean they didn't know what was in store. What they'd be expected to do.

"How many casualties?" I ask.

"Nine on their side. Twelve captured. None of us."

"Good." I wish I'd been here to dust a few myself, but I'm not that handy with a speargun.

Damon shows me around. The crew quarters in the freighter have been sealed and drained to provide a place for the smugglers to live; all the floors are at an angle, but other than that they've outfitted them very comfortably. Flatscreen TVs, DVD players, stereo systems, queen-size beds. Beanbag chairs seem to be the furniture of choice, and posters of naked porn stars the interior decoration. The galley has a walk-in freezer full of blood products, ranging from your basic A through O to more gourmet fare like hemovore ice cream. No shortage of chemical recreation, either; there's a whole cabinet full of magicked beer, whiskey, and even a bale of marijuana.

"I didn't think pires smoked this stuff," I say.

"They don't. Fire messes with the spell that lets drugs affect hemovores and lycanthropes, so they soak the pot in the booze and get it into their system that way. They call it ganja juice."

"Ah, the ingenuity of the American stoner," I mutter. "Federal laws don't stop you, why should supernatural ones?"

Then Damon shows me where the women and the lems were kept.

The lem cells are just big featureless metal boxes, empty shipping containers. Lems don't need food or water or bathroom facilities, so none of those amenities were supplied. They do sleep, but the smugglers had thoughtfully provided a floor for that.

The women's facilities bother me a lot more. Again, no bathrooms or beds, but the floor is littered with hundreds of small plastic vials the size of a pill bottle. Many of them have been crushed, but I pick one up that's still whole. There's a tiny rime of something reddish brown in the very bottom.

"This is how they fed them," I say. "Minuscule amounts of blood, doled out carefully. Enough that they wouldn't go berserk, but keep them in a weakened state."

Damon nods. "I need to get my samples back to the lab to verify, but I've already found traces of sorcery in the vials. I think they were drugging them, too."

Of course they were. Wanted to keep them nice and docile, not to mention disoriented. Until it was time for that long, dark march through the muck of the bottom to the shore of their new country. A country they wouldn't get to see much of for a long, long time.

If ever.

When we raided the Black Port, we didn't find any women *or* lems; we must have caught them between shipments. That's a piece of very bad luck, but I don't have the luxury of adjusting to someone else's schedule. I'm on one of my own, and every time the moon rises it gets a little tighter.

"There's plenty of forensic evidence," Damon says. "I can definitely prove they housed illegal lems here."

"How about the pire women?"

Damon frowns. "Harder to do. Lems have the sorcerous equivalent of a serial number, but the pires don't. We can make a case for the drugs we found, but we really need a material witness to verify the smuggling."

Which means Csilla. And she was too scared to even name the people involved—no way I can get her to testify against them. I just hope they haven't made the connection between her and this raid.

"What about Tair and the Don?" I ask.

"Sorry. Haven't found anything to indicate the presence of a thrope down here, at least not in a long time."

So did I just prevent my two suspects from fleeing the country, or screw up a chance to apprehend them? I shake my head, flinging little water droplets off my hair. Damn it, I can't seem to catch a break, let alone an escaped prisoner and an insane Godfather.

"Have you got any *good* news for me, Eisfanger?"

And now a smile spreads across his wide, ruddy face. "I think I just might, actually. Take a look at this." He opens a rubberized pouch on his belt and pulls out a small plastic evidence bag.

Inside is what seems to be a piece of charred wood. "What is it?"

"Trace I found under one of the airplane seats. Didn't seem to belong there—fire is something they wouldn't have any use for down here."

"So where's it from?"

"I think a lem brought it in. There are muddy tread marks all over the place—they must have given the lems boots to keep them from damaging their feet on the march here. The wood could have been caught in one of the boot treads."

"So, maybe from a ship that burned and sank?"

"No. It's not waterlogged. It must have come from the surface, not the bottom."

I think about that. From a campfire, maybe? That would suggest some kind of outdoor site—but pires don't need to keep warm. Maybe a fireplace—I've seen pire-occupied houses that have them simply for ornamental value. But why would a lem foot be stomping around in an ornamental fireplace?

Damon must understand the look on my face, because he says, "I'm going to run some tests on it, see what else it can tell me. I'll try to come up with a location for you."

"Thanks." I realize I'm shivering, which shouldn't be a surprise; I'm cold and wet and hundreds of feet below the surface of the water.

But looking around the dark, hollow shell that so many desperate women must have passed through, I don't think the temperature has anything to do with it.

I stare at the pire sitting on the other side of the interview table. He's manacled at the wrists to the table itself, which is bolted to the floor. His name is Orrick Lynch, and his file says he's over four hundred years old. He's sort of pear-shaped, with a fringe of gray hair on an otherwise pale, bald head, and he's got a bushy gray mustache. His eyes are dark and very, very cold.

"So, Orrick. I understand you've been running a little import–export business. Seafood?"

No response. Just a flat, unblinking stare.

"Yeah. See, I have a problem with that. And while we may not have caught you with the goods this time, we have more than enough to charge you, anyway."

When he speaks, his voice is rough and accented with German—Austrian, I believe, rather than Swiss. "You do not know who you are interfering with."

"Sure I do. *La Lupo Grigorio*. But the Gray Wolves and I have an understanding. They *gave* you to me, Orrick. Because I'm doing a favor for them. They've got this problem with a runaway Don, and *nobody's* better than me at hunting down a suspect."

He mutters a single word in German under his breath: *"Bluthund."*

Good, he knows who I am; that'll make selling this easier. "They want him back pretty badly. They didn't give you up easily, but hey—they can always relocate, right? Plenty of ocean floor out there, plenty of old freighters they can sink. The aircraft fuselage might be a little harder to come by, but the Wolves own their fair share of junkyards. And the labor's free."

I lean over the table, a big smile on my face. "But here's where it gets interesting. See, you can play the same game they can. Want a little payback, plus a re- duced sentence? I can make that happen. Just think of me as a bribable referee in a really nasty play-off game."

For a second I think he might actually go for it. But then something shifts in his eyes and he shakes his head, slowly. I don't know how many of his four centu- ries he's spent on the wrong side of the law, but long enough to know you don't survive by turning on your masters.

I didn't think he would, but it was important I try. It increases Csilla's chances, makes it less likely she'll be blamed for the raid.

But it doesn't get me any closer to finding Tair.

ELEVEN

I wouldn't let Charlie come with me to the Black Port.

He wanted to. Maybe he even had a right to. But Eisfanger warned me there might be booby traps, sorcerous ones specifically designed to prevent lems from escaping. "If Charlie trips one of those, he could find himself mind-wiped or worse."

But it's not like my partner's going to let me forget about it.

"So, what part of *personal enforcer* do you not understand?" he says as I drive. We're headed for the Mix and Match, though I'm not really sure why. "I can break it down for you, if you'd like. *Enforcer* stems from 'to enforce,' as in using force in the pursuit of a particular goal. I'd like to point out that it's kinda difficult to *use* such force unless the conveyor of said force is actually *present*."

"Wow. You sound like a really pissed-off, macho version of Obi-Wan Kenobi."

"Then there's the word *personal*. I realize this is a term you don't have a lot of familiarity with, since it usually pops up next to words like *relationships, feelings,* or *hygiene*—"

"Hey!"

"—so I'll try to keep it simple. *Personal.* As in *your* person. *Your* health, *your* safety, your *life*."

"What's wrong with my hygiene?"

"Again, it's not like I really care whether or not you get attacked underwater by pire smugglers, because in order to kill you they'd have to go to *unbelievable* lengths—like, oh, yanking a *hose* out of your mouth—"

"If you'd spent an hour trudging through rusty seawater, you'd stink, too. And wherever you're going with that hose crack, I'd advise you to pick your next words *very* carefully."

"—so do me a tiny, minuscule favor, all right? The next time you decide to put your life at risk in a hostile environment—interior of a live volcano, middle of a buffalo stampede, jumping off a tall building—at least give me the option of, I don't know, actually *being in the same general vicinity!*"

He glares at me. I watch the road, trying not to grin. He's adorable when he's overprotective. "If I *had* let you come along, you'd smell like this, too."

"I suppose."

"Probably would have ruined that suit."

"I wouldn't have worn the suit."

"What, so I'd have to see you naked? No thanks. Once was enough."

"Swimming trunks."

"Oh, sure. Pin-striped, no doubt. With lapels."

"Don't be ridiculous."

"Hey, the last time I saw you without pants you stuck a fedora over it."

"That was your idea, remember? Which was pointless, anyway, since there *is* no it."

It's true—golems are sexless, or at least lacking any visible equipment one way or the other. "I have a delicate constitution."

"Yeah, and the heart of a young girl. Mounted on a plaque over your desk."

We've arrived at the Mix and Match. It's just before noon, so there's no one around. I park across the street and stare out the window at the front door.

"What's on your mind?" Charlie asks.

"A little piece of charred wood."

"Right, that splinter Eisfanger found. He come up with anything?"

"Not yet . . ." There's something nagging at me, something other than a golem with a maternal complex.

Something about the boots.

Mob guys are greedy. Iggy found a way to double his profits by doubling his smuggling. I can understand him not wanting to damage the lems by marching them across the seafloor in their bare plastic feet, but heavy-duty footwear costs money. He wouldn't let the lems keep them, he'd reuse the same ones over and over as long as he could. So why didn't we find a pile of dirty, muck-encrusted boots in the Black Port?

Because they were back at the lem factory, waiting for the next batch of lems to tie them on. "Hey, Charlie? In that lem factory that we never found—you think it was possible there was a large pile of waterlogged, muddy boots lying around?"

"It's possible. But I never saw such a thing."

"Of course not. How could you, if you were never there?"

So they were either in transit or stashed in a closet. But wherever they were, somebody had to have transported them from the Port, and transferring a load of a hundred or so filthy, foul-smelling leather boots from a sealed environment on the seafloor up to the surface and into a boat would be a major pain; the best way to do it would be to use a fishing trawler with nets and a winch—

No. I'm not thinking like a wise guy. The best way to do it is to send the boots back the same way they came: on somebody's feet.

I dig out my cell phone and call the lab. "Damon? The tread marks you found—were they headed toward or away from the large air lock?"

"Uh—I'm not sure. Just a second, I'm sending you all the photos from the site."

The phone chirps, letting me know they've arrived. "Thanks," I say, and hang up. I flick through them quickly, until I find what I want. There are a lot of tread marks, many of them overlapping, but most of the ones I can clearly distinguish have the toes pointing toward the air lock. Not lems coming in; pires waiting to go out.

My phone beeps at me. Eisfanger, calling me back. "Jace? You didn't give me a chance to tell you what I just found."

"Does it have to do with pires wearing the boots the charred wood came from?"

A long pause on the other end. "That would make sense," he says slowly. "I interrogated the wood. It had been crushed by something both heavy and organic— not a lem. It was telling me the boot *itself*—the leather— was unnaturally heavy."

Which makes perfect sense. The boots doing double duty again: use them as foot protection for the lems until they get to the Black Port, then zap them with a spell to increase their weight before strapping them on the women. After all, you don't want your merchandise making a break for it in open water, right? At night, in the darkness and swirling murk, a good swimmer might just be able to get away.

Unless, of course, she's wearing concrete overshoes.

An old Mob trick from way back, with a supernatural twist. You're marching with the fishes now; use steel cables and a padlock instead of laces and you can't get them off, either. Like chaining your bike to a lamppost. Keep your possessions safely stuck in the mud, where it's a constant struggle to move and they'd never even consider running away.

I didn't think I could get any angrier about this, but I was wrong. I'm starting to understand a fundamental truth about Thropirelem, and it's an ugly one: Being tougher and stronger than human doesn't mean you suffer any less. It just means that the pain and hardships that get thrown at you get worse in direct proportion to how much more you can stand. There's an old saying that goes *God doesn't give you any more than you can handle.* In that case, whatever God's in charge of this universe either's a real bastard or has a great deal of confidence in the endurance of his subjects.

What I'd really like to do is take the Crown Vic I'm sitting in and ram it straight through the front doors of the club—but that won't solve anything. So instead I put it in gear and pull out with a screech of tires.

"Where we headed?" Charlie asks.

"I don't know. I'll tell you when we get there."

I focus on the boots again. They travel in a loop, from the lem factory to the Black Port to wherever the women are being kept to the lem factory. "Charlie, does the lem-making process involve burning anything?"

"No."

So the charred wood must have come from wherever the women were stashed. Someplace private, someplace controlled. Not too isolated, because they have to get the women to the club and back. Not in the club itself, because that would be too risky—the club's a dispatch point, where they can shuffle the women in and out. But they wouldn't be holding the women too far away from the club, either, because long transit times cut into profits.

I shouldn't be obsessing about this. I should be concentrating on finding Tair, not searching for a prostitution ring. But I just can't let it go; I'm so close, I can practically smell it . . .

I've been circling the block the Mix and Match is on. Suddenly my nose is full of the odor of old smoke, even though the windows are rolled up.

On the far side of the block, directly across the alley from the club, is a burned-out tenement.

I slam on the brakes. "The hell?" Charlie blurts.

I'm already halfway out of the car. "Sorry," I call over my shoulder.

He catches up to me before I reach the front door, or rather the sheet of plywood nailed over what used to be the front door. "You think this is where the wood came from?" he asks.

"I'm thinking that pires, being daylight-challenged, are awfully fond of tunnels." I draw my gun.

I hear a thin susurrus of metal on metal as Charlie pulls his Roman-style short sword from the scabbard inside his jacket. "Front or back?" he says.

"Let's try the back."

It's not hard to get in. There's a blackened fire escape that Charlie boosts me up to and I let down for him. We enter through a broken window on the second floor.

The inside is a mess. The stench of a burned-out building hangs heavy in the air. The charred corpses of furniture lay strewn about, some of them barely identifiable. Pigeon droppings streak the blackened floor with random splotches of white and gray. The structural integrity of the upper floors seems seriously in doubt, so we carefully make our way down what's left of the stairs.

More recent trash litter the rooms on the main floor. A rat scurries out of the corner at our approach, disappearing into a hole in the wall.

"Nothing here," Charlie says, his voice low.

"Didn't think there would be. We need to go lower."

A little searching and we find the door to the basement. It's made of metal, it's set into the concrete foundation of the building, and it's locked.

Charlie sighs. "You're going to shoot it, aren't you?"

"No way to get it open without making a racket, is there?"

"Not that I can think of."

"Relax. I had Eisfanger whip this up for me." I pull a long, thick metal tube out of my pocket and attach it to the muzzle of the Ruger. It takes a minute and involves three different clamping screws. "It's called a silencer. Makes the gun less accurate, but the sound-dampening material it's stuffed with has been mystically enhanced. Eisfanger claims it'll make less noise than a door slamming—if, you know, it doesn't explode and take my hand off."

Charlie takes a discreet step backward. That's one of the things I love about him: No matter how protective he is of my safety, he still lets me take chances he doesn't approve of. Then he complains about it afterward.

I aim at the lock and pull the trigger.

A real silencer is nothing like what you experience on TV, and makes a heckuva lot bigger bang than that little *pffffft!* you always hear in spy movies. The noise this one makes is like neither; if the genuine article is a sudden cry of "Hey!" and the fake one is a loud *"Psssst!,"* then this is an "ahem," a polite little cough by an old lady who really doesn't want to cause any fuss. Which is doubly weird, because the bullet tearing the guts out of the lock should have made quite the racket all by itself—I guess that little heart-to-heart chat Damon and his creation had was really effective.

The door swings open.

We creep down the concrete steps. Not much light, but I can still make out the general shape of things. Big furnace to our right. Bare cement walls, black iron pipes, tin heating ducts. Silvery electrical conduits. Something that looks like a gigantic water heater and probably is.

But it's not what I'm seeing that's important. It's what I'm smelling.

"Over there," I whisper. I point at the furnace. We approach it slowly, carefully. There's a big metal hatch in the side, probably meant for maintenance.

"When's the last time you saw a locked door on a furnace?" Charlie growls.

I use the same key I used on the last door, and it fits just as well. Charlie yanks the door open.

The furnace is just a shell, concealing a rough-edged hole in the concrete floor. I can see metal rungs inside, leading down. Charlie goes first, not giving me a chance to argue, and I follow.

The sub-basement is one big, echoey chamber. I can see a closed metal door at the far end, no doubt leading to the tunnel that connects this place to the basement of the Mix and Match.

The rest of the room is taken up by cages.

The cages are roughly seven feet square. Each one holds exactly two things: a cot, and a naked female pire.

It's daytime, so they're all out cold. Pires don't lapse into comas while the sun's up, but they aren't exactly light sleepers, either.

"We found them," Charlie says.

"No. No, we didn't." I keep my voice low as I head across the room. "Because then all these women would go into the system, and get deported. Which would mean everything they've gone through would be for nothing. And some of them—more than you might think—will wind up doing it all over again, just for the chance at a new life. Or unlife, I guess."

I reach the door on the far side of the room and try it. Unlocked. It leads to a tunnel, just like I thought, but there's another door in the tunnel itself, to another room. It's open, too.

I'm hoping for a guard. Maybe even Iggy himself. What I get when I yank the door open, gun in hand, is a dressing room.

The room is maybe twenty feet long by ten wide. It's got four vanity tables with mirrors, the tables crowded with makeup. The walls are lined, floor-to-ceiling, with racks of clothing. Lingerie, leather, rubber, fur. Every kind of uniform and costume a kinky customer might want, from naughty nurse to stern librarian, plus outfits to wear to and from the club.

But the pires themselves they lock up naked. What's the point in dressing your Barbies when no one's playing with them?

Charlie walks in behind me. He looks around, then looks at my face. "Oh, boy," he sighs. "Okay. Before we get started, I want to make one thing absolutely, crystal clear."

"What?" I snarl.

"*You're* doing the paperwork."

"For what?"

"For whatever rage-induced mayhem we're about to inflict."

I take a deep, deep breath. "We?"

"Yeah." One word, but the weight Charlie gives it almost makes me smile. It's a weight that crushes any sort of doubt as to where he stands.

Right by my side. No matter what.

"Yeah," I say. "Let's go do some *inflicting*."

We march down the tunnel. It's a nice tunnel, or at least one with potential. Fluorescent lights, concrete floor, raw plywood for walls, with that freshly built, new-home smell. Some drywall, a little paint, maybe some carpet, and you've got yourself a cozy little half-block stretch of heaven.

With hell on either end.

The tunnel leads to a ladder, and at the top there's a concealed door. It comes as absolutely no surprise to me that the door opens into a stall in the ladies' room. The door to the stall is self-locking, with a sign that reads OUT OF ORDER on the front and spring-loaded hinges so it closes automatically. The toilet is full and disgusting and there's no paper, just to make sure no one's tempted to use it anyway.

Charlie and I pause at the door that leads into the club itself. I can't hear anything, but there may not be anything to hear; the club is closed right now, after all.

But there's probably somebody upstairs.

I stop and consider my options. I've got enough to bust Iggy right now, but not without sending the women back where they came from. That's not going to work for me.

So I do the only thing I can think of.

I tell Charlie what I have in mind, and then we walk out of the ladies' room. I stride over to the bar and grab a bottle of 151-proof rum from the well. I start to splash it around, and when that bottle's empty I find another one and repeat. I'm on bottle number three before the door in the back opens and Iggy walks out. "What," he says pleasantly, "the hell are you doing?"

"Renovating. I'm thinking some orange, some yellow, and a whole lot of black."

His eyebrows go up. "You're going to burn down my bar?"

"That's right. With you in it."

He smiles. Iggy's no stranger to the shakedown, and he knows scare tactics when he sees them. "Well, you do what you gotta do——"

I shoot him in the knee.

Blows his kneecap right off. He bellows, the impact spins him around, and he lands flat on his face. He's a thrope, but I'm using silver-tipped bullets; that wound isn't going to magically heal like a normal one would. I've just maimed him for life.

"You—you *cazzo cagna*!" he gasps. "What the hell did you just do to me?"

"I shot you. Painful, isn't it? Not as painful as burning alive, but I understand a thrope can survive that. Usually."

What comes out next is just a string of Italian, but I'm pretty sure I get the gist. "Shut up and listen, Iggy. See, this is the only solution I can come up with. Because I'm not going to let those women you have caged at the end of that tunnel get shipped back to whatever hellhole they managed to escape from, and I'm *definitely* not letting you hold on to them. So the bar goes, *you* go, and the women go free. Best I can do."

"No! No, look, it doesn't have to be like that——"

I'm already looking around for a pack of matches.

TWELVE

"You can't do this," Iggy gasps.

Matches are proving hard to find—the tobacco industry isn't as big with the supernatural races. "Give me an alternative."

"I'll let them go. All of them. They can walk away, no strings attached."

"That's a nice sentiment, Iggy. How's it going to work on a practical level? They don't have papers, they don't have money, they have no place to stay."

"I'll sweeten the deal. A hundred grand, divvied up among them. Got it in a safe upstairs. They can stay in a hotel."

"Mmmm." I pretend to consider it. In fact, it's pretty much what I was going to ask for—but it's always better if the person you're shaking down makes an offer. Gives him the illusion of control. "All right. Give the safe combination to my partner, and he'll go up and get it. But before you do, you better call upstairs and let them know he's coming—otherwise, you won't have anyone *left* to call."

He digs out his cell phone with shaking hands and

punches in a number. "Joe? Yeah, it's me. Listen, there's a lem coming up. Don't argue with him, don't give him any trouble. He's getting something from the safe. What? Just do it, you dumb sack of shit."

He snaps the phone closed. "Go on up. Door's open."

I take the phone from him, drop it on the floor, and step on it. "Charlie? You heard the man."

And that's pretty much that. The women wake up groggy and confused, and it takes a while to explain the situation to them. But Csilla's there—which is a huge relief—and she helps. We get them dressed in the least sleazy outfits we can find, call a hotel, then have them send a shuttle bus over to pick everyone up. I check that the bus has one of those extendable sunshields they use to get pires from building to cab in daylight.

Charlie ensures that the wise guys behave by confiscating any weapons or phones they have. The safe, as it turns out, has twice as much money as Iggy quoted, but I only take what was offered. Wise guys are all about greed, but they like to think respect is more important. Not taking all their money might buy me a little.

When the bus arrives, Csilla stares at me with tears in her eyes. I'm a little embarrassed, but when she hugs me I do my best to hug her back.

"I will not forget this," she says.

"Do your best to try," I say. "You'll be happier."

I give her a bag full of cash, make sure she has my number, then watch her duck under the sunshield and dart to the bus. Once she's in, it pulls away, its windows tinted too dark for me to see that there's anyone inside at all.

Good luck, ladies. Welcome to America.

"Feel better?" Charlie asks as we drive away.

"A little."

"Good. Now can we get back to work finding Tair?"

"Sure. Any ideas?"

"Not so much."

"Me, either." I sigh. "Well, *that* bout of euphoria's over . . ."

"Good thing, too. You were starting to get giddy."

We go back to the office. Our one solid lead having sputtered out, we go back to doing the kind of police work that never gets much attention on TV shows or in the movies. We look through files, we make calls. Gretch has a mountain of stuff on the Gray Wolves, but we restrict ourselves to anything pertaining specifically to the Don. The file on Tair is much thinner, but then he's technically only existed for a short length of time.

We go do some fieldwork. Talking to informants, checking places the Don was known to frequent, just hitting the street and shaking things up, hoping something will fall out.

Nothing does.

That's how it is sometimes. You work the case, you probe all the angles, you stay alert. And the case sits there and mocks you, a cold, unresponsive thing about as revealing as a block of oak. You *know* that everything you need is there, locked inside the grain of the wood; but you can't locate the tools necessary to get at it, so you wind up trying to carve the damn thing open with your fingernails.

"Hey," Charlie says. We're back at the NSA offices, in the cafeteria, on either side of a table covered with piles of paper and two open laptops. "This might be something."

I look up from my laptop. "What?"

"Says Ignacio and the Don had a falling-out last year."

"A serious one?"

"Nah. It's pretty hypothetical, actually. Thirdhand

story caught on a wiretap about some kind of ongoing territory dispute. Seems Iggy might have taken somebody else's side."

"Any repercussions?"

"Doesn't seem to have been. Notation says the dispute was resolved amicably."

I shake my head. "Wise guys. They do this stuff all the time, back and forth, arguing over who gets the bigger cut. But why would the Don go to someone he didn't trust?"

Charlie shrugs. "Because he's nutty?"

"No, that would probably make him more paranoid, not less. Maybe he thought Iggy would jump at the chance to get back in his good graces."

"That makes it sound like he knows what he's doing."

"I know, I know—"

"Speaking of which, what the hell are *you* doing?" Charlie glances down at my hand, and I follow his look.

I've been fiddling around with a pencil in my left hand. At some point I must have subconsciously decided the point wasn't sharp enough, so I've been rubbing the edge of my thumbnail up the cone to the tip.

Which wouldn't be worrisome, except that the pencil is a third shorter than it was ten minutes ago, and there's a little pile of wood shavings on the table.

"Aw, crap," I say.

"Lucky it wasn't a pen."

I take a look at my thumbnail, then all my nails. Sure enough, they're visibly longer than they were when I got up today, and a helluva lot sharper. "Lucky I didn't have an itch."

"I take it this isn't normal?"

"For a grizzly, maybe. For a human being, definitely not. My nails break when I type too hard."

"Huh. Then why the expression *Hard as nails*?"

"Because *Hard as screws* is unclear and sexually suggestive."

"If you say so."

Great. In the war for my body, the thrope forces have taken my fingernails. What's next, establishing a beach-head on my earlobes?

I'm still feeling jumpy, restless, all wound up. It doesn't look like we're going to get anything else accomplished and my shift is over.

So I decide the best course of action is to go dancing.

I'm willing to admit I'm a little manic by this point. I call Xandra and Gretch and even Eisfanger, but not Cassius. I'm worried what might happen if I'm around him in a social setting, and I've got enough on my mind as it is.

Eisfanger can't make it and Xandra is busy, but Gretch agrees to get a sitter and show up. Charlie, of course, is determined to stick with me for the duration, but that's just fine; Charlie's a great dancer. His natural grace gives credence to the theory that *T. rex*es evolved into birds.

We go to a place called the Duke of Juke, with a live big band and a dance floor the size of an Olympic swimming pool. I wear a black skirt, heels, and a loose-fitting blouse with plenty of breathing room; I feel like I'm sweating before we even get in the door. Charlie wears a black suit with chrome pin-striping, a fedora with matching hatband, and spats. Blood-red tie, silver stick-pin. Sharp enough to put your eye out.

And then we hit the floor.

The band is called Merry Miller and the Jive Doggies, and they do know how to swing. Charlie and I get out there and cut a few carpets' worth of rug. The band plays the classics, starting off with "Swing, Swing, Swing";

you know, the one with the drums going *boom bada boom bada boomdy boomdy boom!* And then the horns wail, loud and brassy, and the drums just keep pounding away in the background. It's in every movie with a swing dance scene I can think of—you'd know it if you heard it. In fact, I've heard it so many times I'm sick of it.

But not tonight. Tonight that big bass backbeat gets my pulse going and my blood pumping, and I just cut loose. Charlie manages to keep up, but then, he's leading. Mostly.

It might seem weird that I could go out and enjoy myself after a day like the one I just had, but that's a cop's life: You grab your joy where you can get it, and you leave the horror at the office. Otherwise, you'll hit burnout faster than a marshmallow at a cookout.

I should be celebrating, anyway—today was a win. No lems were destroyed and a bunch of desperate women were given a new chance at a new unlife.

I even got to shoot someone.

Which, despite all the jokes, I don't actually enjoy doing. Or never used to, anyway . . . but it seems that's not true anymore. Blowing off that smug, slave-trading, pimp-doggy's kneecap was the most fun I've had in a long time, and that scares me deeply. So—no matter what I may be telling myself—tonight is less about celebrating a win and more about denying a loss. About trying to affirm that I'm still *me*.

For at least the next two nights, anyway.

I do my best to try to dance myself into a state of exhaustion . . . and it doesn't work. I've been going full-tilt for a dozen songs and I'm not even winded. It's Charlie who finally signals he needs a break, and not because he's tired, either.

"I thought you said you were gonna trim those things," he says. He holds out his hands, and I see multiple small gashes on his plastic skin. Little crescent-shaped cuts, made by yours truly.

"I did," I say. "I'm sorry, sandman. Ah, geez, you're hourglassing all over the place."

"Little duct tape will fix it. Be right back."

Gretch is waiting at a table by that point, and I head over and throw myself into a chair. "Gretch! Glad you could make it."

"My pleasure, Jace. You seem to be enjoying yourself."

"Yeah, well . . ." I stare at my fingernails ruefully. "I don't think Charlie's hide is having quite as much fun."

"Ah. You're still experiencing lycanthropic symptoms, then?"

"Just a little claw growth."

"How about aversion to sunlight? Or garlic?"

"Not that I've noticed."

"Mmm. That's not necessarily good."

"I've got another treatment coming up tomorrow." I'm doing my best to catch the eye of the waiter; I'm parched.

"You may want to move it up. This isn't an exact science, you know."

"So people keep telling me." I finally get the waiter's attention and order a pitcher of water, a shot of tequila, and a beer. Gretch has a glass of sangria, which here means blood and wine mixed together.

"So who's looking after Anna?" I ask.

"Two special agents and a professional nanny," Gretch says, just a touch coolly.

Guess I can't blame her for overreacting a little. I tactfully change the subject. "I don't suppose any new intel has come in on Tair or the Don in the hour and a half since I last saw you?"

"I'm afraid not. However, I think we've ruled out the

possibility that they may have fled via the Black Port; Damon went over the site very thoroughly and is sure neither of them was there recently."

I nod glumly. "I know, he said the same to me."

"Did he?" She frowns. "I knew that. I must have forgotten."

Which is something normal people do, but not Gretch. She notices everything and forgets nothing— especially not about a current case. "Hey. You all right?" I ask.

She gives me a smile as bright and taut as a sail in a summer breeze. "Of course. But I'm afraid I'm having a few symptoms of my own."

Right. After over a century as an immortal pire, Gretch is now aging six months for every year Anna does. Normally, Anna's father would shoulder the other half of the time-debt—but since he's dead, Cassius has taken it on. They're both still vampires, with all the advantages and limitations thereof, but their biological clocks have been restarted—kind of—and that presents in odd little ways.

"Oh? Like what?" I ask.

"Breathing, for one. I found myself doing it today, on the elevator, for no reason at all."

Pires don't need oxygen, but that doesn't mean they don't breathe; they still have lungs, and they use them to move air over their vocal cords while speaking. But the regular rhythmic in-and-out that living beings take for granted isn't normal for them—they have to actively will it to happen.

"Huh. Anything else?"

"I—no. No, that's about it."

She's lying.

And I don't know what bothers me more, that she's hiding something from me or that I can tell. Keeping secrets is Gretch's business, after all, which means either my own senses have become super-acute or her skills are degrading. Neither is good news. Plus, there's the fact that Gretch herself was one of the first people exposed to the Ghatanothoa meme, the same one that drove the Don crazy: subliminal footage of an Elder God, spliced into a recording of a ritual sacrifice. Looking at said deity full-on produces an instant mummy, a leathery-skinned immobile husk with a still-conscious brain trapped inside it. The few known cases at one point had all been found to be irretrievably insane, presumably a consequence of the condition itself; there's a medical condition called "locked-in syndrome" that mimics it, but doesn't have the side effect of immortality.

That presumption was wrong. Turns out the mental instability was just as fast to set in as the paralysis, which shouldn't have come as much of a surprise; madness and Elder Gods seem to go hand in tentacle.

Gretch was paralyzed for most of a week.

She recovered, just like almost everyone else did once the big G went back where he came from. But magic, as I keep hearing, isn't science. It's never 100 percent predictable. There are still hospital wards in most countries filled with the immobile bodies of those the cure didn't fix, pires or thropes trapped inside their own insanity for the rest of time . . .

But even the ones who were cured didn't neccessarily escape unscathed. Worldwide, cases of mental instability have shot up in both the pire and thrope populations—and the symptoms can take weeks or months or maybe even years to appear. Gretch might be okay . . . but then again, she might not.

Lovely.

Charlie arrives and sits down, nodding hello to Gretch. His hands are now striped with black swaths of tape, which blend in well enough to his skin tone to almost be invisible. He'll have to have the plastic skin of his hands replaced—which he does on a regular basis anyway, but it still makes me feel guilty.

And damn it, I still want to dance.

So I do what comes naturally: I go out and get what I want. There's a pire in a zoot suit sitting at the next table by himself, and I ask him if he'd like to hit the floor. He grins and says, "Sure."

And that's where things get out of control.

I haven't really danced with anyone other than Charlie or Cassius since I got to Thropirelem, and apparently I never understood just how careful they were being with me. But then, they both know I'm human—and my current partner apparently doesn't.

Swing dancing covers a wide range of styles, from East Coast to West Coast, from Balboa to Collegiate Shag, from Lindy Hopping to the Charleston. It can be done close in, body-to-body, or it can be done with the partners only touching hands or not touching at all. Depending on your preference and level of skill, it can be as easygoing as a foxtrot or as strenuous as Russian gymnastics. The pire I'm dancing with is clearly fluent in many styles, and the first little while we spend together is him trying to figure out exactly how good I am. That's normal, with a new partner—you're trying to sync up, to get into the same groove.

I'm pretty good. But tonight, I feel like I'm more than pretty good—I can match him move for move, no matter what he throws at me or how quickly he changes things up. So after a while he stops testing my limits and just cuts loose, figuring I can handle it.

If you've ever seen any vintage swing-dance footage—guys like Frankie Manning or the Ray Rand Dancers—then you know just how extreme some of those moves can be. Bodies get whipped up, down, and sidewise, between the legs and over the head, sometimes around the hips like a hula hoop. I'm in good shape—but thrope bite or not, I'm only human. My partner isn't—and he's a lot stronger, faster, and closer to indestructible than me.

He's swinging me backward and trying to get me to do a midair somersault when I feel my wrist snap. I holler in pain and land badly, and he immediately lets go. Charlie's by my side in an instant, with the pire stammering apologies and Charlie ignoring him completely. My wrist hurts—a lot—but it's my own damn fault. I assure the pire I'm okay, and Gretch rigs a splint at our table. I never knew she had any medical training, but Gretch is full of surprises. Once the wrist is properly immobilized, we decide to call it a night.

Charlie's holding the car door open for me when my phone rings.

"Well, at least we know the Don's still in town," Charlie says.

We're at a restaurant called the Slaughterhouse. It's a choose-your-own-supper spot, big in the thrope community. They specialize in chicken, rabbit, and veal, but also offer some higher-priced dishes for the sophisticated palate; according to the chalkboard out front, tonight's special is deep-fried guinea pig.

Inside, the most popular dish seems to be dead mobster.

There are three of them. The first vic's in the kitchen, lying on the floor next to a row of cages that makes it look more like a prison than a restaurant. His head's about six feet away from his body—decapitation is one of the sure ways to kill a thrope or a pire.

I kneel down and examine the corpse. "Edges of the cut are clean—single swipe. Sword or maybe meat cleaver."

"No weapon in his hand," Charlie points out. "Probably an ambush attack."

I do a quick search of the body, find half a dozen silver-edged throwing knives in a thick, rune-inscribed bandolier. "Warded sheath, looks like." Thropes prefer not even being around silver, but they need it to fight their own kind; the right spell will let them carry a silvered weapon without ill effects, but it requires a special permit and they're hard to get.

ID in his wallet says he's Joey Piccolo. The look on Joey's face is one of confusion, which is understandable when you realize that the last thing he probably saw were the tips of his own shoes from a very strange angle.

The other two victims are in the main dining area. The scene here is a lot messier, since the weapon used was a blunt one. The first body is slumped over a table, still seated. Another thrope, and a big one. He's wearing a heavy trench coat, which when pulled aside reveals chain-mail armor and a silver-edged machete in a warded sheath. Neither of them saved him from having his head bashed in by something heavy and made of silver.

"Bodyguard number two," I say as I check his wallet. "Vincent Spuzone. The one that stays close. Chain mail to turn him into a living shield—anything gets chucked at his boss, he makes sure it hits him instead."

"Which is why he's still seated," says Charlie. "Hitter took him out from behind so he wouldn't be a problem, then went after the primary target."

We walk over and examine the last body. You don't see many overweight thropes, but this guy obviously worked at it. At least three hundred pounds of flabby flesh stuffed into an expensive suit. I'd tell you what he looks like, but there isn't much left of his face to describe. He's sprawled out on the floor, with bits of his skull and brain decorating the walls and tables in a radius of at least ten feet.

I pull a wallet bulging with hundreds out of his pocket. I already know who he is, but it's good to verify. "Phillip Ulzano. Local gourmand and capo in the Falzo family."

"So now the Don's going after his own people?"

I shrug. "Paranoid schizophrenics often attack the people closest to them. But this was more than just a random bout of violence."

"Yeah. The guy with the throwing knives was lured into the kitchen and killed first. Fast and silent, too."

"And then the other bodyguard was taken out. Leaving Ulzano alone and unprotected—but that's not all. Look at the footprints in the blood, Charlie."

He frowns. "Which ones? The place was full of people eating, and everyone panicked when the mayhem broke out. All I see is a big red muddle."

"In here, yeah. But check out the path between the kitchen and the dining room."

Charlie does. "One set of thrope prints. Heading from the dining room *to* the kitchen. Which means that after bashing Ulzano's brains in, the killer left through the kitchen."

"Tracking little bits of frontal lobe along the way. But the kitchen wasn't exactly blood-free, and Joey the knife-thrower had to have been killed *first*. So why no tracks leading *out* of the kitchen?"

"Because the guy with the sword never entered the dining room. He took out Joey, then waited."

"Yeah. For the *other* killer to finish off Ulzano and his pal, after which both left through the kitchen."

"Tair and the Don," Charlie says.

"You think?"

"Eyewitnesses are scared, but we got a partial description from a woman. She only saw one of them and he was in half-were form, but it sounds like the Don. Said he was swinging a baseball bat wrapped in metal wire. Mob guys call that a Silver Hammer."

The word *swinging* reminds me of my wrist, and I touch it gingerly. The splints—which I suspect are actually thin teakwood stakes designed to inflict suffering, not alleviate it—are still firmly in place, held there by some of Charlie's black duct tape.

"Still hurt?" Charlie asks gruffly.

"Not really. Itched like hell for a while, but it's calmed down now. Just a little sore."

"We should get that looked at."

"After we're done here, okay? I'm fine."

And I am. Still feeling sort of wired, but the pain's almost gone. We go back to the kitchen and take a closer look—the arterial spray from the decapitation was messy, but once the body hit the floor it mostly made a single large pool. The killers avoided that, but they weren't perfect; there's enough spatter to outline two sets of bloody footprints leading to the loading dock in the alley.

"Must have had a vehicle parked there," I say. "We'll see what Eisfanger can turn up once he gets here."

While we're waiting, I take a look at what's in the cages. They've mostly got smaller animals, ranging from mice—mice? What the hell do you make out of mice, rodent McNuggets?—to bigger animals like pigs. But not all of the livestock is quite as mundane. "Charlie? Is that what I think it is?"

"It is if you think it's a kangaroo."

"Kangaroo. This place serves *kangaroo*?"

"Either that or the owner got shorted on his order of koala."

I shake my head. "I can't believe it. I mean, who could *eat* that?"

"I don't know. I have a hard time with the idea of eating, period."

Considering that Charlie's animated by the life force of a long-dead *T. rex,* that's kind of strange—but his body is made out of minerals, not meat, and lems have no stomachs. I do, though, and it feels like forever since I last ate . . .

My gut gives a strange little lurch. Magic has a way of shaking up your assumptions, Charlie and his distaste for meals being a prime example. Here's another: I'm a vegetarian—with the notable exception of sushi— and right now I'm starving. Why?

Because the smell of blood is making my mouth water.

"You all right?" Charlie asks.

"Yeah, fine. Hey, why don't we wait outside, huh?"

"Sure. Whatever you want."

THIRTEEN

I get an NSA field medic to take a look at my wrist when we get back to the office. He tells me my wrist is fine, that the break has healed nicely.

Which took about three hours.

Eisfanger verifies what we deduced and is going to run further tests once he gets the bodies back to the lab. Gretchen tells us that Phil was an important capo, one of the Don's trusted inner circle, and at one time even in line to be consigliere. He made his living as a loan shark, the old-fashioned kind that breaks your legs when you miss a payment; looks like he's moved down a few links in the food chain.

We do all the usual stuff you do when you're trying to break a case, but none of the other witnesses knows anything—not that they'll admit, anyway—the physical evidence has all been collected, and speaking to Phil's associates is a waste of time and energy. It's been a long day and I should be exhausted, but I don't feel the least bit tired.

My co-workers are all worried about me. I can *smell* it on them. Nervousness, affection undercut with fear.

I don't know what it's like for a normal person experiencing imminent thropehood, but for someone with my training in spotting psychological cues it's as blatant as them screaming in my face. Even Charlie's restrained body language seems exaggerated and grotesque, a parody of concern. I bolt for the security of my apartment like a wounded animal hiding in a cave.

Charlie escorts me home, then bids me good night. Which might seem odd, considering how protective he's been lately—but then I realize he hasn't gone home himself, he's just sitting outside in the Crown Vic, parked across the street from my building. Maybe I should get him a baby monitor for his birthday.

I'm too wound up to sleep, too restless to read or watch TV. It's still dark out, so Gally is in human form and asleep. I'm tempted to wake him up and take him for a walk, but then Charlie would insist on coming along.

These cravings are driving me crazy. I pour a can of tomato juice into a bowl, add as much salt as I can stand, and heat the whole thing up in the microwave. Drinking three glasses of it in a row calms my stomach down a little, but does nothing to settle my nerves.

I call Xandra.

"Hey," I say.

"Jace? I just got up." She sounds a little sleepy.

"Got a minute?"

"Yeah, I guess. What's up?"

"Ah, nothing. I'm just feeling a little—I don't know, jumpy. If you need to get ready for school that's okay—"

"No, there's no school today. I can talk."

"Yeah, well, I'm not sure I can. Howl at the moon, sure, but anything more civilized might be beyond me."

"You sound pretty amped."

"Amped? Is that what the kids are calling it these

days? Yeah, amped is pretty much where I am. Also wired, charged, and high-voltaged. Plug me in and I could probably power most of the eastern seaboard."

"Wow. You sound like my friend Sonya when she's had too many Red Bulls."

"Red Bull. That's funny. We have Red Bull on my world, too, did you know that? Except ours doesn't have any bull blood in it. At least, I don't *think* it does—I've never actually checked the ingredients. But that would be highly bizarre and probably clot since our anti-coagulant technology is nowhere *near* what yours is. Hey, do you know what kangaroo tastes like?"

There's a pause. "Umm," she says. "Bouncy?"

"That's kind of what I was thinking. Bouncy. Springy. Jump-up-and-downy. Probably give you hiccups. Ha."

"Jace. You're freaking me out a little."

"Am I?"

"Yeah. I really think you should talk to Uncle Leo."

Uncle Leo. Everybody calls him that, except for the kids who call him Grandpa. If I become a thrope and join the Adams pack, will I start calling him Uncle Leo, too? That wouldn't be so bad.

"Jace!"

"What? Huh?"

"You were whining."

"I was *not*! I bitch, I fume, I rant—sometimes I even pun—but I do *not* whine!"

"No, I mean you were *actually* whining. High-pitched whimpering sound?"

Oh, God. "Uh—that was Gally. He wants to go out. So do I." I realize how that sounds and add, "For *completely* different reasons, okay?"

"Uh-huh. Maybe you should come over."

"Maybe. No. I don't want to bother anyone. Would it bother anyone? Maybe I could."

"You've gone from whining to dithering."

"I have, haven't I? That's not like me. But then again, neither is thinking about kangaroo steaks." I force myself to focus. "All right, all right. I'll come over, talk to Leo. He'll know what to do, right?"

"Of course. Uncle Leo *always* knows what to do."

I sneak out of my apartment the back way, through the stairs.

There's no good reason to ditch Charlie, but I do anyway. Part of me recognizes that this is not entirely rational behavior, but that part seems distant and not terribly important. What's vital is to keep moving, keep hidden, and search out what I need.

No, not *search out*. Hunt.

I wave down a cab a few blocks away and get it to take me to the Adams suburban enclave. It's all I can do to not leap out and run instead.

It's dawn by the time I get there, and the household is awake and bustling. The air seems full to bursting with early-morning smells, everything from wet grass to brewing coffee. I guess Xandra must have told Leo I was coming, because he's waiting for me at the front door. He's wearing an oversize purple bathrobe, and his feet are bare.

"Jace," he says with a warm smile. "I'm glad you're here." He doesn't go inside, but instead steps off the porch and motions for me to follow him. He leads me around the house and into the backyard, where the pool is now hidden by a white plastic cover.

Leo sits down in a lawn chair, beside a patio table, and I do the same.

"What, you're afraid I'm no longer housebroken?" I say. It's chilly enough that I should be shivering, but I feel more overheated than anything. I shrug my jacket off and drape it over the back of my chair.

"No, but I sense you'd be more at ease outside." He's watching me carefully, with a look I recognize: He's trying to figure out just how far gone I am. I wish I could tell him.

"Yeah, good call," I admit. "God, I'm *starving*—"

The back door opens and one of the many small, grandmotherly women who seem to live at the Adams residence appears. She's got a plate piled high with—

"Though you don't eat meat, I understand that eggs are okay?" Leo asks. "And cheese?"

"Yesthatsfine," I croak, and then I'm digging into what looks like an omelet made from a dozen ostrich eggs and about a pound of cheddar. God bless you, Leo.

He keeps his eyes on me while I chow down. I never thought protein could taste so good—I finish the whole thing in a disgustingly short period of time and then sit back, panting like I just ran a marathon.

"Feeling a little better?"

I burp. "Yes. Thank you."

"It's difficult, this part," he says. "The urges, the cravings. The feeling of being out of control. But it will pass."

"Sure, along with my interest in salad bars. But I'm not *ready*, Leo."

"Are we ever ready for the truly important changes in our lives? No. Marriage, the birth of a child, the death of a loved one—they are all things that must be experienced to be understood, and no matter how much we prepare, we are always surprised. And this is a very good thing, Jace. It is the essence of freedom to be surprised. Without the new there are no challenges, nothing to be learned, no way to grow."

"Yeah, absolutely. Got any more eggs?"

He laughs. "Give it time to settle in your stomach. The hunger you feel, it can be controlled. Mastered."

A horrible thought strikes me. "Is this what it's like to be a thrope? To be *hungry* all the time?"

"No, no—these are temporary symptoms, I assure you. Your body is changing, and that requires energy. Fuel."

Which means the more I eat, the more ground the thrope virus gains. Suddenly I'm not quite as ravenous. "Right. Of course."

"It's not all bad, Jace. There are advantages, too, many of them." He closes his eyes and tilts his head back, inhaling hugely through his nose. "You smell that?"

Hesitantly, I do the same thing. An explosion of scents fills my head, so abrupt and overpowering that I gasp: chlorine tang from the pool, grass damp with dew, a hundred flavors of pollen as the plants wake up and yawn; food aromas from my plate and inside the house; insect pheromones in a bewildering array of odors I have no names for; the animal musk of a houseful of thropes, each with their own distinct signature. Leo, being the closest, is the strongest, and carries the indefinable but definite smell of authority.

But that's not all. There's another scent, masked somehow, wrapped in a nullifying cloak like a thick quilt thrown over a ticking clock. And now I'm getting a sense of direction, of distance; the house full of thropes is over *there,* and Leo is *here,* and that annoyingly faint, muffled scent is *that* way, at the edge of the wooded area—

My eyes snap open.

It's Tair.

I expect him to bolt as soon as I become aware of him, but he doesn't. Instead, he steps out from behind a tree and regards me calmly. He's wearing black sweatpants and a black fleece hoodie, sneakers on his feet. He looks more like he's out for a morning jog than running from the law.

I'm already on my feet, but Leo stays seated. He growls. It's a deep, menacing sound, and its meaning is clear: This is my turf.

"Calm down, Leo," Tair says, but I notice he doesn't come any closer. "This is a friendly visit."

"Jace Valchek is under the protection of the Adams pack," Leo says. His eyes have gone bright yellow, his canines are longer, and both his hands are now hairy claws. "You will not harm her."

Tair smiles and holds his hands up in mock surrender. "Wouldn't dream of it. And hey, what's with the cold shoulder, Leo? I thought you'd be happy to see me."

"You are not who you appear to be," Leo says. "And you smell like you're not even here."

"Ah, that. Just a charm to keep me off the radar— didn't want to run into any problems while Jace and I have a little chat."

"Are you *kidding* me?" I say. I have my gun out and pointed at his chest in a second. "You're under arrest. Lie flat on the ground and put your hands behind your head."

Tair chuckles. "Yeah, no, I can't really do that. You know why I'm here, don't you, Leo?"

"I never imagined you'd be so foolish."

"Foolish? Hey, that's no way to talk about tradition."

"Get *on the ground. Now.*"

Leo shakes his head. "You can't be serious."

"As a case of Hades Rabies, Leo," Tair says. "I invoke *sange ucenicie.*"

I've experienced it before, but there's nothing quite as frustrating as aiming one of the largest handguns in existence at someone and being treated like I'm holding a pickle. Not even a big pickle, more like a sad little gherkin the other pickles tease. "Lie *down,* goddamn it! You *know* what this weapon can do!"

"Jace," Leo says, turning toward me. "I'm sorry, but he has invoked *sange ucenicie.* It is his right." He looks deeply troubled, but his eyes have faded back to their old color.

"I don't care if he's invoking the ghost of Christmas past! Now get down on the ground or I *swear* I'll shoot you—in the knee, if I have to. You wouldn't be the first mobster I've put a bullet in—not even the first in the last twenty-four hours."

"No, you won't," Tair says. "In fact, you can't."

I aim at his foot. Not as bad as the knee, but still guaranteed to put him in a world of suffering and blow off several toes at the very least. I pull the trigger.

I *pull* the trigger.

I pull the trigger, goddamn it, except that I don't. It's not that I've had a change of heart, either—I still want to, I just can't. My finger refuses to tighten, no matter how hard I try.

Leo gets to his feet. He stalks toward Tair, who takes a few oddly formal steps toward Leo. They stop, practically nose-to-nose.

"You will do this thing right," Leo snarls. "By the old rules, by the ancient standards. You will not use her, you will not abandon her. She is your responsibility, and I hold your life hostage to her well-being. No matter who you once were, no matter what you once meant to me, my pack will hunt you down and rend you throat-to-belly if you fail her in *any* way. Do we understand each other?"

"We do."

"Well, *I* don't," I say. "What the hell's going on?"

Leo mutters something in another language under his breath. It doesn't sound complimentary.

"Now, Leo," Tair says. "That's uncalled for. Whatever you may think of me, I take my responsibilities in this matter *very* seriously. I mean, I'm risking a lot here."

Maybe it's just his foot that's got the magic whammy on it. I point the gun at his elbow and try to pull the trigger. No good. I try the chest, the head, the crotch. I try using my other hand, different fingers, my thumb. Nothing works.

"Stop that," Tair says. He sounds more annoyed than threatened. "Look, I'll tell you what's going on if you just quit waving that thing around, all right?"

I shove the gun at Leo. "Here. It's easy to use. Just point it at him and yank this little lever here."

"Listen to him, Jace. He has important things to tell you, and I cannot interfere." Leo gives Tair a scowl that a thunderhead would be proud of, and stalks back toward the house, his purple bathrobe flapping in the early-morning breeze.

"What?" I'm stunned. Leo would *never* turn his back on me, that much I'm sure of.

"Ready to listen, Valchek?" Tair says. He settles down in the lawn chair Leo just vacated. "You may not want to hear this, but it's got to be said."

I surrender to the inevitable and sit down myself. I shove my useless, rebellious firearm back in its holster. *"Talk."*

"The lycanthrope pack structure is more than just an imitation of wolf hierarchy. It's mystical as well as biological, and like all magic systems there are rules. Magical rules—just like evolutionary ones—tend to be based on principles of survival. Not just survival of the individual, but survival of the species. And midway between the two, survival of the pack."

"I'm not a thrope, Tair. Not yet."

"No, but you have had blood drawn by one—me. I'm sure others have explained to you the mystic link we have as a result, and what that entails." He grins. "Sorry, unintentional pun."

"Nobody told me that meant you could control my actions."

"Then you weren't talking to the right people." He leans forward, rests his elbows on his knees. "To be fair, it's something that's been mostly forgotten. Hundreds of years ago, if a thrope attacked a human he'd make sure to finish the job; survivors were rare, because the last thing a pack wanted was a transformed human murdering his own kind every full moon and giving them a bad name, or worse yet tagging along after the group and expecting to be adopted like a stray puppy. But, as thropes and humans became integrated, that happened more and more often. So procedures were established to fix the problem, procedures that were implanted mystically and passed down from generation to generation. Sorcery-enhanced instincts, you could call them."

"What sort of procedures?"

"Come on, Valcheck. Tomorrow night's the last one before the full moon. You're going to go from a two-legged animal to a four-legged one. You're going to have to learn a whole new set of skills, and it's not like there's a manual available online. That phrase you heard, *sange ucenicie*? Its literal translation is 'blood apprenticeship.' It means that since I'm the one who infected you, I have an obligation—a *duty*—to show you the ropes. So to speak."

"Right. So I'm what, your *intern* now? You whistle, I fetch? I don't think so."

"You're not paying attention. This is *magic*, all right?

You don't have a choice. Like I said, there are rules—and one of them is *No killing the teacher*. Assassination and learning just don't play well together."

"Neither do I and escaped convicts. If I can't shoot you, I'll just have to let someone else do it." I pull out my phone.

He knocks it out of my hand with a swipe that's almost too fast to see. "No one likes a tattletale, either. Are you ready for your first lesson, or do I have to *spank* you?"

I glare at him. I have the overwhelming urge to put my fist through his face, or maybe rip his throat out with my bare teeth. I could try, but I'm pretty sure all that would happen is a great deal of frustration and a lot of swearing. Leo wouldn't appreciate that; there are kids in earshot.

"What's this all about, Tair? You almost kill me, you partner with a Mob boss who's off his rocker, then show up and start playing high school guidance counselor? What the hell's your game?"

The look he gives me is hard to read: some mixture of uncomfortable, irritated, maybe even a little guilt. "Look, Valchek, I know this might be hard for you to process, but there's more to who I am than 'Dr. Pete *good*, Tair *bad*.' I'm not some cartoon villain made of pure evil. I had the same family, the same friends growing up as the man you knew. Everyone has darkness in their heart, Valchek, and me and Dr. Pete had exactly the same amount in ours. Only difference between us is I actually did the things he was always capable of."

"Dr. Pete dedicated himself to saving lives. You take them."

He sighs. "So do you, Agent Valchek, so do you. And you do it for a paycheck, same as me."

"I don't kill unless I have to—"

"Neither do I. I just *have to* more often than you."

"Did you *have to* murder those bodyguards at the Slaughterhouse?"

"Let's keep this on track, shall we? This is about you, not me."

"Really? Because a second ago you were getting all emo about how you're misunderstood and that you're really a *nice* psychopath once people get to know you—"

"Well, I am." He smiles at me, quite disarmingly. "And believe it or not, I do have a certain sense of responsibility. Yes, I put your life at risk—though I was pretty sure that guard would choose to save you—and yes, I made you a lycanthrope against your will. I regret that, but circumstances forced my hand and I can't undo it. So—despite the fact that you want to erase me from the face of the Earth, despite the fact that you're currently leading a manhunt to throw me back in prison, *despite* the fact that the smart move would be to stay as far away from you as possible, I'm still going to try to prepare you for life as a thrope. Whether you want me to or not."

For a moment I almost believe it. Then I remember how good Tair is at manipulation, and how he never does anything without his own best interests at heart. "Yeah, sure. How selfless and noble of you. Tell me, this whole teacher/student/thrope thing—how's it work once I'm comfy with my new all-body hairstyle? Does the mystical link stay in place afterward? Is there some kind of animal dominance instinct that gets ingrained, so after this I'll *always* be Scrappy-Doo to your Scooby? Because if that's the case, no thanks."

He gets to his feet, slowly. He looks at me with resignation. "No, Jace. That's not it at all. Once I'm through teaching you what you need to know, we're done. No strings—or leashes—attached. Not that you'll ever believe me."

"Sure I will. As soon as the Tooth Fairy verifies your story, we're good to go—"

And then, with no warning, his hands are around my throat.

I can't breathe. All my FBI training, every martial arts move I ever studied, it all gets shoved out of my brain in a surge of primal instincts that are equal parts panic and rage. I flail, I claw, I kick—I'd bite if I could, but I can't reach anything with my teeth.

He ignores it all. His eyes are locked on my own as he methodically chokes the life from me, his face as serious and intent as a man performing surgery.

The world goes gray. His eyes, boring into mine, are shifting to a feral yellow. The rest of the universe fades away at the edges, until all I can see are those two glowing golden eyes.

And then I can't see or hear or feel anything at all.

FOURTEEN

The afterlife isn't like anything I imagined.

I'm on a bus. I'm sitting next to a chubby, almost-bald black guy who looks kind of familiar. "Lot of different ways to prepare kangaroo," he says.

"Oh, no."

"Kangaroo steak, kangaroo casserole, kangaroo fricassee, kangaroo consommé—"

"You've *got* to be kidding."

"—kangaroo omelet, kangaroo shish kebab, kangaroo stir-fry—"

"Look, I refuse to believe that what's waiting in the Great Beyond is a *Forrest Gump* rip-off."

"Kangaroo 'n' rice, kangaroo 'n' taters, kangaroo 'n' dumplings—"

I look around. "Hello? Driver? You can let me off here, please. I don't need to hear the whole menu."

"—kangaroo sushi, kangaroo ice cream, kangaroo à la king—"

And then everything gets all swirly the way things do when you've combined too much tequila with not enough food, and the bus and Kangaroo Guy fall away like a dream when you're not quite awake yet; when you realize that hey, that wasn't real at all, I was asleep and now I'm waking up and opening my eyes and—

And this isn't what's supposed to happen when you wake up.

I'm a wolf.

Of all the senses, the one we most take for granted is kinesthesia. That's the sense of our own body, the overall, constant feeling of simply existing in a container made of flesh and blood and bone. It's constantly telling us that we still have a head, a torso, and the appropriate number of limbs.

Right now, my kinesthesia is telling me something very different.

Everybody knows what a wolf looks like, so I won't go through a laundry list of body parts. You'd think the weirdest thing would be having a tail, but it isn't; that comes in second, with number three being the ability to consciously move my ears.

Number one? I now have junk.

Male junk, I mean. Bald dude in a turtleneck, kielbasa, Mister Boing Boing. I could go on—the only word with more euphemisms is *drunk*—but that's not going to make it go away. It may be hairy, it may be lupine, but it's dangling between my legs and it wasn't there when I woke up this morning.

I blurt out the equivalent of "What the *goddamn*—" and naturally, it comes out as a high-pitched whine. I'm frozen in place, too freaked out to move—I'm not sure I even know *how*—and then I realize that what I'm staring at is worse.

I'm looking at my own body, lying sprawled in a boneless heap on the grass. Its eyes are open, and the same blazing yellow that Tair's were as he—

As he killed me.

"You're not dead, Valchek," Tair says. The voice is inside my head, and sounds just a little tired. "This is part of the process. Call it a test drive—a little time behind the wheel before you get your license."

I've had some experience with magical telepathy, so I know how to respond. "And you had to *throttle* me to do this?"

"Technically, no. We could have used meditation to get you into the right frame of mind, or I could have done it as you were falling asleep—really, anything that put you into a half-conscious state would have worked. But all of those things require your cooperation, and I just don't have the time to get it."

"So you—you *evicted* me?"

"It's temporary, believe me. You think I *want* you in my head?"

"You arrogant piece of—of all the things you've done, this has to be the—"

"SHUT *UP!*"

The roar is so loud, so all-encompassing, that it's more than just sound; it's pure fury, a blast of anger like opening a door to a room that's on fire. All my new senses go away, leaving me alone and stunned in a void with his words echoing in my nonexistent ears.

I shut up.

When he speaks again, I can still hear the anger in his voice, but at least he's not bellowing anymore. "I know you don't want this. That's hard for me to accept—but back when I was a resident, I studied cases of human beings born deaf who, when the technology to give them hearing was developed, decided they didn't want it. That fascinated me. I thought at first that they were rejecting something new out of fear, but that wasn't the case. It was because they realized that in many ways our limitations define us—not because of what we can't do, but because of how we *respond* to those limitations. Deaf people responded by creating a language, a *culture* of their own, and that was what they were trying to protect. Have you ever seen deaf people communicate? They use facial expression as much as hand movement, something thropes can't duplicate— our faces just aren't as expressive. It's—it's a wonderful thing to see. It was one of the things that made me want to study human medicine.

"So I understand that you have valid reasons for wanting to stay human. But Jace—that's just not an option, not anymore. No matter how much you hate me, no matter how scared you are, you have to face that fact.

"You're a smart woman—don't you want to *learn* about this? Don't you want to be prepared? Because what's happening to you is not going to be like anything you've ever known. In the old days, before these protocols were established, people would go insane from the experience. They'd slaughter their own kind, give in to their darkest impulses and go on wild killing sprees. *I don't want that to happen to you.*"

And then, silence.

I think about what he's just said. *Really* think about, not just react emotionally, which is what I've been doing since I got on this lycanthro-go-round. While I'm volatile at the best of times, I'm not a flake; when I do something *really* stupid, it's usually after careful consideration.

So I consider. And come to the same conclusion I would have reached earlier, if my head hadn't been overloaded with pre-full-moon jitters plus two kinds of supernatural viruses locked in a struggle to the undeath.

"Uh—thanks?" I say—or think, I guess.

"Let's just do this, all right?"

"Do *what,* exactly? If you don't mind me asking?"

"This."

The world comes back, and it's moving. Really moving, zipping past in a blur, and I realize it's because I'm running.

No. Not running. If that feeble, two-legged totter I used to do was running, then this is something entirely different. This is as far past that as ballet is past the hokey-pokey. This is a four-stroke engine operating at peak efficiency, a smooth never-ending cycle of impact and motion, pure kinetic elegance. It's like all the hyperbole of every car commercial in the world come to life and injected into my bloodstream.

"Wha-ha," I manage.

"Shhh."

We must have left the Adams yard and gone into the woods at the edge of the property. Northwest rainforest streams past, towering firs and pines, gigantic primeval ferns, thickets of blackberry bushes twice the height of a man and as dense and thorny as a Hollywood contract. Smells flood into my nose, too: aromatic conifers, damp earth, rotting tree stumps, animal musk, moss.

It takes me a moment to realize that even though I'm experiencing it, I'm not actually *doing* it; I'm a passenger, not the driver. "Uh, this is *great,*" I think carefully. "But when do I get to—you know—"

We skid to a stop in a slide of wet leaves. "Take over? Congratulations, Valchek—you lasted all of a minute before your natural tendencies kicked in."

"Well, you did say this was about me learning—"

His chuckle inside my head sounds just like it does

on the outside. "Relax. We'll get to it, all right? But I wanted us to be in a good location."

And then, just like that, I'm in charge.

I fall down.

Tair bursts out laughing. I'd scowl if I knew how to work a muzzle properly.

"Take it slowly," he says. "The instincts are there. You had four legs yourself once, way back in your evolutionary history. Just let them do their job."

I try. I lie still, feeling my legs quiver, then just think about *being* on all fours without focusing on how to get there.

To my surprise, it works. I'm standing on my own four feet. Swaying like a milk-drunk toddler, but still upright.

Walking is harder. It takes a few attempts before I can relax enough to let my hindbrain control the process without thinking about it, but it feels amazingly natural once I get the rhythm.

"Okay," Tair says. "Let's go for a run."

"What? I just learned how to *walk*—"

He sounds amused. "Agent Valchek, are you backing down from a *challenge*?"

I growl, both in my head and my throat. It feels good.

"That's what I thought. Don't worry—I'll start you off."

Then he's the one at the controls again, and we're off.

Bounding, bounding, over the forest green . . . we build up to a good clip, not as fast as we were moving before but still pretty quick.

"Ready?"

I feel like a teenager riding shotgun in a race car; we're heading into the first big curve, going a hundred miles an hour, and the driver just took his hands off the wheel.

I grab it.

And then I'm running, *really* running, for the first time in my life.

Afterward, I collapse on a bed of moss with my paws up in the air, panting. "Wow," I manage. Even my thoughts are out of breath. "That was amazing."

"Well, you didn't run into any trees."

"What? Come on, I did great."

His tone is grudging, but I think I hear some pride in it, too. "You did okay. At least you'll be able to move without losing control."

No, it's not pride I'm hearing—it's pride I'm *feeling*. I'm in Tair's mind as well as his body, after all—and if my experience with Cassius is any indication, then spill-over of emotions while we're linked like this is inevitable. Emotions, and maybe more.

I might never get another chance like this. I have to take it.

I reach out with my own thoughts, my own sense of self. Finding his equivalent isn't difficult; it's the center I'm currently wrapped around, the landlord on the main floor of the house I'm visiting. I probe gently, cautiously, searching for an opening—

"Valchek? What are you doing?"

"Nothing," I murmur. "Just looking around."

There. A chink in the armor, a soft spot that yields when I push. I slip inside—

It's not what I expect.

Cassius manifested as a crimson web, an immense and intricate structure representing his many centuries of existence. I thought being inside Tair's mind would be similar, but it's not.

It's a multicolored sphere, pulsing like a planet-size heart. Below me are continents of verdant green, rivers of blazing orange, oceans of deepest purple: Google Earth on serious drugs. Everything's shifting, moving, all at different speeds. A snaking line of yellow writhes frantically over a slowly morphing black mass, something blue and amoeba-like bulges and contracts near the equator, waves of pink shimmer in concentric rings from the poles. It's beautiful and hypnotic and almost makes sense.

My attention is drawn to one particular feature, a large circle midway between the equator and the North Pole. It's the only element that isn't in constant motion, and it's a clean, pristine white. My instincts—which, at the moment, are pumped higher than they've ever been—tell me it's important.

I touch it.

I'm only in contact for a second before Tair violently ejects me. I'm thrown out of his mind and into a scary, gray nothingness for an agonizing moment before some kind of psychic gravity kicks in and sucks me back into Tair's brain where I was before.

But that was long enough.

What I saw there, what I experienced, was love.

A true psychopath is incapable of feeling love. That requires empathy, compassion, the ability to connect with other people on a deep level. Psychopaths lack those abilities, which makes them view other people largely as objects. The best definition of love I've ever heard is that someone else's happiness becomes more important to you than your own; since to a psycho other people aren't completely real, the concept of someone else's happiness is meaningless to him—let alone the possibility of it having more value than satisfying his own needs.

That's not what I experienced. I only touched it for the briefest instant, but there was no mistaking what I encountered. I'd seen behind the mask of his public persona, and what was there was deep and genuine and very carefully hidden.

"Tair" is an *act*.

"You do *not* have my permission to do that," he growls.

"Do what? I was just trying to get a feel for my surroundings—"

"Your surroundings aren't my frontal lobe."

"Is *that* what that was? I was gonna go with amygdala, maybe the hippocampus."

"I think this lesson is over."

He heads toward our starting point at a quick pace, firmly in control, yours truly relegated to the backseat. He could put me in the metaphysical equivalent of the trunk—like he did when he was yelling at me—but for some reason he doesn't. I decide to take advantage of it while I can.

"So—where's the Don, Tair?"

"Leave the Don out of this. This is between you and me."

"Yeah, wish I could. But the Falzo family has other ideas, as does the NSA. Anyway, you're the one who started this hairball rolling."

Greenery blurs past. We bound off boulders, under fallen logs, over bushes. I'm already missing it.

"And I'll stop it, too. But you have to stay out of my way."

"Why should I? Because you gave me a little how-to lesson after slashing my leg open in the first place? Yeah, I'm *so* grateful."

"I wasn't lying when I said I owed Arturo. What he's going through right now . . ." I feel the mental equivalent of a head-shake. "He needs my help. It's a very personal debt of honor, Jace. I can't explain any more than that."

"Then tell me one thing, Tair. How is helping a crazy werewolf kill people making *anything* better?"

There's a long pause. "I won't defend his actions, Jace. I can't justify any of it. All I can say is that whatever Arturo is doing, I *have* to look after him. No matter what the cost is."

"You owe him, I get that. But it's my job to bring him in, Tair. To bring both of you in."

No response.

He doesn't say anything else until we get back, and then he stops at the edge of the yard. My body isn't where I left it, but it hasn't gone far; it's back in the lawn chair, head lolling to the side like a passed-out party-goer.

The person who no doubt put it there is sitting in the other chair. Xandra.

She knows we're there. She meets my eyes, but it isn't me she sees. It isn't me that's putting that stricken look on her face.

"Uncle Pete?" she says. It's the voice of a little girl.

And then there's this tremendous *whoosh* and everything turns topsy-turvy and I'm plummeting at about a thousand miles an hour. Luckily, my skull breaks my fall—my own skull, the one I've been pouring scotch, caffeine, and bad decisions into for most of my life.

I blink and straighten up in my seat. I can still see the outline of Tair's shape in the shadows, yellow eyes gleaming—and then he's gone.

"Uncle *Pete*!" Xandra wails, and dives out of her chair. She's in half-were form before she hits the ground, and full wolf by the time she reaches the trees.

"Xandra!" I call after her, but it's too late. She hasn't

seen or talked to her uncle since she visited him in the hospital, and he was pretty banged up then. All she's had since he was replaced has been secondhand reports, filtered through older relatives and the NSA. No matter how grown-up Xandra thinks she is, she was close to Dr. Pete, and on some level she feels betrayed and abandoned. I can't blame her for going after him, but I hope he gives her the slip. I don't know what it would do to her to find out what he's become.

Then I think about what I discovered today, and realize I don't know exactly what he is, either.

I'm chilled to the bone, but I don't want to leave until Xandra gets back. I go up to the house, where I'm let in by a yawning six-year-old still in his pajamas. I find Leo in the kitchen, and he pours me a large mug of freshly brewed coffee without being asked. The rest of the house seems strangely silent, as if someone turned the rambunctious knob down from its usual eleven to three and a half. Everyone from kids to grannies seem to be avoiding catching my eye, and Leo and I have the kitchen all to ourselves.

"So," Leo says. "Are you all right? Did he—*behave*?" He sounds a little anxious and a little angry, a doting father dying to know about his daughter's first date but afraid to ask for details.

"No, Leo. He took me out to the woods and made me do terrible, terrible things. And—and I *liked* it." I wipe a mock tear from my eye. "And then he pulled out this bag of *chipmunks*—"

I've met some champion glarers in my time, but Leo's got the kind of eyebrows that can turn a glower into a lethal weapon. "Jace Valchek! This is—you shouldn't—I was so *worried*!"

"Yeah? Well, maybe you should have thought of that before you threw me to the wolf, Leo. Even if he *was* family."

Now Leo looks miserable. "I'm sorry, Jace. I didn't want to, I truly didn't. But he invoked an old and very powerful ritual, one that's written on our very genes. I could no more deny him than I could resist transforming under a full moon. But he is bound by the same pact, the same ancient rules—I knew he wouldn't hurt you."

"I'm glad you had such confidence. Me, I would have appreciated a heads-up."

"Again, I am so, so sorry. I never dreamed he would come near you, let alone invoke the *sange ucenicie.*"

"Yeah, well, he did. And while he told me what it is and how it came about, he was a little skimpy on details. Fill me in, Leo."

Leo takes a long sip of his own coffee, and then nods. "Very well. The *sange ucenicie* is a sorcerous pact, one inscribed into our very blood; it ensures that no new lycanthrope will be turned and then abandoned. Hardly relevant today, but a few hundred years ago it was necessary."

"Tair covered that. Makes sense—better to have a new thrope prepared than have them run wild. It's very . . . *civilized,* actually."

Leo chuckles. "Yes—hardly the image of our kind that was widespread at the time. But that image was exactly our problem: There were far too many people who still regarded us as murderous beasts, unable to control our savage impulses. The *sange ucenicie* was supposed to help fix that."

I finish my coffee and get up to pour another. "So it's a set of controls—a training program, hardwired in.

Lets the teacher locate the student, stick her in a mental classroom, show her some basic skills." I pace back and forth, restless, the mug in my hand. "What else?"

Leo glances at me, then away. "Dominance. The instruction must be mandatory, not a choice. You have to realize the sort of person this was designed for: uneducated, from a rural area, probably religious. They would initially react with terror and revulsion. The teacher had to be able to instruct his student without her running away or trying to kill him, so there's a certain amount of coercion he can exert."

"How much?"

Leo looks troubled, but not nearly as troubled as I feel. "You can't harm him, but he can't make you do something you normally wouldn't. He *can* force you to listen to him, but what you take from the lesson is up to you. Ultimately, the exchange depends on will—yours, and his."

"You said I can't harm him. Can he harm me?"

"You're his responsibility, Jace. He has rules he must obey as well. Once the *sange ucenicie* has been invoked, he's compelled to instruct you as best he can. He can put you at risk, but only if it furthers your training. And all of this lasts only until the first full moon."

The night after next. "And then?"

"Then the bond dissolves. You are free to do whatever you please. But—" He pauses. "Tomorrow night—the night *before* the full moon—is the most dangerous. It's when he must evaluate you, decide whether or not you can survive in the wild. More important, he has to judge if you're a danger to your own kind. If he honestly believes that to be true, he *can* harm you." Leo meets my eyes. "In fact, he will have no choice. He will be forced to kill you—and he won't need silver to do it, either. That last night, the *sange ucenicie* will let him use his teeth and claws."

Sure. What's the point of a course if there's no downside to flunking out? You don't earn your driver's license, you don't get to drive. You don't earn your fangs and fur, you don't get to use them. Or anything else, for that matter.

I stare out the kitchen window and try to collect my thoughts. Is Tair taking this as seriously as he seems, or is he playing another game? Why is he so intent on sticking by the Don, when the old wolf will probably wind up getting them both killed or incarcerated?

Those are things I should be thinking about, anyway. But what my mind keeps turning back to is how it felt to race through the forest on four legs, swift and sure and impossibly graceful . . .

And then I see Xandra stumble out of the woods.

She's naked, of course, having run right out of her clothes; Leo's spotted her, too, and is already shrugging off his bathrobe and handing it to me. I rush out of the house and meet her halfway across the yard, wrapping it around her. She's crying so hard she can't get any words out, so I just hug her—carefully, because she's still got a double row of razor blades sticking out of her skull—and tell her everything will be okay. Sometimes, that's all you can do, whether it's true or not.

She finally calms down enough to talk, and by that time Leo's showed up with a mug of something hot. Cocoa, from the smell. He hands it to her, pats her on the shoulder sadly, and tells her he'll be inside if she wants to come in and talk. Then he leaves us alone; like any good patriarch, Leo knows that sometimes the best way to be supportive is to back off and let people have their space.

We sit down in the same lawn chairs. I can feel about a dozen pairs of eyes peering at us from windows—while the rest of the pack is keeping their distance, everybody's intensely curious about all the drama.

Then I just wait. She sips her cocoa and sniffles, wipes her nose against the sleeve of the robe like a kid. She won't meet my eyes.

"You know what the worst thing was?" she finally says. "He smelled like Uncle Pete. *Exactly* like him."

"Whatever he did, whatever he said, that's not your Uncle Pete."

"I know. I *know*. But—I just miss him *so much,* Jace."

"I do, too, sweetie. I do, too."

"I couldn't catch him. He was too fast."

"Yeah. He sure can run, can't he . . ."

FIFTEEN

I don't have too much trouble sneaking back into my apartment the same way I'd left. Charlie's good, but he's only one guy—and he wasn't expecting me to leave on my own.

The sun's up, so Galahad should be in doggy form—but he doesn't greet me at the door, which is what he usually does when he's in four-legged mode. Odd. "Gally?" I call out.

He appears in the bedroom doorway, and I relax. "There you are. Everything okay?"

He looks at me uncertainly. He whines. And then he turns around and goes back in the bedroom.

Thinking something must be wrong, I follow him. Nothing amiss, nothing out of place. I don't get the sense that anyone's been here that shouldn't. Gally goes to the farthest corner away from me and sits down with his back to the wall. His mouth is closed, his eyes worried.

Then I get it. I sink down on the bed. "Oh, Galahad. It's *me*, okay? I might smell a little funky, but it's still good old Jace—you know, the one that scritches that spot at the base of your tail? The one who feeds you bacon, even when I shouldn't?"

And now he looks a little happier. His ears are too floppy to go up, but he sits a little straighter. His tail thumps on the floor, hesitantly.

I sigh. "Bacon."

A few more thumps, louder and faster.

"Bacon bacon bacon."

And then he's jumped up on the bed and is slobbering all over me, his usual boisterous self. Ah, well—I may not have his undying loyalty, but at least I know it can be bought. I dig out the next best thing I have around, pork-flavored doggy treats, and give him a handful. He'll have to wait until we hit a restaurant for the rest of his bribe.

I get undressed and get into bed. Sleep is a tiny little town in a faraway country that I can't quite remember the name of. I do some tosssing. I do some turning. Gally endures it as long as he can and then abandons the bed with a reproachful look and pads out into the living room. I can hear him jump up on the sofa.

Too much to think about. Too many things I should be doing. Too many scents in the air. Not enough Jace to go around.

Not enough Jace, period.

I've always had a very strong sense of who I was, a secure self-image. That image changed as I got older, but there was always a core that stayed true. I knew what was important to me, I knew what I valued and what I didn't.

For the first time in my life, I feel like that might be changing.

But if it is, it won't be without a fight. I don't meekly accept what life shoves at me. I don't give up at the first sign of opposition. I hang on with a stubborn persistence that makes even my enemies grudgingly respect me.

But this is a different kind of battleground, and it's got me worried. I need to stay in touch with that part of myself that I've always most taken for granted, the part that defines me as human. I'm not even sure what it is, let alone how to hang on to it.

But I think I know who might.

I finally give up, roll out of bed, and get dressed. Grab a leash and collar, get it on Gally. Take the elevator down into a way-too-bright day; I'm glad I thought to bring sunglasses.

Charlie rolls down his window when we walk up. "Morning," he says.

"Morning. Can we skip the whole thing where I pretend I'm outraged that you were out here all night and go for breakfast instead?"

"Sure. Only thing I like better than missing sleep is watching you chew and swallow."

"Ooh, someone's a little cranky. How about we go for a stroll in the fresh air first?"

"Yeah, sounds good."

He gets out of the car, says his usual hello to Galahad, and off we go. It's a cloudless day, and I find myself sticking to the shade whenever possible; it's not the heat of the sun that's bothering me, it's the brightness. By the time we've gone around the block, my eyes ache and I've got the beginning of a migraine.

And I'm really, really thirsty.

We head to a local diner with outdoor tables. I get the breakfast special, order extra eggs, and feed my bacon to Galahad. I also go through three glasses of tomato juice and almost empty the saltshaker. Charlie watches all this without comment—but then, eating is a mystery to him, anyway. When we're done I take Gally back home and get a baseball hat with a brim to further shade my eyes.

We get to the office around ten. Cassius and Gretch aren't in yet—they work long hours, but they're on a pire's schedule and sleep at least part of the day. I sit down in my office and write up a formal report describing what happened between Tair and me—the *sange ucenicie* doesn't seem to interfere with the passing along of information, for which I'm grateful. Being forced into a submissive role is bad enough, but having to keep my mouth shut would have made it much worse. I may be stubborn, but I don't let pride get in the way of work; I recognize when I need help and have no problem in asking for it.

Except, you know, when I decide to sneak out in the middle of the night like a teenage girl and ditch my partner.

I take a deep breath, call Charlie in, and 'fess up. I blurt out the whole thing, trying desperately to justify myself by saying things like, "I didn't plan on doing any of this, it just sort of happened," and "I'm going through all of these changes and they're affecting my judgment," and the always useful "I'm really sorry and it won't happen again please don't hate me."

He listens to all of this without saying a word. He considers me levelly for a full minute afterward, and I wonder if I've finally gone too far. How can you expect your partner to trust you when you do something like this? I feel terrible.

Finally, he reaches into his breast pocket, pulls something out, and hands it to me. For one awful second I think it's his badge, but that's not it at all.

It's my cell phone.

"You must have dropped it someplace," he says. "Just like you—not really paying attention."

I stare down at the phone. The last time I had it was just before Tair swatted it out of my hand. But—

"Wait," I say. "That's—you—*what*?"

"That's what I love about working with you, Valchek. Your eloquence."

"But—but—*but*—"

"And your motorboat impressions."

"Charlie, if you were there, *why didn't you arrest him*?"

"Thought about it. But you clearly had something going on that I didn't want to mess up. Whatever the deal was, Leo seemed okay with it. So while you talked with Tair, I talked with Leo. He explained everything. I was going to see if I could nab Tair when you two got back, but he didn't give me a chance. So I faded."

"Why didn't Leo tell me you were there?"

"I asked him not to. I know how cranky you get when you think someone's reading over your shoulder."

I'm speechless. I don't know whether to be impressed, pissed off, or grateful. "You," I finally say, "are one helluva partner, Charlie Aleph."

"Yeah, I know. So now that you've gotten that off your chest and I don't have to deal with guilt-laden, furtive glances all day, what are we gonna do about this guy?"

I slump back in my chair. "I don't know. Wait for him to contact me again, I guess, and try to set a trap."

"That what you want?"

The question surprises me. "What I want doesn't matter, Charlie. He's an escaped felon and a killer. Whatever happens to me, that doesn't change."

"So I should have grabbed him while I had the chance."

"No. I mean—you did the best you could, under the circumstances. And even if you'd grabbed him then, we still wouldn't have the Don. This way we can prepare, do it right."

"*Right* meaning non-lethally."

"If possible, yeah."

What I don't say is: *I'm glad you didn't try to arrest him when you had the chance, because then I'd never have gone for that amazing dash through the woods, and I'd never have gotten that look behind the mask of arrogance Tair puts on like a disguise.* I don't say any of that, because I'm not sure I'm willing to admit it even to myself.

But it's true.

I know Cassius isn't going to be happy about what happened with Tair, and I'm right.

He's pacing around his office while I sit. I've never seen him pace—he's always calm and in control. It's unnerving.

"I can't believe you let him get away," Cassius says. "You had him, he was *right there.*"

I'm glad I haven't mentioned that Charlie was there, too—he'd be in even more trouble than I am. "I tried, all right? It's this *sange ucenicie* thing—it wouldn't let me."

"I should reassign you."

"What? No! Look, Leo explained the rules to me—Tair can't make me do anything I normally wouldn't, I just can't harm him. Which is fine, because we need to take him alive anyway, right?"

"Yes. I suppose we do."

"Then nothing's changed. We set a trap, with me as bait. The next time Tair makes contact, we take him down."

"If Charlie had done his job, that's exactly what would have happened."

I shake my head. "I told you, this isn't his fault—I

got away from him, that's all. What, you don't think a mere human is *capable* of eluding one of you mighty supernatural beings?" I don't play the human card very often, but there's no way I'm letting Charlie take the fall. The only mistake he might have made was in trusting his partner, and I'm not going to repay that by getting him in trouble.

"I'm not questioning your capabilities, Jace. I'm just worried about you." He hesitates. "I think we should advance your schedule. Give you another treatment."

"I don't know if I'm ready for that."

"I see. So you've decided you'd rather be a werewolf than a hemovore. I understand." He sounds angry, which is also unlike him.

"Oh, please. Give me a little credit, will you? You think one little walk on the wild side is going to make up my mind for me? Yeah, he showed me a very small slice of what being a thrope was like, and I won't say it didn't have its attraction. But *I'm* the one who decides, Cassius. Not Tair, not you, not a damn virus. And right now I am still very much rooting for the home team—which, in case you're unclear, is the old-fashioned human one."

"I'm sorry if I misspoke. But we're treading a very fine line here, and in order to ensure that the process we've started is successful, we need to balance the two forces fighting for dominance in your body. Your experience with Tair has no doubt bolstered the thrope side; I simply want to counter that."

He's right, I know he's right. So why am I so resistant to the idea? Am I *afraid* of Cassius now? Is it the *sange ucenicie*, affecting me in some way Leo didn't foresee? I don't know—I just know that right now, the last thing I want is another out-of-body experience. What I *do* want is—

"I want to see other people," I blurt.

Cassius looks at me. Raises an eyebrow.

"Real people, I mean. Non-supernatural. People who don't howl at the moon or avoid the sun or think silver was created by the Devil. People like me."

Cassius shakes his head. "There aren't any people like you, Jace. For which I am thankful. But I understand what you're saying; it's natural to seek comfort in the familiar when surrounded by the strange. Frankly, I'm surprised you haven't asked me about this earlier."

Cassius likes to support human causes, and the one pseudo-date we've been on was when he took me to a charity event sponsoring human-created art. I didn't really connect with any of the people I met there, and the fact that one of them was an ex-flame of Cassius's put me off even further.

But I feel a craving for human contact—genuine human contact, with my own kind. Call me a racist or a speciesist or whatever you want—I just know it's what I need right now. And I know Cassius is the person who can make it happen.

"So?" I ask. "You can help with that, right?"

"Of course. In fact, I can take you there right now, if you'd like."

"There? There's a there?" For some reason I hadn't thought of a specific location—I guess I just assumed he'd ask me what sort of person I'd like to talk to, then arrange it.

"Yes." He opens a cupboard, takes out a gray hooded daymask, matching gloves, and goggles. "It's not far. Or would you prefer to discuss logistics for trapping Tair first?"

"No. No, now is fine."

"All right. You'll have to leave Charlie here, though."

"Why?"

"I'll explain on the way." He's already halfway out the door.

The problem with Charlie is that he's black.

That sounds racist, but it's not—well, not exactly. Golems are filled with different-colored sand depending on what sort of job they're designed for; that job is usually defined by the spirit of the animal they're animated by. Most lems are slated for heavy physical labor, which is yellow. Office workers are the same, but it's a lighter shade. Those are generally powered by some sort of beast of burden, like a bull or a horse.

Black volcanic sand is the designation for enforcer. Police officers, soldiers, bodyguards. They're powered by carnivores—lions, bears, even snakes. Charlie's a special case, made by government shamans by distilling the essence of a *T. rex* out of crude oil.

And the humans are scared to death of him.

"Lems were designed to help humanity," Cassius tells me as he drives. He isn't wearing the daymask yet—his car windows are heavily tinted, naturally—but he's slipped on the gloves. "For a long time, that's exactly what they did. But as the thropes and pires became increasingly dominant in society, that changed. Lems grew more and more independent, less willing to be weapons or slaves. And they saw which way the world was going."

"So they jumped ship? Declared allegiance to the other side?"

"No. They elected to be neutral. They refused to fight for humans against the supernatural races, and vice versa. But by the time they came to that decision, it was too late—the human race was in decline. There was nothing that the lems could have done to stop that, either; it was simply the natural progression of economics and politics."

I look out the window. We're driving through a part of town that's not exactly picturesque; sagging gray houses, concrete-block fences, yards overgrown with weeds. Thropes in half-were form, standing around in groups of five or six, passing around a bottle and what looks like the carcass of a goat. It's not even noon.

"Okay, so they don't have a lot of faith in lems—I can understand that. But neutral's still better than active opposition, right?"

Cassius gives his head the barest shake, staring straight ahead at the road. "That's not the problem. Enforcement lems are a relatively new development—they've only been around a few decades. Before that, soldiers were the same yellow that laborers are now."

I think about that. "And black lems are made from predators."

"Yes. On some level, humans equate them with thropes or pires."

Which makes sense—but the more I think about it, the less I like it. "There's more to it than that, isn't there? When I headed that strike force going after Stoker, they had no problem with a human target."

"Enforcement lems can't afford the luxury of not engaging with a particular group. They were the first lems to be used *against* humans."

Now I get it. In their eyes, Charlie is worse than a deserter—he's a traitor. No wonder they don't want him around.

We turn off one squalid street and onto another one. We're at the edge of a semi-industrial area, lots of boxy warehouses and heavy equipment behind chain-link fences. I can hear the grind and chatter of machinery in the background like the soundtrack to a robot musical. Cassius drives right to the end of the street, where another fenced-off industrial lot sits. This one has better security than most: Razor wire glints along the top of the fence, and there are security cameras on poles every thirty feet or so. There's even a concrete guardhouse by the front gate, though there's no sign or corporate logo.

Cassius pulls up and puts an ID card into a slot in a concrete pillar. I can't see anyone through the mirrored glass of the guardhouse windows, but apparently Cassius passes muster; after humming for a moment, the slot spits his card back out and the gate swings open. Cassius drives inside.

"Welcome to the Seattle Enclave," he says.

A continuous line of row housing on either side, all the way to the back of the lot. Blocky gray concrete building in front of us, windows barred with rusty iron. Peeling paint on the houses, nothing taller than two stories. Between the houses and the central building is a patchy, half-gravel lawn. There are people outside sitting on folding chairs beside front doors, a few attempting a game of bocce on the largest patch of lawn. I don't see any children.

"This is where they live?" I say. The place looks and feels like a prison. "Since when was being human a crime?"

"They're not locked up, Jace. The security precautions are for their benefit—in fact, they insisted on them."

We pull up and park beside the central building. There are a few other cars parked there, none of them new, most of them with iron grilles over the windows. This isn't a prison—it's a reservation. A reservation full of scared, isolated people.

My people.

SIXTEEN

Cassius pulls on his daymask and goggles, tucking the edges of the fabric into his collar. "I don't normally come here when the sun is up. The buildings have many windows, none of them tinted. They like lots of natural light."

The mask turns him into an anonymous stranger in a suit. A faceless representative of authority, of the world that drove these people to this place. Yeah, not creepy at all.

We get out. Everyone's looking at us, with the careful blankness reserved for newcomers who haven't demonstrated yet whether or not they're a threat. I met a number of "unenhanced"—as the supernaturals refer to them—humans at the art benefit, but I don't see anyone I recognize. Cassius heads for the main building, and I follow.

The front doors are glass, and the lobby is about as grim and depressing as I expect. Industrial carpeting, bland pastel walls, Naugahyde waiting-room furniture. A gray metal elevator door in one corner, and a wood-veneer desk with a plump, dark-haired woman in her fifties in the other. But the flatscreen monitor she's looking at is brand new, and she greets us with a smile and a nod. "Hello, David. Shouldn't you be in bed?"

"Hello, Teresa. I'd like you to meet Jace Valchek. Jace, Teresa McKeever."

Teresa's eyebrows go up, but her smile gets wider. "Ms. Valchek! A pleasure—I've heard so much about you. I was wondering when you'd come and see us."

"I've—been pretty busy," I say. I feel embarrassed, as if she's a relative I've somehow let down. "Work. You know how it is."

She nods. "I do. This place keeps me hopping, I'll tell you that. But you're always welcome here—" The monitor beeps at her softly, and the look on her face becomes one of mild consternation. She glances down, then back up at me, then down again. "Oh, my," she says. "This isn't—this *can't* be right—"

"I'm afraid it is," Cassius says. "But her first transformation hasn't occurred yet. Because of her special circumstances, we may be able to reverse it."

Teresa looks at me, concern and something else warring in her eyes. Concern wins; she comes around the desk and envelops me in a stout, matronly hug. I'm not much of a hugger, so it catches me off guard. "I'm so, so sorry, my dear," she says, then pulls back to regard me at arm's length. "How did it happen? Are you all right? How are you holding up?"

"Uh—I'm okay," I say. "Did you just get an e-mail about me or something? Is my health status on the Internet already?"

"Oh, no, nothing like that. We just have extremely sensitive wards in place—my equipment identified you as a thrope. A very new one, too."

That makes sense—no one would have better mystic alarm systems than these folks. Humans have a natural affinity for manipulating magic, more so than the supernaturals; I'm guessing this place is protected by more than just fences and security cameras.

"How can we help, my dear?" Teresa asks. She takes a step back and regards me gravely.

"I'm not sure," I say honestly. "I just felt like I needed to—I don't know, *reconnect*."

Teresa nods. "Of course, of course. Well, you've come to the right place. David, you'll be all right out here?"

"I'll wait in the car. Jace, Teresa will show you around. Take as long as you like."

"Yeah, okay."

He turns around and leaves. I watch him go, feeling a little like a kid being dropped off at kindergarten.

"So," Teresa says. "What has David told you about us?"

"Not much. Just that you're the officially sanctioned Human Enclave for the Seattle area, and you like to stay off the radar."

"That we do, that we do." She motions to me to take a seat, and chooses to sit down beside me instead of returning to her desk. "We're somewhat . . . *cautious* in our approach to the outside world, Jace. Despite being protected by federal law, we still have enemies. People who see us as remnants of the past that should be eliminated, or people who simply want to use us for our abilities or our blood."

I think about the Purebloods, the pire equivalent of white supremacists, and nod. And then there's Japan, where human blood is an expensive black-market item controlled by the Yakuza—who keep underground blood farms pumping out product from human captives. "I know, Teresa. Believe me, I understand why you'd be careful about outsiders."

"Yes. Well." She looks a little uncomfortable now. "David's vouched for you, and that's good enough for us. He's been our greatest ally—really, I can't think of another person who's done more for us in the last fifty years."

I'm not sure how to respond to that. Cassius certainly appears to care about the plight of the human population, but I'm a little unsure of his motivation. The cynical side of me says he's just trying to appease his guilt, to make up for the sacrifice of six million humans to an Elder God in 1945, a sacrifice that Cassius himself was involved with. The even more cynical side thinks he just wants an ongoing supply of human females, because that's what floats Cassius's boat.

Six million corpses. Hard not to compare it to what my world's Hitler did, except the Allies here had a much better reason—the deal they made gained pires the right to procreate, thereby saving their entire race from eventual extinction. That doesn't make what they did any less horrifying or easier to excuse, but it does make it a little easier to understand. In my world we dropped atomic bombs on two different cities, killing over two hundred thousand people, most of them civilians. How many lives did it save, by ending the war quickly? There's no way to know. Every pire born since 1945—not just in this country, but worldwide—wouldn't exist without the deal the Allies made with Shub-Niggurath, and that will continue to be true for presumably centuries to come. Was it justifiable to kill millions of one race to ensure the existence of billions of another?

I don't know. I suspect Cassius doesn't, either. But every time I look into the eyes of Gretchen's baby, Anna, I'm glad she's in the world.

That being said, I'm still a tourist. I wasn't here in 1945, but Teresa's parents probably were. She might have very different views on the subject, and I don't think I'd want to argue with her. I wonder just how much she knows about Cassius's involvement—he'd been head of the NSA for a decade by then. I've always wondered just how deep his responsibility for the massacre ran, but I've never had the nerve to bring it up. Some elephants are just too big, no matter what room you're in.

"I know what you must want to see," Teresa says. "We just got something in, too—a very special find. I won't spoil the surprise."

"Actually, I have no idea what I want to see. Like I said, I'm not even sure why I'm here."

She studies the look on my face, and then a smile breaks out on her own. "David hasn't told you what we do, has he?"

"Do? Not specifically, no."

"David, David, David . . . if he kept his mouth any more closed, his lips would grow together." She stands up abruptly. "Well, you're in for a treat. Just stick close to me—as I said, we have very sensitive wards in place. You don't read very high on the lycanthropic scale, so we should be fine as long as we stay together."

She bustles over to the elevator and presses the call button. The door slides back smoothly and silently, and we step inside.

She presses the only destination button on the panel, marked with the words DISPLAY FLOOR. The elevator begins to sink. It goes down farther than I would have expected, but I shouldn't be surprised; pire architecture leans heavily toward sub-basements.

As if reading my thoughts, Teresa says, "There was a lot of disagreement over where to house the exhibits. Some of us—including me—thought they should be on public display, out in the open. Out in the light. But a lot more people voted for security. They won."

The elevator door slides open.

I have an idea of what I'm going to see—all the talk

of displays and exhibits leads me to believe this is some sort of gallery of human art, similar to the charity event Cassius took me to. In the back of my mind, I'm envisioning a dusty subterranean warehouse, kind of like that scene at the end of *Raiders of the Lost Ark* but underground.

I'm very, very wrong.

The space we step into is huge, a vast, cavernous room big enough to park a fleet of 747s in. The roof is easily thirty stories high, and the far wall is the length of a dozen football fields away. But it's what the room holds that's truly amazing.

The room is a patchwork of environments, each of them a fully realized microcosm complete with terrain, weather, and vegetation. But that's just set dressing; it's what they surround that takes my breath away.

Directly in front of me, the Sphinx regards us impassively from her sandy bed. To one side, the distinctive spires and minarets of the Taj Mahal gleam a pristine white; the curving stone walls of the Roman Colosseum flank the other. For a second I feel like I've just stepped into a theme park, or maybe some newly opened stretch of the Las Vegas Strip. But these aren't three-quarter-scale copies, they're full-size. And they're not the only structures on display, either.

"Oh my God," I say. "Are these—are they *real*?"

Teresa smiles at me again, but this time her smile is a little sad. "No. Not in the way you're thinking. But in another sense, yes, they are. *More* than real, in some ways."

"Can I—can I touch them?"

"Of course," she says quietly. "That's what they're here for."

I step over the narrow concrete lip that separates the Sphinx exhibit from the tiled walkway. My feet crunch in the sand. I walk up to the Sphinx and gently, reverently, lay a hand on the pitted stone surface. It's rough and cool and dusty and very, very real.

"This isn't a reproduction, is it?"

"Yes and no. The real Sphinx, the original, is still in Egypt. But that's also exactly what you're touching—if the sun were up in that part of the world right now, the stone would feel warm."

"Magic."

"Yes. Basic animism, amplified to a high degree. At the center of the exhibit is a small piece of the original, still linked to its point of origin by a spell. It's like a lens, focusing and projecting the essence of the Sphinx from there to here. You'll notice our version still has an intact nose."

So not the Sphinx itself, but the spirit of the thing, astral projection applied to the soul of an object instead of a being. It makes perfect sense, actually; animism doesn't make such petty distinctions. Its central tenet is that everything has a spirit, and in this world that seems to hold true.

"Welcome to the Archive of Human Works," Teresa says, pride in her voice. "We may use magic to enhance our displays, but it was one hundred percent human effort and ingenuity that built them in the first place."

I rejoin her on the walkway. She heads to the left, past the Taj Mahal. "We have links to some of the most impressive feats of human engineering in existence. Some of the exhibits are incomplete—we just don't have the space to display, say, the Great Wall of China—but we have a representative sample on display."

Sure enough, between the exhibits a section of the Great Wall is visible, encircling the entire room as if it's protecting us from attack by marauding moles. I see a few people in gray short-sleeved uniforms strolling along the top looking like neither Chinese guards nor tourists, more like janitors who stumbled out of a space–time warp. Custodians, I guess.

I feel like a bug who just hit history's windshield as Teresa shows me around. I've never been to any of these places, but I've always wanted to go, and now here they are: the stepped pyramid of Chichén Itzá, surrounded by jungle greenery; the stone terraces of Machu Picchu, set into a very authentic-looking mountainside. And in the middle of a grassy plain, the ancient monoliths of Stonehenge.

"This is astounding," I say. I'm feeling more than a little awe. "But it must take an incredible amount of sorcerous power to maintain. How do you do it?"

"I'll give you a hint," she says with a mischievous look in her eye. "One of these exhibits isn't a projection."

I look around, trying to be analytical instead of overwhelmed. It comes to me almost instantly, more from instinct than conscious evaluation. "Stonehenge. Has to be."

"Very good. You can feel the power radiating off them, can't you? This entire site sits on a ley line, and the stones are plugged right into it. A mystic energy source, very ancient. It cost a fortune to have them shipped here, but it wouldn't have happened at all without a great deal of political maneuvering. Luckily, we had someone on our side."

"Cassius."

"Yes. It would have been impossible without his support."

Yeah. An incredible gift, one that would seem to cement my boss's position as patron saint of mankind.

Except I can't help thinking that by giving the Enclave such a powerful mystic artifact, he's also created a very powerful ally.

"You said you had something come in today—this wasn't it, right?"

She chuckles. "No, it was much smaller. These are the big-ticket items, but we archive important human objects from all over the world. I'll show you."

She leads me to a stairwell that goes even deeper, presumably to prevent putting a door in the Great Wall and spoiling the illusion. It leads us to another room, this one not nearly so grand—it's essentially a long hallway, lined with floor-to-ceiling drawers and shelves, each holding a discrete object. Some of them I recognize, some of them I don't.

"We concentrate on things that have some connection to human history or achievement," Teresa says. "Each one is carefully cataloged and then treated by our shamans. They use magic to strengthen whatever traces of the object's creator or user remain."

We go to the end of the hall, turn right, go down another hall, turn left, then turn right again. The place is a maze, lit with tiny halogen spotlights trained on the walls. It has the cool, dry air of a climate-controlled environment, and the soft carpet underfoot deadens our footfalls into nothingness.

She finally stops before a row of white-fronted drawers and peers at the label on the front. "Ah. Here it is—I was afraid they hadn't finished processing it yet."

She pulls the drawer open. Inside is a pair of glasses, round wire-framed spectacles.

"Go ahead," she says. "Pick them up, but be careful."

I do. Nothing happens for a second, and then I feel a tingle in my hand, up my arm. Suddenly I'm not holding a pair of spectacles anymore; I'm holding some-one's hand. I can see him, even though he's clearly not there—it's like a vivid hallucination, one that's both real and not real at the same time.

It's Mahatma Gandhi.

He smiles at me but doesn't speak. He doesn't have to—that quiet smile on that gentle brown face, the warmth of his hand in mine, is more than enough. I feel his presence, his serenity, his intelligence; he's just as aware of me as I am of him.

I swallow, afraid to say anything. Gandhi's the rea-son I became a vegetarian, though I haven't embraced a nonviolent point of view the way he did. But that doesn't mean I don't respect it; it just means he was a better person than me. That's not exactly news—he was a bet-ter person than most.

"Is this—are you his ghost?" I ask.

Gandhi doesn't answer me, but Teresa does. "No. What you're seeing is an echo, a kind of emotional after-image. A trace of his persona, transferred to something he wore for many years."

"He *feels* real."

Teresa nods. "I know. That's the point. We want to showcase the very best the human race has to offer, and we want people to connect with that on a personal level. To illustrate who we are and what we can accom-plish."

Reluctantly, I let go of the glasses, letting them drop a few inches into their padded cases. Gandhi fades away, and I'm sorry to see him go.

"That was amazing," I say.

"We're very lucky to have them. Gandhi didn't be-lieve in material possessions, so there aren't many arti-facts linked to him left. He gave these to an Indian army colonel named H. A. Shiri Diwan Nawabin in the 1930s; the colonel had asked for a keepsake, for inspiration. Gandhi gave him these, saying they had given him the vision to free India."

I shake my head, feeling a little stunned. I came here hoping for a way to hold on to my human side, but this is all too big; it's history and legends and monuments, not on my scale at all. "Do you have someplace a little less . . . impressive? Someplace we can sit down and have a cup of coffee?"

"Oh, absolutely. We've got a nice cozy café set up in Lenin's tomb."

I blink. She laughs. "Sorry. I can see you're a little shell-shocked. Come on, we'll go to the lounge."

She closes the drawer and leads me farther into the maze of hallways, but this time we come out at an elevator. It takes us back up to the main building and a room on the top floor full of tables and comfortable overstuffed chairs, flooded with sunlight from large glass panels in the roof. There's a cafeteria-style kitchen to one side with two people I can see bustling around and filling steamer trays with food; they both glance at us when we come in, but then look quickly away. There's only one other occupied table, an elderly couple having a meal. The man ignores me, but the woman studies me with outright suspicion.

We get two coffees and find a seat. I notice that Teresa picks a table as far away as possible from the couple.

"No offense," I say, "but—other than you—people here seem a little standoffish."

Teresa blows on her coffee to cool it. It's something I haven't seen since I got here, since pires ignore temperature and thropes seem to have a much higher tolerance for extremes. It's oddly endearing. "Yes, well, there's a certain clannish attitude that's prevalent. We know pretty much every human face within a hundred miles, and anyone new is viewed with caution."

"You knew who I was, though."

She looks a little uncomfortable. "Yes. Well, there are other factors at work, too."

I blow on my own coffee. "It's not that they don't know who I am. They just don't trust me."

"You showed up with Cassius. That gives you a lot of credibility."

I look over at the kitchen workers and catch one of them looking back with a carefully neutral expression that I've seen before. It's the one worn by a prisoner staring at a guard, a mask that projects neither disrespect nor submission. It's a look that says *I'm waiting to see what you do next. I might be your friend, I might be your enemy, but don't expect me to show my cards before you show yours.*

"Not enough, apparently," I say.

Teresa notices where I'm looking and shrugs. "They didn't see you arrive, that's all. Believe me, your boss gets a lot of respect around here. If you knew everything he's done for us—" She breaks off abruptly, trying to hide it by taking a sip of her coffee. I'm not fooled.

"Like what? Besides the artifacts?"

"He helped set this whole place up. There were a lot of human refugees after the war, and he did a lot for them. During the war, too."

"During the war? How?"

"I—I can't really say. It's all classified."

I realize what she's talking about. Six million humans perished at the end of World War II, and the world at large thinks the death toll was due to a sorcerous virus released by Hitler's shamans. But the truth is far darker: The bodies that were burned for health reasons in government-constructed crematoriums were in fact being ritually sacrificed.

And they weren't dead, either.

I uncovered this during my very first investigation on this world, and I've never quite forgiven Cassius for it; as head of the NSA back then, he was part of the power structure that condemned those people to a horrible death. Teresa sounds like she knows the truth, too, and probably more of it than I do. But she doesn't seem to blame Cassius for his role—if anything, she seems grateful.

The old couple in the corner abruptly get up and leave. The man throws me a glare as they stalk out the door, and I suddenly realize why they're so hostile.

I'm a collaborator.

Cassius can be forgiven because of all the good he's done for the human cause, but me? I've made a choice. I'm a cop who works for the enemy. I was brought here to hunt my own kind, and that's exactly what I've done. I've made a name for myself as the Bloodhound, and the people living here are all too aware of who really holds my leash. They don't see a friend of Cassius; they see a turncoat.

Maybe they're right.

I finish my coffee and stand up. "Thank you for your time, Teresa. For what you've shown me."

"My pleasure, Jace. You're—" She hesitates. "You're a good person to have on our side. I hope everything works out for you."

She was going to say *You're always welcome here,* but she stopped herself. Which is good, because it wouldn't be true. In fact, after the first full moon I may never be allowed to set foot in here again.

"I hope so, too," I say. "I really do."

SEVENTEEN

"Jace? I didn't expect you back so soon," Cassius says as I get in the car. He's taken off his mask and gloves.

"I'm a quick study. Let's go."

He can tell I'm upset, but he doesn't pry. He knows me well enough to understand that I won't keep it bottled up for long, and he's right. We're no more than half a mile away from the Enclave when I say, "That place. It's not a museum, it's a mausoleum."

"Is that how it felt to you?"

"Hell, yes. Those people were *scared*, Cassius. I could . . . I could *smell* it."

"They're doing the best they can."

"Are they? They've built a bunker on top of a tomb and they're filling it with history. That's not the act of a healthy society—that's the quiet despair of a people who have given up. They're trying to preserve the best of humanity because they think there isn't going to *be* a humanity pretty soon. They don't have any faith in the future, so they're putting all their energy into capturing the past."

"There's a lot worth preserving."

I make a deeply irritated growling noise. "That's not the point! They're acting like—like there are no new challenges, there's nothing left to accomplish. Like the game is over and all that's left to do is count up the points and put the board away. They're *beaten,* Cassius. And that's—that's not something I can stand to be around."

"Is that all there was to it?"

"No. They've practically deified you, but they don't trust me. Teresa was nice enough, but she was the only one I talked to. And I could tell that my condition made even her very nervous."

"Most of the Axis forces in World War Two were thropes."

"That's not it. Pire or thrope, it doesn't make any difference—it's strictly an *us versus them* thing. What matters is that I came to this world a human being, and I chose to work for the other side."

Cassius is quiet for a moment. "I'm sorry, Jace. I'd hoped it would go better."

"Did you?" I snap. "Or did you think good old predictable Jace would react *exactly* the same way she always does? That I'd see how pathetic those survivors huddling in their self-made prison compound were, and decide I'd be better off as a member of the winning team?"

His voice drops several degrees in temperature. "You're overwrought. Understandably so. So I'm going to let you think about what you just said before I respond to it."

The icy steel in his tone stops me. He's right, I'm getting overemotional. I force myself to cool off and think, and realize that Cassius would never try to manipulate me into turning against my own kind. It wouldn't work, for one thing—I'm too stubborn to switch sides, regardless of how badly my team may be losing, and Cassius knows that. He also knows that if he ever attempted something like that, I'd see through it and he'd lose my trust forever. Accusing Cassius of being manipulative doesn't bother him, but accusing him of doing it badly is just insulting.

"I'm sorry," I say, but my voice is sullen. God, I haven't felt this bitchy since I was a teenager. "You were just trying to help."

"And failing, obviously."

"No. You helped me realize something, by showing me the alternative. I don't want to become like those people, trying to relive past glories; I want to go forward. I want to *fight* for who I am, what I am. I'm ready for another . . . *whatever* the hell it is you're doing to me."

"Inoculation seems the most accurate term."

"Okay, fine. Once we get back to the office, you can inoculate the hell out of me."

He doesn't respond to that, and I can't bring myself to look at him; I'm afraid I'll see a big grin on his face.

And strangely enough, I'm having a hard time keeping one off my own.

We do it the same way we did it last time. I take off my shoes, socks, and pants and lie on his couch, and he kneels beside me. "This time, try to keep it to under a gallon, okay?"

"I know what to expect now, Jace. I promise you, I won't lose control."

"All right, then. Let's get this over with." I'm trying my best for a firm, businesslike attitude, but I can already feel my heartbeat racing. And was that a *quiver* in my voice?

He leans forward and touches his lips to my skin. A shiver races through my body. *This is a medical procedure,* I tell myself. *This is a medical procedure.*

His teeth sink into my flesh. The first time it happened

I gasped, more from shock than pain. This time, I barely feel it. But when he starts to drink, the sensation is much more intense than before; it feels like my very life is draining away.

And just like last time, I can't move.

Panic explodes in my chest. *He lied. He's going to turn me whether I like it or not. I'm going to die, right here and now.*

But I won't stay that way.

I do my best to fight the fear, to tell myself I'm over-reacting. It doesn't do any good. I've been nervous and tense all day and this kicks that tension right over the edge. I'm taking big, raspy gulps of air like I'm drowning, but he either doesn't notice or doesn't care. A very distant and small voice in my head is trying to convince me this is only the thrope virus responding to an attack, but it's just a whisper on the other side of a door compared with the storm of terror that's howling inside my skull.

Then even that's gone, and all that's left is the panic.

"NO!" Whatever pire sorcery is paralyzing my body, it seems to break with the yell. This time, I don't try to pull Cassius free.

I backhand him with my right fist, across the fore-head. This is a stupid thing to do, as the bone that lies behind the forehead is extremely solid and dense while the bones that make up the hand are not. And pires are notoriously resistant to damage, anyway.

It sends him flying across the room. He smacks into a bookcase spine-first, about three feet off the floor, and tumbles to the ground with a hail of literature bouncing off his head and shoulders.

Last time, I took off my jacket before we started. This time, I didn't.

I don't go for the gun. I draw my scythes instead. I'm

not aware of it, though, just like I'm not aware of how I got from one side of the room to the other, snapping the blades open along the way. But I must have been moving awfully fast, because I have the edge of a silvered blade at Cassius's throat before the last book hits the floor.

The scythes were a gift from a thrope admirer when I first got to this world. They're made of ironwood, each of them about two feet long, with a silver spike on top and a recessed, spring-loaded blade that locks open at a forty-five-degree angle. Eighteen inches of razor-sharp, steel-cored silver, able to decapitate any thrope or pire with a single swipe. I'm trained in the Filipino fighting art of kali, which uses twin batons without the blades, and I'm very, very good at it. With the blades thrown in, I'm death in high heels.

And right now, I'm about a heartbeat away from killing my boss.

He doesn't try to defend himself, which is good. Fast as Cassius is, I've got the drop on him; I could take his head off before he could so much as twitch.

So he doesn't. Instead his fangs recede and his eyes shift from red to their usual deep blue. It's enough to make me hesitate, but the storm that's raging in my brain is far from over. *Killhimkillhimkillhimkillhim* is pounding in my ears, drowning out every conscious thought.

"Jace," Cassius says. "Jace, there's no need. I submit. You've won. It's *over*." His voice is gentle, humble. I've never heard him sound like this before, never, and it's enough to confuse the animal that seems to be in control of my body at the moment.

But the blade stays where it is. The point of the second stick is jammed into his chest, right above his heart. One hard shove and he's dust.

"Listen to me. Listen. I'm not your enemy. Try to remember, Jace. Remember who you are, who I am."

"Other," I snarl. I don't recognize my own voice.

"No. That's the virus talking. You're human, Jace. *Human.*"

"You're not," I growl. My muscles tense. He's an abomination, an unnatural *thing,* and I'm going to *end* him—

"Kill me and humans suffer," he says. His voice is soft but urgent. "I'm on their side, Jace. I'm on *your* side. Please."

"Sure you are. You're on the side of *all* humans. They're just too *valuable* to *waste.*" I press the scythe harder against his throat. It cuts into his undead skin, ever so slightly, and a thin line of crimson appears along the edge of the blade. My eyes widen at the sight of it, and a crazy kind of thrill pulses through the pit of my stomach.

"I did what I could to help them, Jace," he whispers. "But I couldn't save them all."

And that damps down the bloodlust, just a little. Just enough to make me pause.

"I used my influence as head of the NSA. Assigned 'protected asset' status to as many as I could. Gave them charms that made them immune to the plague."

My breathing is slowing. The red haze over everything is fading to pink. "What?"

"It's—no one knows, Jace. I'd be charged with treason if anyone ever found out."

And now the rage is definitely subsiding. It's not because of some sudden rush of affection, or even the shock of new information; it's because he's done the metaphysical equivalent of rolling over and baring his throat by sharing his secret. It's exactly the right thing to do, because it speaks to the thrope microorganisms in my bloodstream on a level they understand: A member of my pack has chosen to forgo execution by exposing himself to my fangs. In this moment, I'm the alpha; the implicit agreement he's offering states that in return for his life he's now subordinate to me, and with the knowledge I now possess that's not just a metaphor.

I pull back the blade and the other stick with hands that are suddenly shaky with the aftereffects of adrenaline, and step back. I sit on the floor like a small child, thumping straight down on my butt.

"I—I believe you," I say.

He gets to his feet, slowly but gracefully. A single drop of blood is tracing its way down the side of his Adam's apple. When he speaks, his voice is back to its usual self-assuredness. "Don't. I lied in order to break the blood-frenzy. But considering that you were about to *end* me, I think I deserve a little leeway—"

"No. You're lying now. Teresa refused to blame you for your role in the 1945 massacre, and now I know why."

He straightens his tie and glances away. "Teresa is simply grateful for the assistance I've provided over the years."

I've got my breathing under control now, and in a minute or so I might actually be able to stand up. "You *told* her, didn't you? Even though it was the worst possible thing to do. Whatever cover story you sold the humans you were saving, you told her the *real* reason behind those 'anti-plague' charms you were distributing. How old was she?"

Cassius looks at me for a long moment before answering. "Eighteen."

"You *wanted* her to betray your confidence. You wanted her to tell the whole human community that the human race was being slaughtered not just by Nazi thropes, but by the Allies. You wanted to be hated, to be punished. It's what you thought you deserved."

"That's . . . that's absurd."

"No, it's human nature. Which, despite the fact that you drink AB-negative milk shakes and go into anaphylactic shock at the sight of a garlic lover's pizza, you still have. Teresa doesn't blame you, but you sure blame yourself—and even at eighteen, she was wise enough to recognize that. She's never told anyone, has she? She's kept your secret all these years."

All this time I thought Cassius was one of the people in charge—maybe even a ringleader. But he wasn't. He was doing the exact opposite, using his position to save as many people as he could while hating himself for not doing better.

"I keep forgetting," Cassius says quietly, "that you've been trained to analyze how people think. Every now and then, you remind me. And astound me."

"Just . . . doing my job, Caligula. I've still got one, right? Even after the whole attempted-assassination bit?"

He steps over, extends his hand, helps me to my feet. "I don't hold your actions against you, no. Your contact with Tair strengthened the virus, and it was a lot more aggressive in defending its gains. I'm not sure how much good I did."

I look him right in the eye. "I am. And I guess it'll just have to do, won't it?"

He doesn't answer.

There's a knock at the door. Charlie's voice says, "Hey. If you two are done wrestling, we've got another crime scene. Looks like Tair and the Don again."

I'm already headed for the door, but Cassius grabs my arm and stops me. "Your clothes?" he says. "And you might want to reholster your weapons, too."

"Oh, right."

This time when I come out of the office everybody is studiously not looking at me, especially Charlie's lem buddy, Seymour. I pretend to not notice everyone not noticing me, and stride toward the elevator. Charlie's right behind me. "Another murder. Construction site."

I hit the DOWN button. "Victim?"

"Francis Aggamonte, also known as Frankie Eggs. Another one of the Don's guys."

"Yeah? We better find Arturo before his own crew does—at this rate, they'll kill him out of sheer self-defense."

I get the rundown from my laptop as Charlie drives. Frankie Eggs isn't a capo, but he is highly placed—his file says he launders a lot of Mob money through a number of companies, including a construction firm and a trucking outfit. People who disagree with his business practices have a habit of disappearing.

I squint at the screen and rub my temples. I haven't recovered from the "inoculation"; my head throbs, I'm parched, and I'd gladly lick the sweat off a fat man at the gym for the salt. I feel like the PMS Fairy just hollowed out my skull and used it for a toilet bowl. "Okay. Phil Ulzano was a loan shark. Frankie Eggs laundered money. Both were people Don Falzo trusted at one time, and now both are dead."

"Yeah. Revenge?"

"For what? These are his own guys, not rivals. Besides, if he wanted any one of them killed, all he'd have to do is order it." I shake my head and immediately wish I hadn't. "Maybe the crime scene will tell us something."

The crime scene doesn't tell us much.

Not at first. Frankie Eggs met his demise on one of his own construction sites, which at the moment is just a big pit in the ground with a scoop shovel and two dump trucks in it. The body is in a trailer a little way away, sprawled on the floor. There are multiple thrope tracks in the mud around the trailer, and muddy paw prints inside. Lots of spatter, too.

"Well, the Don doesn't mind getting his hands dirty," I say. We're standing just outside the open door, looking at the body. We've haven't touched anything yet.

"If it was him and not Tair," Charlie says.

"I don't think Tair was here," I say. "I'm not sure why—it just doesn't *feel* like it."

Damon Eisfanger pulls up in one of the NSA's white vans. He gets out with his kit in one hand, already wearing gloves. "Hey," he says. "Another wise guy?"

"Yeah," I say. "We haven't gone in yet."

Eisfanger nods, hands us both pairs of little paper booties, and slips his own on. "Let's take a look at what we've got."

The trailer is one of those little on-site offices construction sites have, with a coffeemaker, a couch, a desk, a few chairs, a small TV, and a DVD player. From the looks of the desk, Frankie was doing a little Bane while watching a movie.

"Truest Grit: Down and Gritty," I say, looking at the DVD case on the desk as I snap on my own pair of gloves. Charlie doesn't bother—he doesn't have any fingerprints to leave. "Huh. Xandra was talking about this just the other day."

"He died watching the Duke," Eisfanger says. "Not such a bad way to go . . . Okay. Position of the body tells us he was facing the door when he was struck. First blow was probably the killing one—hit him right between the eyes. You can see the striation marks from the wire on the skin—I'm betting they match the marks on the previous vic."

I nod. "So he was hit from the front while standing in front of the door. Ambush attack—someone knocks, he answers, gets a bat to the skull for his trouble. But that's not the only wound."

"No. He was struck multiple times, on the shoulders, rib cage, and arms. Looks like a frenzy."

"Yeah. Indicating rage and loss of control. There's just one problem."

Eisfanger raises his snowy eyebrows in a question.

"Frenzy attacks are personal. It's an attempt either to inflict as much pain as possible—in which case he would have stuck to the body—or to completely obliterate the victim, in which case he wouldn't have struck the head only once."

Eisfanger frowns. "You're right. It doesn't make sense."

"It does if you're trying to send a message. He wanted the body quickly identified, which is why he left the face relatively untouched instead of turning it into paste. The savagery of the beating afterward is—" I shake my head, slowly. "I don't know. It might be some kind of irrational behavior, it might be intended as the message itself: *Stay away from me or suffer the consequences.*"

Eisfanger opens up his kit and starts doing forensic shaman things to the body. Charlie and I search the trailer.

The desk drawers are locked, but the key is on a chain dangling from Frankie's belt. I open them up and rummage around. Bills of lading, invoices, a copy of *Hairy Rumps and Furry Bumps,* a bottle of cheap whiskey. And a black leather zippered case, which is disappointingly empty. It has staggered pockets lining either side, obviously intended to hold credit cards or ID.

"Take a look at this," I say. "Wish I knew what used to be in it."

"I might be able to grant that wish," Eisfanger says. He takes the case from me, selects a vial and a small, feathered rod from his kit. He dusts the case lightly with powder from the vial while murmuring an incantation, and a row of ghostly white rectangles slowly coalesce into being about three inches above the case. Eisfanger grins.

"Spiritual trace," he says. "Recent, too. I'd say these were removed very close to the same time Frankie was killed."

I peer at the images hovering there, but they're translucent and hard to focus on. "Some kind of picture ID, I think. Are those lems?"

"Give me a minute," Eisfanger says. He selects another instrument from his kit, a bird skull with a long, thin beak. He uses the beak like a pair of tweezers, reaching out and carefully closing it around one of the rectangles, then pulling it away from the others. The other cards immediately dim, but the one Eisfanger grabbed gets brighter, more solid. He brings it up to eye level and rotates it so it's vertical.

"That's a union card," I say. "Local One Twelve. What's a construction site supervisor doing with a bunch of union cards for truckers?"

"Something he's not supposed to," Charlie growls. "And whatever it is, the Don thinks he can do it, too."

"Except this time," I say, "maybe we can get there before he does."

Eisfanger pulls all the data he can from the case, and sends it to Gretch. She calls me within minutes. "The cards are forgeries, but good ones. They correspond to lems who are on the union rolls, but are undocumented otherwise. Most likely illegal workers with no official right to exist."

"Lems who are in the Gray Wolves' pocket, in other words. Any other correlations?"

"Yes. Almost three-quarters of these lems were the subjects of truck hijackings in the past six months. Expensive electronics items, mostly."

"But nobody thought to check if the lems might be involved?"

I can almost hear her shrug over the phone. "Every case was investigated by local law enforcement, but a lem with a union card is assumed to be legitimate. None of the robberies involved the same driver, so there was no suspicious pattern."

"They didn't use just one inside man, they used a bunch of them. With a state-mandated death sentence hanging over the drivers' heads to keep them in line." I sigh. "Plus, they probably built the damn things in the first place. You've got to hand it to the Mob—they really put the *organized* in organized crime."

"And now Don Falzo has the same lems under his control. What do you think he'll do with them?"

"There's no way to know." I pause, thinking hard. "But we do know what the Wolves were using them for, and there's no reason to think they'll stop. It looks like Frankie gave out the cards as needed, probably only when a lem was actually making a run. They didn't use any of the drivers more than once. So it's possible that one of those unused cards is actually sitting in a lem's wallet right now, and he's getting ready to be robbed."

"Very good. I'll cross-reference that with trucking schedules of high-end electronics and compare it against the previous robberies. We should have a good chance of predicting where they'll strike next." She pauses. "However, it's unlikely this will get us any closer to Tair or the Don."

"Maybe not," I admit. "But it should get us somebody in custody that we can lean on. Somebody that knows

something. We just have to keep following the trail—
sooner or later, it'll lead us to who we're hunting."

It turns out that figuring where the hijackers will strike
next is even easier than that. Cops handling the case
have labeled them "the Overpass Gang," because that's
their MO. They rig a couple of ropes to the underside
of a bridge and hang there until the truck drives underneath. Then they drop down, commandeer the cab, and
get the driver to pull over so they can take his load.

On my world, that would be the kind of thing that
would only happen in a movie. Risky, improbable, dangerous, requiring an insane amount of timing, guts,
stamina, and acrobatic skill. Here, it's the kind of thing
a teenager might do for kicks.

Plus, they have an inside man. The driver marks the
top of the truck in some way to make it easy to spot,
and tells the gang exactly what route he's taking and
when. I'm guessing he also slows down a fair bit when
driving under the bridge, and there might even be a
rope or something slung over the top of the truck that's
easy to grab—easy for a supernatural, anyway.

One of the lems on the phony ID cards is driving a
truck full of LCD TVs to Portland tonight. There are a
number of overpasses between here and the Oregon
border, but the gang tends to stay close to Seattle, which
narrows it down. I've eyeballed all the possibilities, and
we've got teams surveilling every one. Charlie and I are
about a block away from the one I think is the most probable, parked where we can see the overpass but aren't
obvious.

"The thing I don't get," Charlie says, "is why they're
going to this kind of trouble. Why not just have the guy
pull over? He's working for them, right?"

I take a sip of my takeout coffee. "Plausible deniability. They have to make it look like a real robbery to keep any heat off the drivers. They probably don't trust the lems to keep a lie straight, so they go through all the motions of the real thing. Plus, they have to leave enough evidence behind to convince a forensics tech like Damon—scratches in the metal, stuff like that. He could tell in a minute whether or not a thrope had actually jumped from an overpass onto a moving truck."

Charlie grunts. That's partner-speak for, *You're right, which irritates me.*

"Hey," I say. "I think we're on."

Two thropes in half-were form emerge from the shadows beneath the overpass, each with a coil of rope over a hairy shoulder. They bound over the guardrail, lope up the incline to the top of the overpass, and within a minute have two ropes secured under the bridge, attached to the guardrail on either side. They climb down hand-over-hand and spend another minute rigging some kind of tarp between the ropes, giving them an improvised hammock to lie in while they wait for their target. Two big hairy spiders, ready to leap.

A set of headlights appears in the distance. An eighteen-wheeler, shifting gears as it approaches, slowing down.

"Showtime," Charlie says.

EIGHTEEN

As the truck passes under the bridge, the two thropes drop down onto it. I can hear the double *thump* from where I'm sitting a block away. One of the thropes is already scrambling over to the cab when we pull in behind them, Charlie at the wheel.

Two large Agency SUVs pull across the road in front of the truck, blocking it in. Red and blue lights flare into brilliance and two enforcement lems step onto the pavement, arms cocked to hurl six-foot steel javelins through tires or even the engine block.

The truck screeches to a halt. Charlie and I are out of the car in seconds. The thrope on top of the cab freezes, caught red-pawed, but the one still on the freight box tries to make a run for it, leaping toward the rear—and landing directly in front of Charlie.

Charlie lifts one hand to shoulder level. Shows the thrope the shiny silver-coated ball bearing he holds, rolling it slowly around with his thumb and middle finger. Smiles.

"If you run now," Charlie says, "you won't run later. Or ever again."

The thrope reverts to human form, going from hairy predator to a skinny barefoot guy wearing baggy pants and no shirt in seconds. "Hey, this is all a misunderstanding," he says. He's got a wise-guy accent—how about that.

"Yeah, yeah," I say. "That's me, little Miss Understanding. And what you need to understand is that you're under arrest. Get down on the ground with your hands behind your neck."

I walk around to the front of the truck while Charlie cuffs him. The other guy has also decided to be reasonable and has climbed down from the cab, standing in the glare of the truck's headlights with his hands in the air in fully human form. He's wearing baggy cargo shorts with oversize pockets and a warded bandolier, loaded with wooden stakes and silver-edged throwing knives. He looks Latino, with short-cut black hair and a thin mustache. His bare chest has more scars than you usually see on a thrope, too.

He doesn't seem particularly upset at being arrested, staring straight ahead. His eyes have that dead look that means he's disconnected himself from the situation, a trait shared by psychopaths and professional soldiers.

He smells out of place. Foreign. What I'm picking up is probably the result of a different diet from a different culture, suggesting he hasn't been in the country long. But there's more to it than that.

He also smells *dangerous*.

I don't really know how else to describe it. It's something pheromonal that makes the hair on the back of my neck literally stand up. This guy is a killer, about as far from a guy who boosts trucks as a major-league pitcher is from a kid in a sandlot. He doesn't belong here, not by a long shot.

"What's your name?" I ask him.

No answer. His eyes flicker toward me, then back, just enough of a response to acknowledge he's aware of my presence. Nothing else. I try again, and this time I might as well be talking to the truck.

We take the thropes into custody, and when they've been taken away we lock up the driver, too. He looks as frightened as a ten-year-old caught shoplifting, and I know he must be much younger than that. We've got to take him in; he's the weak link, the one most likely to talk.

But I hate myself for doing it.

The lem's name is Billy Beta. He's the sandy color typical of most lems, but under the harsh glare of the fluorescents in the interrogation room it's almost white. He sits in a chair bolted to the floor, hands in his lap, eyes downcast. He looks vaguely ashamed, like a dog that's made a mess on the carpet.

I interview him alone. I start by sitting across the table from him, looking through some papers, not talking. Most people, that'll amp up their antsiness, make them fidget. Lems, of course, are different; they tend to be naturally still, so all Billy does is sit there like a rock.

But I can see the worry in his eyes. And after a few minutes he says, "Can I go home now?"

"No." I pretend to study some more documents. Billy, of course, has no documentation; about the only pieces of paper connecting him to the rest of the world are two forged pieces of ID—union card and driver's license—and the company-issued credit card they gave him for gas. But he isn't necessarily educated enough to even realize he needs anything else.

Lems don't have a childhood, as such. They come into the world fully formed, able to walk and talk and think. They don't know anything about the world around them, but they learn fast. It takes them around two weeks to pick up the basics of civilization, including language—but that's usually two weeks spent doing intensive training in everything from object identification to behavior protocols. Illegal lems are lucky if their creators park them in front of a television and slip in a *Sesame Street* DVD.

What Billy *has* been taught to do is lie.

"Did I do something wrong?" he asks. He doesn't sound like a kid; he sounds like a slightly apologetic, raspy-voiced man in his mid-thirties. I wonder what animal was used to animate him; my files say illegal lem operations often use medium-size animals like sheep or goats.

"Yes, Billy, you did." I give him a long, cold look. "You got caught."

"I'm just a truck driver," he says. I'm sure they made him rehearse that one. He says it again, for emphasis. "I'm just a truck driver."

I'm also sure his creators have hammered home the penalty for being an illegal lem. Billy may not be educated, but that doesn't mean he's stupid; his survival instincts are just as strong as any living being. He's about as close to a true innocent as I'm going to find outside a nursery, and if I do my job the way I'm supposed to he'll be thrown away like a defective appliance.

"Here's the way things are," I say abruptly, putting down my stage dressing. "Your bosses lied to you. They told you that all you had to do was drive the truck, slow down when you got to the overpass, and not resist when the two thropes stole the truck. They told you not to talk to anyone unless you had to. They told you they were the only ones you could trust. *But they lied.*"

He looks at me, opens his mouth, then shuts it again. His jaw clenches. Yeah, I'm leaning toward goat. Or if I'm really unlucky, mule.

"But here's the thing. They don't give a *damn* about you. You're just a tool to them, and when they're done with you they'll—" I stop. *When they're done with you they'll sell you, whereas when* we're *done with you, we'll destroy you.*

I take a deep breath, let it out, then go on. "It's your bosses I'm interested in. The ones who told you what to do, what to say."

"I know what a boss is."

"No, you don't. You know what an *owner* is. All a boss can do is fire you—an owner can do whatever he wants."

"Like kill me?"

"We won't let that happen."

"So *you* own me now?" He's not being sarcastic. It's an honest question.

"No. Listen to me, Billy. Listen to me *very carefully,* okay?" I put as much sincerity as I can into my voice, and he reluctantly nods. "You don't belong to *anyone.* You're a truck driver. You live on your own, at the address on your driver's license. You work for a company called Reliable Trucking. Right?"

So far, he's with me. "Yes. I just drive the truck."

"But the people who own the trucking company are criminals. They tried to get you to break the law. They *threatened* you. So you did exactly what you were supposed to. You did what a *regular citizen* would do."

"I did?"

"Yes. A *regular citizen* would report the crime to the police. The police would arrest the criminals and take them to jail, where they would never bother *regular citizens* again. All the *regular citizens* would be safe."

He thinks about that. "Safe," he says. "No more . . . bosses. But—" He looks troubled. "No more bosses, no more truck. And I—"

"—drive the truck, I know. There are a lot more trucks in the world, Billy. Reliable Trucking doesn't own them all. You'll be able to get another job, and a better place to stay." Because, of course, the address on his license is bogus.

"I'm not sure," he says. "That sounds . . . good. But I'm not like you—I don't know all these things you do. I wouldn't know how—"

"That's okay. I have a friend who can help. He'll get you into a safe house, make sure you're protected. All you have to do is tell him what you know about your *former* bosses."

I stand up and open the door. Charlie walks in. "Hey, kid," he says. "You all right?"

"Yes."

As I step past Charlie into the hall, he whispers, "I thought you were supposed to play the Bad Cop. What are you gonna do now, bake him some cookies?"

"Thought I'd go find some puppies to kick. Also, shut up."

I close the door softly behind me.

He talks to Charlie for a long time. I spend it grilling one of the thropes, the guy with the Jersey accent who tried to bolt. Unsurprisingly, he has nothing to say and demands a lawyer. I keep at it for a while, but he's Mafia to his greasy core, and even facing a ten-year stint in Stanhope doesn't faze him.

I've been saving the Latino thrope for last. Letting his paranoia stew for a while, wondering what I'm getting from the other guy. When I finally walk into the interview room, we've had him for a couple of hours.

He's manacled to the table, but he still manages to look like he's lounging, legs crossed in front of him, body language relaxed. So much for making him nervous. He gives me a slight smile when I sit down.

"Well," I say. "You're something of a mystery, aren't you?"

He meets my eyes, but there's no confrontation in them. Mild curiosity, no more.

"No ID, no prints in the system. Do you even speak English?"

No response.

"Of course, that doesn't mean we don't know who you are. What your friend is saying more than makes up for what you aren't."

His smile gets a little wider. He knows I'm bluffing.

"He's impressed, that's for sure. But then, he's an amateur compared with you. Hell, even *I'm* a little impressed."

The smile shrinks. It's not much of a victory, but I'll take what I can get.

"But only a little. You ex-military types are all the same. Think you're death on two legs because you've had some training and seen some action. Big deal. Anyone can be tough when they've got a whole army behind them."

It's a calculated insult, and it hits home. His eyes get flatter, his smile disappears entirely. Pack loyalty is part of a thrope's genetic makeup; add battlefield camaraderie to that and you've got a big, shiny button with PUSH ME written on it projecting from his forehead.

But I only get to push it once, because right then the door opens and a well-dressed pire steps in. I can smell the lawyer coming off him from across the room. His suit is the deep, smooth black of money with no conscience, and his eyes are about the same. I guess you could call him handsome, if evil were your thing.

"Special Agent Valchek? I'm Mr. Ortega's legal counsel. Here's the necessary forms." He tosses a few sheets of paper down on the table in front of me. "If you'd be so kind as to free my client?"

I pick up the documents and examine them. My prisoner's name is apparently José Ortega, and according to what I'm reading he's to be released immediately. He's a Panamanian national on a diplomatic visa—that's all the information I can glean.

"Hold on," I say. "He's under arrest for armed robbery, and is a suspect in an ongoing investigation into organized crime. You can't just traipse in here and hand him a get-out-of-jail-free card—"

The lawyer pulls out and displays a professional smile. "I'm afraid I don't traipse, Special Agent Valchek. And I don't mind waiting while you verify my paperwork."

"I'll do that," I snap, and stalk out of the room.

But I'm just dragging my feet, and he knows it. Twenty minutes later Ortega is free, and I'm in Cassius's office demanding to know what the hell is going on.

"It's out of my hands," Cassius says. "Political pressure from over my head. Whatever connections Ortega has, they run deep."

"You've got to be *kidding,*" I fume. "Since when does the Mafia have enough clout to jerk around the National Security Agency?"

"Since someone in Washington doesn't want Panama angry at us. Someone who probably owes somebody else a favor. This is politics, Jace; the Gray Wolves are masters at cutting deals and collecting favors, and they just called one in. It happens. The question is, why is this one thrope so important?"

"I don't know. But I'm going to find out."

I meet with Charlie in the break room. He gives me the rundown on what Billy Beta told him.

"It's like this. He's six, maybe seven weeks old. Knows enough to get around in public without drawing attention to himself, answer a few basic questions. Mainly, he knows about driving a truck."

"Yeah, I got that."

"But the thing is, a new lem is like an information sponge. They soak up everything around them really quick and don't forget any of it. They can tell you all kinds of stuff, you just have to know the right questions to ask."

"Oh, the *right* questions. Silly me, I had this whole list of *left* questions I was going to bombard him with."

"Turns out they were using him as a driver on more than just the one run. Most of the time, he was hauling meat in reefer trucks from a meatpacking plant out in Bellingham."

"Yeah? To where?"

"Restaurants, mostly. Including the one our friend Phil Ulzano got whacked in."

I nod. "Makes sense. They've got the workers, might as well put them to work. Probably get higher prices for experienced lems when they sell them off."

"Now, here's the really interesting part. He also made regular runs to the city morgue."

That one stops me short. "The morgue? What the hell for? Jesus, have we stumbled onto some kind of cannibalism ring, too?"

Charlie shakes his head. "I don't think so. Pire corpses aren't edible, they mostly just instantly rot or turn to dust.

Thrope flesh would be instantly identifiable to another thrope—no way you could slip it into a dish without them knowing."

"Sure, but what if that's what they were paying for? That biker gang we dealt with in Alaska were known to eat other thropes."

"Yeah, but those were *zerkers*. Half beast, half drug addict, all outlaw. You can't compare them to ordinary thropes."

I shrug. "Hey, a few days ago I didn't know there were thropes willing to eat *hamsters*. And now—" Now I've developed a craving for deep-fried kangaroo, so anything seems possible.

"Nah, I really doubt it. I know you organic types like to consume all sorts of bizarre flesh products, but cannibalism is really rare. Goes against pack instincts, or so I'm told."

"So why the visits to the morgue?"

It's Charlie's turn to shrug. "Beta said he was dropping crates off, not picking them up. Maybe somebody wanted to give their side of beef a decent burial."

I pause. "Wait. That almost makes sense. A lot of lems are animated by the life force of cattle, right?"

"Sure. Meat goes to the marketplace, soul goes to the lem factory."

"So why aren't lem factories all right next to slaughterhouses?"

"Because they don't have to be. Biothaumaturges collect the life force and store it in temporary containers before transporting it to the factory. Tricky process, though—that's why skilled lem activators are in such high demand."

"Maybe Beta wasn't delivering meat to the morgue—they already have plenty of that. Maybe he was delivering lem juice."

Charlie considers that. "And then it goes from the morgue to the lem factory? They have to be getting the stuff from somewhere."

"Yeah, and what better place than a choose-your-own-live-entrée restaurant? Siphon off the life force, serve up the carcass, ship the extract to the factory."

"But why via the morgue?" Charlie asks.

"I don't know. Equipment, maybe? Good cover for hauling dead things around in crates? Or maybe they just needed another cutout between the two points, like the Mix and Match club for the prostitution ring. Muddy the water in case they're busted."

Charlie tilts his fedora back on his head, something he does when he's thinking hard. "Or maybe they just didn't want a lem driver knowing the whereabouts of a lem-production facility. Old habits, right?"

Right. Lems being able to reproduce is the big buga-boo of thropes and pires alike, some kind of atavistic fear of an unstoppable tide of sandy Frankensteins ava-lanching over the whole world. And considering that not too long ago Charlie and I prevented an evil shaman from using lems to do pretty much that, I can't say their paranoia is entirely unfounded.

I finish my coffee and get to my feet. "Come on. I think it's time we paid a visit to the city morgue."

If there's one thing I know about Tair, it's that he never does anything without his own interests firmly in mind.

So while it might seem like I'm constantly haring off on tangents instead of chasing my primary target, what I'm doing is perfectly logical. I'm following the money. Tair just isn't wired to sign up for a doomed cause; if he's helping the Don run around town killing people, he has very good—and no doubt profitable—reasons for doing so. So far I've uncovered the outlines of a pretty massive operation, one that ranges from international pire trafficking to hijacking to illegal lem production, all of it linked. What I haven't figured out is how Tair thinks he'll come out ahead in this; all he's done so far is to piss off the largest organized crime syndicate in the country and get the NSA hunting him. A lot of money is no doubt changing hands, but I can't see how Tair is planning on getting his paws on any of it.

That's fine. I'll just keep kicking over rocks until I find the one he's hiding under, and then—*sange ucenicie* or not—he's mine.

But in the meantime, I have to go home and walk my dog.

I know, I know, the glamorous life of a crimebuster. Charlie's familiar with my routine and doesn't complain when we stop on the way to the morgue. "I'm in no hurry," he says as he pulls up to the curb in front of my apartment building. "Everybody gets there eventually."

"Wow. Philosophical *and* morbid. You're a real ray of sunshine today."

"Just go get the damn dog," he growls.

So I do—but I run into Xandra outside, pressing my button impatiently. "Hey, X, what's up?" I say.

"You were supposed to meet me here?" she says, doing that teenage thing where she asks a question and accuses you at the same time.

"Oh. Right. We have that movie deal tonight. Well, the problem is—"

"You're working. Still."

I give her a hapless shrug. "Sorry. The case is heating up. This is just a pit stop to go drain Gally's bladder, and then I have to take off again. But tell you what—why don't you come on in and start without me? You can hang out with Gally, watch one of the movies, gorge yourself on junk food—I *know* that backpack isn't stuffed with homework."

I also know this is pretty much an irresistible offer, since half the reason Xandra hangs out with me is to get out of her own house. Not that there's anything wrong with where she lives; it's just a teenage thing, the desire for independence, for a place where you don't have to follow someone else's rules.

I have rules, too, of course. But mine tend to be the *Don't drink my scotch, don't let Gally eat anything that will kill him, don't tell your folks all the stuff I let you get away with* type of thing. Not quite independence, but close enough to provide a comforting illusion. And, of course, I have the convenient habit of abruptly leaving her alone for hours on end. I can see her mentally calculating which of her friends she can invite over and then kick out before I get back.

"Yeah, okay," she says. I unlock the door and we go in.

That's when my phone starts to ring.

NINETEEN

I glance at my phone's screen and see that it's Gretch. "Hey, Gretch."

"Jace. I have some . . . sensitive information for you. It's best if we talk face-to-face."

I follow Xandra to the elevator, get on with her. "I'm at home right now. Charlie and I are on our way to the morgue after I walk the dog."

"On your way to the morgue after you walk the dog? That sounds like a euphemism for something unspeakably obscene."

I chuckle. "Well, it's not. Can it wait until we get back?"

"Certainly. But I'm actually very close to you—why don't I just drop in and we can have a quick chat? Won't take but a moment."

I frown, glancing at Xandra. The two of them aren't a great mix, and I'm only going to be here for a few minutes. Well, maybe a little longer—my stomach's starting to growl again. "I don't know if that's such a good—"

"Fine, I'll see you in a few minutes." She hangs up.

I stare at my phone for a second before I put it away. "Now, *that* was weird," I mutter.

"What was?"

The doors open and we step out. "Gretch," I say. "First that joke, then insisting she come over. Something's not right."

Xandra gives me a roll of her eyes so pronounced I can practically hear them spinning in their sockets. "*That's* for sure. Maybe that stake up her ass punctured something vital."

Have I mentioned Xandra and Gretch don't get along? "Be nice," I say. "Gretch does a job that would turn most people's brains to mushroom soup and their souls to hard little chunks of coal." I pause. *Mmm. Mushroom soup . . .*

I unlock my door and step inside. Gally's already there, barking excitedly; the sun isn't down yet, so he's still in dog form.

I'm a little worried about Gretch, actually. This isn't the first time she's seemed a bit off, and she *was* one of the very first people affected by the Ghatanothoa footage. Delayed onset of symptoms is entirely plausible, too.

"Uh, how would you feel about taking Gally for his walk?" I ask. "Gretch and I have to discuss some work issues. I'd really appreciate it."

She sighs. "Yeah, sure. C'mon, Gally—we know when we're not wanted."

Gally gives her a bright-eyed, panting look that says, *Not wanted? I don't know what that means. Does it mean baloney? Will there be baloney? Baloney is my friend.*

She grabs the leash and slips out, pouting. I call down to Charlie to let him know what's going on and that I'll be a few minutes more. He says he'll stay where he is.

Gretch shows up a few minutes later. I buzz her up

and go back to making what started as a quick snack and mutated into some sort of epic sandwich too large to fit into my mouth.

I let Gretch in when she knocks, a squeeze bottle of mustard in one hand and a jar of pickles tucked under my arm. "Hey," I say. "What's going on? You sounded a little—"

"I didn't want to be too forthcoming over the mobile. Jace, it appears you've stumbled onto something much bigger than we thought."

I put down the mustard and open the jar of pickles. The whiff of dill and vinegar that wafts out is overpowering, so I put the lid back on. "You're talking about the guy from Panama?"

"Yes. It seems our investigation has stirred up things on not just a local level, but also an international one. Are you aware of the South American lem trade?"

I open the jar of pickles again. Still overpowering. I close it. "Not really."

"Panama is a hub. It's where many illegal lems are shipped to, and from. Nasty place. The Gray Wolves do a lot of business with them, and it looks like they've imported some help."

I open the jar again, hold my breath, and dive for a pickle. Success. I yank it out, close the jar, and rinse the pickle under some tap water. "Okay, I'm with you. Paramilitary, right? A merc to deal with their Don problem?"

"That's what I thought. But I have a contact at the CIA who's just told me something far more troubling." She pauses, eyeing my sandwich. "Good Lord. Are you really going to attempt to *eat* that? It looks as if it were constructed over several years by Egyptian slaves."

"It's a work in progress." I cut the pickle into long slices and balance them on top of what I've already got, then add a slab of smoked cheddar. "So what's your fellow spook have to say?"

"Two things. First, that someone very high up is pulling strings to get us to walk away from the investigation— the lem part of it especially. Second—our Panamanian friend isn't alone."

I slather some mayo on a piece of bread. "Meaning what, exactly?"

"He came into the country with twenty others. A squad."

I frown. "Huh. That seems excessive. Even if the Don is a real badass—and so far he seems to be— twenty-one guys is overkill. Something else must be going on."

"Indeed. My contact couldn't say anything more, but he hinted strongly that we should be very careful about political ramifications—both local *and* federal."

I regard the sandwich with a mixture of pride and fear. "So our upcoming trip to the city morgue should be as low-key as possible."

"I'd advise keeping it under the radar, yes."

The buzzer sounds. Xandra's back already? I figured she was good for twenty minutes, at least. I let her into the building, then turn back to Gretch. "Okay, so what's your take on this? Who wants us to back off, and why?"

Gretch taps one elegant red fingernail against her chin as she thinks. "I would say that *La Lupo Grigorio* are trying to protect their investment in the lem trade. A good way to protect an investment is to buy insurance— which in this case would be someone with political access."

Sure. The best way to win friends and influence people is with cold, hard cash, and the Gray Wolves have plenty of that. Their shopping list generally contains members of the legal profession, from cops to prosecutors to federal judges—and sometimes even higher.

"So the Wolves own someone and we're getting a little too close for comfort," I say. "Any idea who it might be?"

Gretch shakes her head just as Xandra knocks on the door. I open it and she and Gally saunter in. "Hey," she says. "Forgot to bring a plastic bag for his you-know."

"Hello, Xandra," Gretch says.

"Hey," Xandra says. Her voice is neutral, but Gally knows better. He whines, which I translate to *Uh-oh. The you-know is about to hit the fan.*

"I love dogs," Xandra says, rummaging in a drawer for a plastic bag, "but man, can they *poop*." She glances over at Gretch. "Whoops, I'm sorry. I probably shouldn't say things like that around you."

Gretch frowns. "And why is that?"

"Well, you know. It must be a century or so since you've cleaned out the old colon."

Time stops. Okay, it doesn't really, but a few glaciers mosey through the kitchen while I'm processing what Xandra just said. Hoo, boy. I think my apartment just went to Defcon One. Or Two, or Zero, or whatever number is really bad and implies imminent global destruction.

Gretch smiles, ever so slightly. Butter wouldn't melt in her mouth, but you could cut glass with what's coming out of her eyes. "A hundred and twelve years, five months, seventeen days. But if I ever have another bowel movement, I shall be sure to think of you."

"Uh, speaking of which, Gally looks like he has to go pretty bad," I interject. "We should—"

"I've always wondered about that," Xandra says. Her voice is light, but I know aggression when I hear it. "Is there, like, some kind of final purge? Or does that last steak-and-kidney pie just sort of sit there for the rest of eternity and *rot*?"

"Good question," I say. "We'll get back to you on that—"

"There's something I've always wondered about, too," Gretch says. Her voice is like silk. "When you're at home, do you use glasses and cups, or simply drink from the toilet?"

"Have you ever *seen* a sandwich *this big*?" I blurt desperately. "I mean, *wow,* look at the *size* of this thing! It's ginormous! It's huge-mongous! It's . . ." I falter as they both ignore me completely and stare at each other like two samurai waiting for the other one to make his move. ". . . it's gonna wind up all over this kitchen," I say wearily.

"Why don't you run along?" Gretch tells Xandra. "The adults would like to talk."

"I'll leave when I feel like it."

"Am I going to have to strike you on the nose with a rolled-up newspaper?"

I step between them and open the silverware drawer to get a knife and fork. "'Scuze me. Rescue mission. Probably hopeless, but I gotta try." I sit back down at the table and carve off a mouthful, then sit back and chew. Might as well enjoy the show.

"You don't intimidate me, Gretch. I know all you pires think thropes are just hairy, disgusting animals, but I'm *proud* of what I am."

"And what would *that* be, besides a rude and ignorant child?"

"I'm Jace's friend!"

"This sandwich is *really* good."

"I'm her friend, too. But I don't attack her *other* friends out of spite."

"I was worried about the sauerkraut. It was a gamble. But I think, in the end, the risk paid off."

"No, all *you* do is pass judgment on everyone you know! Well, what are you going to do *now,* huh? *Jace is gonna be one of us!*"

Silence.

"Ah," I say. "So *that's*—"

"I wouldn't be so sure," Gretch says.

"What do you mean?"

"She's being treated. She may not become a thrope at all."

"What?" Xandra looks at me, stunned. "No. That's impossible. Nobody can do that."

"My mistake. I'm sure you're *much* better informed than a national agency full of the most experienced and powerful shamans in the world. Isn't that right, Jace?"

I manage a weak smile. "Well, she is pretty bright."

The look on Xandra's face is equal parts disbelief and betrayal. "What's she *talking* about, Jace?"

"It's . . . experimental," I say. "It's a treatment using pire blood as a kind of antibody serum for the thrope bite. It's not guaranteed."

"Pire blood? So you might become one of *them*?"

Okay, *that* was the wrong thing to say . . . "Look on the bright side. It might just kill me instead."

"I can't believe this. You'd risk *dying* instead of becoming like *me*?"

Never underestimate the teenage capacity for melodrama, or for making any crisis all about them. I love Xandra dearly, and she's usually very levelheaded—but she's still a high schooler, surfing those stormy teenage hormone waves and trying to figure out most of life for the very first time. I can't blame her for feeling like I've stabbed her in the back. "Hey, give me a little credit, okay? This isn't about becoming a thrope, or a pire. This is about me trying to stay *me,* all right? I didn't choose to get infected."

"*Infected?* Is that how you think of it?"

Oh, well done, Jace. *Excellent* use of exactly the right term.

"This is becoming extremely tiresome," Gretch says. "If you're the friend you say you are, you should care about what's best for Jace."

"What, and you think risking her *life* makes the most sense?"

"She's an officer of the law, Alexandra. She risks her life every day."

Xandra glares at Gretch. I notice that her fingernails seem to have gotten a lot longer in the last minute, and her eyes are starting to take on a yellow tint. Not that Xandra could take Gretch in a fight, but a scrap between them could break something—like my entire apartment. "Let's just calm down, all right? Everybody take a deep breath—"

"Gretch doesn't breathe, Jace? Remember? Or eat, or use the bathroom, or any of that other messy stuff us *living* people do. You really want to be like *her*?"

What I really want is to eat my sandwich, but I can't say that without giving Xandra more ammunition for her argument—not that she seems to need any extra. She hasn't even pulled out her big gun yet—

"I thought you wanted to *help* Uncle Pete."

Uh-oh. *Blam.*

"How is this not helping—"

"If you were a thrope, you *know* you could bring him back."

Gretch gives her head an exasperated shake. "That's absurd. Jace's condition has nothing to do with your uncle's."

"You don't know everything! You didn't know about the *sange ucenicie!*"

"The link is irrelevant. The ceremony to eliminate the Tair persona didn't work. Your uncle is *gone,* and he isn't coming back. Jace becoming a thrope won't change that."

Even for Gretch, that's cold; Xandra must have really pissed her off. Xandra just stares at her, breathing a little too hard, her upper lip twitching into the beginnings of a snarl.

Gretch crosses her arms. "Jace and I have more important things to do than indulge in childish agonizing. Let's make this simple. We both know this is going to end with you making a dramatic exit—shouting or crying or both—so let's get on with it, shall we? Have your tantrum, storm out, and let us get back to work."

And that, oddly enough, seems to cool Xandra right off. Which could have been exactly what Gretch wanted.

"I told you, I'm not a child," Xandra says. "I'm just someone with something called a heart. If you can still remember what that is." And then she turns around and leaves without another word, taking Gally with her. She doesn't even slam the door.

"Hoooo, boy," I say. "That could have gone better."

"I apologize. That was unprofessional of me."

"No, it was *very* professional of you. If, you know, your profession was character assassination."

"She needs to recognize reality."

"No, she needs to be exactly what she is. And right now, that means confused, angry, sad, hopeful, and just a little irrational. You know—a teenager."

"Fair enough. And what about you?"

Good question. What do I want to be when I grow up? Or grow fangs? "Damned if I know. Probably damned if I don't, too. Hey, what's the official position on that, anyway? Do all good thropes go to heaven? Are pires still eligible for a halo and a pair of batwings?"

Gretch smiles. "Depends on who you ask. The Catholic Church recognized thropes as part of God's creation centuries ago, but it took longer for them to admit pires might have souls, too."

I hew off another chunk of sandwich. "Yeah? What finally convinced them?"

"Empirical evidence. Animist magic relies on the spirits that reside inside most things, and it responds to pires as well as it does rocks. Defending the proposition that a boulder had a soul while an intelligent and principled being did not proved virtually impossible and was abandoned by religious scholars long ago."

"Well, that's a hypothetical weight off my chest. How about afterlives? What do I have to look forward to?"

"Opinions vary."

"Well, what are you gonna do? Life's a bitch and then you die and then yadda yadda something something. Or not."

"Succinctly put."

"Can't talk anymore. Eating."

"For what it's worth, I hope your treatment provides the desired results."

"The concept of an immortal me scares you, too, huh?"

"More than I can express."

"Well, thanks for dropping by. Anything else I can do for you? Let you set my dog on fire, maybe?"

"I'll see you back at the office."

"Mmmpph. Diz uh *guh* sanwish."

After I demolish my own creation—and yes, I eat the whole thing—I get a call from Charlie telling me that Xandra spotted him in the car and abandoned Gally with him. "She seemed upset," he tells me.

"No kidding. I'll be right down—I just talked to Gretch and she's got some new information."

I bring Charlie up to speed as I take Gally to finally do his business. "So we're on the right track," I say.

"Yeah. Right between the rails with a freight train coming."

"You want to back off?"

He chuckles. "Hell, no. Last argument I got into with a big chunk of moving metal was the first decent scrap I've had in years."

It takes me a moment to realize he's talking about the time I shot him. "Excuse me? I almost wound up catatonic after that, and now you're saying you *enjoyed* it?"

"Enjoyed would be going a little far. It was . . . challenging."

"I can't believe this." I shake my head. "You think you know your partner . . . Well, at least now I know what to get you for Christmas. I'll just hit you over the head with a shovel a few times."

"Better get someone else to do it. You can barely press two hundred pounds."

"Maybe I'll use a pickax, instead. Or should I save that for a special occasion, like the birthday of the guy who invented duct tape?"

Charlie shrugs. "Nah. I like to spend that with my folks."

"All right, to the morgue we go. Remember what Gretch said: We have to tread lightly. If this is political, the people involved will be extremely jumpy. As soon as we make our presence known, they'll be destroying evidence and trying to distance themselves."

"Sounds like a good argument for going in heavy to me."

I think about that for a second. "You know, you're right. Screw it, let's hit 'em with everything we got."

"I hear you've got a shovel."

"Quiet. You'll ruin the surprise."

We park in the lot for the King County medical examiner's office, better known as the city morgue; long black vehicles flank us on either side, meat wagons for the coroner. The morgue deals with suspicious deaths for the city of Seattle and King County and employs around two dozen people, who handle everything from violent homicides to unclaimed bodies. The building looks like an old factory, made of whitewashed brick and several stories tall with an enormous smokestack looming over it. On-site crematorium, of course. We get out and locate the employees' entrance, a gray metal door with a small sign over it and a battered intercom. I hit the buzzer and somebody lets us in without talking to us.

"Terrific security," I say. I yank open the door, and we step inside.

My breath catches in my throat and my heartbeat stutters. The place is chilly and damp and smells of formaldehyde, but that's nothing new; I've been in morgues before.

But this is the first time I've ever smelled death.

I don't mean decomp. That's repulsive, but it's really just decaying packaging. Rotting plants can stink just as bad as rotting flesh. No, what I'm talking about is death *itself*. The presence of absence. The impression that something whose only reason for existing is to oppose life is nearby . . .

"Jace? You okay?"

"Do you smell that?"

He sniffs the air. "Disinfectant?"

"Never mind."

We walk up to a bored-looking security guard, who checks our ID and then goes back to his magazine. I'm going to ask him for directions to the coroner's office, then decide against it; sometimes you can find out more by just wandering around and poking your nose into things than by following protocol. So I just march off like I know where I'm going, with Charlie at my side.

It's a big, spooky place. Long hallways, lots of doors, walls covered with so many layers of gray industrial paint they seem like geological formations. Doorknobs made of brass that probably date back to the 1920s. Overhead globe lights with drifts of dead bugs at the bottom, tiny graveyard eclipses at the fixtures' south poles. The air is cold and still.

"You have a plan?" Charlie asks. "Or are we just gonna jump the first guy we see?"

"Thought we'd look around a little, get a feel for the place. Then we go knock on the coroner's door and see what we can dig up."

"See, I *knew* you had a shovel."

"Shut up."

The hallways are all deserted. Maybe everybody's taking their coffin break at the same time. We find a stairwell and take the flight going down; there are always more interesting things in the basement.

The drop in temperature as well as altitude tells me that the bottom floor is where they actually store the cadavers. More hallways, more doors, with signs painted in gold script over pebbled glass: AUTOPSY ROOM ONE and X-RAY ROOM and FORENSIC PROCESSING.

And then I smell it.

Not death—that's still present, but by now has become a kind of constant background scent, like the subliminal hum of a machine. No, this is a scent I recognize, though I can't quite place it. My brain associates it with other smells: tequila, sweat, makeup, and . . . gunpowder?

It's strongest right outside FORENSIC PROCESSING, so

I grab the knob and open the door. There's a young woman in a lab coat with long dark hair pulled back in a ponytail sitting on a stool, who looks up from the bone she was peering at on the stainless-steel table before her. She recognizes us as soon as we walk in, though she tries to hide it. "Yes?" she says.

"I'll have a scotch on the rocks," I say. "My partner will just stick with the rocks." I give her a mock frown. "Whoops. Sorry, for a second there I was confused about where I was. This is your *day* job, not your night gig."

The woman looks at me with resignation in her eyes. Her nameplate reads FARADAY, but I know her better as my friendly neighborhood bartender.

The one from the Mix and Match.

TWENTY

She doesn't bother trying to deny it. "Yeah, I have another job. So what?"

"So your other job is working for a mobster named Iggy Prinzini."

"I don't work for him. He just owns the bar."

I give her a second to realize how stupid that sounds, and let her try to fix it. "I mean, I guess technically he's my superior, but I don't work *for* him. I don't—whatever else he does, I'm not connected to any of that. I'm just a bartender."

I nod. "Sure. Hey, that sounds kind of familiar, doesn't it, Charlie?"

"What, *I'm just a bartender*? Yeah, sort of. That's not quite it, though."

"No. It was more like, *I just something something.*"

"I just pass the buck?"

"No . . ."

"I just walk the duck?"

"Not quite."

Charlie taps his forehead with one shiny black finger. "I got it. *I just drive the truck.*"

Faraday goes just a touch paler. Her heart rate accelerates. She *smells* scared.

"That was it," I say. "*I just drive the truck.* Where did we hear that, Charlie?"

"From that lem we busted. You know, the one working for Iggy Prinzini."

Faraday looks trapped. Her eyes dart right, then left. No place to go.

"Funny kind of coincidence," I say. "See, this lem had two jobs, too, and *both* of them involved working for Iggy. How about you?"

"Am I under arrest?"

"Do you want to be?"

She swallows. "No."

"Good, then pay attention—there *will* be a test later. Now, where was I . . ."

"Two jobs," Charlie says.

"Right. And one of these jobs, Ms. Faraday, you and a certain truck-driving lem did together. He dropped things off, and you picked them up. Right here, in this building."

She doesn't admit it, but she doesn't deny it, either.

"Now here's the interesting part. Doing one job for a guy like Iggy can be explained a number of different ways. Maybe you were threatened, maybe you didn't know what was really going on, maybe you planned to go to the cops. Doing two jobs, though—that opens you up to charges of conspiracy. Makes you look like you were in on planning the whole thing. A good prosecutor can really rip you a new one with information like that."

"But—but all I did was pour drinks!"

I shake my head. "All Billy Beta did was drive a truck. But he knew what was going on, what he was part of. And so did you."

"Okay, so I knew something was going on upstairs.

Some kind of gambling deal. But what was I supposed to do? This is the *Mob,* okay? I say anything and I wind up *on* a table in here, instead of beside one."

She seems like she's telling the truth, which is definitely a point in her favor. Maybe she is; maybe she had no idea about the prostitution ring and honestly thought all Iggy had going on was a betting parlor. It makes a certain amount of sense—for a really good cover, you need some people on the inside to believe it, too.

"Let's say you're telling the truth. If you were only truly involved in one operation—*this* one—it would go a lot better for you. But do *not* try to convince me that you were working for Iggy at two different locations and didn't know the score at *either* of them. That would be like calling me a moron, and I get enough of that from my partner."

"I mean it in a loving way," Charlie growls.

"So Billy Beta delivered the crates, and you received them. That much we know. But we're a little sketchy on details about what happened after that. If you want to help yourself, a little information about the next step in the process would go a long way."

She looks around the room, as if there were something on the shelves or lying on a stainless-steel counter that could help her. No luck. She looks back at me, thinking so hard I can almost hear it.

I hold up one finger as she opens her mouth. "Before you say anything," I add pleasantly, "I should clarify. *A little sketchy on details* means we know *some* things for sure, there are a few things we're *not* sure about, and a couple more that we're guessing on. But here's the important part. If you lie to me about something we know for *sure*? That's your first, second, and third strike. You don't get any more chances to play me. You're *done.* Okay?"

Her mouth closes. She nods. Whatever spin she was about to put on the truth, I just smacked it down into the dirt. She doesn't know what to do next, but I sense she's a little too scared to gamble. She's either going to lawyer up, keep her mouth zipped, and hope the Gray Wolves don't kill her anyway, or tell me what she knows and hope I can protect her.

Her eyes flicker from me to Charlie and back again. This time I notice something off about it; it's not that she's looking *for* something, it's more like she's trying *not* to look at something. And the one place she's very carefully not looking is right in front of her.

I glance at the bone on the table. Too long and heavy to be human. Cow, maybe?

"Hey, Charlie?" I say. "What's the best kind of medium for storing golem life force?"

"Astral plasma. It's like a super-condensed, mystically enhanced kind of blood. Highly unstable, needs constant attention from a biothaumaturge or it'll degrade."

"And what do they store this astral plasma *in*?"

"Trees, mostly. Specially grown ones with hollowed-out storage space—you need a dense but living container to embed all the protective wards in or the life force will just kind of bleed away."

I lean down and peer at the end of the bone. It's got what appears to be a large hole drilled in it, a hole I'd guess goes almost all the way to the end. "How about a nice, dense bone that *used* to be alive? Think that might work?"

Charlie considers it. "It might. Probably leak a whole bunch and wouldn't last that long, but you could use it for a few hours."

"Long enough to transport it from a restaurant to a lem factory, I'll bet." I straighten up. "But you'd need a professional to put together the right kinds of wards—

someone with training, and access to equipment. Right, Ms. Faraday?"

She looks subdued now, but she doesn't answer. Not good. I've got her, but I need more than a prisoner. I need a willing source of information.

I look around the room. Lots of shelves, lots of equipment, the usual weird assortment of science and sorcery: an autoclave, a comparison microscope, a Shinto shrine with several ashen cones of burnt incense in front of it, a stack of reference books that range from the mystic to the technical. Also a waist-high, glass-doored fridge with a can of Beefy Fizz and a paper bag visible inside—her lunch, no doubt. There's a paperback lying on top of the fridge, with the shiny, solid appearance of a brand-new purchase. *Wolf's Eye,* by Margaret Atwood. I'm guessing that on Thropirelem, Atwood's a thrope, but I'm going to go out on a limb and assume she's also still as much a feminist here as she is on my world. And that, finally, gives me the lever I need to tip Faraday in the right direction.

"You know what?" I say. "I believe you—about the bar, I mean. Not that you were completely innocent— you're obviously not stupid, you must have known *something* was going on—but I don't think you knew what was actually happening. You weren't part of it."

"I wasn't. I really wasn't."

"I mean, you didn't have any *reason* to suspect it was anything other than a bookie joint, right? You knew Iggy was a player, so it made sense that there were all those women around. Kind of strange, though—a lot of them were pires, and you never saw the boss with one of those. They were just *around*."

"We had a lot of regulars," she says, but I can hear that little note of self-doubt in her voice. I'm not the one she's trying to convince.

"Sure. Regulars who never stuck around long. Regulars who never seemed to buy a drink, regulars who just sort of drifted through and back again. Kind of strange how they just seemed to always be *there,* right?"

She frowns. Her eyes wander up and to the left as she accesses a memory. "I'm not—what are you saying?"

"Did you ever notice that they seemed to arrive without walking through the front door? Or sometimes the other way around, that they came in through the front and then vanished? I mean, I know the place gets busy, but you're an observant person, right? If I'd picked up on that, even subliminally, it would have bugged the hell out of me. I would have tried to convince myself that I was imagining things. I would have resolved to keep my eye on one of them and *prove* that I was wrong."

And there it is in her eyes. A flash of guilt, followed by a quick suppression of panic.

"You *did,* didn't you? You picked one out, you kept track of her, and then she just sort of disappeared, didn't she? How'd you explain that to yourself?"

"I—it's a busy place. I can't keep track of everyone." Not quite a denial, more like a justification.

"But you can keep track of who's coming through the front door. And even though you were sure she never used it, somehow she was back in the club again."

"What's this have to do with—with anything?"

"There's no bookie joint upstairs, Ms. Faraday. That was a cover, too. What Iggy was running was a pire trafficking operation, smuggling illegal female immigrants into the country and putting them to work as prostitutes. There's a tunnel between the Mix and Match and the basement of the burned-out tenement across the alley, and it was full of women in cages. *That's* what you were helping Iggy hide."

Her eyes widen. She doesn't want to believe it. "Yeah, sure." She gives a shaky little laugh. "And he was the one who killed JFK with a silver bullet, too, right?"

I grab her arm and yank her off the stool and onto her feet. "Hey!"

"Let's go," I say. I march her out the door, my hand on her elbow.

"Are you arresting me?"

"Probably. But first, we're going to do a little show-and-tell."

I'm half convinced that it won't be there anymore, that Iggy will have removed any and all incriminating evidence. Turns out I'm also half right: All the clothes and other supplies are gone.

But the cages are still there.

The acrid stench of bleach hangs in the air, stinging our eyes. I show Faraday the tunnel, but she's barely paying attention by then—she keeps looking over her shoulder at the long, cell-filled room.

"Satisfied?" I ask. "Or are you one of those paranoid types that think the government builds stuff like this to con innocent civilians?"

"Oh, my God," she says. She looks so horrified I almost feel guilty. "I didn't know. I didn't—"

"What's your name, Faraday?"

She looks at me like I just asked her to do some kind of complex equation in her head. "Crystal. Faraday."

"Yeah, I got the second part myself. Look, Crystal— maybe you didn't know exactly what was happening, but you knew *something* was. Right?"

She clutches her arms around herself tightly and nods. She looks like she might be about to burst into tears.

"And you didn't do anything about it. You're going to

have to live with that—but today's your lucky day, because I'm going to give you the best shot you'll ever have at making peace with this. You really feel bad?"

Tears start rolling down her face. "You have no idea," she chokes out.

"Then let's sit down and have a conversation. And at the end of it, I promise you, I'll tell you something that will make you feel a whole lot better. All right?"

"All—all right."

"Let's go."

She stops halfway down the long room of cages. "Can I have a moment, please?"

I nod.

Crystal Faraday hugs herself a little tighter. She looks from one side of the room to the other. Forcing herself to take in every little detail. Not denying anything, not any longer. She doesn't flinch, or hurry. She didn't want to know about any of this, but now that she does, she's not going to let herself forget. No matter how much it hurts.

It takes her a full minute. At the end of that time, I have a great deal more respect for Crystal Faraday than I did before.

"Okay," she says quietly, wiping her face with the back of one hand. "Now we can go."

Charlie and I don't take her downtown. We take her to this little out-of-the-way diner I know about, where they serve shoestring fries with jalapeño mayo to dip them in and a decent cup of coffee. We put her on one side of the booth and me and Charlie on the other; I don't want her to feel trapped. She doesn't order anything except a glass of water, and I think she's feeling more than a little nauseous.

"I wasn't always a bartender at the Mix and Match,"

Crystal says. She's left her lab coat in the car, and she's wearing jeans and some sort of faded orange T-shirt with a cartoon character on it. "I used to just go there. I was a regular, I guess."

I nod. Not that surprising; bars that specialize in alternative lifestyles tend to hire from within their own community.

"Anyway, I only work part-time at the morgue, and I'm going to school, too. I needed some extra cash."

"Iggy offered you a job?" I ask.

"No, I didn't meet him for months. This was another bartender; he just mentioned they needed some help. I said sure, why not? I was there all the time already."

She gives her head the tiniest shake, as if she's denying something to herself. "You have to understand. I'm studying to be a biothaumaturge."

"Tuition's expensive, I know."

"No, that's not it. My family has money, school is taken care of. I work because—well, whatever I make bartending is *my* money. I earn it, and that means a lot to me. The morgue is mostly for study credit."

"Two jobs and school. Doesn't leave a lot of time for anything else."

She shrugs. "Like I said, if I wasn't working there I'd be hanging out there anyway—the bar, not the morgue. Might as well get paid for it, right?"

"Makes sense."

"What you have to understand is that people in the crosskink community are very secretive. A lot of people don't use their real names, a lot of people never show you the face the rest of the world sees."

"So they're paranoid."

"Paranoia is when you think people are out to get you when nobody is. I wish that were the case, but it's not. We're discriminated against, we're attacked. People call us race traitors. If my family knew about me, they'd never speak to me again."

"So you weren't just afraid of the Gray Wolves—you were afraid of being outed."

"Yeah. I don't know how he found out, but when Iggy learned about my other job and what I was studying, he made me an offer. Only it wasn't really an offer, it was a threat."

I fork some fries into my mouth as I listen. It might be rude, but I'm starving again.

"The morgue has very finely calibrated equipment for draining, storing, and measuring residual life force for forensic purposes. Iggy figured I could repurpose it, use the same technology to make temporary containers for transporting lem energy."

"Bone batteries," Charlie says.

"Essentially. I'd get a delivery of bones once a week, use the equipment to prep them whenever we hit a slow period and no one was around. I didn't charge them, that was done somewhere else—I just got them ready."

I hold up a hand, finish chewing, and swallow before speaking. "Hang on. Beta said all he did was drop stuff off. Once you'd gotten the bones ready, how'd they get off-site?"

"In the garbage. I'd wrap them up and throw them out—somebody would retrieve them after that."

"Don't you have an on-site incinerator?"

"No, just a dedicated crematorium for actual bodies. Everything else is handled by a medical waste disposal company called Envirocrypt."

I glance at Charlie. What passes for his eyebrows go up, just a notch.

"Envirocrypt," I say. "A private garbage collection agency and the Mob—what a shocking and *entirely* unusual juxtaposition of bedfellows."

"Excuse me?"

Charlie grunts. "You'll have to forgive her. Vital information makes her mouthy."

I wipe my lips with a paper napkin. "I think you mean verbose."

"I know what I said."

We wind up Crystal's interview and then see about getting her into protective custody. Things are starting to speed up, I can feel it—or maybe it's just my overcharged primal instincts, informing me that the prey is in sight and the kill is only minutes away. I call Gretch and tell her to get me whatever she can on Envirocrypt; she calls me back only minutes later, as Charlie and I are handing our new informant off to two agents at a safe house. Crystal looks nervous, but not sorry—she's made her choice and plans to stand by it.

"Let me guess, Gretch—Envirocrypt is owned by someone with an Italian last name."

She sounds mildly puzzled. "Sorry to disappoint you, but that's not the case at all. Envirocrypt is a highly respected company that handles all the government contracts in Washington and has branches in several neighboring states. They *are* a family business, but the family in question is hardly one known for its criminal affiliations. Are you familiar with the name Broadstone?"

"Can't say that I am."

"Old money, old in the pire sense. Very rich, very well connected. One of them's a congressman—in fact, that's who's listed as the principal shareholder and CEO of Envirocrypt. Emerson Hearst Broadstone."

This is starting to make sense, and I know Gretch is sharp enough to see it, too. Her dismissive tone is camouflage in case anyone else is listening. Crystal's words come back to me: *Paranoia is when you think people are out to get you when nobody is. I wish that were the case, but it's not.* "Looks like I got it wrong. Thanks, Gretch—we'll talk soon, okay?"

"Absolutely," she says, and hangs up.

A congressman. One with deep pockets and deeper connections. One who's obviously in business with the Mob, knows I'm investigating him, and isn't happy about it. At least now I know who's pulling the strings, though linking Broadstone with the Gray Wolves is going to be difficult at best. He'll have multiple layers of flunkies between himself and whoever's making the actual pick-ups from the morgue—probably lem truck drivers who will simply disappear. I need more ammunition if I'm going to go after this guy, more hard evidence.

What I have at the moment is a bone. Fortunately, I also have someone who might be able to turn that into something a little more useful.

I plunk the bone in its plastic evidence bag down on Eisfanger's steel table and say, "Got something for you."

Eisfanger pulls on a pair of gloves. "You bring me the nicest things," he says cheerfully. "Looks bovine. You hunting cattle rustlers now?"

"It was going to be used as a temporary battery for lem life force. Charlie's hauling a crateful of others just like it down to the evidence locker as we speak."

His ice-blue eyes widen with interest. "Really? Now, that *is* interesting . . . organic-sourced calcium as a mystical substrate instead of living wood. Warding would be tricky—not to mention unstable—and it wouldn't be nearly as energy-efficient—"

"Strictly short-term and leaky as hell, I know. What I need is any other information you can pull from it."

He eyes it thoughtfully, scratching one ruddy cheek with a pale, stubby fingernail. "I'll see what I can do."

He goes over to a rolling steel cabinet, opens a wide, thin drawer, and considers the interior. "Are you looking for anything in particular, or just going on a forensic fishing mission?"

I pull up a rolling stool and straddle it. "I'm not sure. Would finding the fingerprints of a prominent congressman be expecting too much?"

He makes a decision and selects an instrument, a wishbone inscribed with tiny, intricate *kanji* symbols in scarlet and a miniature steel cylinder projecting straight up from the head. "I *will* dust it for prints, but I sense you're being ironic."

"You won't find any prints—not obvious ones, anyway. The person who gave it to me has forensics training."

Eisfanger places the wishbone on the table and opens another drawer. Pulls out a twelve-inch length of very thin but stiff wire, with an eyelet at one end and a tiny screw at the other. He screws the wire into the wishbone's cylinder with a thumb and forefinger. "Then we're unlikely to find any trace or transfer. But that's okay; the essential nature of the bone itself may give something up."

I sigh. "Like what? A fondness for grass? A lifelong relationship with a milking machine?"

He takes a third item, a small glass vial, from a shelf. He pops it open and dumps the contents into his hand: a six-inch length of crimson thread with a tiny bead at the end. He ties the thread to the eyelet at the end of the wire, giving him something that looks a little like a miniature fishing rod with a Y-shaped handle.

"I'm hoping for something both more and less specific." He takes a long tube down from another shelf, and pulls out a rolled-up length of parchment. Once it's unfurled I can see that it's a map of the United States; Eisfanger places small paperweights at each corner to hold it down. "Cattle aren't generally big travelers; dairy or beef, they usually spend most of their lives on one range. That gives them a real geographic affinity for the place."

He takes the bone out of the evidence bag and places it on the table beside the map, then strips off his gloves. Holding the wishbone between the thumb and forefinger of one hand, he lowers the dangling bead into contact with the bone and starts muttering an incantation. Animist magic is mostly based on either Shinto or African shamanism; what's coming out of Eisfanger's mouth sounds more like Swahili than Japanese.

After a minute, he raises the bead, then moves it over the map. It sways gently back and forth, then seems to tug south and west. Eisfanger lets it guide him over the Virginias, the Carolinas, Georgia, Florida . . . and right off the edge of the map.

"Huh," he says. "Our cow isn't local."

He grabs another map and tries again. Starting in Mexico and moving southwest once more, gliding over Guatemala, Honduras, Nicaragua, Costa Rica . . .

And then it stops dead.

"Panama," Eisfanger says. "Huh. I would have guessed Argentina."

"Argentina isn't an international trade center for the illegal lem trade." I'm staring at the little bead, stuck to the map like it was glued there. "But Panama is. And somebody that owns a cattle ranch there is supplying a local restaurant here. And using not just the flesh, but the bones and spirit of the animals. Makes sense—but none of this ties Congressman Broadstone to what's going on."

Eisfanger sets the miniature divining rod down on the map. "A congressman, huh? Going after the *big* game. Dangerous."

"I'll bring him down."

"Don't doubt it. You pretty far along the trail?"

"No, just got the scent, actually—"

I stop. I stare at Eisfanger, my mouth open. I'll give Damon credit—you embarrass him, that complexion of his goes from ghostly pale to blazing red in about half a second; that's what happens now, when he realizes what's going on.

"What—what are we *doing*?" I say. I'm aghast.

"Talking shop?" he offers weakly.

"Yeah, but not as *colleagues*. We were talking shop *as thropes*." I'm still aghast. In fact, I may be *multiple* ghasts at this point.

"I'm sorry—it wasn't intentional!" If Eisfanger had a tail at the moment, it would be between his legs. "I—it's just—I fall into it naturally when I'm talking with another thrope—"

"I'm not a thrope!"

"I know. I *know*. But—well, you *smell* like one, and I wasn't thinking—"

"Stop. Talking."

I can't believe it. Tair enrolls me in thrope kindergarten, Xandra's ready to help me pick out curtains for my new kennel, and now the people I work with are acting like my humanity is already obsolete. It makes me so angry I want to—

Oh, no.

It's happening. I can feel it. My bones, wanting to twist and shift. My teeth, aching to lengthen. Every inch of my skin prickles with the fur about to erupt from its surface. The fury I'm feeling is the beast clawing its way out of my soul.

"Jace!" Damon says. "You—you look like you're about to—"

Everything comes into abrupt, incredibly sharp focus.

I can see every single thing in front of me in minute, high-resolution detail, the colors so bright and vivid they're surreal. Sound amplifies and divides into a hundred discrete rustles, squeaks, thumps, and scrapes, everything from the buzz of the fly in the hall outside to Damon's heartbeat a few feet away. And the *smells*—my God, the smells. Aromas and odors I don't even have names for, just impressions—things that smell heavy or purplish or jingly or smooth.

"This—this is a bit much," I manage to croak. I look down at my hands, amazed they aren't hairy yet.

"You're having a prechange episode," Damon says. "Tomorrow night's the full moon. I understand they can be intense, but it won't last. It won't be like this when—" He stops.

"When what?" I gasp. "When I'm a thrope, right? Or maybe you mean when I'm dead. Or a pire. Maybe I'll get to have these sorts of delightful conversations with Gretch and Cassius instead."

Damon's smell changes. He smells . . . *guilty.*

No, that's not it. He smells like he's hiding something, something I should know but don't, a secret that's . . . *tragic,* yes, the twin scents of doom and inevitability twining around each other, the bitterness of regret, the whole thing wrapped in a layer of compassion and just a touch of hope.

I grab Eisfanger by the lapels of his lab coat. He's a sturdy, muscular guy, but I whip him off his feet and around into the wall with even thinking about it. He yelps in surprise.

"You're hiding something from me," I growl. "What is it? Something about my condition?"

"Just calm down, please. You're not in control."

"Tell me or I'll show you just how out of control I am." I'm not bluffing; I'm ready to rip him and his lab apart. Instinct is driving and it's locked the rational part of my brain in the trunk.

Eisfanger knows it, too. I'd like to think he respects me enough to consider me a genuine physical threat—even without the novelty item I call a gun—but he's probably more worried about damage to his lab. "You should talk to Cassius," he says carefully.

Instinct doesn't bother with careful processing and analysis; it just leaps ahead. "Not my condition, my *treatment*," I say. "The tests Cassius had you do. It told you something."

He looks into my eyes for a second and then glances away. He's afraid, but not of me; he's afraid of something he knows. Something tragic.

It sinks in slowly. I let him go and take a step back. "Am I going to die?"

"No," he says quietly. "Cassius is."

TWENTY-ONE

The thrope symptoms that rode in on a tide of anger wash out again with a cold surge of shock. "What?"

"The treatment he's devised requires a great deal of sorcerous power. He's fueling it with his own life force. He thought he could do it and still survive, but the thrope virus is proving too strong. He can still beat it, but it's going to take everything he has."

I sink back onto the stool. Suddenly everything seems smaller, diminished, hollow. My vision is blurred, my hearing's fuzzy, it's all very far away. No more super-senses, just the regular old world; I don't know if it's a relief to have it back or a disappointment.

Then the planet goes sideways and decides for me. Damon catches me before I fall off the stool, and lowers me carefully to a sitting position on the floor. "Take it easy," he says. He sounds concerned, but he smells like an ordinary lab tech again. "You're going to need to lie down. We should get you to the infirmary."

"No, no." I try to get to my feet and find it takes all my strength. "No infirmary. I'll just—just go home." If I don't pass out first.

Damon calls Charlie, who shows up thirty seconds later. He asks what's wrong with me, gets the short version from Damon, and agrees to take me home if I promise to lie down and get some rest. I don't tell him about Cassius, and neither does Damon; I'm too exhausted to go into it and Damon obviously doesn't believe it's his decision to make. He's right.

I think about it as Charlie drives me home. It's not that there's any good reason to keep it from him, it's more like I'm so overloaded I'm not sure what to do. Charlie will be supportive regardless—the only thing that can overcome his loyalty to me is heavy-duty magic, and even that's not a sure thing. But how is he going to take it when I tell him that in order for me to survive, Cassius has to die?

Charlie'd kill him, of course. Dumb question.

I'm so brain-dead that for a minute I'm actually worried Charlie might try to do that. Then reason seeps in and it becomes blatantly obvious that not only would that not solve anything, it's the sort of basic logic that a clever orangutan wouldn't have trouble with. I decide the best course of action would be a short nap, and when I wake up I'm on my couch.

Charlie's sitting in a nearby armchair, reading a newspaper.

"Whuzza time?" I say, yawning and sitting up.

"You've been out around an hour. I took your shoes off."

"Thanks."

"You're welcome. You know you talk in your sleep?"

I glare at him and stifle another yawn. "Do not."

"I distinctly heard you say, 'Waffle my carborundum.' "

"You're a terrible liar."

"You put a lot of emphasis on the *waffle* part. It was almost obscene."

"I need coffee. In the sense that fire needs oxygen."

"I thought you might. In the kitchen."

I get up, stretching, and stumble into the kitchen. It must be after dark, 'cause Galahad is in there in his human form, dressed in yellow sweatpants and a HELLO BATTY T-shirt, his brown-and-white patched hair standing up in unruly tufts all over his head. "Jace!" he says joyfully, and twitches his butt from side to side in a tailless happy-dance.

"Hey, big guy," I say. "Still glad to see me, or are you going to go all weird on me, too?"

"Weird!" he says, grinning and nodding. It's like living with the world's biggest toddler, I swear. Whatever uncertainty he was feeling toward me, it seems to have resolved itself in my favor. I guess he figures that no matter how strange I might smell, I still feed him on a regular basis.

And then he does something he's never done before.

He holds his arms up and straight out, looking like he's trying to do a bad sleepwalking impression, then spreads them a little wider. He looks expectant and a little hesitant.

"Hug?" he asks.

They say a dog's love is unconditional, that dogs will never judge you. But that doesn't mean they aren't capable of judgment; it doesn't mean they can't see when you're down and need some of that unconditional love. That would describe me, right now.

Me, giving my dog a long, ferocious hug and trying not to bawl my eyes out.

So after I've wiped my eyes and gotten my coffee and given Gally an entire bag of pork rinds, I open the door that leads between my kitchen and my living room and see Charlie with a knife to his throat.

Holding it and standing behind him is Tair.

Don Arturo Falzo sits on the couch, dressed in a natty plum-colored suit that even Charlie would admire. He's got his legs crossed, a matching fedora perched on the end of his knee. He looks at me and smiles, an old friend dropping by unexpectedly to say hello.

My jacket is hanging over the back of a chair a few steps away, with both my scythes and gun inside. But the blade of the knife is pressed against the plastic skin of Charlie's throat, and Tair can decapitate him in the time it takes me to twitch.

Galahad growls, deep in his throat.

"Gally, *no*." The last thing I want is for my loyal but not terribly bright dog to be ripped to pieces defending me.

"Hello, Agent Valchek," Don Falzo says. "I apologize for our rudeness in showing up without notice, but we really needed to talk to you privately."

He doesn't sound crazy at all, but that means nothing. He seemed fairly lucid the first time I met him, just before he told me about the demonic footwear conspiracy. "Congratulations, you have my attention. I didn't think it was even *possible* to sneak up on Charlie."

"We cheated," Tair says. "Black-market stealth spells from Nigeria. I know a guy."

Charlie doesn't bother threatening either of them. He just stays very still and very quiet, focusing all his energy on waiting for that one second when Tair drops his guard. It's something predators do, willing themselves to become part of the landscape, making themselves so unremarkable that the prey forgets they're even there. Charlie thinks of it as a Zen thing; I tell him he's just channeling his inner rock garden.

However you look at it, though, I don't think it'll work. Tair's usual relaxed arrogance is gone, replaced by an intensity I can feel from ten feet away, no doubt heightened by the *sange ucenicie*. No way he's going to let himself get distracted.

Not when this is the night he decides if I get to live or die.

The Don takes his fedora and places it on the couch beside him. He uncrosses his legs and sits a little straighter. "Before you do anything rash, I should tell you that we're not here as enemies. In fact, we have a proposal for you—we think you can do something for us, and we have something to offer in return."

"I'm listening."

The Don smiles and spreads his hands in the air. "What we have to offer, first of all, are some facts. In fact, we'll give them to you for free."

"How generous."

"As you can see, my mental faculties are sound. They were never disabled to begin with."

I glance from the Don to Tair. He nods.

"Why?" I ask. "Why go through all the playacting?"

"Because I was in a very precarious position," the Don says. "Thropes age slowly, but we do age. Every year there's a new challenger trying to dethrone me and take my place. The last few years, I've sized up my probable opponents ahead of time and had them eliminated before they could make their move. But that only works for so long."

"The families got wise to you," I say. "They knew a shift in power was inevitable, and they decided to back someone new. Someone they protected from your preemptive strikes."

"Yes. So I was forced to take a different route."

"By pretending to be crazy? How does that help?"

"Several ways. It gives you an advantage in that

people don't know how to react, how they should treat you. You become an unknown quantity, and people always fear the unknown. The ones who don't fear you don't take you seriously, and that's good, too. But most of all, it gave me an excuse to meet *you*."

"Me? Why me?"

"Because you don't give up. Because you're very good at what you do, and once I put you on the trail I knew you'd follow wherever it led."

Wherever it led . . . son-of-a-*bitch*. "The murders. They had nothing to do with you trying to escape the country, or revenge. You wanted me to bust Iggy Prinzini."

"Ignacio is being groomed—quietly—as my replacement," Falzo says. "The smuggling operation he's running is very successful. He's made some powerful allies, too. My only hope was to discredit him, hurt him enough that he would no longer be seen as a viable successor."

"So pick up a phone. Drop a dime on him."

"Please. Informing on a family member to the authorities? It goes against our deepest-held beliefs. No, all I could do was create opportunities for him to fail."

"And make sure I was there to capitalize on them."

"Which you did wonderfully well." He tilts his head in acknowledgment. "You've dealt serious blows to several facets of his operation."

I did more than that. I blew Iggy's kneecap off, which effectively took him out of the running as far as becoming top wolf went; Mafia thropes are notoriously unenlightened when it comes to employing the disabled. But that means the Don got what he wanted long ago—why keep killing when I'd already taken out his main opponent?

I think I know. "And along the way, you killed a number of Prinzini's supporters."

Falzo shrugs. "If I hadn't, they would have tried again next year with someone else. I needed to do more than eliminate the competition, I needed to change the playing field."

I shake my head. "Then you failed. You may have bought a few more years, but you're a thrope, not a pire; sooner or later this will happen all over again, except you'll be even older and weaker."

He leans forward. "You think I don't know that? I do, believe me. A man in my position, he has to be looking at who's going to be filling his shoes when he's gone. Used to be it would be passed down through blood; my offspring would inherit whatever it was that I built. But the Gray Wolves figured out a long time ago that wasn't the best thing for the organization itself."

I know what he means. Thropes have big families, which means multiple siblings waging war over who gets what. Plus, a powerful parent doesn't always translate into powerful children; too often they grow up pampered and overprotected, whatever genetic advantages they've been given weakened by a soft and indulgent environment.

"I understand the rules," Falzo says. "Why they are what they are. But over time, any system can become corrupted."

"You should know."

He gives me a cynical grin. "Yes, very true. And *because* I know this—among many other things—I should have a say. A voice in the decision as to who will be the next Don."

"What decision? I thought it was all done by some sort of contest."

He waves one hand contemptuously. "Pfah. Do you

believe everything you're told? The Trials are as filled with treachery as any other endeavor we undertake. Survival is the only true rule. No, if the other families decide to support a particular candidate, that is the candidate who invariably wins. So far, I have had that support."

But not anymore. "I take it you don't agree with their choice of replacement?"

He scowls. "Ignacio Prinzini is not fit to be Don. He thinks only in the short term. The deals he's struck have made him powerful, but his alliances will not hold. He thinks once he's in charge he can consolidate his power base, but he's wrong. He won't last a year, and then the families will tear themselves apart trying to gain dominance over one another."

Funny how often people in power are convinced that the world will go to hell unless they're around to hold the reins. It's a convenient rationalization, one that lets you think of yourself as an altruist while brutally suppressing anybody who might threaten your regime.

What's more interesting, though, is that the Don is talking like he thinks Iggy is still a threat. "One thing I don't understand. Why didn't you just go after Iggy yourself? Take him out directly?"

"You think I'm afraid of him?" He chuckles again. "Not so. But he's very good at not being found, which presents problems. In fact, since I put you on his trail, he's vanished completely. I don't suppose you killed him?"

"No," I say, and leave it at that. Better if the Don doesn't know Iggy has become Limpy—it makes me more valuable to him. "Okay, you admit your time is ending, and you're not a fan of Iggy. So *who*—"

Ah.

"Who else?" Tair says.

I sigh. "All right, I think I'm up to speed. I finally know what's going on and exactly who the players are. There's just two things I'm still a little unclear on."

"Ask away," Tair says.

"Why are you *here* and *why do you have a knife to my partner's throat?*"

"To ensure you would give the proper attention to my proposal," the Don says. "You see, Tair and I have reached something of an impasse. Ignacio has used his political connections to bring certain outsiders to town. Normally I would have the resources to deal with these individuals myself, but, the circumstances being what they are—"

"—on the run from the law and hunted by your own people—"

"—we thought it wisest to seek an alliance of our own."

Outsiders. Political connections. There's only one group in this situation that fits that description. "You're talking about the paramilitary unit from Panama."

He looks pleasantly surprised. "She's as good as you said, my boy."

"Told you," says Tair. I wonder if he's proud enough of his *sange ucenicie* star pupil to let me live.

"This group," the Don continues, "are not mere soldiers. They are a death squad, tasked by the Panamanian government with the elimination of military insurgents. They are not assassins; they are butchers. Their job is not just to murder rebels, but to kill a rebellion. They do so through torture and terror, and they are very experienced."

"I can see why you might be a little worried. Is that what this is all about? You want us to protect you?"

"In a way." The Don's mouth is set in a grim line, but

there's a savage joy in his eyes. "I want you to help me kill them."

There's a long, pregnant pause.

"Okay," I say.

Tair grins. "Congratulations. You pass."

TWENTY-TWO

There are times when you just have to look around your-self and wonder, *How the hell did I get here?* Usually followed by, *And what the hell do I do now?*

You might think I had one of those moments in my apartment, with a renegade thrope holding a razor-sharp blade to my partner's throat and the head of one of the Five Families casually suggesting I help him eliminate a paramilitary death squad from South America.

Nope. Sorry.

It speaks to the high level of weirdness in my life that my second meeting with the Don registered as mostly business-as-usual, with a side order of adrenaline due to the threat to Charlie's life. No, I didn't have one of those WTF moments until around three hours later, long after Don Falzo convinced me that Iggy's political connec-tions meant I couldn't take this to the NSA. Long after he persuaded me that the only way to take the death squad out without civilian casualties was a lightning-fast surgical strike on where they were holed up.

Long after the Don made me an offer, and I didn't refuse.

Which, I suppose, answers the question of *how* I got here, though it doesn't do much for *What the hell do I do now?* And *here* is pretty bizarre, all by itself . . .

I'm hanging upside down in a tree, completely dressed in black. I've got on a radio headset and I'm looking at our target through a pair of high-tech night-vision binoculars. Our target being a building that looks like the result of a drunken fling between Buckingham Palace and a 1920s bordello: one ostentatious mansion, heavy on the Gothic architecture, surrounded by large, well-kept grounds. An old structure, built by old money.

Congressman Broadstone's house.

"I'm in position." Charlie's voice, coming through my earpiece.

"Wish I could say the same. All the blood's rushing to my head."

"Thrope stuff?" Charlie sounds a little worried.

"No, I'm upside down."

"Why?"

"I thought it would make me look all cool and ninja-y."

"No one's supposed to be *able* to see you."

"Ah. I knew there was a flaw in my plan. Also, I slipped."

"In fact, the whole *point* of being a ninja is not to be seen."

"Fortunately I have this nifty safety harness, which is why I'm dangling instead of plummeting. Thanks for asking."

He sighs. "If it doesn't cut into your busy dangling schedule, you want to tell me what you see?"

"No lights in the lower floors. One light on in the second, east corner. Sentries haven't come back from their sweep yet."

I have to admit, Broadstone using his own place to house the death squad is a stroke of genius. Plenty of room, isolated, fairly secure. They can come and go as they please, and the local residents' own preconceptions mean all they see are groundskeepers or domestic help. Perfect cover.

However, this is a congressman's house, not a military base. He has security cameras, spotlights, motion sensors—but he's not equipped to fend off a serious assault. Or at least he wasn't until he imported twenty-one ruthless Third World assassins; now he could probably hold off a small army.

So we're not going in as an army. We're a commando team: two thropes, a lem, and me. I'd like to say I'm their big gun, but in fact I'm their *only* gun. The death squad will probably be armed with bows, but a thrope's speed and strength make that just as deadly as a rifle; a well-trained werewolf archer can send a flurry of razor-tipped arrows at you as fast as a semi-automatic handgun, and with more accuracy.

So we have to make sure they don't have a chance to use them.

"Time to make my entrance," the Don says. He doesn't have a headset, but he's broadcasting through a hidden mike in his collar. Getting onto the grounds was relatively easy—thanks to the stealth spells Tair provided—but the house itself has more sensitive mystical wards. That won't matter to the Don, though, because he's not going to try to sneak in; he's going to walk in the front door.

He presses the buzzer for the front gate, identifies himself. Says he needs to talk to the congressman in person. Falzo sounds urbane, confident, in full control of his faculties. He says he's alone, means no harm, wants to make a deal. They let him in.

Lights go on across the main floor. There are lots of

windows, which means both Tair and I have excellent views—me of the main-floor study where the meeting will no doubt take place, him of the front door.

Tair reports in. "Sentries just passed my position. Still undetected." The sentries rove in pairs, but we think the Don's arrival will push that number up. I'm proven right a few seconds later as Tair says that two more pairs have just loped off into the night, one to take up position by the gate, the other to support the initial two. That makes six outside.

Tair watches four more thropes slink from the house to the gate to escort the Don inside. Falzo stays silent until he's actually in the house, when he says, "Ah, such a reception. Six of you to look after a frail old man? You flatter me."

So, six more in the room with the Don to make sure he doesn't try anything crazy—because, of course, for all they know that's exactly what he is. That makes twelve. Nine unaccounted for, possibly asleep.

This is not going to be easy.

I try to focus, get myself under control. I tell myself that these are the worst of the worst, that they specialize in the most ruthless kind of state-sponsored terrorism; they wipe out entire villages just to make a point. Look up *evil* in the dictionary and you'll find these guys staring back at you.

"Coming your way," Tair says. "Do it now."

I take a deep breath and let it out slowly. Put away the binoculars and take out my gun. Hope Eisfanger's silencer keeps working as well as it has so far.

And when the two sentries lope past underneath me, I shoot both of them in the back.

Silver-tipped bullets. At this range, instant death for thropes. I've killed people before, but this is my first execution. Somewhere on the other side of the estate, Tair is doing the same but with two silver-tipped arrows. Four down, seventeen to go.

I don't know how I expected to feel—guilty, disgusted, numb—but what I didn't expect was *this*.

I enjoy it.

I just killed two men without ever knowing their names, without even seeing their faces. And not only am I fine with that, I can't wait to do it again; joy surges fiercely, followed by a deep sense of satisfaction. It's both thrilling and fulfilling, the thrill of the kill.

"*And* the instigator of bad poetry," I mutter. I shouldn't be surprised. I've got the virally induced instincts of two predator species thrashing around in my bloodstream, after all. The harsh truth is that right now, me committing murder is going to be like a lion mainlining catnip.

Good. That might just be what it takes to survive this.

"Shish kebab times two," Tair whispers in my ear. He doesn't try to disguise his glee; he came to terms with his darker urges a long time ago.

I don't bother to reply, focusing on the conversation I'm hearing between the congressman and the Don. I'm positioned in the trees edging the gardens at the back of the house, with a good view of the study through a large window. I can see the congressman—a tall, thin thrope wearing a yellow sweater—enter the room with the Don and his escort. Then he draws the curtains, and all I have is the audio feed:

BROADSTONE: I'm surprised to see you here. It doesn't seem very . . .

FALZO: Rational? I assure you, I know exactly what I'm doing. The only one here who's deluded is you.

BROADSTONE: Oh?

FALZO: Ensuring that the Golem Bill won't pass is a mistake. Both personally and politically.

BROADSTONE: I don't see how. It will ensure certain businesses *remain* in business. And that they remain profitable.

FALZO: You refer to your arrangement with Ignacio Prinzini. Yes, I'm sure the immediate consequences will be favorable for both of you, especially financially. But it is not a situation that can last indefinitely. Now that the lems have their own country, lem rights will continue to expand. Allying yourself with anti-lem forces dooms your political future. Or are you so blinded by greed you can't see which way the wind is blowing?

BROADSTONE: There's nothing wrong with my vision *or* my political instincts. For instance, I see *exactly* what the future of the Gray Wolves holds: a change in leadership. Or am I mistaken?

FALZO: (chuckling) You may be. Right now you're wondering, *Why is this old man here?* Either I'm out of my mind . . . or I'm here with a counter-offer. And you're listening very carefully because—if I'm *not* crazy—then I must have something very, very enticing. Something so good I'm willing to walk into a house filled with dangerous people—people whose sole reason for being in the country is to *kill* me— based on it. Would you say that's accurate?

BROADSTONE: That sums it up nicely.

FALZO: Very well. Then here is my offer.

He pauses. "Charlie, *go*," I say. I unclip my safety harness and drop to the ground.

So try to imagine this: You're a thrope soldier, doing guard duty at a gate. A big steel gate, set into stone pillars sunk deep into the ground. Stone walls nine feet tall on either side. You're on higher alert than normal, because the guy your unit was sent to kill just walked up to that gate and surrendered himself, which is all kinds of wrong and stinks of a setup.

And then you see the Cadillac roaring up the street straight at you.

First thing you do is put several razor-tipped arrows through the windshield. The windshield is heavily tinted so you can't actually see the driver, but you have plenty of time. And you—and your partner—are both excellent shots.

Except the arrows do no good. The Caddy—a huge monstrous thing, painted a bright purple and with enough chrome on it to blind a showgirl—keeps coming. As it gets closer, you see through the arrow-damaged windshield that it doesn't appear to *have* a driver. What it has is some sort of pole lashed horizontally to the steering wheel, the ends sticking out of the open windows on either side of the car, with ropes leading from the pole's tips toward the rear of the vehicle. They remind you, absurdly, of reins.

You realize that the Caddy is going to smash directly into the gate. You don't have time to alert anyone—all you can do is dive out of the way in the last second before impact, still peppering the car with arrows in hopes that you'll hit something vital.

The car smashes into the steel bars. Amazingly, the gate holds, bringing the Caddy to an abrupt halt.

A large shape flies through the air, over the car's roof.

In a flash of uncharacteristic inspiration, you realize that someone was crouched on the Caddy's trunk, guiding it with the ropes. They probably put a brick on the accelerator first, then popped the car into gear with another rope attached to the shifter once they were in position. The Caddy's sudden stop has catapulted this mysterious rider through the air and inside your perimeter.

All of this bursts into your consciousness with the brilliance of sudden revelation, in the fleeting instant before the shape lands a few feet away and resolves itself into the outline of a large, well-armed golem.

And those are the last thoughts you—and your partner—ever have.

I can hear these events occurring in stereo, coming through clearly via Charlie's audio channel and—more faintly—live in the distance. At the same time, I'm still listening to Broadstone and Falzo's conversation as I sprint toward the rear of the house.

FALZO: I will let you live. In return, you will vote *against* the Golem Bill, and urge as many of your peers as you can to do the same.

BROADSTONE: Excuse me?

FALZO: Your career, in the aftermath, will be uncertain. If it were up to me, I would proffer the hand of friendship—even though I find many of your actions to be without honor—in the spirit of continued cooperation and mutual benefit.

BROADSTONE: I don't—what was *that*?

It's funny how often our first instinct is to actually *look* for a potential threat, even if doing so isn't the wisest move. The thrope soldiers inside the study know that; Broadstone doesn't. Even though the sound of Charlie's arrival comes from the other side of the house, Broadstone still pulls aside the drapes and looks out, just as I trip the motion sensors and the security lights come on.

I put three bullets into the window. Not into the congressman—I'm aiming high and at an angle, just trying to shatter the glass.

Turns out I needn't have bothered; a snarling thrope comes sailing through a second later, all tangled up in the heavy drapes. He slashes them to pieces in seconds, but that's all the time I need to see that he's not the Don. I put him down with a single shot. Assuming Charlie took out his two, that leaves fourteen, with five more right in front of me—two of whom I can see, now that one of the drapes is gone.

I shoot one, slamming him into the far wall. The other dives for cover. I can't see the congressman or Falzo, but I can hear plenty of snarling and smashing going on. A second later another thrope flies through the window, doing pretty much what the first one did; I repeat myself, too.

I've got a good view of the whole study now, and from the open door into the hall I'd say the good congressman has fled. The Don is in half-were mode, a gray-furred monster seven feet tall locked in combat with two other thropes. He's got a silver blade jutting from one shoulder and his left ear is gone, but other than that he appears to be winning; I say that because there's one headless thrope corpse already at his feet, and a second later he uses his jaws to add another.

I vault over the sill to help him out, but he doesn't need it. He yanks the knife out of his shoulder while dodging a swipe from a silver-edged sword, and takes out the last one with a thrust to the heart.

"Only three of them?" I say. "Geez, you *are* getting old."

He leaves the blade buried in the thrope's chest and signs, *In my youth they would not have touched me, let alone drawn blood.*

I hear the unmistakable sound of a heavy door being smashed in. For a second I wonder where Charlie found a battering ram, then mentally shrug. He's resourceful that way.

Nine left.

"Hey, Charlie?" I say into my headset.

"Hang on," he snaps.

Sounds of mayhem ensue. "Yeah?" he says a moment later.

"Try throwing them out the windows. Works like a charm."

"I'll keep that in mind. Tair?"

"Present."

"Working my way upstairs. Be ready."

I nod at the Don. "Come on, let's try to find a back staircase. I want to get up there ASAP."

I doubt your friend needs help.

"Help? I just want to show up while there's still a few left."

I believe I'll try to find the congressman and finish our discussion. I have a feeling he'll be in a much more reasonable frame of mind. He springs out the door and down a corridor.

Charlie's voice: "Tair. Second floor. Two windows to the west of the one over the main entrance." *Crash!*

"*Got* him."

I find the back stairs. The rest of the unit must be quartered in the guest bedrooms, that light I saw on in the east corner. I orient myself, figure out which direction I need to go.

"Second floor, fourth window," Charlie growls. *Crash!*

"*Nailed* him," says Tair. "Lot of windows in that room."

"It's a hall."

"Oh, that makes sense."

I creep up the stairs. When I reach the top, I find

myself in a long, dark corridor, with green light spilling around a corner at the very end of it. I advance slowly.

"Hey," says Tair. "Think you'll make it to the third floor?"

"Maybe. Why?"

"If I had a little more lead time, I could take them out before they hit the ground."

"You want me to look for a skylight while I'm at it? Pitch 'em straight up, make sure they're framed by the moon?"

"Could you? That'd be *swell.*"

I make it to the end of the hall, peer around the corner cautiously. The light's coming from an open doorway. I can hear a low muttering from inside the room: the congressman's voice.

"This is getting boring," Tair says. "I think I'll let the next one run a little."

"You let one get away and I'll make you *eat* that bow."

I approach the doorway. Inside, Broadstone is kneeling beside a small stone altar. The green light is coming from an object on the altar, though I can't tell what it is— the congressman's body is in the way. His muttering resolves into a low-pitched chant, words in a language I don't know—but one that sounds horribly familiar.

High Power Level Craft is a type of magic only governments have access to. It's Thropirelem's equivalent of atomic weapons, a way to contact other dimensions— dimensions a lot scarier than this one. It's what was used at the end of World War II to give vampires the ability to have children, what Aristotle Stoker used to raise the continent of Mu and get the attention of an Elder God. It's as dangerous as a dozen high-yield nukes but a lot less stable, and the last thing you want in the hands of a corrupt politician whose back is against the wall.

"Stop right there," I bark in my best cop voice. "Utter one more syllable and I'll kill you where you kneel."

He falls silent. Something hangs in the air, heavy and oppressive. Something's watching me from every direction, like there are eyes just below the surface of the walls, the floor, the ceiling, studying me through a thin veil of reality.

Not just eyes. Mouths, too.

"Turn around!"

He does, shuffling awkwardly on his knees. He's holding something in his hands: an oddly shaped black rock, its outline almost organic, like an amoeba frozen between seconds. There are runes carved into it, and they're pulsing with a mucus-tinted glow that's hard to look at. So I look at Broadstone's face instead—and wish I hadn't.

He's in half-were form, his head that of a wolf's. But with every pulse of light his flesh becomes almost completely transparent, and the fanged skull underneath is the jet black of obsidian instead of bone.

"Put the rock *down*."

When he sees my gun, he gives a bark of laughter. A half-were can't speak; its mouth isn't shaped right for it. But I guess the language the congressman was chanting a second ago wasn't designed for a human mouth, either, because he goes back to snarling and grunting whatever incantation he's started.

I can't just shoot a congressman, dirty or not; the paperwork would be hell. So I shoot the rock instead.

It drives the thing into his belly—a Ruger Super Redhawk packs a *big* kinetic wallop—and he goes backward, knocking over the shrine.

But he doesn't shut up. And he doesn't drop the rock.

Something rips its way into the world.

It's long and black and serpentine and has eyes all

over it. Mouths, too, round toothy ones like a leech's. It's not entirely *here*, though; its outline shifts and blurs like smoke or a movie moving in and out of focus. I try putting a bullet into the thing, but the round goes right through it without any effect.

I drop the gun, draw my scythes, and snap them open.

I know, I know. If this interdimensional snake monstrosity can ignore a big-ass silver-tipped round, what good is a silver blade going to do against it? Probably nothing at all.

Which is why I go after the congressman instead.

He's flat on his back, holding the rock up and away from his body, still chanting. I pincer him with the scythes, impaling the backs of his hands. The tip of each blade stops dead against the rock itself.

Silver interferes with most magic, but HPLC is in a class by itself. Whatever eldritch energy is flowing through the rock, it channels itself straight through the blades, along the shafts, and up my arms. I see my own skeletal hands, the bones a charred black, through my translucent skin—and then the two streams of energy come together, somewhere in the middle of my chest. I'm pretty sure I heard somewhere that crossing the streams was bad . . .

It's a horrible sensation. Something foul and black is filling me up, not my lungs or stomach but my skeleton, like all my bones have been hollowed out and now someone is injecting tar into them, tar filled with the ashes of a thousand corpses. I scream.

And Broadstone drops the rock.

I don't know if it was me diverting his mojo or just the pain of having silver embedded in his flesh, but the rock thumps onto his chest and then slides off onto the floor. The green light dies. The snake-thing howls in frustration and folds itself back into whatever Hellrealm it calls home, not so much fading as getting farther away while staying in the same place, until it vanishes into the nonexistent distance.

And me? I manage the extremely badass maneuver of not passing out. I stumble backward a step, pulling my scythes out of the congressman's hands, and say shakily, "So *there*."

And then I sit down, kind of suddenly. Yep, they're definitely going to make me the star of an action movie, with me doing cool stuff and spouting clever one-liners immediately afterward. Maybe there'll even be explosions behind me I can walk away from without looking at. In slow-mo.

Broadstone sits up, slowly. He's reverted to human, and looks about as drained as I feel.

"Touch that rock again," I say, with as much authority as I can muster, "and both your hands are coming off at the wrist."

He stares at me, despair and frustration warring in his eyes. Despair wins. He slumps back against the ruins of the altar, cradling his bleeding hands against his chest. The energy surge seems to have shorted out my headset, because I can't hear Charlie or Tair anymore.

It doesn't matter, though. The congressman and I just sit there and glare at each other until Charlie finds us, a few minutes later.

"All clear," he rumbles. "Tair just took out the last one. Radio not working?"

"Fried," I say. "Where's the Don?"

"Haven't seen him. Tair, have you—" He stops and listens. "Sure. What a surprise. I'll let her know."

He gives me a hand standing up. "The Don's with Tair. Seems they think it's time to leave—in fact, they already have."

"Leaving us to clean up. Lovely."

"You—you are in *enormous* trouble," Broadstone says. He seems to have regained a little of his composure and thinks he can bluff his way out of this. He's a politician, after all—I would have been disappointed if he hadn't at least tried.

"No, we're in the *presence* of someone who's in enormous trouble," I say. "And that would be you, you slave-trading, demon-summoning pimp *wannabe*. I am going to find the deepest, darkest off-the-books cell and *bury* you until you're putting in your fangs with *Polident*."

"We'll see," he says. "It's my word against yours, after all. You have no evidence, and your allies have fled."

"Yeah," I say, pulling out my phone. "How entirely unexpected. My, my, whatever shall I do." I hit the second number on my speed dial. "Cassius? You have them, right?"

The congressman's face gets a little paler. I snap the phone shut and smile down at him. "What, you really think I'd put my *trust* in those two? In an operation like this? The NSA has been backing us up all the way, so far back in the shadows that even Don Falzo couldn't smell them."

I shake my head. "Thropes don't have the market cornered on being sneaky, you know. But after a few thousand years of being a professional spook, I'm pretty sure my boss does—and *I'm* a fast learner."

TWENTY-THREE

The NSA cleanup team arrives and we leave. The congressman goes into custody for "debriefing"; that means he vanishes with a plausible cover story for a few days while Cassius decides what to do with him. The NSA crew will disappear the bodies of the death squad and make sure nothing gets into the papers. All neat and clean and tidy—but going in we had no such guarantees. The one brief phone conversation I'd managed to have with Cassius—after ditching the thropes for all of two minutes—was barely enough to convince him to let me run this op from the inside, without his active participation. There was no time for details, just his promise that he'd hang back as long as he could. Everything after that had been thrown together on instinct and luck.

But it worked. We have the congressman, Tair, and the Don. Everything after this is a matter of figuring out who to charge with what—and what deals can be struck.

"I'm sorry," Atticus says. "I really don't get why I'm here."

He's wearing a track suit of pale yellow today, giving his rounded bulk the somewhat unsettling suggestion of a giant baby chick. He gives me a puzzled smile and spreads his hands, as if to say, *What? I'm just sitting here waiting for the Easter Bunny.*

"Well, that's the thing, Atticus. I'm not exactly sure, either. Why don't we try to figure it out together?"

His oily pompadour gleams under the interview room lights. He shrugs affably. "Sure, no problem."

"First off—I want to apologize for any disrespect I showed you when I was your, ah, *guest.* I had no idea *you* were actually consigliere, not Dino. My bad."

"No sweat. People make that mistake all the time, you know? I like to hang back, not be too confrontational."

"Sure. Anyway, our intel analyst set me straight. In fact, she was the one who insisted on this meeting."

"Yeah? And who is *she* exactly—"

The door opens. Charlie shoves two more wise guys inside: Louie and Dino. They're both in cuffs, hands behind their backs.

"And here are our other two *guests,*" I say. Charlie steps back into the hall, shutting the door behind him. "All four of us together again, just like old times. Louie, how's your gut? All healed up, or do you still leak when you eat soup?"

"The hell is this?" Louie growls. "I want a lawyer, *now.*"

"And I want a double cappuccino, no foam, with just a dash of vanilla. But we're both gonna have to wait, y'know?"

Dino just stares at me impassively. He knows what's going on, and figures his only option is just to endure it. He's right—mostly.

"To answer your question," I say, "the woman who arranged this little reunion is the mother of the one person who's missing. You know, the really short one?"

I can see them get it. They all react differently. Dino

gets even more stolid, withdrawing completely, while Louie gets aggressive and Atticus tries to be conciliatory.

"Hey," Atticus says. "No harm done, right?"

"I said I want my goddamn *lawyer*!"

"I mean, she's fine, okay?"

"You *fucks* can't get away with this."

"Louie, please. Come on, we never planned that part of it, you know? It was an accident, pure and simple."

The door opens again. Cassius and Gretchen walk in, Gretch closing the door quietly behind her.

"Who are you?" Atticus asks. "You her?"

"Yes," Gretch says.

Louie glares at both of them. "And who the fuck are you? The *daddy*?"

"No," Cassius says. His voice is very calm. "I'm David Cassius, director of the National Security Agency."

Atticus nods, looking a little relieved. "The boss. Okay. I understand *my* boss is also enjoying your hospitality right now?"

"He's in our custody, yes," Cassius says. "But that's not why I'm here."

"No? Then why—"

"Moral support," Cassius says.

Gretch steps behind Atticus. A thin loop of silver wire slides out of her sleeve. It goes around his throat and disappears into the fat of his neck so quickly I barely see it at all.

This is not what I expected.

I thought we were just going to throw a scare into them. Hurt them a little, terrify them a lot. But as it happens, right in front of me, I'd be lying if I said I was all that surprised. Part of me knew exactly what was going to happen—and just didn't want to admit it.

You know that scene in *The Godfather* when the fat guy gets strangled? This is just like that, except it goes on a lot longer. The only expression on Gretch's face is a slight smile. I think about her recent odd behavior and realize I was way off base.

Gretch isn't crazy. She's just really, really angry, and the strain of hiding that has made her seem a little distracted. Not anymore, though. At the moment, she is completely, totally focused on the bastards responsible for threatening her child's life.

Dino tries not to react to what he's seeing, but his face keeps getting paler. Louie tries to shift form and howls in pain when the silver in the cuffs stops him. He backs away into the corner, eyes wide and horrified, watching Atticus choke to death.

I don't do a damn thing.

When Gretch is done, the wire disappears up her sleeve again. She meets Louie's eyes, then Dino's. "Any questions?" she asks.

"No," Louie croaks.

"No," Dino whispers.

Gretch turns and leaves without another word.

"I think we should move these two to another interview room," I say to Cassius. My voice is a lot firmer than I feel. "This one needs to be cleaned."

"Good idea," Cassius says. "I'll take care of it."

I study Tair through the one-way mirror. He's back in an orange prison jumpsuit, manacled to the table in front of him. Even though I should be invisible behind the glass, he's looking right at me with a slight smile on his face. Letting me know he's aware of me, that our link is still strong.

Tonight's the full moon.

The door opens and Cassius walks in. It's only the second time we've been in a room alone together since I found out that he lied to me about my treatment, since I learned that in order to save me he's going to have to die. I have no idea what to say to him, either; the events of the last day are still catching up with me.

"Good work," he says. "We've recaptured Tair, we have the Don behind bars, and we broke the spine of a major Gray Wolves operation."

"We also piled up a lot of dead thropes."

"All on their side. Anyway, I've come to expect a certain amount of collateral damage where you're involved. It seems to be the price of admission to the Jace Valchek Experience."

I know what's coming; that undertone of regret in his voice broadcasts his intentions as loudly as a stack of Marshall amps. He's going to admit it.

"There's something you need to know," he says. "I wasn't completely honest with you concerning your treatment."

I resist the urge to say *I know*. I don't want to get Damon into trouble. "When are you ever?"

"One last treatment, and I can guarantee you won't become a thrope. But—"

"But what?" Here it comes.

"But Tair has to die."

"Excuse me?" I manage.

Cassius looks carefully neutral. "His assistance in your treatment is still necessary, but it doesn't have to be voluntary. Human beings are protected under federal law; infecting one against his or her will carries a heavy penalty. That includes mandatory participation in any rehabilitation process."

"Wait—you want to *force* him to help? Even if it *kills* him?"

He looks away, through the window at his prisoner. "I don't *want* to, Jace. But it's the only safe option."

"For me, you mean. What about *him*?"

Cassius studies Tair, his eyes cold. "The law was written with social and emotional integration into thropehood for the victim in mind. But I have the authority to interpret it as I see fit—and though it's never been done before, *curing* your lycanthropy meets my definition of rehabilitation."

"That's not what I mean and you know it. You can't just *execute* him!"

"I'm not. I'm saving your life."

My life, which once again has gone off the rails with someone else driving the locomotive. "Yeah? What about *your* life? Or unlife, or whatever the hell you call it?"

He frowns. "I'm not—"

"Don't even try. I already know the treatment is going to be fatal for someone—*you*. Is that why you wanted Tair alive? So you could put him up as a sacrifice and save yourself?"

"I don't know why you care. He's the one who violated you, remember? The one who almost killed you?" Cassius tries to keep his voice as cold as his eyes, but I can hear the anger creeping in. "He's the one who tried to make you into a *beast*."

He almost spits out the last word, and I finally see something so big, so *obvious,* that it never even occurred to me. "Oh, my—this isn't even *about* me, is it? This is a thrope/pire thing. Dracula versus the Wolfman. Who does that make me, Abbott or Costello?"

"Don't be stupid."

"Wouldn't dream of it. I'm a lot of things—reckless, sarcastic, mouthy—but stupid isn't on the list. Neither is *likes to be manipulated* or *willing to let others make important decisions for her.* And especially not *willing to let other people die in her place.*"

"It's not that cut-and-dried. There's a possibility that either Tair or I might survive—but you definitely will."

"That almost sounds like the truth. I say *almost* because I'm really not sure what the truth would *sound* like coming from your mouth—I'm not sure I've ever even heard it. Maybe it comes out all squeaky, like someone who's just inhaled helium. Maybe it has a ridiculous accent. Or maybe it's in a language you don't even fucking *speak*."

"I'm not lying—"

"How the hell do I know that?" I yell.

Tair's gaze had drifted away from the window, but now it snaps back, looking right at us. He grins. Even if he couldn't feel that through our link, I'm sure he heard it. And right now, I don't care.

"Tell you what," I say, forcing myself to calm down. "Why don't we go ask the condemned man how he feels about this? Doesn't that seem fair?"

I push past him and into the hall, then into the interview room.

Tair's grin is still there. "Hi, honey—glad you're home. How was your day?"

"Better than yours," I say. "Let me ask you something, Tair: How would you feel about dying so someone else could live?"

He laughs. "Is this about poor, poor Dr. Pete? That ship has left the dock, Jace. Didn't even get out of the harbor before it went down, either."

Behind me, I hear Cassius walk in and close the door behind him.

"This isn't about that," I say. "This is about me, and what you did to me."

His smile turns rueful. "Ah. Time for a little retribution, huh? Well, I guess I have it coming. Do your worst."

"How brave," Cassius says. "Considering your link means she can't physically hurt you." He's suddenly between Tair and me, having moved so fast I could barely track him. Leaning right into his captive's face, deadly serious. *"But I can."*

"Sure," I say. "In fact, he can kill you. See, my boss here has done the impossible—he's come up with a way to *reverse* the effects of lycanthropic infection."

"Right," Tair says. "With a little help from the Tooth Fairy? Or did he go straight to the top and ask Santa?"

"No. He bit me."

"If he had, you'd be dead."

Cassius is still staring into Tair's face from around eight inches away. When he speaks, his voice is controlled and flat. "No. I used a biothaumaturgic feedback loop. Carefully controlled viral release, directly into the original site."

Tair frowns. "How'd you monitor?"

"Zanzibar cellular enchantment, modified with a Tetsuo aura harness."

Tair's frown turns thoughtful. "Direct control? For that kind of viral load? Take one helluva lot of focus . . . Spengler was working on something like that four years ago, but it was purely theoretical."

"Now it's not."

"No," I interject, "it's not. It's in my bloodstream. My own three-sided biochemical war, with four possible outcomes."

Tair's a trained biothaumaturge; he doesn't need any more of an explanation. "You'll wind up either human, pire, thrope, or corpse." He nods. "That's with a level playing field. But now you have *me,* don't you?" He looks up at Cassius, gives him a hard smile. "Much easier to win a war when you've got one of the generals hostage, isn't it? Run that same spell through me, get control of my forces, make them do whatever you want. Of course, you'll need to override my own nervous system."

"Of course," Cassius says.

"Which will be like routing lightning through the wiring of a house. Destroying everything it surges through. Unless you've found a way around that?"

"No. I can barely shield myself."

"Not a bad plan; if I were in your position, I'd do the same thing. No, wait—I'd just *kill* me. Nice easy way to break the link and cure Jace. Except you *can't* now, can you? That happens and the pire virus wins too easily. Jace says good-bye to tan lines and solid food. She'd never forgive you for that, would she?"

"I might," I say. "At least he asked before he bit me."

"I apologize for my atrocious table manners," Tair says, and deliberately looks away from Cassius and at me. "However, I may be able to make it up to you. Your boss may be clever, but he's still not a medical expert. I am. There are two factors he's failed to consider, and they change the situation quite radically."

He lifts one manacled hand, holding up a finger. "First of all, the fact that you're not native to this reality. You've adapted, but on a very basic level you're subtly different. It's why you developed Reality Dislocation Trauma when you first got here. That's interfered with our link, made it unreliable. You wouldn't know that, though, since you have nothing to compare it with."

He pauses. Whatever the second thing is, he doesn't want to talk about it. But he forces himself. "The other factor is that the Shinto spell I interrupted when I escaped has also had an effect. A lingering one."

"You're lying," Cassius says. "Like you said, that ship has sailed."

"Yeah, well, it got a lot farther than I expected. In fact, it's still out there, somewhere on the horizon . . ." His voice trails off. "I'm not entirely *myself* anymore. I find myself thinking about things from the past a lot, and sometimes it's not my past. It's *his*." The look on his face is—well, haunted. Haunted by a ghost of himself.

"Really messed with my brain at first. Felt like an invasion, like losing control. But the thing is—most of those memories are pretty good. Happier. Better than what I've got, anyway . . ." He shakes his head, as if to clear it. His voice and face harden. "What I'm saying is, your precious Dr. Pete isn't entirely gone. And he—*I* think it's causing enough additional mystical interference that I can consciously weaken the link between us."

I'm not sure I believe him, or what difference it makes if I do. "What effect would that have?"

"Well, if the link were severed completely before the first full moon—by, let's say, my death—then the thrope virus in your bloodstream would die as well. Instantly. Would have been a good solution before your boss chomped you—now, not so much. But *weakening* the link, that'll confuse the virus. It'll slow down, stop multiplying. Leave itself vulnerable to attack. In other words, it'll have much the same effect your boss wants to achieve—*without* flash-frying my neural net."

Cassius's response is to turn around and leave the room.

It's the last thing I expected, confusing enough that I chase after him, catching him halfway down the hall. "What the hell? Where are you going?"

"My office." He's still moving, heading for the elevator. "We need to talk, and that can't happen with him in the same room."

"Why? Because you can't plan someone's murder while looking him in the eye?"

"No, I have no problem with that. *At all*."

The two lems and two thropes in the elevator take

one look at Cassius's face and all decide they'd rather take the stairs; we have the car to ourselves as we continue our argument.

"You heard him," I say. "What do you think?"

"I think he's lying. He's using your affection for Dr. Pete to manipulate your emotions and the mystic link to affect your judgment. You need some time and distance to think this through."

"I'm a little short on time this week. Could I maybe get an advance?"

"Just—just give it some consideration, all right? Look at all the angles."

It's hard to argue with advice like that, so I clam up and do some hard thinking for the rest of the elevator ride. I'm still thinking as we walk through the office and up to his door.

And then, as we step inside, I've got it.

"He's telling the truth about at least one thing," I say. "His memory."

"Oh? And how do you know that?"

"Because he mentioned my RDT. *And Tair never knew about that.*"

Cassius shakes his head. "It doesn't make any difference. We can't kill him and we can't trust him. The surest way to handle this—"

"No," I say flatly. "I won't have the cost of saving my life be someone else's, especially not like this. If part of Dr. Pete is still alive inside Tair, it would be like killing two people to save one. I won't allow it."

"Then that leaves only one option."

"You sacrificing yourself? You destroy enough of the thrope virus to eliminate it as a threat, and burn yourself out in the process? No. I can't accept that, either. The general is *not* going down with his troops."

"It's not ideal, I know. I can't guarantee you'll survive it, but your chances are good. I'm sorry."

I frown. "You're sorry my chances are good?"

"No. I'm sorry for this."

And then his fangs are in my throat.

TWENTY-FOUR

I should have known.

Cassius is an extremely old vampire. He's clever, he's experienced—his middle name may as well be *cunning.* Combine that with a job that's made him a master of the double cross and you get someone both willing and able to betray me if he thinks it's the right move.

Apparently, the right move in this case is suicide.

A major pire whammy slams into my brain the instant after the fangs go in, locking every muscle I have. I'm a statue, frozen with my hands half raised and my head tilted to one side where I instinctively tried to twist away. This time I can't talk, can't even blink.

No, I think. *No, don't do this.*

But what I think doesn't matter, not anymore. This is Cassius's decision. Cassius's life.

Cassius's sacrifice.

It's different from before. He's not holding back. He's done his initial reconnoitering, established his beachheads. It's time for the final assault.

Blood throbs from my throat into his mouth. Something like electricity radiates from where his lips touch my neck, crackling through my entire body. It hurts, in that achy, sick kind of way you feel when you have a high temperature. Sweat breaks out on every inch of my skin, and vertigo lurches through my belly and head. I feel like the whole room is an elevator that just headed for the basement.

The war is on. It's the fight of my life, and I'm not even involved—I'm just the battlefield. I'm horrified and angry and more scared than I've ever been in my life . . . but even that's not up to me. Everything's slipping away, getting far and distant in that feverish, delirious kind of way when you can't tell if you're dreaming or awake. In another few seconds I'm going to start hallucinating or pass out, and there doesn't seem to be anything I can do about it.

I refuse to accept that.

My body may not be returning my calls, but I still have my mind. I think. I think, therefore I something something something . . . what? Focus, Jacinda, focus. Focus on something. Folk us. Sum thing. Math is a sum thing for folk like us. Hah.

He tilts me back, lowers me gently to the floor without ever losing contact with my neck. Now all I can see is the off-white of the ceiling, just like a movie screen before the lights go down. Ah, there they go now . . .

Today's feature is *Battle for the Bloodstream!* coming to you in glorious ValchekVision 3-and-a-half-D. It's a cartoon. Little animated vampires flying batwinged biplanes are strafing squads of big-eyed werewolf troops driving furry tanks that look like giant stuffed toys. It's very entertaining and funny, but the landscape is jarring—it's all computer-generated and hyperrealistic, which wouldn't be so bad if it weren't also biological: The ground is wet, red flesh, the trees are made of bone, the rolling hills the troops are swarming over are huge living organs, livers and lungs and hearts, all of them pulsing and glistening under the pale glow of a sun that's half crimson and half yellow. Who am I supposed to be rooting for again?

Oh, right. Me.

I've got to do something—and I realize what. It'll take every bit of willpower I have and I still might not pull it off, but I have to try.

I concentrate. Draw on whatever reserves might be hiding somewhere inside me. Put everything I have into it, straining so hard I might just give myself an aneurysm at the same time.

Slowly, ever so slowly, my eyes close.

The movie goes away. I know it'll come back any second, though, so I take my faltering will and reach out with my inner senses the way I did the first time Cassius treated me.

The vast scarlet web of his consciousness flares into existence in front of me, just as enormous and intricate as I remember. Yellow sparks flash and flicker throughout it, like a swarm of fireflies that have blundered into a spider's trap. Abstract representations of the thrope virus he's fighting reports from the front. This isn't the battle itself, though; it's the pire High Command. My boss's big brain.

Exactly where I want to be.

I dive straight at it. I need to convince him this isn't the way to go, and the direct route is the only way left. I have to make him *listen*.

Easier said than done. He's juggling an unbelievable number of variables at once, coordinating a fight involving millions of soldiers on a microcosmic battleground that would probably be the size of a planet if the troops were human-size. As soon as I make contact I can *feel* him, but it's like trying to talk to lightning;

ironically, he's operating on too big and too fast a scale to even be aware of me.

So I do what I did before. I *push,* going deeper into his psyche, and this time I slide right past his defenses. He's too busy fighting on a physical level to spare any attention to the psychic.

Once again, I feel the pain at the core of him. This time, I get more than a brief taste, and I can appreciate just how *big* his suffering is.

That's the only way to properly describe it, too, by its size. It's not intense, not in the immediate way agony is; it's *vast* instead, like an ocean of melancholy. The incredible weight and weariness of a being who's lived too long, seen and done too much. You know that feeling you get when you're so tired you're not tired anymore? Like that, multiplied by a hundred. It's like he hasn't slept in years.

This is how he feels all the time.

No wonder he wants to die, no wonder he's willing to trade his life for mine. He's felt this way for so long, he can't remember what it's like to feel any different. I'm just giving him a convenient excuse to kill himself.

Except I won't let him.

You might think that's selfish of me—and maybe it is—but I *am* a trained psychologist. No matter how depressed someone is, no matter how deep or unrelenting their pain may seem to be, there's *always* more to the picture. Situations change. Things get better. The human mind, no matter how stressed, still retains a capacity for joy. If Cassius truly felt this bad every minute of every day, he would have offed himself long ago. This may be the bulk of his day-to-day existence, but there have to be moments of light in his darkness. There have to be things that keep him going, that give him hope or peace or pleasure. I just have to find them.

So I go deeper. Push into the center of the crimson thicket, the interconnecting threads getting denser and denser until they tie themselves in knots, a tangled sphere of thought at the center of his being. What I need is in there.

I flow inside like a ghost—and see that I'm not the only one.

They hang suspended in an endless white void. Women. Some are pretty, some are not, but all are beautiful. There are multiple versions of most of them, differing by age, from girls barely out of their teens to ancient crones. They're arranged in a great circle, facing outward, like soldiers protecting a perimeter.

And at the very center of that circle is me.

I'm wearing that ridiculous panda shirt I was using as sleepwear the night I was dragged into Thropirelem. At least he isn't remembering the vomit stains all over it, which is how that particular encounter ended—but he *is* remembering; that's what all this is, what all these women are. Memories of women he's known—*human* women. Women whom he's known, whom he's watched get older, whom he's watched die. Over and over, throughout the centuries. There are quite a few, but considering Cassius's life span there should be a lot more. Strange, but I don't have time to figure it out.

I will myself forward between two of them, flow right up to my own image, and stop. As much as I hate magic, it has a certain intuitive logic to it that I'm starting to get. If I want to talk to Cassius, my best bet is right here; merging with his own memories of me will plug me into his conscious thoughts, open a channel of communication. I have no evidence for this theory, no proof at all—but I know it'll work.

I reach out and touch my own face.

Memories flood through me, but I'm ready for that.

What I'm not ready for is the oddness of seeing myself through somebody else's eyes, of getting not only visual memories but emotional ones.

I watch myself over the months Cassius and I have known each other. All the details he's noticed and I've forgotten: the way I stand, the little crinkles at the corners of my eyes when I smile, the glee that hides just below the surface when I get him really good with a zinger. He admires my body but doesn't obsess about it. He spends a lot of time looking at my eyes and he has every single time I've ever laughed memorized.

He's in love with me.

The enormity of that fact overwhelms me. He's not infatuated, it's nothing as simple as a crush. He's watched me, thought about me, dreamed about me—it's all there in the flow of his memories. He's following an old pattern, one he's all too familiar with, one he tries to resist and always fails. A pattern of fascination with women like me: fierce, smart, strong . . . and human. Survivors. The last members of a dying race that just won't give up.

It goes beyond physical attraction. It's my *spirit* that he can't stop thinking about, the way I refuse to back off for anyone or anything. He respects that, admires it, and those feelings have deepened and grown into something more. His job means he can't always be honest with me, and he hates himself for that—but if lying to me means keeping me alive, he's willing to swallow the guilt. There's more than a little martyr in Cassius; after a very long life, there's a part of him that's determined to die doing something good. Something noble.

Something like saving the woman he loves.

"No," I whisper. Or try to, at least; but my body is so very far away I can barely feel it, and I don't know if I even *can* talk in this place. But I *have* to—I have to make Cassius see this isn't the only way.

Cassius. I think loudly, instead of trying to talk. *David. I won't let you do this. I* won't*!*

He hears me. There's this sensation like a whale slowly turning around behind the glass of an underwater habitat to regard me. *Jace.*

You got it, Caligula. What the hell do you think you're doing?

Saving you. His mental voice sounds nothing like his normal one; it's much deeper, richer, more nuanced. I suddenly feel like the blond surfer boy I see behind Cassius's desk every day is no more than an elaborate sock puppet. *And now you know why.*

I don't know how to respond, what to say. There's a level of honesty here that most people never get in a relationship even if they're married for fifty years, and Cassius and I have had a grand total of one date. I know, with absolutely no doubt at all, how he feels about me— it's how I feel about *him* I'm unclear on.

But apparently that doesn't matter, either—because he can feel my uncertainty without me saying a word.

And he doesn't care.

This isn't a negotiation. He sounds a little sad. *Too bad, considering how good I am at those . . . I'm not trying to guilt you into loving me back, Jace. You weren't even supposed to know. I just want you to live. That's all. No games, no deals, no trades. Just* live.

He means it. Cassius's last big manipulation, his final sneaky double cross, is to save my life without letting me know why; he almost pulled it off, too.

Too bad I'm so good at screwing up other people's plans.

No. Forget it. I know *now, so all bets are off, you*

hear me? Die now and this becomes nothing but a massive screwup. I know, you know I know, and there is no way you're going to shuffle off to whatever vampire afterlife exists and leave me holding a gigantic bag of guilt!

Jace. It's too late.

What?

I know how much you love ruining other people's plans . . . but I'm afraid this time you're going to have to accept the inevitable. He produces a hollow mental chuckle. *Not that you will, of course. But it's over.*

Over? But—

There was no other way. No other option. I've defeated the thrope virus, Jace; my viral forces are so decimated, your own defenses will finish them. Your body is yours again. His voice is getting fainter, like he's talking to me while walking away. I can feel my senses coming back, the memoryscape fading to black.

Good-bye, Jace. I love you.

The connection is weakening, but it's still there. I have time to say something, but I don't know what to say.

I'm still trying to find the words when I feel him die.

TWENTY-FIVE

I come back to myself. I'm lying on the floor of Cassius's office. He's lying beside me, and my head is cradled on his arm.

I push myself up groggily on one elbow. I feel a little drugged, but otherwise fine. Cassius is . . .

Cassius is still dead.

His eyes are open. They're back to their normal brilliant blue, not red. His fangs have receded. He's not breathing, of course.

But he hasn't turned into a pile of dust and bones, either.

I don't hesitate. I roll on top of him and start CPR. The old Bee Gees song "Stayin' Alive" starts playing in my head, just like it's supposed to, and I time the thrusts to his chest to the beat.

It's the time-debt sharing with Gretch's daughter, it has to be. As long as she's growing and aging normally, so are Gretch and Cassius—each one at half the same rate.

Half a life is better than none. Half alive means he has at least half a life to be saved, and I'll be *damned* if I'll let him go without a fight.

Hah, hah, hah, hah, stayin' alive, stayin' alive . . .

"Come on, damn you," I mutter. "You think I'm going to let you go all noble and self-sacrificing on me now? Come *on*, you bastard. *Fight, goddamn it!*"

Any second now he's going to turn into a pile of dust. My hands are going to go right through his breastbone as it crumbles into ancient, yellowing fragments.

Thrust. Thrust. Thrust. The Brothers Gibb continue their falsetto wails inside my brain and I wonder if I'll ever be able to hear that song again without having some kind of breakdown.

"You. Will. *Not*. Do. This. To. *Me*," I gasp.

Come on, Caligula. How about Anna? Her mother will have to take on Anna's time-debt herself, and I'll be the one dealing with the fallout whenever Gretch gets another gray hair. Not a pleasant prospect to look forward to, right? Plus, she might start a war with Bosnia or something.

I can't do this, okay? Not on my own. Yeah, half the time I didn't know what was going on in that ancient skull of yours, but you always had my back, didn't you? You were always on my side, even when I didn't know it. You've always done your best to save lives, even if that meant making hard decisions.

I don't want you to go, okay? Please. Please *don't go.*

I'm crying as I keep thrusting against his chest. I don't know how long I should keep going, I don't know when I should give up. I guess that's just something I've never learned.

And I don't learn it now.

I stop, eventually.

I don't know how long it's been. All I know is that the front of my blouse is wet from tears, my wrists are sore, and his body still hasn't crumbled away to nothing. It must be the time-debt enchantment; maybe Cassius even knew his corpse would continue to age at a half-normal rate, fulfilling his obligation to Gretchen's child. That would be like him—honoring a deal even in death.

I put my head on his chest and cry. I blew it. I couldn't save him.

And then, with my ear flat against his body, I hear it. *Ba-thump.*

A heartbeat. A single heartbeat.

I sit bolt upright. Stare down at him.

His eyes flicker. Close, then open again.

"Jace?" he whispers.

"Don't die," I snap. "You hear me? Do *not* die. *Again,* I mean."

"I—" His eyes close. He's gone again.

I pound on his chest some more. His eyes are still blank. No good. He's only got a flicker of life in him, and I've got to fan that into a flame. I need—what?

A jump start. Cardiac paddles. Except Thropirelem's medical technology is *way* behind my native reality's and they've probably never heard of using electricity to restart a heart. No good.

I'm not thinking about this the right way. This is magic, not medicine. He's only half alive, but he's half undead, too. He needs—what? What's the mystical equivalent of a shot of adrenaline?

I bend down and kiss him.

It's all I can think of. Sleeping Beauty, Snow White, all those fairy-tale clichés. I just hope he doesn't turn into a frog.

I can taste my own blood in his mouth. His lips are warmer than I expected—and after a moment, they twitch.

He kisses me back. Slowly at first, like he's waking up and not really sure what's going on. When he figures it out, he pulls back and says, "Whuh?"

I grab his wrist, press my thumb against the radial artery. There's a pulse there, but it's slow and weak. I can do better.

I stick my other hand behind his head and pull him up for another kiss. This time I put a little fire into it.

His pulse surges. Just a little, but I can tell.

He pulls away again. "Jace, what are you—"

"Saving your life, stupid." I kiss him again.

This one goes on for a while. He doesn't pull away, either—he's figured out what I'm doing. Because he's smart and all. Yeah, that's what's going on.

It's not like we're enjoying ourselves or anything.

His pulse is still slow—half the speed of a living human, of course—but it's steady. Good job, Jace. Guess I can stop now.

Uh-huh.

The thing about kissing a pire? They don't have to breathe. I still do, which is why when I finally pull away it's with a gasp. I'm straddling his torso, one hand behind his head, the other holding his wrist.

"You did it," Cassius says. His eyes are about eight inches away from mine. "Thank you." He's doing his best to put some formality into his words, to give me an opportunity to back off with some dignity.

Like hell.

This time I kiss him like I mean it. And I do.

There's a whole conversation that goes on during that kiss. Questions, tentatively asked and forcefully answered. Suspicions confirmed, apologies offered and accepted. Our relationship undergoes a complete overhaul in a few intense moments, a total renovation of the structure we've built between us. Walls come crashing

down, doors get ripped off and thrown away. It's powerful and scary and makes me feel like screaming in glee
like a kid on a roller coaster.

When we break apart this time, it's for more pragmatic
reasons.

"Now?"

"Yes."

"Here?"

"Couch."

"Clothes—oh."

Don't ask me who said what. I'm not sure and I don't
really give a damn. We're kissing and unbuttoning and
tugging and we wind up tangled together with the cool
smooth leather against our bare skin. I'm on top and he's
looking at me like he's trying to burn every last detail
of my body into his memory. I realize what he's doing
and put my hand gently over his eyes.

"Stop," I say softly. "Don't do that. I'm not going
anywhere."

He nudges my hand away. Smiles at me, a little ruefully. "I'm sorry. Old habits die hard."

"So do I. Now stop thinking about how I'm going to
die someday and make me feel *alive,* okay? Starting
with right . . . *here.*"

I move his hand. It's all the invitation he needs.

When I first got to Thropirelem, I had an ill-advised
and drunken fling with a werewolf. Nothing kinky, no
fur on the bedsheets, but it was still my first time with a
supernatural lover. Unfortunately, it was also my first
time with magic-enhanced booze, and my memories of
that night are fuzzier than the guy I slept with. Still,
what I can remember is . . . enthusiastic. Athletic, even.
Thropes are stronger than human beings even when
they're not in were-mode.

This is nothing like that.

I read a sociology paper once that stated there were two features that human beings always find sexually attractive, that turn people on no matter what kind of society they live in. Two factors that apply universally across all cultural boundaries—one for males and one for females. For men, it was youth; for women, it was status.

Cassius is both, all wrapped up in the same package. He's got the body of a twenty-year-old surfer, though his tan has faded somewhat after a few centuries in the shade. A swimmer's body, long and lean and muscled in that elegant way that reminds me of racehorses. Smooth, soft skin, cool but not cold. Long, clever fingers.

But this is no college boy, fumbling his way around in the dark. His touch is experienced, sure, firm. He knows a woman's body the way Jimi Hendrix knew a guitar, and he plays with just as much joy. He has me gasping halfway through the first song and he hasn't gotten to the solo yet.

I do a little strumming of my own. He smiles in a way that makes me breathe a little bit harder, and I give him a kiss that makes what I did before seem like a great-aunt's birthday smooch.

He slides me around and over and now we're side by side, necking like teenagers in the backseat of an old Chevy. I can feel the strength behind his tenderness, the power he's holding back, and it makes me crazy; I want it, I want my whole body wrapped around it, and I want it *now.*

And that's exactly what I get.

Everything gets a little slippery. Inside, outside, time, skin, senses . . . it's an overwhelming cocktail of sensation and emotion, feelings sliding into and over and under one another, playful tongues and rough joy and salty urgency. The taste of his nipple, caught between my teeth. His tongue, tracing its way around my belly button. Biting my own lip. Him inside me and me inside him, lips and tongues and trembling eagerness. Everything spiraling up into the inevitable, me making far too much noise and not giving even a single damn. His own orgasm a minute later, staring intently into my own eyes the entire time. I feel utterly connected to him, joined not just at our hips but at our gaze, a completed circuit with a surge of pleasure cycling through it in an endless loop.

It fades, eventually. Neither of us wants to break the moment by speaking. I finally, reluctantly, look away. "*Damn,* Caligula," I pant. "When was the last time you got *laid*?"

"Turn of the century."

"Which one?"

"You're hilarious."

"I know."

We both shut up again.

And there it is—the dreaded awkward silence. I've just shared one of the most intimate moments of my life with this man, and now we're realizing neither of us knows where this is going to go next. He's my *boss,* for God's sake. And of course, there's the great unspoken truth that both of us know exactly how he feels about me . . . and neither of us knows how I feel about him.

"So," I say.

"Is this the part where I regret surviving after all?"

"No. This is the part where I thank you for saving my life. Even if you were kind of self-destructive about it."

"I think you've already returned the favor. Though I have no idea how you pulled it off."

"Oh, come on. I may have been enthusiastic, but I don't think I actually *detached* anything."

He sighs. "This is what I get while basking in the afterglow? Puns?"

"You want a more serious answer? Simple. Sexy hot woman magic. I'm a master practitioner."

"Ah. It's all clear to me now."

"You're just lucky I held back. Could have blown the top of your head clean off."

"I believe, in fact, that's exactly what you did."

I grin, and snuggle onto his chest. "Damn straight . . ."

Which is when the door opens, and Charlie walks in. He looks at us. We look back.

"You two done?" Charlie says. "Or do I have to get a firehose and a pry bar?"

EPILOGUE

I'm not sure what I should do now.

The case has been wrapped up. The Don's out on bail, and Gretch tells me the murder charges against him may not stick; Arturo's too wily to be caged that easily. A deal will be struck, Falzo will stay free and in charge, and his accomplice will probably take the fall. In the meantime, Tair stays in custody while the higher-ups negotiate—which means Cassius disappears behind a wall of NSA lawyers and I'm left to do paperwork while Charlie sharpens some choice remarks about my new relationship.

I'm exhausted and elated, pumped up and strangely let down. Too much has happened and I need at least a week to just sleep and let everything filter through my subconscious while my body readjusts to being human again. I'm expecting big, weird dreams, but all I get is twelve hours of near-coma followed by a total lack of appetite. Considering how many calories I was werewolfing down before that, I don't mind a little break.

I take Gally out for a long walk, the kind where I let

my mind wander along with my legs. I feel . . . unsettled. Like something's missing.

That bothers me, because the list of suspects is both long and troubling. Am I missing the heightened senses of a thrope? The bloodlust of a pire? The chance to truly belong somewhere that came with Leo's offer to join the Adams pack? Now that Cassius and I are finally together, I could be missing him—or I could be feeling a supposed loss of independence. None of those things feels right, and all of them do.

It starts to rain, that light kind of drizzle that's so common in the Northwest. I flip up the waterproof hood on my jacket and keep going, past the big plate-glass windows of a bar. Lots of people inside, laughing and drinking and talking. Mostly pires, it looks like—lots of wineglasses filled with red.

Gally senses my mood, comes up and licks my hand. I should really get him home soon—the sun will go down in less than an hour, and I forgot to bring his big-boy pants. "I'm okay," I sigh. "Just a little—I don't know."

I think I'm starting to, though. I've carved out a niche for myself in Thropirelem; I've got a career, a home, friends. A dog. Even—though it's a little hard to believe—a relationship.

But I don't have anything that's really *mine*.

It was visiting the Seattle Enclave that did it. I was looking to reconnect with my humanity, but I didn't fit in there at all. This whole experience has made me realize just how alone I really am; there's no one on this whole planet like me.

But then, I guess the same could have been said about me before I came here. We're all really a species of one, aren't we? Locked inside our own heads, trying to understand how all these other odd beings around us think, trying to figure out why they do what they do. And that's okay, it really is, because we all learn how to deal with it in our own way. We learn, we adapt, we overcome. Maybe we find happiness, maybe we don't, but it's *always* possible; there's only one thing that's guaranteed to stop us, and that's giving up.

I don't do giving up.

So. Internal pep talk over. Disgustingly optimistic attitude being enforced with gritted teeth. Next question: How do I *beat* this?

I think about it all the way home.

"Hello, Tair," I say. "How are they treating you in here?"

He gives me one of his easy smiles. "No complaints. No assassination attempts, anyway."

I nod. He's back at Stanhope, with more charges against him pending. The interview room is the same one we talked in the last time, and he's chained to the same steel post.

He studies me intently. "I know why I'm here, Valchek. Why are you?"

"I wanted to give you an update on my condition."

"Ah. Not really necessary, is it? I mean, I felt the link dissolve. Give my congratulations to Cassius, will you? I really didn't think the old neckbiter could do it."

"I'll pass that along."

I'm not sure how to do this, but that's never stopped me before. I take a deep breath and say, "I want to talk to Dr. Pete."

He stares at me. Blinks. Then his eyes roll up and his head sags forward like someone who's just fallen asleep. When he talks, his voice is hollow and spooky. "Jaaaaace. I am here. Speeeeak."

"Yeah, that's a laugh riot. You sing and dance, too?"

His head snaps up. He grins with only the whites of his eyes showing. "No, but I'm working on my ventriloquism. Want me to make your pants talk?"

"Not particularly. And stop staring at the inside of your own head—it's creeping me out."

His eyes slide back to normal. "Tough audience."

"I meant what I said. Please."

He frowns. "Look, it doesn't work like that. It's not like we're two different people, okay? Just two sides of the same coin. I'm him, he's me. Same way vision works: two points-of-view, coming together to form a three-dimensional image."

"So you're a complex person now, instead of a sociopath? Lots of layers, someone with real depth?"

He grins. "Couldn't have said it better myself."

"That's because I'm a trained psychologist. And as such, I can tell you your explanation is bullshit. In fact, it's exactly the kind of glib, self-serving rationalization that a sociopath would come up with, making you sound sympathetic while denying any real responsibility for your actions. Nice touch with the vision metaphor, though."

He shrugs. "I liked it."

"The thing is, if you and Dr. Pete were truly integrated, you'd be presenting with a very different affect: more guilt, less denial. I don't know if he actually exists as a separate entity or if you've just acquired some of his memories, but if there was any chance he was actually *in* there, I had to try. I owe him that much."

He studies me coolly, and I study him back.

Waiting. Hoping.

"What do you want me to say, Valchek? What were you *expecting*?"

"I just want the truth."

He snorts. "What good would that do? You'll never

trust me or anything I say. Even if I *was* completely honest, you wouldn't believe it."

"Try me."

He looks at me with thinly veiled anger. I don't blame him. After all we've shared, the risks he's taken on my behalf, I'm rejecting him for the interloper who's taken up residence in his head. For a weaker version of himself that somehow wound up happier. I can see how much Tair hates him, the kind of hate only a sibling can have for a more successful brother or sister. His hate is a wall—and unless I can get through that barrier, I'll never know if Dr. Pete is behind it or not.

I stand up. "Okay, I guess I see your point. Good luck with your appeal."

I'm at the door, my hand raised to knock so the guard can let me out, when he speaks. "Hold on."

It's not Tair's voice.

I stop. Turn.

The voice is weary, sad, with none of Tair's cockiness. "Jace."

My eyes are stinging. "Doc—Dr. Pete?"

He looks up at me with eyes full of pain. Starts to raise his hands and is brought up short by the manacles. "Jace. I'm—I'm a little confused. Why am I chained up? Did I—did I *do* something?"

"It's—complicated," I say. "What's the last thing you remember?"

He shakes his head in bewilderment. "I don't know. My memories are all mixed up. Sorcery?"

"Yeah. You got stabbed with the Midnight Sword. It changed your history and threw your physical body back in time a week. The new you has made some . . . *questionable* decisions in his past. A lot farther back than just a week, too."

He nods. "That's why everything's so jumbled up. Tair.

That's the alias I used when I worked for the lem Gray Market."

"I've been working on getting you back. Tair kind of sabotaged that."

"I'm sorry, Jace. I've done—I've done terrible things."

"No. *Tair's* done terrible things. He's not you, okay?"

"But he is, Jace. That's what's so horrible . . ."

I take my seat again. "I'm not giving up on you, Doc. We'll get through this together, all right?"

"I appreciate that, Jace." He pulls himself together with a visible effort. "How have *you* been doing?"

Good old Dr. Pete. Always thinking of others first . . . "I'm doing fine. Just wrapped up a case."

He gives me a wry smile so familiar it makes my chest hurt. He lifts his manacles a few inches off the table and says, "Put the bad guys in jail, huh?"

I laugh. "I guess."

"I don't care about that, Jace. I don't know how long it'll be before—before I'm not *me* again. So don't tell me about work. Tell me about *you*."

And I do.

I tell him about Galahad, and how glad I am to have him. I tell him about Xandra, and how much she misses him. I tell him about Gretch's baby, and the new dance steps Charlie's been patiently trying to teach me.

I don't tell him about Cassius.

"Sounds like you're integrating well," he says. "That's good. That's really good."

"There's something else, too." I hesitate. "You told me, when you were first treating my RDT, that I needed to put down some roots. I've been thinking about that a lot lately, and I finally made a decision."

"Which is?"

"I've started a dojo—that's a martial arts gym, basically. Just a rented space in a dance studio on Sunday afternoons, for now."

"Martial arts?"

"Yeah. It's something that means a lot to me, but I can't really train with experienced pires or thropes; the skills they have rely on more strength and speed than humans possess. So I figured I'd start with people who know nothing about martial arts and teach them what *I* know, concentrating more on leverage and tactics. Wily human stuff."

"How's that going?"

"Got six members so far—well, five and a half. Xandra, a thrope bouncer who likes to pretend he's a pire, two recent immigrants who are determined to never be physically abused again, one genuine human in her fifties, and my dog."

"You're teaching *Galahad* kung fu?"

"What can I say? I seem to attract strays—and besides, he's a good benchmark. If I can teach *him,* I can teach anyone."

"Oh, I don't know about that. Some people just can't be taught."

"That sounds like a challenge. Or are you saying I couldn't teach *you*?"

"No. I'm saying some people are just goddamn *idiots*."

I know that smug tone all too well. And I have a sinking feeling I know what he's referring to.

He leans forward, his eyes intent. "I mean, come *on,* Valchek. I told you I couldn't be trusted, and you *still* fell for it. Oh, poor, poor Dr. Pete, I'm so glad you're back. Now let me tell you all about my depressing, pathetic life."

I stare at him for a moment.

And then I smile.

"Nice try," I say. "Smooth transition, too. But you're not going to fool me again."

He laughs. It's an ugly sound. "Again? Don't you mean *still*?"

"No. I know who I was just talking to, and it wasn't you. I was wondering why you would let Dr. Pete out, and now I know: So you could yank him back in again and make me feel betrayed. Because then I'd never trust you again, would I? If the *real* Dr. Pete ever tried to talk to me, I'd dismiss it as a trick. You're sabotaging any future attempts by him to get out, trying to make him feel isolated and alone. And there's only one reason you'd do that—because you're afraid of him. Which means he's a *lot* stronger than you're letting on."

"Sure. Keep telling yourself that. I can't wait for your next little heart-to-heart with me—I mean, Dr. Pete."

I stand up again. "I'm not giving up on him, Tair. You hear me, Doc? *I am not giving up on you.* I'll be back, okay? We'll talk again, I promise."

"Ooh, I can't *wait,* sweetheart. Kisses." He puts as much perverse venom into his words as he can, but I just grin and rap on the door for the guard. Venom, I can handle.

I leave the prison feeling better than I went in. There's still hope; there are still possibilities, waiting to unfold.

It's Sunday morning. Time to go home, get into some comfortable clothes, and go teach a few people how to kick ass.

It's what I do best, after all.